History tells us that an 18-year-old boy named Raymond Jones walked into a record store in Liverpool, on Saturday, 28th October 1961, at around three o'clock in the afternoon, and asked Brian Epstein, head of the record department, for a disc called 'My Bonnie'. "I'm afraid not," said Epstein, shaking his head. "Who's the record by?"

"A group called The Beatles," said Jones.

The fabled meeting is said to be what first prompted Brian Epstein to seek out the then relatively unknown Liverpool beat group, become their manager, and steer them on to worldwide fame and fortune.

However, an increasing number of people now say the meeting never took place and that Raymond Jones never even existed.

What's incontestable is that it was Brian Epstein who first recounted the story in his autobiography—*A Cellarful of Noise*—published in 1964 at the very height of '*Beatlemania*'.

Brian Epstein's influence on The Beatles was paramount and it's highly unlikely we would have ever heard of the 'Fab Four' were it not for him and all that he did for the group.

So what really did happen all those years ago? And why would Brian Epstein base the legend of The Beatles upon a lie?

Much of what follows is true...

Also by Tony Broadbent

London 'Creeping' Narratives
The Smoke
Spectres In The Smoke
Shadows In The Smoke

Short Stories
'As to: An Exact Knowledge of London'
A Study In Sherlock

'The Remaining Unknowns'
The Mystery Box - Mystery Writers of America

THE ONE AFTER 9:09

A MYSTERY WITH A BACKBEAT

Tony Broadbent

PLAIN SIGHT PRESS | Davidson NC

PLAIN SIGHT PRESS
P.O. Box 909
Davidson NC 28036
www.plainsightpress.com

Publisher's Note: This is a work of fiction. Apart from well-known historical figures and well-documented events, the names, characters, places, and incidents portrayed are the work of the author's imagination. Any resemblance to actual persons, living or to businesses, companies, events, institutions, or locales is completely coincidental.

Cover Design & Image: Tony Broadbent
Book Design: The Book Designer | Pulp

The One After 9:09 | Tony Broadbent
ISBN 978-0-9963722-9-9
Library of Congress Control Number: 2015942440

1. The Beatles 1960-1963–Fiction. 2. Brian Epstein 1934-1967–Fiction.
3. Great Britain–Society, teenagers, popular music–1960-1963–Fiction.
4. Historical-Mystery–Fiction. 1. The Title

For John, Paul, George, and Ringo
And Brian Epstein and George Martin

And Sam Leach

And anyone that's ever loved The Beatles

CHAPTERS

Afterward

Author's Acknowledgements

This is unashamedly a historical novel, not a work of history.

And so even though it's based on extraordinarily well-known figures and exhaustively documented events, it is nevertheless a complete work of fiction.

The story, herein, as well as the names, characters, places, and incidents portrayed, are the work of the author's imagination and any resemblance to actual persons, living or dead is completely coincidental, even if somewhat inevitable.

The mystery, as ever, is all.

Bigger Than Elvis

Brian Epstein glanced down at the entry in his desk diary. "Spike? Is that your real name?"

"No, Mr Epstein, it's not, no. It's what everyone's called me since I was a kid." The young man wrinkled his nose, ran a hand through his thatch of dark brown hair. "Me dad always used to say I was that daft, I should've been on *The Goon Show*. And it, sort of, stuck, like."

"The...the *Goon Show*?"

"Yeah, you know, on the radio. Spike Milligan. Peter Sellers."

"It was...they were never really my cup of tea."

The boy looked around the office—at the Spanish bullfight poster, beige walls, venetian blinds, the lightwood furniture, and burnt-orange seat cushions on the couch. And he had to admit it was all very nice, if you liked that sort of thing. "Well, Mr Epstein, sir, you must've been the only one in all of England who wasn't mad keen on the Goons."

They were separated in age by no more than eight or nine years, yet it might as well have been thirty or forty—a million. They were generations apart as they looked at one another across the cavern of years, the posh, poised businessman and the well-scrubbed scruff.

Brian Epstein smiled affably. "Would you mind, awfully, telling me your real name? I'd like to know whom it is I'm thanking. Who you are, where you come from, because...I...I want to reward you."

"But as I explained to Mr Makin, that's not necessary."

"Yes, I've spoken to Rex Makin. But I feel the circumstance calls for me to do something more...something special."

"All I did was agree to help. As a favour, like. As both Mr and Mrs Makin have been very good to me and me mum, since me dad died."

"Yes, he told me about your father. I'm so sorry. I know a couple of other young people that have each lost a parent. It can't be easy."

"It isn't. But what's this all about, Mr Epstein, sir?"

"Er...Spike...?"

"My name's Raymond, Raymond Jones."

A shadow crossed over Brian Epstein's face as he thought of the awful night, in Hamburg. He suppressed a shiver. "The thing is, Raymond, I...I really can't thank you enough for what you did."

"I didn't do anything, Mr Epstein. Really, I didn't."

"But I was there, Raymond. I saw what happened with my own eyes. You kept it all from ending before it had ever really begun."

"I'm sorry...I don't follow."

"They're going to be bigger than Elvis. The Beatles...John's group...one day they're going to be even bigger than Elvis Presley. I know it, Raymond. I see it so clearly. They have the talent...the..."

Spike was on firmer ground here. "Yeah, they're great, no one to touch them. But there's hundreds of groups all round Merseyside...all of them dead set on beating The Beatles in the next *Mersey Beat* Popularity Poll."

"Yes, I write a column for *Mersey Beat* and know the editor, personally. And I'm very well aware of all the talent in Liverpool. It's just that The Beatles are different. They're special. They have something even more important than talent. They have *charisma*. One can't take one's eyes off of them. And as The Beatles become more and more famous, I want to ensure you're a part of their story...forever."

"I'm sorry, Mr Epstein, I still don't follow."

"I want to make you part of the legend, Raymond. One day I'll tell the whole story. Write a book so people will know what really happened. And I'll say you were there at the very beginning and that it was all down to you that I went out and discovered The Beatles."

CHAPTER ONE

Sam Leach

"LADIES AND GENTLEGERMS, welcome to the Iron Door Club and 'Rock Around the Clock'...Liverpool's first ever all-night rock session. Now, to open the show, we proudly present the best group ever to come out of...Where did you say you come from, lads?"

Terry McCann, minder-cum-compère, threw a wink at his boss, Sam Leach, standing down by the side of the stage. Johnny Rocco and The Jets were making their first professional appearance anywhere and Sam was as nervous as a newly neutered cat the band wouldn't be up to scratch. But there was no time for a snappy comeback line. The Jets' drummer bashed a cymbal, yelled "Onetoofreefawr!" and led the group straight into 'Rock Around the Clock'.

Terry laughed, ran off stage, waving to the crowd.

"You know, Tel," Sam shouted. "I'm sick to death of that bloody song, but they don't sound too bad, do they? Clever of them to start off with it, I should've thought of it myself and I will next time."

The club had barely been open half an hour and the dance floor was already one heaving mass of beat fans. Sam shook his head in wonder. "I knew they'd come in droves if I gave them what they wanted." He waved at a poster on the wall. Read it aloud. "'TWELVE GROUPS FOR TWELVE HOURS. PRICE: ONLY SIX SHILLINGS AND SIXPENCE'. But that's me. Isn't it? Sam Leach, the only Liverpool music promoter who'll never get rich, because he always gives it straight back to the fans. Who else has the balls to turn this old 'Trad-jazz only' dive into Merseyside's very first Mecca of rock 'n' roll?"

"Nobody's got your balls, Sam," Terry said. "And even if they did, none of them have got a pair of trousers big enough to fit them in."

Sam sniffed. Nodded. How true. "I don't know how much I'm paying you, Tel, but give yourself a bonus." Suddenly feeling peckish, he turned, his eyes alighting on a fresh-faced teenager with an unruly mop of hair. He called the lad over. "Here, Spike. I know, I said you being the new boy meant you had to get your feet wet, but I didn't mean for you to go swimming in your soddin' clothes. When I sent you outside to check on the size of the queue you obviously didn't see the great, big, bloody umbrella by the front door did you? You've got to learn to use your head in the music business. Anyroad...do us another favour, will yers? Pop upstairs and get Tel and me some hot dogs...lashings of tomato sauce, onions...whole lotta mustard. And get one down your neck, too. You look like you could do with it."

Beat fans were still pouring down the stairs into the huge basement cellar that served as the dance floor. Glory be, thought Sam, there must be well over five hundred of the lovely buggers and The Beatles aren't even due on until eleven. He turned and shouted into Terry's ear, "You know, Tel, I think it's going to be a very successful night. And, unless I'm very much mistaken, I hear the sound of cash registers a-ring-a-ding-dinging."

Sam sang along to 'Hound Dog'—the Jets' third number—and when Spike handed him a hot dog in a paper wrapper, he paused, curled his lip and mumbled, "Thank you, very much." Then he bit the head off his hot dog and yelled, "This is the life...rock 'n' roll!"

They'd all just finished wiping their fingers on the greasy wrappers, when a youngster ran headlong into Sam and began dashing up the stairs. Terry caught hold of the boy's jacket. Sam caught hold of boy's arm. "Hold your horses, young 'un. Where's the soddin' fire?" The boy, no more than fifteen, turned, shaking with fear. "Hey, didn't I speak to you earlier, outside, in the queue? What the devil's up?"

"It's that gang of Teds from St. Helens. They're out to get me. So I gotta get out of here, mister. Or I'm a dead 'un, for sure."

"Not tonight, you're not," Sam growled. "I'm sick to death of that bunch of layabouts and all their bloody nonsense. But they won't get near you tonight, I promise. You just trust to me and my lads, okay? Good. Terry, a word in your ear."

"Yes, guv, what can I do you for?"

"We're not going to have another kid getting himself booted to death as happened over in Garston, last month. Whether it's Teds with their duck-arse haircuts or Leather-boys on their greasy-arsed motorbikes, they're all just bloody delinquents, the lot of them. I've had it up to here with them, I have. Go tell the Mean Machine to get themselves ready."

"Consider it done, Sam."

Sam turned to the young boy. "What's yer name, son?"

"Er, Billy. Billy Cook, mister."

"Alright, Billy, you go hide out in the cloakroom with Spike, here, until we get things all set up. Then I want the two of you to come back down onto the dance floor so the St. Helens gang can all cop eyes on you. And when they do, you just get your arses back up the stairs, dead sharpish, and let them follow you up into the foyer. We'll be waiting for them." Sam grinned and nodded encouragement, all traces of his earlier humour vanished. Much to his surprise, Spike found himself shivering. Sam peered at him. "You okay with this, young Spike? Only you look so gormless with that funny haircut of yours, the St. Helens mob is bound to think you're a right pushover, too."

"I'm okay, Sam. The Mean Machine on idle was enough to put the frights up me. God knows what they'd do if they really got going."

"Well, if you live through it, you'll be able to scare your grandkids with tales of what you see tonight. Alright, you two, off you go."

SPIKE JONES had only met the club's fearsome collection of bouncers an hour or so before. It wasn't the high point of his first night working for Sam Leach.

"You look like a right twat with your tatty haircut and gear, but Mr McCann says you can handle yourself if you have to. So, okay, Spikey, it's time you met the rest of the Mean Machine."

Even in the dark, at the bottom of the long flight of stairs leading down into the club, the well-built young man in a light-grey, narrow lapel, three-button Italian mohair suit and thin black-knitted tie looked as sharp as a newly-honed razor and just as dangerous. The close-cropped blond hair and baby face did nothing to soften the piggy eyes that stared at him with a look as flat and as desolate as the River Mersey on a winter's day. As if that wasn't enough promise of trouble, the chill young man was flanked by a bunch of equally cold-faced charmers.

"Me? I'm Jimmy Molloy. Them two are me brothers Tony and Timmy. That's Charlie, Larry, Johnny and 'Griff'. Those two over there...built like brick shit-houses...are the Behan brothers, Mickey and Sean. But they're not as nice as we are, so best stay well clear of them. Tall gent, over there, is Mr Butcher, boss of the Mean Machine. If you survive your first night, he might let you call him Kenny. Until he does, best keep clear of him, too."

Spike nodded. His eyes locked on Jimmy Molloy. "I best get about my business, then," he said. "Try and keep myself out of trouble."

"Yeah, you just do that, sunshine," said Molloy, very quietly.

As if on cue, Terry McCann appeared out of the blue to separate the two. "There you are, Spike. Thought I'd lost you for a moment. Thanks, Jimmy," he said, warmly, before patting Spike on the shoulder and leading him back up the stairs. "Don't you mind them, Spike. They're as gentle as little baby lambs, the lot of them. But I thought it best they get a sniff of you while the lights are still up...much safer that way." He thrust a piece of paper into Spike's hand. "Here's Sam's list. Check everything on it. Make sure the numbers tally. See if we have enough hot dogs, Cokes, tins of coffee, packets of biscuits, that sort of thing. Check tickets and pins for the cloakroom. Then go ask Jim, the cashier, if he's got enough change in the box-office. That lot, done, come and help me check out the sound equipment. Then I'll go over the running order of the groups with you. Okay?"

Spike nodded. That was more like it. More of what he'd hoped he'd be doing—getting up real close to where all the live music happened.

TERRY McCANN, Kenny Butcher, and Jimmy Molloy worked out a battle plan. The big iron door to the street was closed, the foyer cleared of people, and Terry led a few of the biggest bouncers downstairs and positioned them near the stage. The Behan brothers then escorted Spike and a very nervous Billy Cook back down onto the dance floor.

The crowd—having just checked out of 'Heartbreak Hotel'—was rocking the whole cellblock as Johnny Rocco and the Jets wailed their way through 'Jailhouse Rock'. Meanwhile, the mob of fifteen or so St. Helens Teddy Boys stood off to one side of the stage, clicking their fingers and shuffling their feet in their own private world—cocksure, duck-arsed lords of all they surveyed. All of a sudden one of them clapped his hands, repeatedly, out of time with the music, and pointed to little Billy Cook pushing his way through the crowd. The St. Helens gang turned as one, began to circle like sharks, and quickly closed in on their prey.

The moment Billy Cook saw he'd been spotted, his nerve broke and he turned and ran for the stairs. Spike spun round. "Billy!" he yelled. Then he set off after him. And so did the gang of Teds.

Billy bounded up the stairs, two-at-a-time, and skidded into the foyer, where one of the bouncers picked him up bodily and bundled him into the box-office.

"Right, gentlemen, start your engines," said Kenny Butcher, in a voice that would've done a BBC outside broadcast commentator proud. "Watch out for knuckledusters, flick-knives, bicycle chains. And remember the fookers in the drape jackets will probably all have fish-hooks or razor-blades sewn behind their lapels, as well."

The Teddy Boys poured out into the foyer, whooping and baying for blood, only for them to come face-to-face with a wall of very stern-faced men. They skidded to a halt. Stood—all bunched together—wide-eyed. A couple of Teds, bringing up the rear, quickly turned tail, ran back down the stairs, but the Behan brothers soon dealt with them. Then there was no going back for anyone. It was all about to go off. And nothing on God's green earth could stop it.

The Teds spat their defiance, spewed out abuse, and gesticulated with wave after wave of two-fingered obscenities.

Then as if in response to some secret signal they all whipped out flick-knives, razors, chisels, and bicycle chains.

The Iron Door's team of bouncers growled—surged forward.

The fight was bloody and brutal, with no quarter given or expected. Leather coshes in hand, Jimmy Molloy led his brothers straight for the Ted he'd identified as the gang leader. The Ted went down in a flurry of blows. Kenny Butcher, a full head taller than everyone else, waded in and knocked Teds flying left, right and centre with his ham-sized fists. The Behan brothers rushed into the very thick of things and hit anything strange that moved.

A Teddy Boy brandishing a Coke bottle ran straight at Spike. He sidestepped, ducked and, as if in slow motion, hit the Ted smack in the belly with a blistering body shot. The Ted went down with a sound of a ruptured inner tube. Spike yelped with pain, sure he'd broken his hand. He flexed his skinned knuckles and was struck by the thought his guitar playing days were over even before they'd ever begun. "Fook it, typical Jones family luck," he gasped. "Right on the soddin' belt buckle." But his blood was up and he shook his head and threw himself back into the fight.

"This can't be happening," he moaned, as he hit out at anybody in a long drape coat or studded-leather jacket—wincing with each blow of his bruised hand. Then, as he was gulping for more air, he caught the glint of a cutthroat razor swinging across in front of him and, with both fists locked together, he lunged forward to block the attacker's arm. "No, you bloody don't," he yelled, catching the would-be slasher hard on the elbow. Then he lost his balance and tumbled to the floor.

Somewhere, way above him, he heard Jimmy Molloy shout. "Fuckin' hell! That was meant for me!" But all Spike could think about was getting up off the floor before he was kicked senseless. "Thanks there, Spikey, you saved me from a right bad haircut."

"Only trying to be of help, Jimmy."

"You still look like a right twat, down there, sunshine, but thanks a bunch, anyway."

"Welcome to the Iron Door," Spike muttered, as he scrambled back to his feet. He turned, grabbed the nearest Ted, swung him round, butted him in the face, pushed him down and kneed him under the chin.

"That's using yer head," someone yelled.

Spike grunted, shook his head to clear it, and when he looked round the foyer again he saw the fight was all but over. What was left of the St. Helens mob were being dragged over towards the club's big front door and dumped outside onto the wet cobblestones. Kenny Butcher's voice boomed out into the night—a Mersey foghorn at full blast. "Don't any of you greasy bastards even think of coming back...just stay home and play with your dolls." Then the not-so-gentle giant turned and slammed the big iron door shut.

The beat fans, still queuing-up outside in the rain, looked on in wide-eyed astonishment as the thunderous sound echoed up and down Temple Street. Then they all quickly huddled back against the wet brick walls as the now very badly bruised and bedraggled band of Teds limped away into the night.

Back inside the club, Sam rubbed his hands together as if wiping away something particularly unpleasant. "Right. Well done, fellas," he shouted. "Cokes and hot dogs, all round."

CHAPTER TWO

Lightning In A Bottle

"How many did you say?"

"There's well over a thousand inside the club, Sam. But there must be another two hundred or so, outside, all still hoping to get in. Jim, in the box-office, is tearing his hair out...what's left of it that is...as the legal limit of the club's nine hundred and we passed that ages ago. Says he's also he's run out of tickets. Asks if he can use your business cards with a number rubber-stamped on them, instead. But as that was half an hour ago, he's probably gone and done it, anyway, knowing him."

"I think that's what they call initiative, Tel. I must remember to get myself some next time I go shopping."

"Er...excuse me, Sam, but I just heard John Lennon's got a problem he wants fixed, like, and quick."

"Hell, that's all I need. It's never anything trivial with him. Okay, lead on, Spike. Got any idea what it's about?"

Spike pushed a way through the crowds. Blue smoke hung everywhere. Rivers of condensation ran down damp shiny walls to mix at floor level with greasy hot dog wrappers, cigarette stubs, and sticky spilled puddles of coffee and Coke. "Not sure, Sam. Something to do with the electrics, I think."

"Great! It's like Frankenstein's bloody castle inside here, as it is. All we need now is a flash of lightning and we'd all go up in smoke."

Spike pushed open the door to the Ladies toilets, pressed into service as a dressing room, and held it open. Sam, not knowing what he was about to receive, but knowing attack was always the best defence, started talking loudly before he was even halfway through the door. "Missed me that much did you, you idle lot. Last Monday and Tuesday nights' money not enough for you, is that it? So now you're back, asking for more. And to think that I've already booked you ungrateful swines for tomorrow, as well as next Monday, Wednesday and Friday. I don't know. The sooner you lot just sod off back to Hamburg, next weekend, and leave Liverpool in peace, the better for us all." He sniffed his defiance and, as an afterthought, nodded a tardy acknowledgement of Spike's display of courtesy. "Thanks, there, Spike."

"There's posh, Sam. You going in for your very own private serfs, now?" John Lennon, sat in a chair by the door, burst out laughing. "And just look at the state of your shoes, Leachy! You could've made a bloody effort to tidy yourself up knowing we were coming."

Sam looked down at his brand new pair of brown suede Hush Puppies, the very latest in fashion and now very much the worse for wear. "Oh, heck, and they were new on today, as well."

"They're dead disgusting, they are, Sam. Me? I wouldn't have let you in looking like that. It definitely lowers the tone of the establishment."

"You can shurrup, too, George Harrison," Sam growled. "Or I might have the Mean Machine tread all over them flash new cowboy boots of yours."

Pete Best patted George on the shoulder. "He didn't mean anything by it, Sam. It's just he's the sartorial one of the group."

"The sarky one, more like it," chipped in John.

"Yeah, we heard about the Mean Machine going into action earlier, Sam. Fearsome, they are. You should send them on a tour of all the Hamburg clubs, around St. Pauli. They'd clean up there, they would."

"Not a bad idea, Mr McCartney, if they could only sing and play, like you lads. But as long as they look after you and the fans outside, and deal with any trouble, I'm happy. So what's the big problem? You're not expecting to get paid in cash money or anything like that, are you?"

John thrust out his hands, begging. "Ohhhh, please don't scold us, Mr Sam, sir. Your bountiful munificence has always been enough for us poor Scousers to keep our humbly homes together." The quavering voice suddenly grew hard. "But now you mention it, you swine, some real pound notes to stuff in our pockets would work bloody wonders."

"It's you that should get stuffed, Lennon. Don't I always look after you boys and always pay you way more than anyone else?"

"Don't lose your wiggie, Sam," said John, waving a finger. "We were only just saying how well things go, when you're running them."

"So, I repeat, 'whistling Jock' Lennon, what's yer big problem?"

John pulled a face. "You tell him, Pauly, you can explain it better than the rest of us."

"Thing is, Sam, we use a lot of American equipment now. We've got a Gibson amp and a Fender amp and the wiring's different to what we have here at home. Normally, we'd have a go at sorting it out ourselves, like. But there'd be bare wires all over the place. And well, with no proper earth wire and with all the condensation running down the walls...if any of it touched any of our leads and shorted out, like...we'd all be..."

"We'd all be bloody dead, Sam. Burned to a bloody crisp," snorted John. "So, what you gonna do about it, Sam? What you gonna do?"

"I heard you the first time, John. I haven't got cloth ears. But as everyone's here to see you lot play, there'd be a full-scale riot if you didn't go on tonight. So just let me think a minute, will yers?" Sam scratched his head and chewed his lip and tried to ignore the growing knot in his stomach.

"Yeah, and silence reigned and we all got wet."

"Guten Abend, Herr Sutcliffe. I was wondering when you'd pipe up from behind your dark glasses and funny haircut." Sam gave the group's bass player a dirty look and continued scratching his chin.

"Shurrup, Stu, can't you see the man's trying?"

"Yeah, he's very trying."

George Harrison piped in. "I'd have had a go myself, Sam, having once been an apprentice electrician, like. But I decided not to, as I was never any good at it."

Sam, lost in thought, looked up at George, and stared. "And what do you call that funny looking haircut when it's at home? You and Sutcliffe look like a right pair of puddings."

"Well, I don't know what Stu calls his, Sam," said George, good-naturedly. "But I call mine, Ingrid, after a girl I met in Hamburg."

"You're a great help, I must say." Sam shook his head, his frustration growing by the second. "I know, why don't I just clap my hands or something and conjure up an electrician out of thin air? Or better yet, wait for a bolt of lightning to put us all out of our miseries. If only you daft sods had thought to think about all this beforehand."

"Well, I don't know if it's of any help, Mr Leach, but I do know a bit about electric motors and step-down transformers. Only, before I managed to get into the Art College, I did a couple of terms at night school doing an electrical engineering course."

All eyes in the room swivelled towards Spike, who'd been totally ignored up until that point. Sam looked at him in amazement and, quick as a flash, spread out his arms ready for acclaim. "How *do* I do it? It's truly amazing, it is. Er, fellas, this is my new personal assistant, Spike Jones."

"Goodness gracious me, a wild Welsh Goon, 'Jones the Spark'. So speak up, serf Spike," said John. "If you can speak English, that is?"

Spike nodded. "Well, both amplifiers look as if they've got single, twelve-inch speakers, so they'll each put out about 20 watts, I should think. Of course, I'd need to take a look in the back to see how they've been wired up. And as you probably got the amps in Germany, I need to see if any sort of step trans-former has been added into the sequence anywhere. After that, it's a question of determining which circuits carry what voltage, matching up their polarities, and making doubly sure every-thing's earthed properly. The one thing you've got to avoid is any chance of live current earthing between your guitars and the club's microphones. As that could kill you stone dead."

"Leachy, give the man a carrot, and quick."

"My only thought," said Sam, "was you could all stand on your rubber amplifier covers and pray. What about it, Paul, will he do?"

"Looks like it, Sam. Yeah. Good one. Pleased to meet you, Spike. I'm Paul, this is George, and that's Stuart and Pete over there. The one pulling those horrible faces, over in the corner, is John. But you probably knew that already."

"Yeah, I saw you the first time you played Hambleton Hall, last January. None of us had ever heard anything like it. The sound hit you right smack in the chest, like a soddin' howitzer. It was dead amazing. The whole place went wild. Absolutely bloody wild."

Paul McCartney and George Harrison threw wary looks at one another—then at Stu. They'd each of them been beaten-up by Teddy Boys after playing Hambleton Hall—they hated the bloody place.

"He'll do, Leachy," said John Lennon, not catching the exchange. "Anyone that loves Beatles that much, is definitely okay with us."

Spike bubbled on, unaware of the pecking order or the rules of engagement. "I always thought I wanted to be an artist, like. But after I saw you play, then heard round the Art College as how you and Stuart Sutcliffe, here, had just sagged off, for good. I did, too. Now all I want to do is be in a group and play rock 'n' roll, like you fellas."

The light banter suddenly turned heavy. "Oh, for Christ's sake," snapped John Lennon. "Not another failed bloody artist blaming us for his poor, misguided life. Next, he'll be telling us he's as sensitive as shite. Throw him back in the Mersey, Sam. Just get rid of him quick, will yer?"

Spike—startled, surprised, stung—shot back. "You might think you're cock of the walk, Mr Lennon, sir, but you'll still fry yer balls off with 240 volts of alternating current going up yer trouser leg."

"Wooah, Johnno, he's got some lip."

"Yuck, fried Lennon balls. That's dead disgusting, that is."

"I dunno, though," mused Paul. "Shuffling off this mortal coil while singing yer balls off sounds dead poetic, if you ask me."

"And just one more thing there, Mr Lennon, sir. If I can pry your shiny new guitar from out of your dead blackened hands, can I keep it, like?" Spike swallowed hard, but stood defiant.

"Bloody hell, all I said was..." But John didn't finish.

"Hey, Johnno, he's okay," shouted Stu Sutcliffe. "Hey, tell us, young Spike, what did old Ballard say to you when you said you were leaving?"

"He told me I was a daft sod for quitting me art studies just to go play rock 'n' roll, especially as I was showing such promise."

"Yeah, well he might be right there, an' all," said a suddenly reflective Stu. "I mean he's a damn good painter, himself, he is, so he knows real talent when he sees it. You know, you should really listen to..."

"Oh, don't start up with all that again, Stu. You've made up your mind to stay in Hamburg with Astrid and do your painting. And bloody good luck to you. As for us, it's grand to have you sitting in with us one last time. Then that's it. Finished." He blinked and turned his head like a gun turret and pointed it straight at Spike. "As for you, Neddy-Spike-Seagoon-Jones, you just do your job for nice Mr Leachy here. And if you even breathe on my lovely little Ricky 'Three-Two-Five', like. I'll bloody cripple you. Have you got that, have you?" John tilted his head back, peered at Spike through half-closed eyes, and gave a slow, sly wink.

Spike swallowed, nodded, tried not to look too relieved.

"Yeah, Sam, he'll do just fine," continued John. "Especially if he stops his gabbin' and gets on with helping our Pauly fix our amps. Because it's soon gonna be time for us to *Mach* some bloody *Schau*."

"Hallelujah," shouted Sam. "Hey, Spike, stop scratching yer arse and go get a screwdriver from somewhere, will yer. And be quick about it, too. You're not a bloody art student, now, you know."

"LADIES AND GENTLEMEN! Beat boys and girls! It's The Beatles!"

The roar was enough to stand your hair on end. Send waves of shivers up and down your spine. Girls rushed the stage, pushing and elbowing their way to the front. Boys just stood and stomped and whistled and cheered.

Paul McCartney ripped into 'Hippy, Hippy, Shake', and the Iron Door was instantly electrified.

Everyone in the club suddenly plugged in to one another. Everyone knowing this was their music, their sound, and their joy. All empty spaces filled. Nothing more needed. And they bopped and rocked and jumped and jived. Everything complete at last. Everyone sharing the same secret; without anyone needing to say a single, solitary word.

Paul whooped and sang and screamed. He shook it to the left. Shook it to the right. Shook it all over. He couldn't keep still. Not for a single, solitary beat. He jumped up and down, back and forth, and threw himself around the stage as if possessed. He gave it everything he had. Then dug deeper and found more and gave that, too. And when he'd finished, he stood gasping for air, lungs heaving, sweat pouring down his face. His black T-shirt stuck to him as if he'd been dipped in steaming black tar. He nodded and smiled, mouthed his thanks, and waved back at the crowd still going wild. Then wiping his brow with the back of his hand, he turned and nodded to Stu, who quietly unplugged Paul's makeshift bass guitar from the lone Gibson amplifier and plugged in his own Hofner bass.

John Lennon stepped forward into the roaring, stamping, clapping, cheering wall of sound and stood for a moment—head back, guitar strapped high on his chest, legs spread wide—peering out into the crowd. The moment stretched and stretched almost to breaking point. He blinked, owlishly, and yelled, "This is rock 'n' roll!" The Beatles' guitars, bass, and drums snapped out a crisp four-bar intro and John's raw exhortation for his girl to come 'twist and shout' momentarily stunned the crowd to silence.

It was unnerving, exhilarating, galvanizing. Unbelievable.

Pete kicked, battered, thudded, and beat at his drum kit. Stu plucked and pulled at the thick strings of his big-shouldered, brunette-coloured Hofner bass. The deep notes throbbing out the same, simple, ever-repeating pattern. Paul, meanwhile, picked and plucked at the three old piano strings on his now unplugged make-do bass, silently hitting two, three and four notes to every note Stu played. It didn't matter the Rosetti Solid 7's jack-plug was now stuffed, uselessly, in his pocket, he was rocking and rolling and he knew his bass runs were getting better and better, each and every time he played.

Eyes glued to the neck of his Futurama guitar, George kept time by banging one foot against the other. Bending notes. Striking chords. Filling here, adding there. Rounding out the group's hard-hitting sound with all the mastery he could muster. Then leaning in towards the microphone, he and Paul, heads together, sang in perfect harmony, fifths upon thirds, echoing John's call to shake up the world.

John—relentless now—driving the song forward with the razor-edged rhythm of his guitar and the raw naked power of his voice—until at last he came to his final call to *"Shake it. Shake it. Shake it."* To the final screaming crescendo *"Aah, Aaah, Aaaah, Aaaaah, Aaaaaaah!"* And to the last brightly jangling chord of his guitar.

The spell lingered on and on and on until the entire Iron Door audience, stunned, wasted, breathless, finally gasped for air. There was a moment's silence. And then the whole place erupted. Whistling. Cheering. Stamping. Applauding. Shouting for more.

"My throat goes dry every time he bloody sings that," croaked Sam. "It's bloody unbelievable."

"Bloody unbelievable," whispered Spike, nodding, swallowing, and wiping the sweat from his brow with his sleeve.

"And there's another hour and twenty minutes of that still to come," Terry said. "Though God only knows where they get all the energy from."

Terry, Sam, and Spike stood by the side of the stage, all but transfixed. Sam's eyes glistened. Standing there, so close to it all was what made all the business hassles worthwhile. It was the one perk he never ever wanted to give up. Rock 'n' roll was such an obsession; it scared him sometimes. It was food and drink. The very air he breathed. Far more important than whatever money he made from putting on such events. Getting a bigger and better hit of satisfaction is what drove him to put on ever bigger and better shows. There was no other feeling like it. At least, nothing else he'd tried had ever come close. And if it also held out the vague promise of a better life than him just being another soddin' accountancy clerk in the Liverpool offices of the English Electric Company, then so much the better.

"Just feel all that electricity," Terry yelled. "It's like the whole place was hit by a bolt of bloody lightning. Everyone was jumping up and down like they were plugged into the wall or something."

"Like lightning in a bottle," whispered Spike.

"Yeah, but how on earth could you ever bottle that?" croaked Sam. "And who's smart enough to do it? The boys all know I want to, but I just haven't got the cash. I will one day, though, by Christ, I will." He stared off into the distance, as if searching for some sign that might more clearly point the way to his dream. Then he blinked and shrugged and slid his eyes sideways at Spike. "Talking of electricity, sunshine. Did you notice that whatever it was you re-wired in them amplifiers, in the end, the boys still all stood on their rubber amplifier covers?" He blew a perfect smoke ring into the air. "You might know a thing or two about electrics, young Spike, and don't get me wrong I'm very glad and impressed you do, but I tell you when it comes to survival, you just listen to old Sam Leach, here. Only, hush-your-mush, now, it's our George's turn to sing."

GEORGE sang. Paul sang. Pete sang. And so did Stu. Then John took back the stage. Until, finally, together, at last, John and Paul threw themselves at 'Money' and brought their rip-roaring ninety-minute set to a close. The crowd went wild again—jumping, stamping, whistling, shouting, clapping, and cheering for minutes on end.

"Fookin' 'A'," yelled Spike as The Beatles left the stage.

"Glad to see that that education of yours hasn't gone to your head, any," quipped Sam. "But, yeah, there's no one in Liverpool can touch them. No one. So, yes, I have to agree with you, fookin' 'A' is right."

"More's the pity, Sam. How in heck do me and The Pacemakers follow that?" A despondent Gerry Marsden turned and looked up at Sam. "Next time, Sam. Do us a favour, will yers, and put us on before the Beats?"

Sam grinned, leaned forward, and clapped Gerry on both shoulders. "But that's exactly why I have put you on next, Gerry, me old son! There's no one else in all of Liverpool, but you, who could follow The Beatles. I promise you, by the time you get to singing, 'You'll Never Walk Alone', you'll have the whole lot of them marching alongside you, eating out of your hand."

"Okay, Sam, if you say so. We'll try knock the sods down, even if we can't knock 'em dead."

Sam signalled for Terry McCann to begin his introduction. Gerry led The Pacemakers out onto the stage to a rapturous welcome from the crowd.

Sam turned to Spike and whispered. "I don't know how I do it, sometimes. Honest, I don't. It must be the way I tell them."

CHAPTER THREE

Easter Rock Fest

The Punch and Judy cafe across the road from Lime Street Station was a favourite hang out. Food was good and cheap, the place stayed open late, and the manager didn't seem to mind if you sat and nursed a cup of tea or coffee for a good couple of hours. The constant stream of people coming and going—all the bustle and noise—only seemed to add to the sense you were somewhere very near the heart of things.

Sam looked up and sipped his tea as Spike bit noisily into a slice of hot buttered toast. "You getting a couple of posters down inside the Cavern toilets is very good. Sticking a few on Ray McFalls's Cavern-mobile, parked outside, is even better." He peered at his young assistant through the clouds of blue cigarette smoke. "But you plastering fifty posters up and down the length of Mathew Street...now that was inspired, even if I say so myself. Just remind me to give you a raise for inventiveness next time I have some cold hard cash in me pocket."

Spike, still munching on his toast, smiled and nodded, and gave a thumbs-up. Sam lit another cigarette with his rolled-gold lighter, took a long drag, inhaled deeply, and blew two long parallel streams of smoke out through his nostrils. He picked a flake of tobacco from his teeth. "There's a definite art to fly-posting. And you've definitely got the hang of it. But as it's not one of them rowdy Students' Panto Days or Fine Arts Balls, you've got to go real careful. People tend to get a bit funny if you make too much of a mess round the place and they think you haven't got the proper education for it. They call it hooliganism, then, not art." The lesson duly given, Sam extended his little pinkie, reached for his cup, and gulped down his tea.

"Perhaps you better know, now, Sam, I also stuck a poster up on Bob Wooler's front door."

Sam all but snorted up his tea. And as he reached for a handkerchief he knocked over his cup, spilling the tea onto the red Formica tabletop. Half-spluttering, half-choking, he tried to soak up the fast-spreading brown puddle with his copy of the *Liverpool Echo*, while dabbing furiously at the tea that'd also splashed down the front of his coat.

"You went and did bloody what?"

BOB WOOLER muttered through his teeth. "I'll have Sam Leach's garrulous guts for garters." Having to scrape off the Easter Rock Festival poster he'd found flour-pasted to his front door, that morning, had been bad enough, but to have then been confronted by another fifty more of the blasted things, plastered up and down Mathew Street, was too much. Now here he was, standing outside the entrance to the Cavern Club, in the midday drizzle, putty knife in hand, scraping the offending rain-soaked posters from off the grimy warehouse walls.

A small compact man with bird-like features, Bob Wooler's carefully articulated erudition and love of alliteration elevated him in any crowd. He was well known around Liverpool's pubs and clubs for his barbed ad-libs—all of them, of course, meticulously pre-planned. He found himself shivering in the cold damp air, but diligently carried on with his muttering and wall scraping. "That conniving character from Consville...that no good do-no-gooder. There's supposed to be such a thing as good manners and civility, in business. Not that Mr Samuel Leach by name, leech by nature, would know that, even if it'd been beaten into him by a superfluity of nuns."

A voice hailed him from the arched doorway that led down to the basement storage cellar that'd been transformed into the Cavern Club by little more than a coat of whitewash and a few lights. "Here, Bob, come on inside and get yourself dry. I'll have Paddy Delaney and the boys have a go at getting the rest of them off, later. That damn Leach...he even managed to get a couple of the damn things on the walls in the Ladies toilets. I don't know about him, really I don't."

RAY McFALL, the owner of the Cavern, was not amused. It'd been a nice orderly scene until Sam Leach had barged his way in and messed things up. To McFall, schooled solidly in accountancy, Leach was nothing more than an upstart maverick promoter whose single purpose in life seemed to be upsetting everyone's applecart with madcap schemes for generating business and publicity. What really irritated him was that Leach's wild, often juvenile antics not only appeared to produce results, they raised the stakes for everybody else. He pulled out a packet of cigarettes, lit one, and then quickly and deliberately stubbed it out. Yes, he and the Cavern could well do without the likes of Sam Leach. And he wondered, and not for the last time, whether any of Liverpool's other promoters felt the same.

He knew very well it was Bob Wooler he largely had to thank for his success. One of the smartest things he'd ever done was to hire the ex-British Railways booking clerk as the Cavern's full-time club compère and disc jockey. Bob owned what was widely considered to be the best collection of 45 rpm records on Merseyside, most of them American imports all but unobtainable through usual channels. Furthermore, not only did Bob have the best line of patter of any disc jockey in Liverpool, he also knew most of the top groups, personally. In fact, it was Bob who'd first suggested the Cavern book The Beatles to play lunchtime sessions. Bob had actually called them 'rhythmic revolutionaries', whatever the hell that meant. But the effect the group had on attendance had certainly woken him up to their box-office potential. The fans had started queuing up hours before the club opened. And that was something he'd not witnessed before—ever. Even the previous week, when he'd booked The Beatles as a back up band for 'The Bluegenes' Guest Night', there hadn't been room enough to swing a drumstick, let alone a cat. The Cavern had been packed to the rafters.

He bent down and picked up one of the posters he'd scrunched up and thrown on the floor and read it again. 'BRITAIN'S FIRST EVER EASTER ROCK FESTIVAL. 30 MARCH — 3 APRIL. NINE SHOWS. THREE VENUES. OVER 4 DAYS OF EASTER'. It was the part highlighting the 'All-Nighter at The Iron Door' on the Saturday that made him narrow his eyes.

"What do you make of it all, Ray?" Bob Wooler asked, shak-

ing the rain from his raincoat and wiping his feet on the big coconut doormat.

"It gives me an idea, Bob. Leachy may have de-faced my van,
but I think there's a way for us to fix his wagon...and for good
this time."

SAM LEACH pushed aside the empty teacups and plates. "Right,
sunshine, let's tally it all up." He totted up the figures scribbled
on the back of a cigarette packet. "Strewth. By my reckoning the
total publicity cost, thus far, for the Easter Festival is nigh on
five hundred quid. Five hundred! After spending that much
money you'd have thought The Beatles would've had the courtesy not to go gallivanting off to Hamburg again. With the lads
topping the bill I'd have been certain to make me money back,
several times over. But I mean to say, five hundred quid! Talk
about 'Britain's First Ever Rock Festival' being right on your
doorstep...what about on my soddin' shoulders?"

"That's a colossal amount of money, Sam, but you're doing
something no one's ever done before. Not here. Not anywhere.
Just think, Sam. Two thousand crown posters, ten thousand
handbills, and that's not even counting all your advertisements
in the *Liverpool Echo.*"

"True, true, those three full-page ads must've cost a hundred
quid, all by themselves." He looked at Spike, a look of bemused
resignation on his face. "But I don't have any choice in the matter, do I, me old mucker? It's the way I'm made. I'm a rebel with
a cause, I am."

"Yeah, but now everyone seems to be copying what you're
doing."

"Again, very true. Only this afternoon, when I was at the
Echo, writing out more ads, paying out more money, that sod,
Ray McFall, walks in, as bold as brass, to put an advert in for the
Cavern. The sly bastard is catching on fast. You've gotta spend
money, to make money. That's why I nipped down Mathew
Street, afterwards, to check up on your handiwork."

"Did you know his people would go and tear down all our
Easter Rock Festival posters?"

Sam nodded. "I half expected it, like, knowing McFall. That's why I had you and the lads ready to splash up another hundred posters as soon as his back was turned. It's the Liverpool way. You always fight fire with a load more fire."

SAM LEACH slammed down the phone. "I don't bloody believe it. Spike! Terry! Someone's only trying to pull the Iron Door out from under me." He sat, eyes going from side to side, desperate to figure out what was going on.

"What the hell's up, Sam?" Terry McCann skidded into the cramped storeroom-cum-office, took the one free chair, and sat down.

"That was Geoff Hogarth, one of the owners of this place. Says his new partner, Billy Glanz, has had a very big offer from someone who wants to take over the entire music franchise for the Iron Door. Says there's going to be a meeting about it tomorrow. And he's not certain, like, but Glanz may have already shook hands on the deal. All of which means, me old muckers, I could be out on my arse and on the street as early as next week. Which would leave me with only the Cassanova and the Merrifield as venues. And there's no way in hell I can put on an all-nighter in either of them."

"Blimey, that's a bit rich," sniffed Terry.

"On the contrary, it'd have me bankrupt and my name ruined for life, and me only twenty-seven years of age. I can't go back on all the promises I've made to the groups. Not now I've firmed up all the bookings...done all the advertising. What in heaven's name would all the fans think, if I didn't deliver on me promises? My name would be mud all over Merseyside."

"What you going to do, Sam?"

"Shurrup a minute, Spike. I'm trying to bloody well think."

Spike and Terry busied themselves around the club. An hour or so later Sam leaned out into the corridor and yelled for them to re-join him. "Here, sit your arses down and listen." Sam stood up, as they sat down, and started pacing back and forth. "I've been racking my brains trying to think," he said, lighting a new cigarette from the stub of an old one. "Then I remembered I'd once overheard, in the Grapes, that Ray McFall used to be Billy Glanz's accountant. It all fell into place, after that. Think about it. Right out the blue, Billy Glanz becomes partners with Geoff Hogarth and part-owner of this very building." Sam slid a Coke out from the nearest wooden crate and knocked off the metal cap on the edge of the table. He took a long swig, handed the bottle around. "So I made a few telephone calls. Took me best part of an hour. Almost didn't believe it myself when I found out what I did." He stopped, stared at the wall for a moment, ran his hands through his lank greasy hair, and then turned, his face grim. "The new offer to operate the Iron Door came from a club owner who's a well known close friend of Ray McFall's, in partnership with none other than our old enema, Bob Wooler, demon-jawed DJ of this parish."

Silence hung in the room like a damp fog off the river.

"You tell me if you think I'm mad. Only, Sam's old nose smells a big rat skulking in a cellar not a million miles away from Mathew Street."

"What the hell are they playing at, Sam? The sneaky backstabbing bastards must've known it'd put you out of business."

"That's the whole point of the exercise, Tel. They're out to bloody crucify me...and at Eastertime, too. It beggars belief. They want me out of the music business and gone for good, with absolutely no chance of resurrection...not now, not ever."

"It's not fair, Sam," piped in Spike. "It's not right."

"Life hardly ever is, me old son," retorted Sam. "And better you learn it now, than sometime in the future when you've got your own arse hanging out in the wind. Here, let me sit down."

Spike and Terry stood up, neither of them knowing what to do or say. Sam sat at his desk and tapped his fingers up and down. Then he looked up, narrowed his eyes, and smiled his most devilish smile. "But I happen to have an idea how to get back at the sods. It might not work, but as I have nothing else to lose it's worth a try." He swept the clutter from off his desk onto the floor, reached for another Coke, knocked the top off, took another swig of the nectar of the Gods and handed the bottle to Spike. Then he reached for his little black address book, picked up the telephone, and got to work.

He called his contact in every one of the groups contracted to play at the Iron Door, over Easter, as well as all the groups booked to play the Cass and the Merrifield. And he told them in plain blunt language what was up. Afterwards, he sent Spike and Terry out on a borrowed motorbike, to track down anyone he'd been unable to get hold of by phone. And, as he'd hoped would happen, every single musician, in every group, said they'd boycott the Iron Door for good if it reopened as a new club under the proposed new management. What seemed to shock everyone was that Bob Wooler had been party to such shady dealing—the general feeling that it was way, way beneath him.

SAM LEACH rubbed the grit from his tired eyes and retied the cord of his dressing gown. It'd been a very long night—but it was now half-past cockcrow and time to telephone Geoff Hogarth, at home, and tell him of the threatened boycott by almost all of Liverpool's top groups if the proposed deal to oust him from the Iron Door went through as planned.

Hogarth was stunned. "Bloody 'eckers, like, Sam. You know even more about this than I bloody do. I don't know as how you found out as much about it all, as you did. Or how you've managed to do as much about it as you've done, in the time, but let me call you back later. This has ruined me breakfast, this has."

"Yeah, it did mine, Geoff," croaked Sam as he put the phone down. He caught sight of himself in the hallway mirror. In the pale light of morning it looked like he'd aged ten years.

It took until lunchtime for Geoff Hogarth to call back. "Billy Glanz went bloody spare when I told him of the threatened boycott, Sam. But he's not daft, he's already gone and put the kybosh on the deal with Wooler and Williams and has promised to stand by my original contract with you. So we're back now to how we were, okay?"

"Yeah. Back to where we all once belonged. Ain't life grand?"

SAM LEACH threw down his stub of a pencil. However many times he did his sums, it added up to more trouble than he could handle. How on God's green could things have gone downhill so quickly after the huge success of his Easter Rock Festival? It was more than just bad luck. It was as if someone had stuck pins in a Voodoo doll and thrown it on the fookin' fire.

The very first Saturday night following the Rock Festival there'd been such a huge disturbance at the Black Cat Club, up-stairs from the Cassanova, that the police had raided the place in force. Busloads of people had ended up in hospital. So the au-thorities told the building's owner to close both clubs down—no argument. And he'd opened up another club, elsewhere. A much smaller venue, much further out of town, that he'd christened, the Valentine's Club. But it was never in the same class as 'the Cass' and business had never really picked up.

Then, suddenly, all over the city, there'd been another out-break of gangs offering clubs protection. The same old threat—cough up money now or your club will get wrecked or worse. Soon after which the Black Rose coffee bar, at the bottom of Duke Street, had been gutted by fire. As he'd said to Terry, "How the fook do you fight that without the entire Liverpool fookin' fire brigade at your back, day and night?"

Even then, ever the optimist, he'd kept on trying new things. He'd put on a special send-off show for Gerry and The Pace-makers, at the Merrifield Club, prior to yet another of their trips out to Hamburg. But the gang-fight that'd broken out that night was as mean and as vicious as any he'd ever seen. It started with fists, quickly progressed to broken bottles and beer glasses. Then the bicycle-chains, razors and knives had all come out.

And with that he was down to two club venues.

A few days later, an even bigger fight had broken out at The Valentine's Club. And even though the boys in blue from the nearby police station, in Cheapside, had arrived quickly, more than a dozen Teddy Boys needed hospital treatment. After-wards, the local chief inspector had strongly suggested he close the club, which of course not being daft he'd done immediately.

All he had left then was the Iron Door.

And with only one club—and the dog days of summer fast approaching—he'd had no other choice but to economise. God, but he hated that bloody word. He needed bouncers for three nights, each and every weekend, but he had no other choice but to let go most of the Mean Machine. Terry and the Molloy brothers had stayed on, at reduced wages, as a favour. Spike, too. And everyone had filled-in when and where they could. But they hadn't been able to contain the fights that broke out the moment their backs were turned. And of course it wasn't long before the fans noticed and began to stay away.

It was a vicious cycle. Fewer fans meant smaller box office takings, which in turn meant he wasn't always able to pay the groups their money on time. It was no way to run a business. So, yes, he'd given up his lease on the Iron Door, before everyone else gave up on him. It'd felt like giving up both his arms and his legs—and that he'd remain crippled for life. So to get back onto his feet, he'd tried to do things on credit. Looked farther and farther afield, in search of new venues. But the more he tried, the more it always seemed all doors were already closed to him or were very quickly slammed in his face.

"BLOODY HELL, SPIKE, you'd think I was a damn leper the way things have been going lately." Sam looked at Spike sitting across from him, in an almost deserted Punch and Judy cafe. "Thanks for standing me the tea. Especially as I haven't been able to pay you a single bloody penny for weeks. So, look, sunshine, I reckon it's time for us both to cut and run. Either that or I go cut my bloody throat."

"Things will get better, Sam. I know they will," said Spike, softly.

"You're as bad as me, you are, Spike. Despite all your mean and moody carryings on, you can't hide it from me, you know. You're like me, you just can't stop running around looking for something to believe in."

Spike, taken aback by the piercing clarity of what he'd just heard, looked at Sam in surprise.

"I'm not just a pretty face, you know, Spike. I've been to the Liverpool College of Life and learned one or two things about people. And I know enough to know you don't need me to show you the way. It was always rock 'n' roll for me, but I've got a tin ear. And what hurts most is I can't play a note or carry a tune to save my bleedin' life. I sound like a broken concrete mixer. Or a dog with a hernia." He smiled, swirled the tea round in his tea-cup. "But you, you go off and find yourself. Go play that soddin' guitar you're always going on about. Or go do some of that artsy-fartsy painting you keep telling people you'd never be caught dead doing ever again."

Spike, his throat suddenly very, very dry, reached for his tea. It was stone cold, but he drank it down in one gulp.

"Yeah, time to go." Sam downed his own tea and wiped his mouth. "Er, got another ciggy by any chance, Spike?" He patted his pockets. "Only, I'm all out."

Spike opened his fag packet, looked inside, and saw there were only two cigarettes left. He closed the packet and held it out to Sam.

Sam opened the pack and, his fingers rippling like he was about to play a piano, took a single cigarette. "Just the one." He passed it under his nose as if it was the choicest Havana cigar, nodded his thanks, and slid the cigarette behind his ear. "See you round, sunshine," he said. And with that, he went out into the early evening rush of Lime Street.

Spike watched him disappear and, as tough and as cool as he liked to think himself, had to fight back the tears welling up in his eyes.

SAM LEACH walked all the way to the Pier Head and stood in the shadow of the Royal Liver Building with the rest of the crowd waiting for the Mersey ferry. He sniffed the air and all but choked. "Ah, the mighty majestic Mersey. Nothing in the world to touch it for having a piss in." A middle-aged woman wearing a headscarf, who'd overheard him, looked at him sharp-ly, hugged her Blackler's carrier bag even more tightly to herself, and edged away.

Sam turned and gazed across the river towards Birkenhead, until the old black, red, and cream ferry finally appeared chug-ging its merry way from out of the gathering gloom. The ferry cut its engines, drifted a little on the tide, then banged up against the old rubber tyres on the side of the pier. Sam waited for the passengers to disembark, paid his tuppence fee, and boarded the ferry. But instead of taking a seat inside, he made his way through the cabin and went and stood out on deck.

Leaning against the rail, he looked down at the dark grey-green river and waited for the ferry to depart. The breeze was strengthening and he knew enough to know it meant there was a chance of storm coming in. He shivered, pulled his coat collar up and, with eyes blinking, peered into the wind. And being away from all the other passengers, and everyone he knew or that knew him, he found himself, quite unexpectedly, at peace. He breathed in again, deeply, but now the Mersey-scented air seemed to help clear his head. He caught the sounds of the waves slapping against the side of the boat and the seagulls screaming and snapping in circling clouds of dirty grey and white above him. "I may be down and out," he whispered, "but I'm not bloody dead yet, am I?"

He reached up and took the cigarette from behind his ear, cupped his hands against the wind, struck a match, and lit up. He drew the smoke deep down into his lungs and blew it out through his nostrils in two long blue streams. The wind snatched at the smoke and twisted it away to nothing. And slowly Sam began to nod his head from side to side, as if keeping time with some unseen rhythm, some unheard beat. Soon he was tapping his foot and drumming his fingers up and down on the top of the scuffed wooden railing. Then he was slapping the flat of his hands hard against the rail in a tightly patterned, re-petitive, driving beat—the waves and the gulls lapping and screeching in concert, all around him. And in a hoarse, gravely whisper of a voice, all but choked with emotion, he began to sing his favourite song—one that he'd always felt could've been especially written for him—Eddie Cochran's 'Summertime Blues'.

The ferryboat's engines suddenly shuddered into life and added a rumbling, rolling, throbbing backbeat. And with two ear-piercing signal blasts of the ferry's high-pitched horn, Sam Leach finally got underway.

CHAPTER FOUR

Mersey Beat

Brian Epstein had telephoned personally—not his secretary. A tiny point, perhaps, but it pleased Bill Harry immensely and he smiled at the recollection of it. 'Would he mind dropping round to NEMS record store, in Whitechapel, for a meeting that would be to his advantage?' Of course, he bloody well wouldn't mind. When someone as important to the city's music scene, as Mr Brian Epstein, manager and owner of NEMS—*Finest Record Selections In The North*—called you with a promise of some extra business, you responded. You might not jump to it, but then again it was only prudent that you not be late for your scheduled appointment.

He slipped into Whitechapel from Stanley Street and made a mental note to straighten his tie and polish his shoes on the back of his trouser legs before he entered the store. As it was, it was all he could do to hold on to half-a-dozen or so large manila envelopes and the big bundle of *Mersey Beats*—Merseyside's very first, very own entertainment newspaper—he had clutched under his arms. Humming tunelessly, he wove in and out of the slow moving late-morning shoppers; all of them bundled up against a wind that was much too cold, even for a Liverpool July. As he hurried along Whitechapel, the flimsy newsprint rippled and flapped a paradiddle as his feet beat out the time on the pavement, but he had no ear for the rhythm or meter of the street. He might write about the music scene, but he was an aspiring journalist and newspaper publisher, not a musician. He left music to others with the appropriate talents.

He sniffed a runny nose into submission and wished he'd had time to run a comb through his unruly hair. Hair, his best friend, John Lennon, had once told him, that looked like he'd got his fingers permanently stuck in an electric socket. But now, with no time to spare and no comb to hand, he stuck a toothy grin on his face, pushed open the door to NEMS, and asked to be directed to the manager's office.

"Mr Harry. Thank you for coming so promptly. I'm sure you must be very busy. Please do take a seat. A Sherry? No? A cup of tea? No? Let's get straight down to business, then, shall we?"

Slim and handsome, with brown wavy hair always perfectly trimmed, Brian Epstein was fastidiously—some might say fussily—elegant. He wore expertly tailored suits, hand-made monogrammed shirts and when not sporting a discreetly patterned silk tie, always wore a silk spotted foulard tied around his neck. He spoke with a polished, almost 'plummy' upper-class voice that showed not the slightest trace of a Liverpool accent.

Bill Harry scratched his straggly 'beatnik' beard, took a deep breath, and was overcome by a heady mix of lavender furniture polish and expensive after-shave. His throat, suddenly as dry as burnt toast, he gasped, "Could I have a glass of water, please?"

"Of course, how unthinking of me." Brian Epstein shot his cuffs, got up from behind his desk, went over to a small side table and poured a glass of water from a crystal decanter. He turned and, with an apologetic smile, handed the glass to his guest. "The thing is, Mr Harry, when earlier, this week, I agreed to take those first dozen copies of *Mersey Beat*, I had no idea they'd sell so quickly. In fact, they all went within minutes of being available. The same thing happened with the two dozen copies I asked to be delivered yesterday."

"It's Bill. Please call me, Bill, Mr Epstein, everyone does. And that's great that is: all sold out, in minutes? That's great, that is."

"The thing is, Mr Harry, excuse me, Bill—and please do call me, Brian—I'd like to re-order a further hundred copies of *Mersey Beat*. I was frankly amazed by all the interest. Young people came in asking for it all afternoon and unfortunately we had to turn many of them away, empty handed. As you may know, I pride myself on giving record buyers a service that's second to none, but I simply had no idea there was such a pent-up demand for news regarding the local music and entertainment scene."

Bill Harry cleared his throat. "Well, there must be over three hundred groups, around Merseyside, all playing rock 'n' roll, country, western, Trad-jazz, folk. There are duos, trios, quartets, even all-girl rock 'n' roll bands. There are black vocal groups and Caribbean steel bands. There's also a flourishing poetry scene. As well as a huge number of works' social clubs that employ hundreds of comedians, speciality acts and show bands."

"How very extraordinary."

"It is, Brian, and it's going on everywhere: town halls, church halls, ballrooms, ice-rinks, clubs, cellars, coffee bars...even cinemas and swimming baths. One local promoter, Allan Williams, even hired Liverpool Stadium to put on a rock 'n' roll show."

Brian Epstein nodded, sagely. "I truly had no idea, Mr Harry. But the question remains, can you immediately let me have an extra hundred copies of your newspaper? And if demand continues, I'll be sure to ask you for more. In fact, I'll order twelve dozen copies of your second issue, now."

The profit to NEMS would be minimal—a penny-halfpenny, half of the newspaper's selling price—but if new fans could be drawn into the store to ask for *Mersey Beat*, he felt sure additional record sales would soon follow. "So, what do you say, Bill? Have we got a deal?"

BILL HARRY grinned a big toothy grin. He'd originally intended to start a newspaper devoted solely to jazz, but when he'd witnessed what was happening, musically, all over Merseyside—in the city, across the river in New Brighton and Birkenhead, up in Crosby and Southport, even as far as Warrington and St. Helens. He knew he had to cover it all and write about the groups and the music, as well as list and advertise the hundreds of shows and dances occurring each and every week. He'd walk his beat, as he called it, like some conscientious local policeman, and bring news of the new sound to music fans all over Merseyside.

And now, here it was, suddenly, all happening for real.

He got to his feet and as he did so one of the large brown manila envelopes slipped from off his lap, spilling its contents out onto the floor. He bent down to pick things up, but his mind was elsewhere, figuring out the significance of Brian Epstein's request. If NEMS was going to commit to one hundred and forty-four copies of *Mersey Beat*, every two weeks, at threepence a time, that would give sales of around one pound, seventeen shillings, and sixpence a fortnight—three pounds, fifteen shillings a month—and all from just one store. Half of the proceeds, of which, would then come directly to him.

And that was even before he counted the potential sales from the main wholesalers: W. H. Smiths, Blackburn's, Conlan's. If he factored in the other twenty-eight stores, clubs, and musical instrument shops on his distribution list, he could well be on his way to selling out all 5000 copies of *Mersey Beat*—the entire print run.

He'd be in profit with his very first issue!

All of it done while still, officially, attending the Art College.

"Well, golly, yes, that's terrific, Mr Epstein, I mean, Brian," he said, shuffling about on his hands and knees, trying to retrieve the photos and typewritten papers that'd spilled out onto the richly carpeted floor. "Er, thank you, I can bring them round myself, later today." He looked up. "Or before lunchtime, if you like? You can even have these copies I was going to drop off at another store."

Brian Epstein, ever the gracious host, came out from behind his desk and began to help pick things up.

BRIAN EPSTEIN smiled. "Here, let me help you with those, Bill." The black and white glossy photos of boys dressed in black leather jackets and tight-fitting jeans had immediately caught his attention. Who were they? Where were they? What were they? He picked up several of the eight-by-ten photographs and studied them. "What very professional-looking, rather unusual photographs...rough-edged and gritty, but so very real...a little outlandish, even. Do you mind if I ask you who took them?"

"Fantastic, aren't they? That one's going to be on the cover of the next issue. A young photographer, named Astrid Kirchherr, took them, over in Hamburg. She lives there, studied at the art school. And as you can see, she's very, very talented. She became a real close friend of the boys, I mean, The Beatles, during their first visit there."

"The Bee...the Beetles, did you say?"

"Yeah, The Beatles...Liverpool's best rock 'n' roll and rhythm-and-blues group. That photo's one of the first ones Astrid took of them. Good, isn't it? They're all friends of mine from the Art College. Well, Stu is. He's the one on the right, in the dark glasses, who looks a bit like James Dean. John is, too. He's the one in the middle. The others are Paul and George and Pete. But they're all of them great guys, great musicians. Got fans all over Liverpool. Boys, as well as girls, start queuing up to see them hours before a show's even due to start."

Brian Epstein carried the photographs back to his desk, laid them out, neatly, side-by-side, and stared intently at the picture that'd first caught his eye. He tried hard not to swallow. The boys in the photo looked so wonderfully magnetic—so rough and tough—so brooding, so arrogant—with a barely concealed promise of aggression—it was quite intoxicating. The boys held their guitars rakishly, but intimately, as if the instruments were integral parts of their bodies. It was, he thought, wistfully, as if they each held the very wand of youth. And for a moment he envied them, even more than he was attracted to them.

"The Beetles? And they're English, you say, not German?"

"No, they're all regular Scousers, all Liverpool born and bred. They've just made a record out in Hamburg, for Polydor. And I tell you, Brian, I think they've got it in them to go all the way to the very top."

He flushed—felt oddly uncomfortable—and suddenly his elegantly furnished office, tailored suit, starched collar, tightly knotted tie all seemed to be constricting and constraining him. The room appeared to be getting smaller and smaller, as he found himself seemingly getting larger and larger—almost like a character from out of some half-remembered book from childhood. Wonderland? Looking glass? He felt so disoriented, he couldn't recall. And his mouth, suddenly, so very dry, he poured himself a glass of water and noticed, with some amazement, that his hand was shaking.

"The Beetles? What an odd name for a group of musicians."

"It's a tribute to Buddy Holly and The Crickets. Only it's not spelt the same as a creepy-crawly beetle, like, it's a play on the word 'beat'...as in a beat of music. John thought it up, he's very clever with words is John."

"Buddy Holly and The Crickets? Oh, yes, I get it, now. Crickets? Beetles? Yes, how very clever. We have 'The Buddy Holly Story' LPs, Volumes One and Two, in stock, downstairs, and in the Charlotte Street store. They sell very well."

"Yes, Buddy Holly's a huge favourite with all the groups."

Brian Epstein slowly tapped a perfectly manicured fingernail up and down on the black and white photograph, the glossy feel of its surface so much like the leather jackets worn by the boys in the picture. The photo showed them sitting on or leaning up against a large wooden structure of some sort. A heavy goods wagon, perhaps, he couldn't be sure. There were words, in German, stencilled on the front of it—a company name in all probability—and the word 'Hannover'. Odd, but he was sure Bill Harry had said, Hamburg. He'd been to Hamburg. He knew all about Hamburg.

THE FIVE BEATLES stared out of the photograph—a study in youthful defiance. Yet they looked surprisingly innocent, even vulnerable. He noticed no one was smiling. The pale young faces marked more by fatigue than joy. Yet he could see a quiet determination there, too—a determination that verged on the insolent. It was odd, but it looked as if they were all waiting for something important to happen. And for the very briefest of moments, he felt he knew exactly what the special event might be, but the thought quickly passed and, beyond the obvious surface attraction, he couldn't think why he should feel so drawn to these five particular young men in the photograph.

He looked again, as if searching for clues, paying close attention to the eyes. The pale, brooding one, in the centre—the one Bill Harry had said was called, John—and the fresh-faced young man standing next to him, holding a white guitar, both stared off into the same unseen future. To the right, in dark glasses, was the one Bill Harry had called, Stu, who looked to be the most self-assured of them all and, as had obviously been his intent, the hardest one to read. On the left, was a rather sullen-faced young man, undoubtedly the youngest member of the group, next to a moody, rather good looking one—with drumsticks in hand and snare drum at his feet—the two young musicians looking straight out at him, unabashed and unmoved.

"The Beatles, you say? B–E–A–T–L–E–S?" He spelled out each letter. He had to admit, it was a marginally clever play on words, but it also seemed to promise something else, although he couldn't think what. He blinked and looked down at Bill Harry, still gathering up his photographs and papers from off the floor. "And they're good friends of yours, these Beatles? Well, when you have a moment, you must tell me more about them, Bill. They sound very interesting." He took one last lingering look at the photos; then pushed them across his desk. How very refreshing it was to have something new and bright to think about. He beamed a warm smile, got to his feet, and began slowly pacing up and down the room. "You know, Bill, I think…I think I can do something for you, in return. What would you say to me writing a little piece…a column's length…for each fortnightly issue of *Mersey Beat*? Just a few words…from the retailer's point of view…that sort of thing. I could review the new record releases. Perhaps, even help make it a little easier for fans to identify and order discs, by also including the relevant stock numbers. I'm sure it would make a very welcome feature in your newspaper. What do you think?"

It was Bill Harry's turn to look off into space. The meeting hadn't turned out at all like he'd imagined—it was a hundred times better. Here was the most important record retailer in Liverpool asking if he might write a regular column for *Mersey Beat*—another first for 'Merseyside's own entertainments paper'.

"It's a good idea, isn't it, Bill?"

Brian's mounting enthusiasm pulled Bill Harry back from his momentary reverie. "Um…yes…Mr Epstein. I think it's a very good idea. A very good idea, indeed."

"Yes, yes. We could entitle it: 'Record Releases by Brian Epstein of NEMS'. What do you think, Bill?"

"I like it Brian. I like it a lot. I really do." And he did, too. He was already enough of a businessman to know how the world turned. He smiled his big toothy grin again; then scratched his chin. "Yes," he said, "why don't we give it a spin."

CHAPTER FIVE

Searchin'

Spike Jones sat on the edge of his bed, in his room, over the front porch of his mother's house, in Huyton, and for what must've been the thousandth time that morning, tried to play and sing along with The Coasters. He'd borrowed a 45 rpm record of 'Searchin' for a few days and had to give it back the following afternoon. He'd pulled the guide arm on the Dansette record player all the way up to the top of its centre spindle, so the disc on the turntable would repeat itself endlessly. Then he'd played it so many times it was as if he'd been trying to learn the group's 1957 hit and the B-side 'Young Blood' all his bloomin' life. The chord shapes C and F were bad enough, but then to be confronted by impossible bloody chords like C7 and B7 and Bb had made for a long and frustrating morning. "Why couldn't they have used an E or an A or a D? I can soddin' well do them." He scratched his chin, peered at the chords someone had hurriedly scribbled out on the back of a cigarette packet and wondered if perhaps they'd got them all wrong. After another hour or so of finger-numbing effort, he put down his guitar to give his fingers and voice time to recover.

He'd taken Sam Leach's advice to heart and was now determined to learn to play the guitar—properly. At one of Sam's gigs, no less a guitarist than Gerry Marsden had suggested he get lessons from Jim Gretty—or 'Grim Jetty' as he called him—at Hessy's music shop. Gerry had said that even though Jim was over thirty, he was one of the best guitarists on Merseyside and had once even won first prize on *Carroll Levis Discoveries* on TV. More importantly, our Jim was the best guitar teacher, going. So with what little money he'd been able to save, as well as some he'd borrowed from his mother, he'd bought the best guitar he could afford—a cherry red Rosetti Solid 7.

He went downstairs, made a cup of instant coffee and a slice of bread and jam, and returned to his room. Then sat on the edge of his bed and started leafing through the latest issue of *Mersey Beat*. Rory Storm and The Hurricanes were on the cover with the news they'd soon be back from their three-month summer season at Butlin's Holiday Camp, in Pwllheli. Gerry Marsden, just back from Hamburg, was pictured in an ad for the Cavern. In the opposite corner was an ad for Jim Gretty. Spike couldn't help but smile. He'd met all these people, at least enough to say hello and have a chat with. True, he hadn't met any bodies quite as lovely as the three girls pictured dancing at a recent event at Litherland Town Hall, but he could dream, couldn't he?

A tiny item in the 'Mersey Roundabout' gossip section caught his eye. The Liverpool Jazz Society was reverting back to its previous 'Iron Door' policy and henceforth there'd be no more rock 'n' roll played at the club. "Bloody hell, Sam," he said aloud to the empty room. "That's enough to make Buddy Holly turn over in his grave. I know they're all still trying to bury you, but that's ridiculous." He threw *Mersey Beat* down on the bed, picked up his guitar again and hit into 'Young Blood', but his fingertips were still so sore he soon had to stop. He reached for his cup of coffee, only to find it stone cold. It put him in mind of the last time he'd seen Sam Leach. He sighed, "Oh, come on, Sam. Don't let the bastards keep you down."

He sighed and went back to *Mersey Beat*. 'WELL NOW-DIG THIS!' said the banner for Bob Wooler's column, but it looked to be a lengthy piece, so he carried on down the page. 'STORM AT BUTLIN'S' reported that Rory Storm had driven fans wild and had been escorted from the ballroom every night by security men in order to protect him and The Hurricanes from the clutches of marauding female souvenir hunters. Spike laughed. Rory was outrageous. Known all round Liverpool as 'Mr Showmanship'. And not just for his bleached-blond hair, turquoise suits, and gold-lamé shirts, but for the raw energy and nonstop excitement of his performances. The amazing thing about Rory, the pronounced stutter he had disappeared completely the moment he started to sing. When, as everyone then agreed, his voice was almost as good as Elvis Presley's. Rory and Sam Leach being the very best of friends, Spike had met the singer loads of times, and had marvelled at how very reserved—normal, even—the man was when not on stage.

At the bottom of the page, right next to an ad for NEMS stores, he noticed a section entitled 'RECORD RELEASES BY BRIAN EPSTEIN OF NEMS'. Like almost every other teenager in Liverpool, Spike listened to disc after disc in the record store's listening-booths before ever putting down a hard-found six shillings and threepence to buy an actual 45 rpm record. In his humble opinion, the Whitechapel and Great Charlotte Street branches of NEMS were the best in the city. They had the best sound-booths and always had the very best record selection. People hung out there for hours at a time. He did, too.

He skimmed the article: EMI's inexpensive new LP label 'Encore' promised the likes of Frank Sinatra, Nat King Cole, Dean Martin, Ruby Murray, and Sir Thomas Beecham for a bargain price of only twenty-three shillings and threepence. 'An asset to any collector and at this price a real bargain', proclaimed the owner of NEMS. "Not for me, it isn't," Spike said, aloud. He ploughed on through Brian Epstein's 'POPS' listings. The Shadows had gone Hawaiian with their new single, 'Kon Tiki', to be followed in September by the release of their very first long-playing album. Elvis's new single 'I Feel So Bad' was going to be available at the end of the month. The George Mitchell Minstrel Singers were going to release their first LP that autumn, before their upcoming Christmas Show.

"Total waste of time," he said, yawning. He stretched and went back to Bob Wooler's piece at the top of the page. 'WHY DO YOU THINK THE BEATLES ARE SO POPULAR?' asked the headline. "Much better," he muttered. "How in heck could I've missed that?" He read Wooler's perceptive comments, nodding his head in mute agreement with almost every line. The Beatles were the biggest thing to hit the Liverpool rock 'n' roll scene and were very definitely its hottest property. "Yeah, there's no one can touch them," Spike said aloud. Then he laughed. 'The stuff screams are made of'. "Yeah, a great line, that, Mr Wooler. Well worthy of old Bill Shakespeare, himself."

SPIKE JONES shook his head. There had to be more to life than just shagging—just had to be. He got to his feet, went to the window, pushed back the lace curtains and, typical for bloody Liverpool, it was raining. What in hell was he doing with his life? His mother had nagged at him non-stop since his father died. Told him he'd amount to nothing, the way he was going on. She'd let up a bit when a friend of the family had helped get him into the Art College. But ever since he'd quit the place, it seemed she'd all but given up on him, too. She still fed him, washed his clothes, gave him pocket money whenever she could, and so at least he had that to thank her for.

He turned, leaned against the windowsill, and stared into his room. Dusty lengths of string dangled down into space. Once upon a time, he'd hung plastic models from the ceiling. Meticulously painted bombers and fighters from his dad's war. He stared at the CND banner pinned to the wall. Tried to remember what on earth had possessed him to hitchhike down to Aldermaston and march through the rain to campaign for nuclear disarmament. He'd even stopped following the ups and downs of Liverpool City—most of the soccer players on the posters on his bedroom wall were long gone, anyway. His eyes slid over the signed photo of Henry Cooper, the second year the boxer had won the ABA light-heavyweight title, and came to rest on the cricket bat standing in the corner. Yeah, he was going to be the next Don Bradman, too, wasn't he? Was he heck? He shook his head at the posters of paintings he'd never ever seen in the oily flesh. Even the pictures of Brigitte Bardot he'd torn out of film magazines were yellowing and fading. As, too, were his school photos. Rows of blurry faces, the names of most of which, he couldn't remember, didn't want to remember.

He looked at the books gathering dust on the bookshelf. At the dark-blue spines of the second-hand electrical manuals he'd bought for evening classes at the local technical college. At the art books on his favourite artists he'd nicked from the Art College library. Cezanne. Picasso. Pollock. Rivers. Rothko. Looked at the pile of dog-eared paperbacks. Camus. Sartre. Kerouac. Orwell. Even, Colin Wilson. Yeah, ever the outsider, he'd staggered through his own plague of know-alls and all of them so bloody brilliant, so bloody sure they'd got all the answers to life's problems. And where had it got old Camus? There was no more asking old Albert, was there? Not since he'd popped his clogs the year before. And where had it all got Spike Jones—ex-schoolboy, ex-art student—current daydreamer? More and more bloody confused, that's what. Weighed down with answers he couldn't even understand the questions to. The only truth he knew for sure—that it was their own roads they'd all written about, not his.

As for his time at the Art College—it'd been one long, never-ending parade of dead boring conversations about nothing much at all. Empty chatter over empty coffee cups that'd gone round and round the soddin' houses, until people had disappeared up their own soddin' backsides. And in the end, wasn't that exactly why he'd left? The fear he was fast becoming just another phoney in a sea of phoneys.

Rock 'n' roll was different. It spoke to him. It was more real than real, sometimes. All life, love, passion, and death resolved in two or three minutes flat. And at the end of each song, you were left with a simple, overwhelming feeling of completeness, of being part of something. He patted his little, green Pye transistor radio; a present from his mum after his dad died. Nigh on every night, since then, lying on his bed, he'd tuned the dial to Radio Luxembourg and listened for hours to the sounds of rock 'n' roll fading in and out like a distant signal from some faraway galaxy.

SPIKE thought about his poor, sad, broken-hearted mum. He knew deep down he loved her, but he didn't know how to show it or how to help. All she did was go out to work. Then spend the rest of her time grieving for someone who was no longer alive. And what good was that if it meant you ended up dying inside and wasting your life away?

What was love, anyway? You couldn't measure it, weigh it, or touch it. It was a nothing. A zero. It was a drag. And yet it'd been like a bloody disease at the Art College—everyone so desperate to pair-up, so desperate to be seen as grown up. The couples always in and out of each other's pockets—promising eternal love. And all of it just play-acting—all of it just dick. Even he'd got sucked into it and without warning had suddenly found himself talking about love and marriage, prams, the whole bloody bit.

It would've been all too easy, too. Yet the plain truth was he'd never once been in love. He couldn't think of anything worse than marrying someone you didn't love. Love had to be real. Otherwise, what was the bloody point? And in his admittedly very short life, there was only one thing that'd ever touched his whole body, heart, mind, and soul, and that was rock and that was roll. The beat did more than make his feet tap—it moved him. The words of hope and longing he'd heard in pop songs had often hit him more deeply, more piercingly, than any so called proper poetry had ever done. Rock 'n' roll might be simple, but it had much to teach you, if you knew how to listen. So, maybe, Sam Leach had been right. All along, all he'd ever really been searching for was something to believe in, someone to love. And there it was—he'd at last managed to put words to the predicament of his life and times. He laughed out loud, but it was without humour.

SPIKE glanced at a stack of canvases standing in the corner. Old paintings of his he'd turned to face the wall the day he'd quit the Art College. He went over, pulled them back, and stared at them. Studies of the River Mersey, of Liverpool's abandoned and decaying docks, of empty buildings and warehouses, and of the old overhead railway—'the Docker's Umbrella'. Vague, impressionistic studies of his mother looking lost, sad and alone. Self-portraits—every single one of them, dark-eyed and dour. A half-finished picture of his dad, based on an old Army photograph—a study in black and grey and khaki, with a single violent slash of red across it.

It hit him then that almost everything he'd ever painted had been in a palette of sooty-blacks, dirty-browns, and cold, flat blues and greys—every single soddin' picture, a sad reflection of never-ending depression. "Fook, what a fookin' miserable life I've gone and made for myself," he whispered, letting the paintings slowly fall back against the wall. He shook his head and let out a long sigh and just stood staring off into space—lost again.

At some point, out of the corner of his eye, his guitar flamed like a beacon in a deep fog and he turned and drifted over to the bed and landed on the copy of *Mersey Beat* still open to Bob Wooler's column on The Beatles: *Rhythmic revolutionaries... An act which from beginning to end is a succession of climaxes... Truly a phenomenon... but also a predicament to promoters! Such are the fantastic Beatles. I don't think anything like them will happen again.*

"Too bloody right, there, Bob. You brilliant old bugger, you."

He thought back to all the stories he'd heard of the rivalry between Sam Leach and Bob Wooler, and chuckled. "The very worst of friends and the very best of enemies," Sam called it. It was pretty obvious though both men loved rock 'n' roll and rhythm-and-blues with a passion, and The Beatles in particular. Wooler couldn't be all that bad, then, could he? After all, he'd been the DJ and compère at Hambleton Hall, that January, when Spike had first set eyes and ears on The Beatles. And as for that bit about nobody being able to touch The Beatles, that's exactly what he thought, too. "But it won't be for want of bloody trying," he shouted as he reached for his cherry-red Rosetti Solid 7 and started 'Searchin' again.

CHAPTER SIX

Spanish Fly

Brian Epstein settled back in his chair and out of the corner of his eye began to watch the young men parade up and down the promenade. A waiter set down a carafe, poured a glass of Rioja, and departed without a word. Over the years he'd been coming to this part of the Spanish coast, he'd developed quite a taste for the local wine and, as he sipped at it, he found himself beginning to relax and for the first time in months. He lit a cigarette, more out of habit than desire, and allowed himself a half smile.

It was his darling mother, 'Queenie', who'd insisted he take himself off to Spain. She said it would help him forget any fears he might have about being in Liverpool at that particular moment in time and, as always, her judgement had been most sound. The warm breeze ruffled his hair and caressed his skin and he closed his eyes and began to drift off. A small cloud cast a shadow across his face and his eyelids flickered, then he sighed, and fell asleep in the sunshine.

He felt his skin start to prickle horribly, from his neck to his cheeks, and he wondered whether the man in the dock felt anything like the same level of discomfort. Even though he'd been permitted to formally identify himself before the Bar as 'Mister X'; his privilege under British law as the intended victim of blackmail; it still felt very much to him as if he was the one being vilified and branded for life, the one destined for prison. He blinked and blinked, but the courtroom and everyone in it was a blur.

HE'D BEEN INVOLVED in an incident in a public toilet, in West Derby, that'd turned unexpectedly ugly and had then become a living nightmare.

"Hello," I said.

"Hello," he said.

"What are you doing out so late?" I asked.

"Nothing much. You?"

"No, nothing much."

Long silence.

He blinked and in the chill overhead light, he saw the docker's broad shoulders, his head inclined, his neck inviting, and he fixed upon the flare of the man's nostrils, his dark eyes, insolent lips, and he swayed with the sickly-sweet remembering of hair-grease mixed with sweat and stale beer. Then he shuddered as he recalled the harsh disinfectant smell that'd assailed his nose and broken into his oblivion and wrenched him suddenly awake into awful, searing pain.

Long silence.

He reached for the edge of the witness box to steady himself, but the sight of his own soft, pink, perfectly manicured fingers made him recoil at the sudden vivid memory of ice-cold water splashing onto him from out of the pit of the urinal trough and soaking him as he lay, all curled up, foetus-like, on the piss-stained concrete floor.

Long silence.

His attacker had emerged from out of the shadows like a fast gathering storm cloud and beaten and kicked him unconscious. Robbed him of his wallet, watch, and fountain pen, even his gold signet ring. Then he'd returned the following day to rob him of his face and his good name. The first menacing telephone call just as he was sitting down to dinner with his parents. Told in no uncertain terms to pay up or else very important people around Liverpool would find out about him being a nancy boy, a ginger beer, a faggot, a bleedin' queer. And that wouldn't do now, would it? No, it wouldn't do at all. Not for a posh businessman with a reputation to keep up—especially when that posh businessman was a pansy-arsed Jew-boy. That had to be worth double anybody's fookin' money.

Long silence.

"No, sir, I have no idea why he attacked me...

"No, sir, I can think of nothing that would have given the accused any reason or cause to attack me...

"No, sir, never at any time did I look at or speak to the accused."

Long silence.

Giving testimony had been the most awful part of the trial. He'd tried to keep all his answers simple and to the point, and not show any emotion; just as he'd been instructed to do; but his story hadn't got any easier with the repeated telling. He'd first had to tell his mother and father; then Rex Makin, the family solicitor; then all the dreadful detectives at the police station. Then he'd had to go through the whole horrible catalogue of events, over and over again, in front of the judge, the jury, both counsels, and all the countless court officials. And, of course, he'd had to give evidence in front of the loathsome creature that'd attacked him and then blackmailed him. The most dreadful part being, the horrid man had been the only one who'd ever looked him straight in the eye.

Long silence.

The police detectives had all but coerced him into setting a trap for the blackmailer. They'd instructed him to return home, wait for the next phone call, and agree to pay whatever sum of money was demanded. Then arrange a rendezvous. The following night, he'd stood in the shadows of a shuttered shop in a deserted section of Whitechapel, not far from NEMS, and waited for what seemed like hours beyond the appointed time. His attacker had suddenly emerged from out of the shadows across the street and approached him: a dark terrible shape, black against the pale yellow street lamps. His hands had trembled and his legs shaken so much he thought he'd die. It'd taken everything in him not to turn and run. Up close, the docker had looked brutish and ugly and the despicable man had even leered at him, as he'd demanded payment. All of which had so disconcerted him as he'd handed over the money in an unmarked brown envelope, that he'd almost forgot to brush a hand back across his ear. The prearranged signal that had the police rushing from their hiding places to make good an arrest.

Long silence.

In the end, the man was convicted of blackmail and sentenced to three years in prison—with no additional penalty for the original assault. A charge best avoided, both learned counsels and teams of solicitors had so deemed before trial, as it might otherwise bring into play the somewhat indelicate question of whether the two parties had been involved in a homosexual act prior to the incident; a far more serious crime. And so the incident of assault had been quietly set aside and by agreement not even entered into evidence.

Long silence.

Only then, as the blackmailer was being led from the courtroom, the horror was again made all too real when the dreadful man had turned and shouted at him and sworn bloody revenge. "I'll get you, you fookin' Jew bastard. I'll do you over good, next time, I will, you fookin' queer. You're already fookin' dead, you are. Dead. Do you hear me, Epstein? You're fookin' dead."

BRIAN EPSTEIN blinked and saw his mother and father sitting quietly in court, day after day after day, all to show their support. How awful it must've been for them. It definitely had to be the last time. He couldn't keep putting his family through such things. He'd make amends, though, he would. He'd pray, then ask for forgiveness, three times, as was the custom, but he knew all too well the shame would remain and the stain of it, haunt him forever. Deep down he knew he was the true guilty party: the one who'd sinned, the one who'd transgressed; and he'd never be able to forgive himself. He knew it with all his heart. And his guilt began to prick at him, unmercifully, from his head to his feet, and as he writhed in quiet torment, he turned and saw the black cloud approaching again from out of the shadows. He cried out. The pain, this time, simply too much to bear. Then was startled by the crash of breaking glass and peoples' shouts and laughter. He blinked and blinked and looked, imploringly, around the courtroom, but everything remained blurred. Then he felt someone pulling and tugging at his sleeve. He began to protest; this really was too much.

"Señor, señor."

There was a shadow hanging over him; shutting out the sun.

"Señor, señor. Excuse, please."

He blinked, coughed, sat up with as much composure as he could muster. "Thank you. Gracias. Thank you. I'm all right."

He must've fallen asleep; his daydream turned nightmare. He shielded his eyes and blinked at the dying rays of the sun. Then he looked down at the glass shards glittering like cheap jewellery in the puddle of red wine. He shivered. The breeze now turned cold. And he resolved to start over again, just as he'd done every day for the last three years. Things had to get better. And with both hands clasped tight together—almost as if in prayer—he gently rocked back and forth, his head nodding in earnest resolution. "Yes," he whispered. "Tomorrow, the sun will shine tomorrow."

"WELCOME BACK, MR BRIAN."

"Thank you, Rita. Have you seen Mr Taylor this morning? Oh, there you are Alistair. Have you a moment, please? In my office."

Alistair Taylor was turning out to be the perfect 'personal assistant'. Quiet and discreet, charming and fun, and always ready to take off his jacket and help carry things in if a vanload of records was delivered. Or go the extra yard when the quarterly overstock invoice review was due. Yes, a very good hire.

"The figures look very good, Alistair. Thank you for holding the fort down, while I was away."

"We all missed you, Brian. Your holiday certainly seems to have agreed with you. You're looking very tanned and relaxed."

"Yes, thank you, Alistair. I am feeling rather refreshed. So, tell me, what's been happening in the Hit Parade? Did John Leyton's 'Johnny Remember Me' perform as well as I said it would?"

"It did, Brian. And just as you suggested we ordered 300 copies and we all but sold out, the first weekend. NEMS were the only record stores in the entire North to have the disc in stock. Just like what happened when you predicted Ray Charles would be 'number one', all around the world, with 'Georgia On My Mind'. I don't know how you do it, Brian."

"I believe I won a gin and tonic off you for that," he said, laughing. "It's true, though, I do know when something's going to be 'number one' and usually on the very first hearing, too.

However, it's far more than just having the right song or the right artist, it's something that says to me, 'that's special and it's going to be a hit'. I mean, everyone knew 'Kon-Tiki' by The Shadows was going to go right into the hit parade; the real gift is being able to spot the more off-beat sort of song or artist before everybody else does." It was true; he did have the knack for such things and it felt good to be back and back in charge. He smiled and looked at his assistant. "Anything else?"

"I've collected all the press releases and promo-copies of the new 45 discs and LPs and put them ready for you, Brian."

"Good, I'll do that first. Then I'll attend to the window displays. This afternoon, I'll go over all the stock with you, so we can get the new orders to the record companies first thing tomorrow morning."

BRIAN EPSTEIN wanted to be alone. Even though it'd been a very long workday and normally he'd have invited Alistair Taylor out to dinner, as a 'thank you', he simply had to be alone. He passed the Beehive, on Paradise Street, a sometimes favourite of his, and walked on to the Basnett Bar, tucked away in a side street, near the Liverpool Playhouse.

The Basnett was one place he could go when he was feeling low, as it was one of the very few places in Liverpool where a homosexual could feel at ease without attracting too much of the wrong sort of attention. Standing off to one side, he sipped his gin and tonic and watched people come and go. He recognised many of the faces, but as ever when in a blue mood he preferred to keep his own company and he soon found himself feeling more and more depressed. He looked up to see a man pushing his way through the door and almost choked. The man was busy talking to someone he'd come in with, his face obscured, but they were the same broad shoulders, same strong neck and chin, thick black Brylcreemed hair. Even the coarse voice was the same one that'd haunted his dreams every night for three years. And suddenly it was as if all the light and sound in the bar had narrowed into a long dark tunnel and he felt dizzy and weak. It was the blackmailer, newly come from prison, standing there, in front of him. He felt he was about to choke and gasped for air and tried to call for help. But he couldn't move. It was as if he was nailed to the spot.

And then it wasn't that horrid, awful man, at all. It was someone else entirely. Someone he'd never seen before. He stared at the man and his companion as they pushed their way to the bar. His sense of relief so absolute it sent him into a sudden vicious spin. The bright lights over the bar fast spiralling him into a dark fathomless void. And in an instant he was overcome by another wave of terror so profound that six weeks of newfound resolve dissolved in as many seconds. In blind panic he almost dropped his cocktail, but ingrained breeding and etiquette won out and he fumbled in his pockets for a half-crown to leave as a tip. He very deliberately placed both glass and coin down onto the marble countertop and turned and stumbled to the door.

"Hello, Brian. My, but don't you look..." But he didn't even hear or see whoever it was had spoken to him. The only thing that filled his mind was the malevolent black shape that seemed ever intent on blocking out both the light and his life. He didn't hear the words spat out in his wake. "Stuck up bitch. Who in hell does she think she is?"

BRIAN EPSTEIN arrived at his friend's flat, in Toxteth, without being at all aware of how he'd got there.

"Brian, what a surprise. When I looked out the window and saw the new model Zodiac, I thought it might be you. Come in."

He'd known Joe Flannery since childhood. Joe was homosexual, too, but their friendship was based solely on a shared love of theatre, stage shows and musicals, film musicals, and sporty motorcars.

"I had nowhere else to go, Joe. No one else I could to talk to."

"That's all right, Brian. I'm glad you came. Sit down. Have a drink. We can talk or I can just listen, whatever you want."

"I've tried everything, Joe, simply everything. The holiday in Spain, a new car, but he's still there, always on my mind. That dreadful, awful man is like a shadow that will never go away. I know he means to kill me, but I don't know what I can possibly do about it. I'm absolutely terrified, but I can't go the police. I can't and won't go through that again. And I certainly can't put my parents through it all again. But I also can't spend my entire life taking lengthy holidays abroad, just so I can feel safe."

"Here, Brian, drink this whisky. You'll feel much better."

"Yes, thank you, Joe. You're too kind. The horrible thing is, you see, Joe, he's due out of prison soon. Yet I already keep seeing him everywhere...across the street, in a shop doorway, in a crowd, in a bar. He's everywhere. I can't work. I can't think. I can't sleep. It's making my life a complete hell. For all I know, he's already out of prison and out there, now, just waiting to attack and kill me. I don't know what to think."

"Think positive, Brian. Think positive or you'll drive yourself mad. That horrible man would be a bloody fool to seek you out and hurt you. He knows he'd be put away for life, if he did."

"But that's the point, Joe, I don't want anything bad to happen to me. I get so worried about it, sometimes, I can't move a muscle, I feel I'm locked up in chains and it's me who's in prison. And yet...and yet...while I'm worrying about something awful happening to me, at the very same time, I want something to happen to me. And I want it so very badly. Oh, I know I must sound completely crazy to you, Joe."

"Brian, calm down, calm down. Everything's going to be all right. Believe me. It'll all work out. Let me top-up your drink."

"Yes, another drink. Maybe that's the answer; just blank it all out. Only, explain it to me, Joe. Why do I always feel like such a misfit? I don't ever seem to fit anywhere. One minute, I'm terrified. The next, I'm bored silly. I don't know what to make of it all or what to do next, but I have to find some way of understanding it all or I'll go mad."

REX MAKIN was by all accounts one of Liverpool's most highly regarded solicitors. He rarely if ever made house-calls, but this morning's summons was but the latest in a long line of requests for him to help clean "the Epsteins' dirty laundry", as he called it. All his clients expected him to clear a pathway through whatever tangled legal thickets they found themselves enmeshed in.

And should a court case ever prove unavoidable, for him then to instruct a barrister on their behalf. Rarely did he disappoint or fail, which was why his services were in constant demand and why he could afford to live on Queens Drive in the affluent suburb of Childwall. He often wondered though whether it was a curse or blessing he happened to live right next door to the Epstein family.

"Rex, thank you for dropping by. Rather than my coming into town, to your office, I thought this a little more discreet. Harry and the boys have all gone off to work, so it's just you and me, this morning."

'Queenie' Epstein, though slender and refined, was a formidable woman in her own quiet way. Nothing in the world was more important to her than her husband, Harry, and her two boys, Brian and Clive. Though, Brian, being her first born, held a very, very special place in her heart.

"It's Brian, again, Rex. No, there hasn't been another incident that I know of. And thankfully he hasn't crashed his car again. I thought the long holiday in Spain would do him good. Help him take his mind off that awful person and all those dreadful threats he made. And for a short time it did seem he was his old self again. Only, now, dear Brian seems more fretful, worried and depressed than ever I've seen him."

He nodded and, although known as much for his piercing gaze as for his discretion, tactfully averted his eyes as 'Queenie' Epstein continued on with her tale of family woe.

"The thing is, Rex, with that awful blackmailer being released from prison very soon, I wouldn't want anything dreadful to happen to Brian. So I was wondering if there was some way of perhaps keeping an eye on him? Make sure he came to no harm. I mean…there must be such people that you can call upon in your capacity as a solicitor?"

"Well, yes, Mrs Epstein, I do have occasion to call upon certain people to help gather information or, as you suggest, keep a close eye on things. The truth is though I usually only employ such people to seek out very specific pieces of information or evidence. This request of yours, by its very nature, would have to be a much more open-ended endeavour. One therefore that might not be inexpensive."

"I appreciate your concern, Rex, and thank you for it, but cost isn't important when it concerns Brian. Please, will you do what you can to help? I know you'll be discreet, but if you'd also indulge me by not mentioning any of this to Harry or Brian, I'd be most grateful."

"Of course, I will, Mrs Epstein, and as ever you can count on my discretion. Why don't we think about keeping an eye on things for a month or so, then we can discuss the matter again? Until then, just leave everything to me and, rest assured, I'll call you if I come across anything I think needs your attention. Will that be satisfactory?"

"As always, Rex. Thank you. Please do whatever you think is appropriate and bill me, personally, whenever you have need."

He drove into the city, a plan of action already forming in his mind. When he reached his office, he told his secretary to hold all calls for five minutes and hurried inside, closing the door behind him. He took a slim black leather address book from his briefcase and ran his finger down the alphabetised scalloped edges until he came to the letter L. He picked up his private line and dialled the number. A man's voice answered after the second ring.

"Lightfoot."

"Harry, I wonder if we could meet? I have a job that requires your special talents. Thursday? No sooner? Okay then, the usual place. Say four o'clock? Good. See you there. Good bye."

BRIAN EPSTEIN stood in the street outside the NEMS Whitechapel store and looked at the window-display he'd designed to promote the soundtrack of the film *South Pacific*. Satisfied, he nodded, and went back inside. Only then did he realise he'd purposefully avoided looking up Whitechapel, to the spot where the police had arrested the blackmailer. He shuddered, but took comfort from the loud click of the brass door lock as it closed firmly behind him. He walked through the classical record department on the ground floor and was tempted to take refuge, amidst the potted palms, in one of the comfortable leather chairs, but knew full well this was one time even the soothing sounds of Sibelius could not heal his troubled heart. He switched on more lights and descended the stairs to the popular record section, down in the basement.

He stared at the sales counter, at the row of listening-booths, at the racks of LP covers all properly categorised. ROCK 'N' ROLL, POP, FOLK, COUNTRY, WESTERN, RHYTHM & BLUES, JAZZ, STAGE SHOWS, FILM MUSICALS, MUSIC OF FRANCE, GREECE, SPAIN. There was music of all types, from all around the world, and all of it now quite meaningless to him. He looked up at the galaxy of stars, at the brightly coloured LP sleeves of the world's top recording artists covering the ceiling—a popular feature he himself had designed. He peered at the famous faces and stared deep into their eyes, almost as if he might find some clue there as to the secret of their success. He shook his head. He was utterly lost and he knew it. Worse, he could see no obvious or immediate solution to cure him of his wretched predicament.

His eyes slid over the racks of greeting cards and paperback books, and on, past, beyond the record counter, to the shelves of long-playing records in their brown cardboard sleeves. His unique filing and re-stocking system had proven so effective, so foolproof, record retailers from all over the north of England had visited the store to see it for themselves. Yet like so many of his so-called brilliant ideas, to him it'd been simplicity itself. He was master of one of the most-successful groups of record stores in the country, but it'd become all too clear it wasn't enough for him and never could be. There had to be something more to life, some other outlet for all his undoubted energy and creativity, but he couldn't even begin to imagine what that might be. It seemed he'd been condemned—for life—to exist in a state of perpetual ennui.

He turned and climbed back up the stairs, switched off the lights, and stood in the darkness, looking out at the deserted and rain-swept Liverpool street.

CHAPTER SEVEN

Fly-Posting The Beat

"Sod this for a game of soldiers," yelled John Lennon.

"Yeah, them an' all," Paul McCartney yelled back.

The Beatles were not happy campers. There'd been no three-month booking at a Butlin's Holiday Camp for them. They'd played over three hundred gigs in the year since they'd first gone out to Hamburg, but they still didn't have two bloody half-pennies to rub together at the end of the week. They were always totally skint.

"Pete, you've got to rustle up some more bookings, even if we do only have to split things four ways now Stu's no longer in the group," John said, flatly. "Ask yer mam if she'll write another letter. Better yet, get her to call someone, as we need the bloody money, we do."

"Money. That's what I soddin' well want," sniffed Paul. "I mean, we can't go on knackering ourselves like this for ever, can we?" He picked up his new Hofner bass and thumbed the strings in quick succession. "I think I'm starting to get the hang of this. At least, something's getting better."

"Yeah, but it can get a lot worse if we can't ever afford to pay off the hire purchase on our amps and stuff from Hessy's." George picked up his dark brown Gretsch Duo-Jet guitar. "At least, no one can ever take my lovely Gretsch off me. It's all already bought and paid for, thanks to that nice Liddypool sailor needing money and wanting to sell it real quick, like. It's welded to my body now, it is. It's part of me."

"Yeah, but welded to which part?" shouted Paul.

"Cheeky monkey," yelled John.

"Okay, John," said Pete. "I'll ask Mo. See what she can do for us. We can always play the Casbah whenever we want."

"Yeah, ta, Pete. Look, we're the best bloody group in Liverpool or Hamburg and yet Bob Wooler's still getting sniggers down the Cavern when he announces us as 'Liverpool's best rock 'n' dole group'. And that's dick, that is. I mean to say, we've even made a record we have."

"Yeah, but as Tony Sheridan's 'Beat Brothers', not as Beatles."

"Don't bloody matter. No other Liverpool group has done a record. Even if it is only the damn Krauts that can buy it at the moment."

"So, what're we going to do about it, John?" Paul asked.

"As I've said, Paul. Sod anyone that's not a Beatle. So let me ask yer, fellas, where we going to?"

"To the top, Johnny," the other Beatles chorused, half-heartedly.

"That's soddin' well not good enough. So let me ask you Scouse bastards, again. Where we going to, fellas?"

"To the top, Johnny," they shouted back loudly.

"And what top is that, fellas?"

"The topper-most of the popper-most, Johnny."

"Yeah, that's more like it," thundered John Lennon. "And don't any of us ever forget it. We're The Beatles. And there's nobody out there, can touch us when we're rockin'. Not now, not ever."

SAM LEACH underlined the name scrawled on his tiny sheet of notepaper. He sucked the last dregs of nicotine from his last but one cigarette, mashed it to a pulp, and threw the stub on the floor of the telephone box. Then he dropped some more pennies into the coin slot and dialled a number. He was trying to reach Terry McCann. And with the telephone receiver in one hand and a pencil in the other, he tapped out a beat on the metal coin box, as he patiently waited for the call to go through.

He'd spent a long weary wet summer trying to climb his way back up the greasy pole of success. It hadn't been easy. One promising rock 'n' roll venue he'd almost set up in Crewe—some fifty miles away—had abruptly fallen through after someone had helpfully informed the local Town Hall that 'Mr Leach had to close two clubs back in Liverpool due to financial difficulties'. After which the only regular venue he'd been able to put to-gether was the much smaller Winter Gardens ballroom, way out in Garston. And even though it'd been very hard won, it'd been even harder to run successfully. It was too close to the Garston Baths—one of Liverpool's more infamous venues. "The blood baths" as they were known, locally, attracted the very same gangs of Teddy Boys that'd given rise to the area's notoriety. And it was only by the extensive—and very expensive—use of the Mean Machine that his paying customers had been able to enjoy anything like a proper evening's rocking entertainment.

He knew without any shred of doubt that certain, unnamed forces were doing their utmost to keep him out of Liverpool's lucrative city clubs. And he certainly didn't need a crystal ball to know who they were. Or even that their ultimate goal was to push him out of the business for good. He could curse them all until the cows came home, but a fat lot of good that'd do him.

What irked him most was that he'd heard on the grapevine that many of the city's more-established promoters had been steadily raising admission prices, while holding down or even reducing the fees they paid the beat groups. Some of the sods even cutting down on the number of bands they offered on any one night. It was the same 'little old merry-go-round' of club owners controlling more and more of the Liverpool booming music scene. How he hated them all for it. His one plan—his dream—was to come up with something so big, so new, it'd blow every man jack of them right out of the fookin' Mersey.

And so, determined as ever to fight his way back into the centre of things, he'd husbanded what little money he'd managed to make from all his many efforts and bided his time and awaited his chance. Then right out of the blue, right out from under everyone's soddin' noses, he'd managed to get his hands on the biggest venue in all of Merseyside, the New Brighton Tower ballroom. A ballroom that could hold five thousand paying punters with ease and still have room left over for them to go wet their whistles in the long-bars situated on its upper floors. It'd been a hugely popular big-band venue before and after the War. But since then, like the War and the old seaside town of New Brighton, it'd fallen out of fashion with anyone who'd just rather rock 'n' roll, instead.

"But what's to stop some clever sod from bringing it right back into fashion, eh? That'd really shake the sods up," he chortled down the phone to Terry McCann, once he'd finished telling him the details of the fantastic deal he'd just made with the Tower's management.

"I tell you, Tel. It's going to be the biggest rock 'n' roll event the north of England has ever seen. I've planned it like a military operation. People are going to be rockin' to Merseyside's top five, biggest and best groups from 7.30 at night, right up until one o'clock the next morning. There'll be licensed bars, open late, and a proper buffet, too. I'll even hire a fleet of special coaches as late night transport to take the Liverpool fans back home through the Mersey Tunnel. Hire another lot to take kids back down the Wirral and on down into the rest of Cheshire. I tell you, it's going to be big, it's going to be huge, and it's only going to cost the fans, five bob, each, to get in."

"That tops everything you've ever done, Sam," Terry yelled down the phone. "It's world class, is what it is. What you going to call it?"

"'Operation Big Beat'," Sam shouted, proudly. "With The Beatles, Rory Storm and The Hurricanes, Gerry and The Pacemakers, The Remo Four, as well as old 'Kingsize' Taylor and The Dominoes, all playing, what else could I bloody well call it?"

BRIAN EPSTEIN sat back in his chair and patted his hair into place. What was it the Americans said? "Another day; another dollar?" Yes, and all very understandable, even desirable.

Yet there had to be more to life than simply making money for the sake of it. At least, now, though, he'd made his father proud. Even his grandfather, Isaac, had been heard to mutter a few words of praise. All because of the sizeable profit NEMS record sales were now generating for the family.

Hopefully, the silly episode in London that'd led to his early discharge from the Army, his brief flirtation with acting at London's Royal Academy of Dramatic Art, and the deeply disquieting incident of being charged with importuning, were now all forgiven, if not entirely forgotten. The slate wiped clean.

Truthfully, he'd already had enough of London to last a lifetime. He couldn't even begin to imagine what might tempt him to return there—at least not in the foreseeable future. For the time being he'd stay in Liverpool. There had to be some as yet unexplored creative outlet for him—somewhere. Books. Art. Music. Drama. Something.

Intimate dinners with men friends and, occasionally, the one or two young ladies he knew well enough to ask out, socially, were all very well. But it all still left him with that feeling of ennui that something was definitely missing in his life. And window-dressing, however much of a winning idea it might be proving for NEMS, could never be enough. He smiled, ruefully. Even being a famous dress designer, one of his very earliest and most cherished ambitions, couldn't have satisfied him at that moment. He wanted—needed—a new and different challenge—something or someone he could believe in—totally.

Even so, Liverpool was so very humdrum. So numbing. He pushed back his chair and paced up and down his office. Perhaps he should simply get away from it all. Escape to Spain forever. Or better, yet, learn to speak Italian and join the international set, as the newspaper 'hickeys' called them. Go off and live in luxury in Rome. Go enjoy the sweet life...*la dolce vita*.

He stopped pacing and leaned back against his desk, his fingertips tapping lightly against the highly polished wood veneer. What was it that he was missing? He chewed at his lip and stared out of the window, oblivious to his reflection in the glass windowpane. He turned and looked at a pile of *Mersey Beats*. Clipped to the front of each issue was a small card bearing the neatly typed legend: 'Reserved exclusively for Mr Brian'. He picked up the top copy and leafed through to his 'Record Releases' column. Yes, writing the column was proving very pleasurable. He checked the two advertisements for NEMS for accuracy and closed the paper. Then for some reason he opened the paper again and looked at it in more detail. There was 'Mersey Roundabout', written, if he remembered correctly, by Bill Harry's girlfriend, Virginia. Followed by some absurd drivel, written by some perfect idiot, under the by-line 'Beatcomber', and more by Bob Wooler who was much too verbose for his taste. The local beat scene the poor man tried to write about with such dramatic flourish wasn't at all his cup of tea. It was all a little too much ado about nothing. Or was it? Would it really be such a bad idea if he actually went and took a look at this so-called, flourishing Liverpool music scene?

Bill Harry had even suggested the wave of beat music occurring in Liverpool must be very similar to what'd taken place in New Orleans, during the early days of jazz. And, it was true. NEMS was supplying local musicians and fans alike with a constant stream of American rock 'n' roll and R&B records. So, even if only from a business standpoint, it couldn't hurt to find out a little more about what was actually happening.

Something pulled at him—a thought—but about what? Who? He tapped his fingers against his chin, shook his head. Nothing. Then the answer was there—staring him fully in the face, at last. He shook his head again. He'd been so full of dread with the thought of the blackmailer's impending release, and then so caught up in the pleasures of Spain, it'd completely slipped his mind. He sorted quickly through the pile of *Mersey Beats*, looking for the issue containing his very first column. And there it was. The photo of—what were they called—The Beatles? He looked at the tiny black and white picture on the cover and shivered at the memory of that first sighting. The Beatles.

He stared at the picture intently, stroked it gently, and the ink rubbed off onto his fingertips. Instead of it annoying him, he rubbed his fingers together slowly, sensuously. Then as if in a dream, he carefully folded the paper and with a last lingering look at the boys in the picture, he placed it almost reverently in the bottom drawer of his desk. And with The Beatles once again centre-stage, in his mind, he picked up the latest edition of *Mersey Beat* and read it through from cover to cover. Twice.

Yes, getting better acquainted with the local beat scene was a very good idea. It was also now a new and suddenly very exciting idea. Was there, perhaps, a chance of him actually seeing these Beatles play that very night or within the next day or two? After all, is not action, eloquence? Pleased at his remembered Shakespeare, he reached for his silk scarf and overcoat.

BRIAN EPSTEIN left the bright nimbus of Whitechapel, turned right into Rainford Gardens, and made his way through the tangle of lanes towards Mathew Street where he hoped he'd find The Cavern Club. He was amazed at how quickly the polish and glitter of the shopping district's shops and stores seemed to evaporate behind him. Even in the dim yellow light of the street lamps, he could see the lane was dirty and strewn with rubbish. He pressed on past the raucous sounds spilling out onto the pavement from the open door of the White Star public house and tightened his scarf around his neck and pulled his coat collar up. Then he veered to the left and found himself having to blink repeatedly as a chill wind threw dust and grit into his eyes.

Mathew Street was a narrow, cobble-lined street, utterly devoid of character, hemmed in on both sides, by grim-faced, seven-story high warehouses. And even though it was already past seven o'clock, there were several goods-lorries and delivery vans still parked haphazardly on the pavements, forcing him to have to walk down the middle of the street. The odour of rotting fruit and vegetables assailed his nose and he reached for a handkerchief to help mask the smell. He noticed that many of the walls and doorways, on both sides of the street, had been defaced by hurriedly painted student rag slogans or were covered in cheaply printed music club posters. One, in particular, advertising some ridiculous event called 'Operation Big Beat', was repeated endlessly, sometimes upside down, which was amateurish in the extreme. Gritting his teeth, he pushed on past a boarded-up bombsite, only to be confronted by dozens more of the offending posters. No, Mathew Street was not at all what he'd expected. And he began to wonder whether searching for The Beatles was such a good idea after all.

A group of laughing teenage boys and girls suddenly erupted from out of nowhere onto the street in front of him and he assumed, rightly, that he'd found The Cavern. There was no lighted sign that he could see. It was literally a hole in the wall. He began to hear the thump of drums and an electrified bass coming up from somewhere beneath his feet, but it all sounded to him very much like a toothache. Standing outside the club entrance, was a tall, dark-haired, thickset man wearing a dinner jacket and cummerbund under an open overcoat. The man, who looked every inch an ex-boxer or sergeant major, peered at him through the gloom and then saluted. And he felt himself shudder and begin to blush; a strange mixture of past disappointments and future desires mingling together. He nodded to the man, but immediately wished he hadn't and walked on past. Perhaps, a drink at the Basnett was more in order. He might meet someone there he knew from the Playhouse. Afterwards, he could even go on to a club more in keeping with his tastes. He shook his head. What had he been thinking of?

The thump, thump, thump of the beat diminished into nothing, as he walked quickly away.

"SAM! Wow! Fancy seeing you at Hessy's...been a long time."

" 'Lo, Spike. Good to see you, too. I wondered when I might bump into you, again. How have you been, me old mucker?"

"Oh, alright I suppose, mustn't grumble. I tried phoning you once or twice, just to say, 'hello', like, but it was always out of order, Sam, and I didn't know how else to get hold of you."

"Yeah, well, that's okay. I haven't been around this way too much myself, lately. And I had the phone cut off for a bit, didn't I? Things got a little bit tight, that's all. But it's back on now, so I hope you haven't thrown me number away or anything."

"No, I've still got your number in me wallet. Though there's nowt much more than an army of moths in there at the moment. But it's so good to see you, Sam." He glanced at the poster Sam was Sellotaping onto the back of Hessy's window. "'Operation Big Beat'? Wow, is that you? Just saw loads of them up and down Mathew Street. The Beatles. Gerry. Rory. That's great, that is. Put me down for a ticket. I'm coming, even if I've got to swim the River Mersey to get there."

"Yeah, it's me ticket back into the big time. Got time for a coffee?"

"Yeah, the Kardomah's next door, I'll go get me stuff. And it's on me, right?"

Sam carried his bundle of rolled-up posters and Spike his guitar, and they went out on Stanley Street, drifted a few steps to the right, pushed open the big glass door into the Kardomah Coffee House, ordered two cappuccinos, and found a table close to the window.

"It's always like the black hole of Calcutta in here, there's never enough light. I reckon it's so you can't see what they put inside their pastries. Anyway, sunshine, what you been doing with yourself?"

"That's why I was at Hessy's, Sam. I've been trying to learn the guitar, proper, like. Just like you told me to do the last time we met."

"Blimey, someone who actually listens to me. That's a first. Here, has old Jim Gretty still got all those guitar chords chalked up on the wall? God bless him, still playing the guitar, and at his age, too. He's a marvel of modern medicine, he is. You any good on that thing?"

Spike held up the guitar by its neck. "Well, I've learnt a few chords, like, but there's a long road to go yet, before I get anywhere."

"Haven't you got any mates to practice with?"

"I did bump into some old schoolmates, at Hessy's. Fras and Dave. Blokes I was at Liverpool Collegiate with. They've got this group, The Persuaders, and were in buying some new guitars on the never-never. Said the last thing they needed was another soddin' guitarist. Did say, though, I could go watch them practice, sometime. *Vivat haec sodalitas*...my arse."

"No one else from the Art College?" asked Sam.

"Not really. There were a couple of groups. But you had to be good to get in. Everyone was real gone man, gone, about modern jazz and beat poetry and stuff. Not my cup of tea. I didn't understand it, for a start. I don't think they did, either, it just made them feel real cool."

"I have to say, actually, that I got no particular kick against modern jazz." Sam did his best to sound posh. And failed miserably. So, instead, he waggled his little pinkie as he slurped coffee from his cup.

Spike laughed, got into the act. "Oh, I say. Do you mean unless they play it too damnably fast?"

They both laughed then. Started singing 'Rock 'n' Roll Music'. Nodding their heads, in time. Sam slapping out the beat on the tabletop, Spike tapping out a backbeat with a spoon. A chorus of irritated coughs and murmurs immediately erupted from the surrounding tables, but the two friends didn't seem to hear—or care.

"Fook, yeah, Sam. It's gotta be rock 'n' roll music...it's just gotta be. I can't seem to live without it. All I want to do, all the time, is be Buddy Holly or Chuck Berry or Eddie Cochran. Me mum thinks I've gone completely off me rocker. But until I can play properly, like, I'm sort of keeping myself to myself. I just keep on practicing and practicing till me fingers bleed."

"You'd better watch it, sunshine, that's unhealthy that is. You could turn into one of them rebels without a cause. After that, it'd just be one long slippery slope into wine, women, and song."

"Yeah. Rum 'n' coke, slap 'n' tickle, and lots of rock 'n' roll."

Sam smiled and peered at Spike over his coffee cup. "You know, I reckoned the real reason no one had seen you was that you'd gone and got yourself a little judy stashed away, somewhere."

"No. No girlfriend, Sam. I had lots at the Art College, like. No, I did, honest, hundreds of them. Only, I got no time for them at the moment."

Sam raised his eyebrows. "All right, sunshine. I'll believe you, but there's millions wouldn't."

"Yeah, well the honest truth is, Sam, I've got no money."

"You go on learning to play that thing and you'll be fighting them off with your guitar strap. Anyway, when the right one comes along, it's not money she'll be looking for, sunshine. I'm telling you, you should get out and chance your arm. You might surprise yourself."

"Chance 'ud be a fine thing," said Spike, ruefully.

Sam smiled. "I did think about trying to get hold of you, once or twice, myself, like, but it seems you moved from that doss house full of art students that you used to stay in. Gambier Terrace, wasn't it?"

"Yeah. Moved back in with me mum after I left college. The sods stopped my grant dead. Can't blame them, I suppose. Anyway, it's just for the time being. I do the odd job to try help out with money."

Sam drained his coffee cup and smiled. "You wanna come back and help me? Do a bit of fly-posting and stuff? Only I can do with the help. Terry's signed on, so has most of the Mean Machine. It'll be like old times. I can't pay much, like. But I'm sure there'll be enough afterwards, for you to treat some judy to a bag of fish and chips and a Coke. Who knows, you might get lucky, get some fish and finger pie." He winked, a devilish look on his face, and Spike nearly coughed up what remained of his cappuccino. "Hey, I'm still a bachelor, too, you know. As I know only too well."

Spike laughed. Sam was a real tonic. And as married as he'd been to his guitar, he knew deep down that Sam had touched on an increasingly sore point. Yeah, a few admiring glances from some bright-eyed little judy would go down a treat—a real treat.

"Yeah, great, Sam. Count me in. And thanks a lot, like."

Sam raised an eyebrow again. "Talking of the Mean Machine. Young Jimmy Molloy has been asking after you. He's even looked out for you round the clubs. Says he's not seen you. Seemed quite concerned. Said he hoped you hadn't been done over by anybody. I didn't know he thought so much of you, but it appears he does. You must've impressed him, somehow, but I can't think how. Knowing him, though, it can't be your haircut or your clothes, could it? I mean he wouldn't be caught dead in cowboy boots, jeans, and a leather jacket like you've got."

"Yeah, well just call me the wild one."

"All right Marlon Brando, time you got on yer bike. Here's a couple of posters you can stick up on your way home. Tomorrow, I'll have a bunch more posters and some tickets you can take over to the Tower Ballroom, in New Brighton. A long sea voyage would do you some good. Put some colour in yer face."

"I get seasick on that damn ferry, Sam," laughed Spike.

"Well don't do it over the posters, there's a good lad. Let me see, now." Sam took out a dog-eared diary from his jacket pocket and a stub of pencil from behind his ear. "Thursday, 26th of October? Right. I've done the English Electric, Civil Service,

Owen Owens's, Lewis's, Rushworth's, and Hessy's, which leaves NEMS. I'll nip across the road. Try and get a poster or two up on the walls. See if I can sell-in a few more tickets. Only it's a bit slow, there, for some reason. Then I'll pop back round Mathew Street to see how many posters them thievin' yobbos from The Cavern have torn down."

"I can stick one on Bob Wooler's front door, again, if you like?"

"Nah, best we show a little decorum. The bugger threatened to bill me for having his door re-varnished the last time. He's got no humour, that one."

"I'll go back down Mathew Street for you, Sam. Only, I was there this lunchtime seeing The Beatles."

"If I'd known, I'd have come with you."

"Yeah, as if that big bugger on the door would have let you in, Sam. As usual, though, they were bloody fantastic. Bob Wooler said as how their record's out in Germany, like, and that we should all rush out and buy it. As if I could afford it. Hey, did you know the Cavern did an all-nighter with The Beatles, last Saturday night?"

"Ray McFall's not daft. He knows a good idea when he steals one. And their record's come out, has it? Good for them. That's what I wanted to do with the boys...and with Gerry and The Pacemakers, too. Record them doing their best songs. Start up me own Merseyside record label. Troubadour Records, I was going to call it. Only, I couldn't afford that, either. Just never seemed to be able to get all the cash together at any one time. Anyroad, never mind...onwards and upwards, eh? So, yeah, save my old legs, will yer, and just nip round Mathew Street and count them posters for us."

"Righto, Sam."

"Then give us a ring in the morning, okay? We can replace them if we have to. But I'm only allowing for fifty posters this time. No good throwing good money after bad. Hey, and thanks for the coffee. Next time it's a mixed grill, at Joe's Cafe...on me. Good seeing you, again, Spike. Ta-ra."

CHAPTER EIGHT

Merry Go Round

"No, Mr Leach, business is off for some reason. Even the men in the furniture department were saying so, this morning. Must be that spot of sun we've had...everyone would rather be out sunbathing."

"The weather's as barmy as the rest of us, Rita. Where would you like this poster up? Over by the R 'n' B record-racks on the far wall or over next to the listening booths? And here's another book of tickets for NEMS to sell. Just tell people The Beatles are playing better than ever since their return from Hamburg."

"Oh they're fab, Mr Leach. All the girls in the store think so. They come in here a lot to listen to records, like. But as they can be a bit scruffy it's not really appreciated. I think they're lovely, though."

"They are, Rita. And so are you. Lovely, I mean, not scruffy. And thank you for your support...I'd fall over without it, I would."

"Oh, you are funny, Mr Leach. Only, I was thinking, like, why don't you take some posters and tickets over to the NEMS store in Great Charlotte Street. Spread the good word."

"Yeah, good idea. I'll do that. Thanks, Rita. Ta-ra, then."

SAM LEACH walked down Richmond Street in the direction of Central Railway Station and turned into Great Charlotte Street. The NEMS store looked smaller than the one in Whitechapel, but any shop in a storm. He pushed open the store's front door.

The first thing he noticed was an impeccably dressed young man standing atop a stepladder. The man was pinning record posters to the wall—all the posters positioned at odd angles. "That's very eye-catching," Sam thought to himself, "must give that a try sometime...but then I already have. Funny that." He coughed, politely, and waited. The young man turned his head

and looked down at him, evidently unimpressed with either Sam
Leach or his tailor. The man slowly descended the stepladder.
"And what can NEMS do for you today, sir?"

The man's patronising tone cut Sam to the quick. "Well, for a
start, sunshine, you're not getting any 'Big Beat' tickets to line
your pockets with." And without even attempting to conceal his
annoyance, he plonked a couple of posters down onto the record counter, sniffed his defiance, and turned to leave.

The man glanced at the posters and said in a voice that
could've cut glass, "Would you please enlighten me as to how
NEMS' registered trade mark comes to be displayed on your
merchandise?"

Hackles up, nostrils flaring, Sam spun round, snatched up the
posters from the counter and, biting his tongue, made for the
door.

"Please do not ignore me," the man said, primly. "If you can-
not furnish me with a satisfactory explanation as to why NEMS
is listed on your posters as an official ticket agent for this so-
called 'Operation Big Beat', I'll have no alternative but to call our
solicitors."

Sam turned with a loud, exaggerated sigh. "Look, pal, you
must be mistaking me for someone who gives a stuff what you
think, but as you must be new here, I'll explain it to you very
carefully. Then I'll get on about my business." He put the posters back down on the counter. "Firstly, NEMS have always
displayed posters and sold tickets for me. Secondly, the manag-
eress of the Whitechapel store personally suggested I come
here. Thirdly, if you want the posters, fine. If you don't want
them, that's fine, too. I really don't care."

The man blinked, touched the knot of his tie, and studied the
posters on the counter. Every few seconds he looked up with
what Sam took to be a look of distaste. Finally, the young man
flicked a hand. "No, I'm sorry, these are definitely not for NEMS.
Please take them away from here and from the Whitechapel
branch, also. Thank you. Good-day."

The man's words hit Sam like a bucket of cold water and he
went from hot under the collar to sweat-covered brow in a matter of seconds. The loss of sales from the Whitechapel store,

alone, would be a tremendous blow. And he tried not to let his anxiety show, as he switched seamlessly from showman to salesman.

"Well you do surprise me, I must say. NEMS receives ten per cent commission on all tickets they sell. Plus, your precious trade name is plastered on five hundred...no, a thousand broadsheet posters all over Merseyside; as well as on another four thousand handbills. And that's not even counting a full-page ad with your company's name on it, in tomorrow's *Liverpool Echo*." He paused. Brought up his big guns. "And how you could even think of walking away from being associated with The Beatles, I don't know. They're only the biggest thing to hit Liverpool since the Luftwaffe bombed the place. Every time they play, they draw crowds as big as if it was an FA Cup match between Everton and Liverpool City. They've even got a record out, in Germany. Am I getting through to you? I hope so, because, I tell you, no one's attempted anything like this, on this scale, ever before. The Tower Ballroom can hold as many as five-thousand kids and the reason it's going to be chock-a-block full to the rafters is The Beatles."

Sam swallowed, his throat suddenly as dry as bleached bone. He'd inflated the numbers of posters and handbills, a little, which was only natural, but the rest of the numbers were real. Yet with all that, the young man didn't say a word, the bugger just tapped his fingers up and down on the counter and slowly re-examined the posters.

"Yes," the young man said, at last. "Yes, all right. You make a good case for the arrangement to continue. So I shall allow it, for the time being. But I must tell you I will be monitoring the situation closely in the future. Very closely, indeed."

Sam breathed a sigh of relief, stepped forward, and extended his hand. "Er, my name's Sam Leach. And you are?"

The man looked almost pained, but shook Sam's hand, all the same. "Brian Epstein," the man said. "My family owns NEMS."

"Well, er, very pleased to meet you Mr Epstein."

"It should be pronounced...'Ep-steen'...Mr Leach. And, yes, the pleasure was all mine."

"THANKS FOR MEETING ME, HARRY. I may have a little job that's right up your alley." Rex Makin took a sip of his coffee and looked over the rim of his cup at the hawk-like face of the thickset man in the belted raincoat sitting across from him.

"Yes, dark alleyways and sometimes even darker hotel bedrooms is about it. What a life? But no matter, it's all in a day's work. That's why I prefer we meet in this old barn of a place. The Kardomah makes it easy to see who's coming and going, not so easy to be seen. So, what is it this time, Mr Makin, sir, another 'watching' case?"

Harry Lightfoot, ex-Liverpool policeman—forced into early retirement, it was said, because of a knee injury sustained while playing inter-divisional rugby—calmly sipped his coffee and waited. Once a detective inspector, now a private investigator for a few of the city's better firms of solicitors, he was by his own estimates making almost three times his old weekly take-home pay. And if you added that to the part-pension he was receiving from the Force, he was doing very nicely, thank you. Yes, waiting had both its merits and its rewards.

"Yes it is, Harry. And as it happens, the party in question has his office just across the street from here. So if you take the job, like, you may well be seeing a lot more of this place."

"I suppose it's just as well I like their coffee then, isn't it?"

Rex Makin smiled and slid a large brown paper envelope across the table. Then he excused himself. Said he needed to go visit the Gents. When he returned, the envelope was laying exactly as he'd left it. But he knew in the short time he'd been away, Harry Lightfoot would've thoroughly perused and digested the contents. He sat down and raised his eyebrows. Lightfoot nodded back, slowly, which meant they could do business.

Harry Lightfoot leaned forward. Said, very quietly, "Would there be any reason for the gentleman in question to suspect the police might have him under observation at the present time?"

"As far as the original case is concerned, Harry, I'm pretty sure he believes all his dealings with the City police were finished with three years ago. But he's all too aware of the blackmailer's impending release. And that's of great concern to both him and his family. But as yet, there's been no formal request for any sort of police protection." Lightfoot nodded, but said nothing. Rex Makin swirled the dregs of his coffee around in his cup and looked up. "I also have no reason to believe he's done anything, recently, that might've brought him to the attention of the City's Vice Squad, if that's what you mean? Though, of course, I have no way of knowing for sure."

"Well, that's easy enough to find out, Mr Makin, sir. I still have one or two friends left on the Force, as hard as that may be to believe. So I'll have a little drink with someone on Vice who still owes me a favour and see what they're up to at the moment. And as for me being seen by your gentleman, it might even do some good if I was a bit conspicuous, at times. It's not how I like to operate, but it might help queer the pitch a bit, if the black-mailer does show up. Talking of which, the photo you've got of said nasty piece of work is a bit too grainy for my liking. So I'll see what else I can get hold of. I don't ever want to be missing that bugger in a crowd."

"Yes. That was taken a few years ago, just before the trial. But just you go careful, Harry. Don't go stirring the wrong pot. Our job is to simply ensure my client's safety. He's scared witless about the threat to kill him, apparently."

"He has every right to be, Mr Makin. But I'll help keep an eye on him for you. And, as always, I will use the utmost discretion at all times. Can I take it then, that it's our usual arrangement as far as my fee and any out of pocket expenses are concerned?"

"Of course, Harry. And thank you for agreeing to help."

BRIAN EPSTEIN stared at the picture of the five Beatles gracing the cover of *Mersey Beat* and moved his fingertips slowly back and forth across the inky surface. As he touched the face of the one in the middle, his hand stilled and he felt the rush of blood to his neck and face and was conscious of his heart beating loud-ly in his ears. "*Oh, carapace, mi cara, amore,*" he whispered.

A noise from the street outside broke into his reverie and he blinked and shook his head and stared at the newspaper's head-line as if for the first time. 'BEATLE'S SIGN RECORDING CONTRACT!' Odd, but even the incorrect use of the apostrophe didn't irritate him. What was it about The Beatles that already made him feel so free? His eyes fell upon the boys' names stacked in a column of type next to the photo. '*Left to Right. Pete Best. George Harrison. John Lennon. Paul MacArthy. Stuart Sutcliffe*'. He spoke the names over and over to himself, memorising them. Then he noticed the issue date was '*July 20–August 3*'. How very odd. It'd all been there, ready and waiting for him, before he'd ever gone off to Spain. Damn his dreadful nightmares for taking him away. He'd always prayed—no, he'd always known there had to be something more to life than his all-consuming fears. Yesterday, his troubles had seemed so close, so overwhelming. Yet here, now, today, for some reason he couldn't quite fathom, they all felt so very faraway, and he felt uplifted, positive even, about the future. How very odd and, yet, how very wonderful, too.

He'd heard of Bert Kaempfert, of course, the German orchestra leader and producer who'd had a world-wide hit with 'Wonderland By Night', but he was both intrigued and then disturbed to read that Kaempfert already had The Beatles under contract to provide four records a year for Polydor, Germany's leading recording company. It appeared, though, that in this instance, The Beatles had merely provided vocals and backing for someone named Tony Sheridan. The article listed several numbers that'd been 'waxed to vinyl', as the writer termed it—the pseudo-Americanism grated upon him, hugely—but he read on. For some reason, not disclosed, The Beatles had been dissatisfied with the recordings and had immediately sold the rights back to the recording company, thereby leaving them still contracted to produce another four records that year. He shook his head. The Beatles definitely needed someone to help them. Otherwise, they'd never get out of their commitment to Polydor.

He made a note to contact Polydor, in London, and place an order for whatever Beatles record had been released. If necessary, he'd even call the company's head-office in Hamburg. Because if that loathsome little man Sam Leach was right and the group really did have a huge following in Liverpool, he could easily count on selling a box of twenty-five copies—perhaps as many as two or three boxes. He smiled. He'd once attended a sales meeting in Hamburg and had very enjoyable memories of several of the clubs along the Reeperbahn. Yes, events might yet conspire to have him pay another visit there. And wouldn't that be delightful?

There was a final paragraph about the group's bass-guitarist, Stuart Sutcliffe, an aspiring artist, who'd apparently decided to remain in Hamburg and marry a German girl. However, the group had no plans to take on another guitarist and had decided to remain a quartet. He hurriedly scanned the photograph again, putting names to faces. Thankfully, it was just as he'd hoped. Stuart Sutcliffe was the one in dark glasses trying very hard to look like James Dean. He smiled. Mr Sutcliffe might've been too arty, too intellectual for his taste, even a little too argumentative. "Good bye, Mr Sutcliffe," he said, wiping both the name and face from memory.

He looked out of his office window and stared down at the people and the traffic going up and down Whitechapel. He sighed. It always looked so very mundane and humdrum and he was about to turn away when he saw a young man in leather jacket, blue jeans and cowboy boots walking on the opposite side of the street. It wasn't the clothes that caught his eye, or even the young man; but the cherry-red guitar the young man carried so very cockily, under his arm. In the flat grey light of a dull Liverpool day it stood out like a fiery signal beacon.

He blinked, went over to his desk, picked up a pen, and wrote on his notepad: 'Call Hessy's Musical Instrument Store'. The shop was only across Whitechapel, on the corner of Stanley Street, but he always preferred to telephone ahead before meeting anyone new. It helped put things on a proper business footing. He nodded. Yes, all in all, a good day, a very good day. And, yes, the sun might very well shine tomorrow.

SPIKE JONES smiled. Life had been a whirl since bumping into Sam Leach at Hessy's. "Was that only the day before yesterday?" he murmured. It seemed like he'd travelled all round Merseyside since then and come back a new person—very much how a butterfly must feel emerging from the confines of a chrysalis into a brave new world. Not that he saw himself as a red admiral or a peacock or anything exotic. He was more a scruffy cabbage white. Still, the plain truth was, after so many months—years even—of feeling sad, confused, and angry about a whole multitude of things he could never quite put his finger on, he was surprised—no, delighted—to find he now seemed to be walking around with a smile on his face all the time. Funny, wasn't it, how a chance meeting could end up giving you a whole new lease on life. Sam was a real tonic. As was Terry McCann, who'd popped up out of nowhere, that Friday afternoon, driving a delivery van he'd borrowed. "Roll up. Roll up. All aboard the mystery tour bus," he'd yelled out the window, as he'd beckoned to him. And off they'd gone, all over Liverpool, delivering tickets and posters to countless shops, offices, and factories. As darkness descended, they'd descended on the town to carry out some highly illegal 'hit-and-run fly-posting' that'd had them all giggling like schoolgirls at the daringness of their deeds. They'd gone to the Grapes, afterwards, for a drink, and followed that up with a mixed grill at Joe's Cafe—all paid for by Sam. After which, he'd gone and topped the evening off by winning the contest as to who could produce the longest and loudest burp.

"Beginner's luck," Sam had said, handing him a ten-bob note.

Truth be told, he'd loved every single mad minute of it. The constant high-spirited banter between Terry and Sam; their unflagging humour; their drive to succeed—regardless of what obstacles got thrown in their path—energised him. Helped push himself out of himself. Even that morning, on the ferry over to New Brighton, he'd somehow felt as if he'd been setting out on a voyage of discovery. He'd found the wind and spray wonderfully invigorating and the distant shore full of unexpected promise. Everything leading up to a welcome at 'the Tower' that'd not only been totally unexpected, but downright overwhelming.

"Good lad, thanks for coming, only we needed more of them posters and tickets for the weekend." The Tower Ballroom's general manager, Tom McCardle, a big, bluff Yorkshireman, had looked up from his desk and given him the expert once-over. "Done a bit of boxing have you, lad?"

"Yeah, sparring with me dad, then at a couple of boys' clubs, youth's clubs." Spike stopped, a look of genuine surprise on his face. "How did you know, like?"

"Done a bit meself, like, in the past," said McCardle, smiling. "You can always tell, in or out of the ring, it's how someone moves. It never goes away. Here, do you want a cup of instant coffee? Only, you look as like you could do with one." McCardle turned towards his open office door and shouted, "Hey, Thelma, fix the lad a cuppa, will you please? Thank you. And I'll have another one, too, while you're at it, like." He pointed a finger at Spike and smiled. "You work for Sam, do you? Well, you tell him he's a bloody genius, he is. Only, our switchboard has been absolutely bloody jammed since he came up with the idea for having his 'Big Beat Operation' thingy, here at the Tower Ballroom. Young girls are ringing up all day long, crying, 'Are The Beatles really coming? Are they really, really coming?' They've all gone completely potty. So tell us, young man, who are these Beatle fellas, then? Because I've not seen or heard anything like it, since the glory days of Joe Loss and his Orchestra."

A pretty, dark-haired young girl, about Spike's age, came into the room carrying two mugs of coffee. She approached the desk, slowly, so as not to spill anything, and placed the mugs down very carefully. "I've already put sugar in for you, Mr McCardle," she said. Then she turned and smiled at the room and casually brushed her hair with her hand. She'd already decided the scruffy young man in jeans and leather jacket was not really her sort. Office girls didn't go out with the likes of delivery boys.

"Thank you, Thelma. This young lad works for Sam Leach...the bloke that's doing 'Operation Big Beatle'. He's brought that pile of posters and tickets, over there. Pop them down to the ticket office, for us, if you would."

The girl looked at Spike with renewed interest. She turned, shuffled things about on McCardle's desk and discreetly moved the mug in his direction. "The Beatles? All the girls here think they're fab. Do you know them personally, then, er, er...?"

Spike took the coffee mug in both hands and nodded his thanks, "Er, Jones, Spike Jones. I've met them, working for Mr Leach, like, but no, I don't know them personally. Not really. But, yeah, they're great, aren't they?"

"Yeah, well I want to meet these Beatle fellas, meself, and shake their bloody hands, whoever they are." Tom McCardle waved his arms up and down like a giant windmill. "I tell you, I've known nowt like it." He beamed, gulped at his coffee, and winced. "How much bloody sugar did you say you put in here, Thelma? Right, thank you, that'll be all." The young girl smiled a dazzling smile at Spike. Then threw him a last long lingering look from the doorway. "Thelma! Posters and tickets!" McCardle waited for the girl to return, pick things up, and leave. He rolled his eyes and took another sip of coffee. "She's really a very smart young girl, but she can be as daft as brush, sometimes." He started pacing up and down again. "Where were we, now? Oh, yes, what I wanted to tell you." He stopped, turned and pointed at Spike again. "You remember to tell your boss, Sam Leach, he's the business he is. You tell him he's the dog's bollocks."

Spike couldn't help but laugh. His dad used to say that when he was out of earshot of his mother. 'The dog's bollocks' was printers' slang for the symbol that combined two dots with a dash. And, as he laughed, Tom McCardle laughed—big, exploding gales of laughter. And suddenly amidst all the hustle and bustle and unexpected warmth of the Tower's office staff, it hit him like a fist in the stomach. He missed his dad more than he'd been able to admit to anyone, including himself. There'd never been anyone to talk to about it. A young man wasn't supposed to get caught up in death. You were expected to bottle everything up, inside. Show a stiff upper lip and all that shite.

As soon as it was polite, he'd finished his coffee. Said he'd best be getting back. Then he'd gone out into the cold crisp cleansing air and stood in the shadow of 'the Tower' and for a good half hour or more, walked up and down and just let the wind dry his tears as the Mersey helped wash away years of useless fookin' anger.

SPIKE JONES, having learned from his dad the best place to fish was wherever the fish are, pinned up a postcard on the upstairs notice board at Hessy's Music Store. The place was as busy as ever, so his advertisement offering his services to any group looking for a rhythm guitarist or anyone interested in forming a group was sure to be seen by masses of people. He stepped back and nodded. The drawing he'd done of his Rosetti Solid 7 guitar wasn't half-bad. The different shades of red coloured pencil he'd used to add texture and depth to the body of the guitar made the postcard really stand out. "At least my time at the Art College wasn't a complete waste," he muttered under his breath. Then he turned and shouted, "Hey, thanks there, Jim." And back, above all the noise, came Jim Gretty's fluting tenor, "That's all right lad, anything to help a fellow musician."

Still smiling, he stood on the corner of Stanley Street and surveyed the mob of Saturday shoppers, then glanced up at the clock outside the Kardomah and saw it was almost three o'clock. He had twenty minutes before his bus was due and he looked at the few coins he had in his pocket, then across the street at NEMS.

He hadn't got the new edition of *Mersey Beat,* yet. So he could read it on the bus home. That decided, he played matador with the traffic on Whitechapel and was just about to enter the store, when a smartly dressed young man strode out of the shop as if he owned the place. Spike took a quick step back and for the very briefest of moments the man looked at him intently with a quizzical smile on his face. "Do excuse me," he said, "I'm late for an appointment." Then he disappeared in a cloud of after-shave. "Don't mention it," Spike muttered in his wake and made his way downstairs to the store's jazz and popular-music record department in the basement. As usual the place was packed and knowing he didn't have too much time he quickly went and stood in line and waited for a sales assistant to be free.

The girl at the record counter looked at him. "Yes sir," she said pleasantly. "What can we do to help you?" She tried to act just as she'd been schooled by Mr Brian, himself, and not be put off by the young man's scruffy leather jacket and jeans. "Everybody," she remembered, Mr Brian saying, "is an important potential customer and should always be treated as such. We must never, ever send anyone away empty-handed, if we can possibly help it. Satisfaction is all. That's the NEMS way."

"Er, have you got a record by The Beatles?" Spike asked. "On-ly, I heard Bob Wooler, the DJ, play it at Hambleton Hall, last Sunday and again at the Cav, Thursday lunchtime. He said it was from Germany. And I was wondering, if you've got it, can I have a listen, please?"

"It's called 'My Bonnie'," she said, smiling. "But, no, we don't have it in stock, although you must be the eighth or ninth person today to come in and ask for it. Is it any good, like? Only, I ha-ven't heard it myself. But they're fab, aren't they, The Beatles?"

"Yeah, there's no one can touch them, if you ask me."

She pointed to the big poster for 'Operation Big Beat' pinned up on a nearby wall. "We've got tickets for that event, on sale, if you like?"

"No, thanks, very much. I've sort of got mine, already, like."

In the true NEMS manner, she persisted. "Well, er, would you like me to order the record for you, then?"

"No, that's okay, I only wanted a quick listen, but, er, I will take a *Mersey Beat*." She handed him a copy from the top of the pile sitting on the counter and he handed her a threepenny bit. She smiled and he smiled back. "But, look, thanks for offering," he said. Then he left.

A slim dark-haired young man in a smart suit came up and stood next to the young girl. "And what did scruffy want, Rita?"

"It was someone else asking for that new record by The Beat-les, Mr Alistair. But he didn't want to order it. He only wanted to have a listen."

CHAPTER NINE

Down The Cavern

"Thank you for making time, Mr Gretty, I see you're as busy here, at Hessy's, as we are over at NEMS."

"It's the same every Saturday, Mr Epstein. There are kids coming in and out all day long. Sometimes they even buy something. So how can I help you? Bernard, the manager, said something about you wanting to talk about local musicians and the such like."

"Yes, I do. Is there, perhaps, somewhere a little quieter?"

"Do you fancy a quick coffee?" I always take a break about this time if I can manage it."

"The Kardomah? Yes, that'd be fine."

Brian Epstein followed Jim Gretty back through the din of voices, guitars, and tapped-at snare drums, and stepped out into the altogether much quieter hustle and bustle of Stanley Street.

"I telephoned Hessy's because I wanted to find out more about this so-called explosion of music groups that's happening all over Liverpool. And, save for Bill Harry at *Mersey Beat*, there's no better person, apparently, to talk to than you. In fact, it was Bill who told me that you not only run your own variety agency and supply bands for all sorts of events, but you also know most of the groups, personally. And it was you, in fact, that'd taught many of them how to play."

"That's very kind of him, but not quite true. It's amazing, but most of the young lads are self-taught. I help out with chords if they come in and ask, like. And I give a free lesson with every guitar we sell. But it's like an epidemic out there, it is. Kids will travel all the way across Liverpool if they think they can get a new guitar chord off of someone or borrow a record of some tune or song they want to learn."

He nodded, took a sip of coffee. "Yes, sales of sheet music, in NEMS piano department, have been growing hand over fist."

"I love it, of course, Mr Epstein, and not just because Hessy's happen to sell guitars and drums and such. No. I'm for anything that helps keep all them youngsters off of street corners. Give me gangs of musicians over gangs of Teddy Boys, any day of the week."

He smiled. Jim Gretty was exactly the sort of person he needed to talk to: warm, willing, and self-effacing. "I couldn't agree with you more," he said. "Do please call me, Brian. May I call you, Jim?" He paused. "So let me ask you, Jim, who are your favourite groups?"

"Let me see, now, er, Brian. There's Gerry Marsden and The Pacemakers. Nice lad, polite, lovely voice, and a very good guitarist. The Fourmost. Nice bunch of fellas and very good musically. Then, of course, there's 'Mr Showmanship' himself, Rory Storm. He and The Hurricanes are probably the most entertaining band, out there, at the moment. I like The Big Three, too. Though I can't stand them, personally, like—a little too pushy for my taste—nevertheless, a great sounding combo. Then, of course, there's The Beatles."

He could barely contain himself. "The Beatles? Yes, I think I've heard of them. Are they any good?"

"Well there's some would say they're the best of the lot. The kids that come in the shop can't seem to stop talking about them. And from what I've heard they're playing better than ever since this last time they got back from Hamburg, especially that young George Harrison."

"Thing is, Jim, say I was looking to get involved in the business, not as a variety agent, you understand, but more in an advisory role, would these Beatles be the sort of group I should take a look at?"

"Well, they're a bit rough round the edges, like, but a nicer bunch of lads you'll never find. I tell you what, though, Brian. I'm putting on *Star Matinee*, a special charity show, at the Albany Cinema, over in Maghull, next week. The Beatles will be playing. I'll get you a couple of tickets, if you like, and you can come and see them for yourself."

"Yes, Jim, I think I'd like that very much. Thank you."

THE BEATLES had been perfectly wonderful. Made an otherwise perfectly dreadful Sunday afternoon tolerable. He'd gone
to Jim Gretty's charity show, out in the suburbs, and found himself sitting next to Bessie Braddock, the local Member of
Parliament, the mayor and a host of councillors and civic digni-
taries. And for three, long, interminable hours he'd sat right in
the middle of them all, trying desperately not to fidget. The variety bill had been a trial of numbing mediocrity—one awful act
after another. An indifferent organist had followed a truly terrible tenor. An unending parade of Trad-jazz bands and country
and western combos had all blurred into one meaningless noise.
Then a lone opera singer had all but murdered two of his favourite arias. The only relief had come when, almost against his
better judgement, he'd found himself laughing along with the
rest of the audience at the ridiculous antics of the local comedian, Ken Dodd. Then, after sixteen almost criminal acts, The
Beatles had at last appeared to close the show and open his eyes.

It all went by so very quickly, he couldn't remember much of
what he'd heard. Only that the music seemed incredibly raw and
alive, even if somewhat deafening. What *had* imprinted itself—
indelibly—upon his memory were The Beatles, themselves. Not
for them, the brightly coloured stage suits and highly choreo-
graphed steps-in-time favoured by other bands. They'd dressed
from head-to-toe in black street-clothes just like the photograph
in *Mersey Beat*. Had simply stood there and played their guitars.
First one singing lead vocal, while the others harmonised, then
they'd all switch roles for the next song. The older members of
the audience hadn't known what to make of it, but the young
ones certainly had and they'd clapped and whistled and cheered
until the compère had finally restored order and all the per-
formers been allowed back to take their final bow. He'd clapped
long and hard, too; sitting forward in his seat, eyes glistening in
the dark, an island of giddy enthusiasm in a sea of politesse; and
with good reason. The Beatles *were* different. It was as if every
act before them was 'the old' and they were 'the new'. They'd
played for no more than ten minutes. But in that time they'd
rocked his world and shifted it about its axis.

He spent a sleepless night staring out through the open curtains at the stars he now knew for sure were twinkling behind the clouds. And the following morning he called Jim Gretty to thank him. Almost as an afterthought, he added, "Jim, I like those Beatles. And I think I'd like to manage them." And there, the cat was out of the bag, but he felt all the lighter for it—relieved—thrilled even. It was the very first step in his new life with The Beatles. The only obstacle, of course, being that The Beatles didn't know it yet. But they would. He'd court them. He'd engage them. Then he'd manage them. After which, he'd show the whole world exactly what it was he saw in them. Nothing less, than such stuff as dreams are made on.

"HELLO? HELLO, BILL. It's Brian Epstein. No, no problem. *Mersey Beat* is still selling very well. And, yes, I'll have my 'Record Releases' column typed up and sent over by Monday morning. How's Virginia? Good." He crossed a line through the name on his notepad and drew a ring round and around the word beneath it. "Bill, I have a favour to ask. That Beatles group, you once talked to me about. I noticed in *Mersey Beat* they're playing at the Cavern Club, not far from me here. Didn't it use to be a jazz club? Yes. Well, as I imagine it now only caters to young people, I've not ventured there myself. But, look, Bill, could I ask a favour? I was wondering if you could fix it up with the people at the club for me to pay a visit? I'd rather not get involved with membership cards, having to queue up, or any of that kind of thing. Could you possibly do that for me? I'd be so grateful. You will? Thank you, Bill. Yes, I'll await your call. Good-bye."

Brian Epstein unlocked the bottom drawer of his desk and took out the copy of *Mersey Beat* with The Beatles on the cover. He brushed his fingertips across the picture and went and stood over by the window and looked out across Whitechapel. To the left, he could see the narrow lane that led through to Mathew Street and he followed it in his mind's eye, his eyes boring through buildings and the tangle of lanes, until they came to where The Cavern was. He imagined himself pushing through a curtain of darkness, but had no idea what he'd be met with on the other side. He'd visited dozens of nightclubs in London, Paris, Amsterdam, Barcelona, and Hamburg. But this pending visit somehow promised to be different and he felt both apprehensive and excited. What did he expect to find there? Would he know it if he saw it? Or was he simply setting himself up for another failure? He stared at the picture of The Beatles again and drew strength from it.

BILL HARRY had been as good as his word. Even the weather had played its part. Early November was usually cold, wet and windy. And here he was, without an overcoat. Even so, he walked briskly down Mathew Street. Not to appear overly eager, but promptness was ever a virtue. He noticed his personal assistant, Alistair Taylor, had to make an effort to keep up with him.

"Bit of a surprise, Brian. Not your usual lunchtime custom."

He narrowed his eyes. Mathew Street didn't improve with daylight. It was still a dark, grubby little street, utterly devoid of character. He turned and smiled, encouragingly. "It's only so we can get some more information on this Polydor record they've released, Alistair. We needn't stay long."

He tried not to look too disquieted as he picked his way between the goods-lorries. Or, indeed, disgusted, as he did his best to avoid stepping on the squashed fruit and vegetables that littered the cobblestones. That would give entirely the wrong impression. Yet, even he saw that, dressed as they both were, in their business suits, they looked more and more out of place with every step they took. He did his best to ignore the inquisitive, almost insolent, gazes of the shop girls, office girls, delivery-boys, and apprentices. All of them stood in a line that stretched down one entire side of the street. Yet, much to his surprise, he found the chatter and swell of voices only added to his own growing sense of excitement.

"This is silly, Brian. Look at the steam billowing out of that hole in the wall. There must be a fire down there or something."

He smiled enigmatically. "We're here. And exactly on time."

Thin wisps of steam surrounded the entrance to the Cavern like a cheap theatrical effect. But the impression it made on him was much more dramatic. It was as the very air itself was suffused with the pounding beat of drums and electric bass. Out of the blue a large man, wearing a dinner jacket and red cummerbund under an open overcoat, stepped forward sweeping out an arm towards them, like a door opening. "You must be Mr Epstein. Please go straight down, sir. We've been expecting you." Paddy Delaney, the club's doorman and chief bouncer, threw a slow salute and smiled. He nodded and said, "Thank you," and tried hard not to salute back.

He glanced over his shoulder to see if Alistair Taylor was actually following him. Then he stepped through the brick-arched doorway and descended into the depths of The Cavern. It felt like he was entering a train tunnel and a blast of hot, fetid air hit him before he had a chance to catch his breath. The place was dark and dank and stank of disinfectant and cheap tobacco and sweat and body odour and urine. He almost gagged, but continued on down the narrow slippery stone stairs to the warehouse cellar. He put out a hand to steady himself and immediately withdrew it when he felt the walls running with condensation. For one panicky moment he regretted being there and was about to turn and push his way back up to the street, when the beat of the music caught and grabbed him—transfixed him.

Boom. Boom. Boom. Boom.

He swallowed—lost for words as much as for air. It was different from anything he'd ever experienced. It wasn't at all like the charity show at the Albany Cinema. It was raw, urgent, almost primal, and it hit him in the chest. Pounded at his head.

Boom. Boom. Boom. Boom…Boom. Boom. Boom. Boom…

"Good God, Brian. What on earth is this place?" Alistair Taylor shouted. But he pretended not to hear and just continued his descent into the depths of The Cavern.

At the bottom of the steps, a man sat at a battered folding canteen table. On top of it were two bowls of loose change. One for silver, the other for pennies. The man looked up and waved him past the line of teenagers waiting to pay their admission money. He pressed on, the crush of tightly packed bodies parting in front of him, as if it too had been ordained.

He was in a low cavernous space made of three, long inter-locking brick arches. It resembled nothing so much as a dungeon in a second-rate horror movie. Undeterred, he moved closer to the source of the sound and light until he found himself at the back of the long central aisle. There was a small stage at the far end with rows and rows of swaying teenagers seated in front of it. He looked around. Both outer aisles were one writhing mass of dancing, jiving, jumping bodies. Then suddenly The Beatles were there in front of him.

Boom. Ba-Boom. Boom. Ba-Boom.

He couldn't speak. He could hardly breathe. He didn't even turn round when he felt Alistair Taylor come to stand by his side. He was already bound in chains, chains of love, and he didn't want to break away from them. Not now. Not ever.

Boom. Ba-Boom. Boom. Ba-Boom…

The sound of The Beatles hammered at him. It was beyond loud; it was physical. The beat thudded against his chest. Went deeper and deeper and became one with the beating chambers of his heart. Became the very lifeblood rushing and pounding in his ears.

Boom. Ba-Boom. Ba-Boom. Ba-Boom.

And suddenly he was through the sound barrier and on into the realm beyond. He became one with the mass of dancing, joyous, revelling bodies and he knew with all his heart the boys on stage were playing, singing, drumming, moving, only for him.

Boom. Ba-Boom. Boom. Ba-Boom…

He felt free. "Oh, my God," he all but cried to himself. "*This* is what it must feel like to feel really and truly free." There was no prickling, no blushing, no dark sweats. Only a joy that coursed through him and buoyed him, and held him tethered, transfixed and deliciously captive. He realised he was grinning like a demented young schoolboy. And as he tried to still the urge to shout his feelings out loud, he felt tears of sheer joy pricking at the corners of his eyes.

The music stopped. The effect so wrenching, he had to shake off a rising feeling of panic he might never hear it again. But as the wave of clapping and cheering slowly subsided, and his heart stopped racing, he found he could breathe once more. He blinked, blinked. Slowly became aware of a smooth, velvety voice. "I have some special news for all you Cavern dwellers." He tried to focus, to listen. It was probably some announcement to do with The Beatles. "We have someone rather famous in the audience today. A Mr Brian Epstein of NEMS Music Stores."

"Oh, damn and blast," he said to himself. That was the very last thing he'd wanted to happen. He felt his skin start to prickle from his neck to his cheeks—the precursor to a shaming, full, red-faced blush. He felt nauseous. Tried to swallow. Did his best to smile. Maintain his dignity. Almost at the point of choking, he nodded, waved a hand for the music to continue. Mercifully, the group's drummer immediately counted out the time on his drumsticks. The pounding beat began again. The sound engulfed him. And in an instant he was transported from the depths of misery to almost dizzying heights of joy.

He stared at the boys on the bandstand. The lead singer was singing, imploringly, of wanting money. But money was the very last thing on his mind, it was The Beatles, themselves, that utterly consumed him and his hungry eyes missed nothing. The boys were all dressed in leather jackets and jeans as in the photographs. Their hair still unfashionably long, three of them with it brushed down over the foreheads. In between songs, they smoked, ate sandwiches, and drank Coca-Cola straight from the bottle. At times, they even turned their backs on their audience and talked and joked amongst themselves. They ad-libbed sarcastic replies to requests and shouts from the audience. Yet they were always surprisingly funny and engaging. Once or twice, without any sort of apology, they even stopped singing halfway through a song, seemingly dissatisfied or bored with their performance. Much to his surprise, he found them no less charming for their outrageous antics. A feeling, he noticed, fully shared by the rest of the audience. The boys had an extraordinary presence. More importantly, they exuded that unmistakable charisma that spelled star quality. The very thing he now realised he'd unknowingly been searching for all the days of his life.

At the interval, he turned, almost breathless, to his still utterly bewildered assistant. "Come on, Alistair. I must go and talk to them. I must." Holding an arm out in front of him, as if to ward off any killjoys, he jostled his way through the crowd to the cramped band-room at the side of the stage. He approached a Beatle lighting a cigarette. "Hello," he said, "I'm Brian Epstein. And this is my personal assistant, Alistair Taylor."

"That must be very nice for you," said George Harrison, grinning. "What brings Mr Epstein and his personable assistant here, then?"

"Your, er...it's about your record, 'My Bonnie'. People keep coming into the store and asking for it. They say you play it, here, at the Cavern."

"Well, I don't play it meself, like," said George, dryly, "but he does. That little short fella hunched over his turntable desperately trying not to listen to what we're saying. Here, Bob, meet Mr Brian Epstein of..."

"NEMS. Yes. Thank *you*, Mr Harrison." Bob Wooler checked the status of the disc he was playing, squeezed out from his little cubbyhole, and proffered his hand. "The Beatles' record of 'My Bonnie'? Yes. I'm the one you have to blame for that. People are always pestering me about how they can get hold of a copy."

He shook Bob Wooler's hand. "Yes, well, I've been on to Polydor Records in...in London and they've never heard of it."

"Yeah, well that's because they know us as 'The Beat Brothers'." It was Paul McCartney. "Hello, I'm Paul. Only, George, here, just said you're Brian Epstein, of NEMS. We've bought thousands of records from your shop. Well, hundreds, maybe. But, er, our record will be listed as 'Tony Sheridan and The Beat Brothers'. We were just the backing group, like. Although we do have a contract with Polydor to do more."

He smiled, a winning smile. "Er, Paul MacArthy?"

"No, that's McCartney. You must've been reading your *Mersey Beat*. I'll duff Bill Harry next time I see him. He's always misspelling me name."

He nodded. "Tony Sheridan?...*and*...'The Beat Brothers'? Yes?" He half-turned. "Alistair, make a note of that, please?"

George stuck his head over Paul's shoulder, grinned. "Would the rather famous Mr Epstein like to hear the record played live?

Because if he did, like, I'm sure we could ask the not so famous
Mr Wooler, here, to oblige. Couldn't we, Bob?"

He smiled, enthusiastically, nodded again. "Yes. Thank you.
That would be delightful. That is, of course, if Mr Wooler
wouldn't mind?"

"It's all work and no play for those of us that toil in obscurity
in the vineyards of pop," muttered Bob Wooler, as he squeezed
himself back into his tiny cubicle. But once The Coasters had
finished their 'Searchin', his dulcet velvety voice purred: "Now
dig this, all you Cavern dwellers, it's time you made this disc,
one of NEMS' best ever, best sellers."

Then he played 'My Bonnie' at maximum volume.

"MR MAKIN, it's a Mr Lightfoot on the line for you. He says
it's important and that you'd know what it would be in regards
to."

Rex Makin closed a leather-bound law book, returned it to its
proper place on the shelf. "Thank you, Marian, I'll take it in my
office." He closed the door, crossed to his desk, and picked up
the phone. "Yes, please, put him through." There was a click.
"Harry? Yes, I can hear you clearly. What can I do for you?" He
listened in silence for a few minutes. "Yes, Harry, I appreciate
the difficulties. Yes, I'm sure you haven't been faced with anything quite like it before. No, I'd like you to continue. But let me
think about the problem over the weekend. Then we can meet
next week. No? You really think we should meet sooner? Well,
let's see, it's almost two, what about the usual place, later? Say,
four o'clock? Okay? See you there then. No, you did the right
thing in calling me. Yes, thank you. Good bye."

Rex Makin rubbed his chin. "Bugger, that Brian," he said.
"Always some new little kink that needs straightening out." He
pressed the intercom button. "Marian, cancel my three-thirty
and four-thirty meetings, will you please. I'll be going out."

THE KARDOMAH was busier than usual for a Thursday afternoon, but the two found their regular table in the back, empty
and waiting.

"I swear I'll turn into a bloody coffee bean, the amount of this stuff I drink when I'm hanging around, watching and waiting." Harry Lightfoot stirred his spoon round the rim of his cup.

"Much better than you having to stand out in the rain or dashing about the City, at all hours, isn't it, Harry?"

"Yes, shouldn't grumble, Mr Makin. But personally I never minded walking the beat, in the early days. It was a much simpler world, back then." He removed a little black notebook from his pocket and flipped it open. Then he took a sip of coffee, licked a finger, and leafed through the pages. He looked up. "I hope it wasn't too noisy, when I called you earlier. Only, I had to pop into the Grapes, quick, like, to use their telephone."

Rex Makin raised a questioning eyebrow.

"No, Mr Makin, I admit I do like a little taste of the malt, now and again. But never when I'm on duty. You know that."

"You always were a good copper, Harry. And there's never been any reason for me to believe, otherwise. Either then or now, despite what happened. So, just put that questioning look of mine down to my never-ending inquisitive nature, that's all."

Harry Lightfoot nodded. "Righto, then, Mr Makin. As I said on the telephone, I've followed your Mr Epstein around all over Liverpool. And I'm certain he's not noticed me, whether I've been on foot or driving in my little black Morris Minor. But there's a pattern, of sorts, I'm beginning to see. At first, I thought, he'd just be visiting his usual haunts. The Playhouse, a restaurant or two, his queer little clubs: The Basnett, Magic Clock, and such like. Only now he also seems to have developed a new passion."

Rex Makin stirred his coffee, nodded, but said nothing.

"This time, it seems to be young kids. Teenagers. I've followed him to West Derby, Knotty Ash, Huyton, even over to Aintree. He doesn't get out. He just sits in his car. Staring at the kids all lining up outside this club or that dancehall. Then when they've all gone in, like, he just drives off."

Rex Makin peered at the private investigator over the rim of his cup. "Did you by any chance look and see what was going on in the places he visited?"

Harry Lightfoot smiled. "As a matter of fact, I did, Mr Makin. I checked the posters pinned up outside each venue and it always seemed to be something to do with this rock and skiffle music the kids are crazy for." He consulted his notebook. "Very possibly, something concerning Beatles."

"Beetles? What like spiders, ants and butterflies and things?"

"No. It's the name of one of the show bands. Only there's dozens of different ones out there, apparently, all with daft, peculiar names. But these so called Beatles was the only band common to every place he visited."

"Beetles? How very odd?" Rex Makin added some more sugar to his coffee. Slowly stirred it round. "So, Harry, what do you think? Is it anything to do with his...how shall I put it...his particular peculiarities?"

"Well, even though I might've done at first, I don't think it's the young kids he's interested in. At least, I've never once seen him talk to one of them. But I did think, like, as it might perhaps be one of these Beatles that he's interested in. To put it bluntly, Mr Makin, they look a rough and ready lot. Then, again, I've not seen him talking to any of them, like, either."

"And you say he's still visiting his usual haunts?"

"Yes, he is. All the usual places, and one or two I suspect that even the Vice Squad haven't cottoned on to, yet. But nothing we need concern ourselves with. I also had that little drink with my friend on the Squad and managed to get my hands on a better photo of our little blackmailing friend. It cost a tenner, but I thought it was well worth it, considering. "

Harry Lightfoot pushed an envelope across the table, his eyes never leaving Rex Makin's face. The solicitor opened the envelope and slid out a photograph, part way. He glanced down at it and shuddered. The flat, dead look of the blackmailer's eyes still sent shivers up his spine—and that just from having seen him everyday at the trial. God only knew what memories of the man's face did to poor Brian. He cleared his throat, slid the photo back inside the envelope and pushed it back across the tabletop. "Yes, that's him. It's one face you don't forget in a hurry. So, where else has our boy been visiting, then?"

"Well, that's just the trouble, Mr Makin. As I told you, it's these music clubs set up for teenagers that worry me. I mean, I've followed your man into the Merseyside Civil Service Club, twice, and that was easy enough. I also went out to Maghull, one Sunday, to a St. John Ambulance Brigade charity show with that comedian, Ken Dodd. And what with the Mayor and Mayoress of Crosby being there, along with scores of other grown-ups, it was a piece of cake; I blended right in. It's the smaller clubs that are the real problem. If they were just playing jazz music, like they used to, I could probably get away with it, maybe. But when it's only office girls and young tearaways that go inside them, I stick out like a roast pig at a bloody Bar Mitzvah."

Rex Makin smiled at the broad-shouldered Harry Lightfoot and suppressed a laugh. "Yes, I can see as how that might be a problem."

"Take this Cavern Club, in Mathew Street, that he went into this lunchtime. At first he used to walk past at night, probably trying to pluck up the courage to go in, but again only when these so-called Beatles were on the bill. I went down once, like, pretending to be a Public Health Inspector, checking up on the food and the toilets. But that fly bugger on the door gave me the eye, as if to say he knew right bloody well I was an ex-copper or some such, and I shouldn't ever bother coming back."

"So there's only so much close surveillance you can do without attracting too much attention to yourself, is that it?"

"In a nutshell, Mr Makin, yes."

"Well since you first called me, Harry, I've been racking my brains. And I think I may have an idea that'll help us keep a wary eye on our Mr Epstein. But only if you're agreeable to it, of course."

Harry Lightfoot leaned forward so as not to miss anything. "This should be bloody well interesting," he said to himself.

CHAPTER TEN

Operation Big Beat

The dense blanket of fog had come up river late that afternoon. No one had expected it. Not even the weatherman on the telly the night before. First report of it was on the midday shipping forecast on the radio. And by mid-afternoon tongues of fog had already moved across Liverpool Bay and were licking hungrily at Wallasey, Bootle, and Crosby. By teatime, both banks of the river and 'the Tower', at New Brighton, were shrouded in a grey-green fog the colour of the Mersey.

All of Liverpool was completely fogbound.

"What the bloody hell did I do in my past life to deserve this?"

"Don't know, Sam, but it must've been something pretty bad."

"Bloody hell, Terry, will you look at that bloody fog."

"Well, I would, like, if I could see anything."

"Alright, smart arse, back inside the Grapes. This calls for some serious drinking. I'm ruined I am, bloody ruined. What time is it?"

Spike glanced at his watch. "Five past, Sam. But no need to worry, I'm sure The Beatles will get through."

"I don't doubt it, Spike, especially with that mad sod, Nelly, driving. No, it's the fans I'm worrying about. What with all the ferries being stopped and most of the busses not running, how in hell they're going to get themselves there, I don't know. You couldn't find the bloody Tower in this fog, even if it fell on top of you. We'll be bloody lucky if we can find it ourselves. The real sod of it is, though, ticket sales have been much less than I'd hoped. You'd think the kids had given up on rock 'n' roll."

"Maybe for one night, Sam. But not in our lifetimes, they won't."

"Thank you, Sigmund Freud. What time is it?"

"Quarter past. What time did Neil say he'd have them here?"

"Half-past. But in this pea-souper, who the heck knows?"

Terry McCann arrived with a tray of drinks. "Look on the bright side, Sam. Just imagine The Beatles and Gerry and Rory all playing their hearts out at 'the Tower' just for us. Cheers."

"I tell you, I'm ruined I am, totally bloody ruined. Cheers. Talking of which, what time is it?"

"Nigh on half past, Sam. Stop yer worrying."

"That's all very well for you to say, sunshine, but..."

A car-horn beeped a tattoo outside in the street and eyebrows shot up in question and hope. Spike was already at the pub door. "It's them. All aboard the New Brighton ferry!" They downed their drinks in a rush, piled out of the Grapes, and into the back of Neil Aspinall's battered Bedford van.

" 'Lo Sam. 'Lo fellas," chorused Neil and The Beatles.

"Get yer arses in quick or we'll all catch our deaths," shouted John Lennon.

"All arses aboard and accounted for, sir," yelled Sam. "Hey, thanks for turning up, lads. At least tonight won't be a complete bloody loss."

"Well, wherever it is we're going," groaned Neil, "I'll see if I can get us there by the middle of next week. Everyone hold on tight."

"Next stop, the Mersey Tunnel," shouted George.

After a few minutes of hurtling through the streets of Liverpool at five miles per hour, Paul McCartney turned to Sam and said, quietly, "Look, Sam, we were talking, like, on the way to pick you up. If this bad weather hits you hard tonight, we'll play for nothing, okay?" Sam turned to John and George who both nodded their agreement. Pete, sitting up front, holding his snare drum on his lap, gave a thumbs-up. Sam coughed and nodded his thanks, his eyes a little glassy. Terry and Spike huddled by the back doors kept their thoughts to themselves.

When the old Bedford van at last entered the approach to the Mersey Tunnel, George yelled out again. "There it is, fellas. You can just make out the Hessy's sign on the side of the building."

"Oooh, Hessy's," yodelled John and Paul in Goon-like voices.

"Ready?" shouted John, "Hessy's Musical Instruments and...?"

"Ra-di-o!" The Beatles all yelled as Neil tapped out the beat on the car-horn. Then they all clapped and cheered.

"We do that every time we pass that sign," explained Paul.

"It's our way of wishing for the day we hear one of our own songs actually played on the radio," added George.

"Where we going to, fellas?" John shouted.

"To the top Johnny," the other three Beatles chorused.

"And which top, is that, fellas?"

"To the topper-most of the popper-most," they yelled in unison as the van rattled on through the Mersey Tunnel.

"We best start by topping the bill at 'the Tower', then," John shouted back. "How much bloody higher can you get than that?"

"You guys could make it all the way to the moon, if you wanted to," Sam said, the lump still in his throat. "Thanks, lads. I won't forget this. Not ever."

"Hey, shurrup will you, Sam. And start soddin' praying, instead. We've got to get to the bloody place in one piece, yet."

"Righto," yelled Sam. "Our Lennon, who art in heaven..."

AN HOUR OR SO LATER, the little blue Bedford van nosed its way slowly across 'the Tower' car park until it bumped up against the kerb in front of the long line of entrance doors. The old, iron tower had been dismantled to provide metal for the War effort. All that was left now was the Gothic-looking four-storey building that'd once been the base of the attraction and even that had disappeared in the fog. The only clue they'd arrived at the right place was the half-lit illuminated sign welcoming people to 'The Tower Ballroom'.

Everyone whistled and clapped and cheered Neil Aspinall who'd driven with his nose pressed hard up against the windshield for the entire five miles from the tunnel exit.

"Ye poor wee sod, Nelly," said John Lennon patting him on the shoulder. "Yer poor wee eyes look as if they've melted intae yer bony cheekbones. Oooh, it looks awfa nasty, it does, and ye'll probably go blind, because of it. But dinna you worry, laddie, ye've only got tae do it another three more times, toneet, before ye can go home to yer poor wee bed."

All the doors of the van burst open at once and everyone piled out, laughing, as eager to get their feet back on dry land, as get on with the night. And it being Sam Leach's night he immediately took charge. "Right lads, its only three flights up. Spike, you give Pete a hand with his drums. Terry, get a hold of the other end of this amp. Right then, fellas, onwards and upwards."

There were only about fifty people in a place that could hold five thousand and to hide his disappointment Sam ran around like a mad man, checking on everything. He checked the stagelights, the four new 'Reslo' microphones he'd insisted 'the Tower' management buy for the PA system, and then checked the dressing rooms and toilets.

He buttonholed Pete Smith, the compère for the night, and told him to start on the dot at 7:30 PM no matter how many people had shown up. "Five or five thousand, we'll give them a show they'll never forget. It looks like it's only going to be sixty people or so, so do your best to get them all jumping and jiving. And remember to tell everyone how very special they are for braving the fog or swimming the River Mersey, okay?"

"Got it, Sam. I'll even tell everyone to keep spreading out, so it looks like there's many more people in the hall."

"That's the ticket. Hey, Spike, got a minute?"

"Yeah, Sam?"

"I need to put that education of yours to good use again. Go double-check those new mikes for me, will yer. I think they're all right, but if anyone's going to get a shock, tonight, you're the only one I can afford to lose." He grinned and poked Spike, playfully, in the ribs.

"Okay, Sam, I'm yer man," Spike said laughing, "but if I go up in a cloud of smoke, tell me mum, I said, I loved her."

On his way backstage, he bumped into Paul McCartney. "Hi, Paul, just going to check the mikes before you go on."

"Good lad. Hey, Spike, what do reckon on these leather trousers we all got in Hamburg, then? They don't make us look too...well, you know, like idiots or anything?"

"No, not at all. I was thinking, like, when I first saw them, how really gear they looked...like Gene Vincent in *The Girl Can't Help It*."

"You reckon?"

"Yeah, with the black leather jacket, 'an all, it looks t'rrific."

"Good enough for a bit of 'Be-Bop-A-Lula'?" Paul grinned.

"Yeah, as if you'd have trouble finding a girl that wants to rock 'n' roll. But, hey, Paul, sing us that one, will yer?"

"Can't, that's John's song, that is. How about, er, 'Long Tall Sally'?"

"Little Richard? Yeah, that'd be great. Thanks, there, Paul."

Mouthing the words of the song, Spike went on stage to check the microphones. He looked out at the expectant faces. There must've been a hundred people or more, girls mostly, milling around, but it was still painfully few. A bank of spotlights suddenly blazed on and off in quick succession and he had to shield his eyes with his hand.

"All right, Johnny Ray, come on down, it's nearly time for the start." It was Sam, still buzzing with nerves, staring up at the huge dome and the still empty dancehall. "What bloody awful luck?" he said, scratching. "But I suppose I can't blame that lot back in Liverpool for all this fog, can I? No. If Allan Williams, Ray McFall, and Brian Kelley have any sense they'll all be tucked up in bed with Agatha Christie and a nice hot cup of cocoa. Knowing the sods though I wouldn't put it past them to have put a curse on me."

"But there's people still coming in, Sam."

"Yeah, but only in dribs and drabs, dribs and bloody drabs...not enough to make a real difference. What's the time?"

"Just gone twenty past. Do you want to delay the start?"

"No, never, the punters have paid for a top class show and a top class show is what Sam Leach is going to give them, even if I go bust doing it. Here, go find Pete Smith and then go tell The Beatles they're on in five minutes. I'll go see what Terry's up to. Oh, by the way, Jimmy Molloy was looking for you earlier, I think he misses you being part of his Mean Machine."

"He wouldn't be seen dead talking to me, in me old jeans and leather jacket, with all them posh-looking judies about."

"You'd be surprised, Spike. As, I said, he's taken quite a shine to you, for some reason. In a brotherly way, of course."

"Well there's no one better to have next to you in a fight."

"You're right there, young, Spike. That's why I call them *Leach's* Mean Machine. It's so they always remember it's me they're supposed to be looking after. Anyway, get on with it you scruffy bugger. I can't afford be seen talking to the likes of you, I've got my own reputation to consider."

"LADIES AND GENTLEMEN, it's time for 'Operation Big Beat'. And to kick off the evening, The Leach Organisation is proud to present...the one and only...the fabulous...Beatles!"

Paul ripped into 'Long Tall Sally' and the tiny crowd rushed the stage and stood rooted to the spot, staring up in wonder at the four Beatles. And soon everyone was stamping and cheering and waving their arms about, making enough noise for a thousand people.

"The number counter on the turnstile says there's already over two hundred kids inside, Sam, even more queuing outside."

"Even more music to my ears, Terry, but just look at them, will yer? Aren't they bloody fabulous? God, what a sound."

"What, The Beatles or the crowd?"

"Both, old son, you can't ever really have one without the other. I think they call it combustion, but there must be a proper musical term for it, somewhere. I'll ask our Spike about it, later, if I remember. The clever sod's bound to know."

The Beatles kept up the blistering pace with two Chuck Berry numbers in a row—John rocking hard with 'Rock and Roll Music' and George rolling straight into 'Roll Over Beethoven'—the group not leaving a single moment between songs for the crowd to catch their breath. And by the end of the third number, as if by magic, the crowd in the ballroom had swelled to over four hundred.

"I'm caught between a rock and a turnstile, I am. But I've got to go downstairs and look for myself or I think I'll burst. I've suddenly got a feeling in my water it's all going to happen like it should. Keep an eye on things up here, Terry. See you in a bit."

Sam bounded down the stairs, taking two or three steps at a time, delighted to see dozens of people dashing up the stairs to the ballroom. He yelled to them that The Beatles had already started playing and, despite all the groans, he was tickled to see that even the slowest of the latecomers picked up speed.

"And the more the bloody merrier," he shouted.

The sight that met him at the entrance hall would stay with him forever. There were hundreds of people clamouring to get into 'the Tower'. The Mean Machine already had things well organised by sorting ticket holders and non-ticket holders into two lines. And when he raced outside he was ecstatic to see the pay-at-the-door queue was the longest by far. He let out a huge sigh of relief. "Thank you, God," he whispered, crossing himself. Even so, when he checked the turnstile counter he was staggered to see that it showed there were over a thousand and forty fans inside. And as he'd just seen for himself there had to be at least that many, still outside, waiting to get in. All of which spelled 'SUCCESS' in great big capital letters.

How had the fans all managed it? He'd barely made it himself and he'd come with The Beatles. And yet, there, in front of his disbelieving eyes, people were still pouring through the doors of the Tower Ballroom on one of the most miserable, fog-bound winter nights in living memory. He went back outside, oblivious to the chill, happier now than he'd been in months. He looked up to where 'the Tower' would've pointed skyward if it'd still stood proud. "Look, I don't know if you heard me the first time, Mister God. But just in case you didn't, like. Thank you, again, from the bottom of Sam Leach's old, almost-stopped-beating-twice heart."

The sudden blast of what sounded like an angel's trumpet made him almost jump out of his skin. "Strike a bloody light," he yelled. "What in heaven's name was that?"

"Hey, 'oop, Sam, it's only little old me and me car-horn," shouted a voice from out the fog. "Is this the right place?"

He spun round to see Gerry Marsden's big grey Humber saloon inching its way through crowds of latecomers. "Hey, careful, you daft sod! Don't knock anyone over! They haven't paid to get in, yet."

Gerry gently rolled to a stop, cut the engine, and switched off the headlights. And even though Sam was standing right in front of the big motorcar, it all but disappeared in the swirls of fog. "Hey, Sam, you should see the crowds we've had to come through." Gerry ran round the car waving his arms in delight. "It's as if Liverpool City were playing at home to Manchester United. The roads are chock-a-block with people. I don't know who the hell you've been praying to, but put in a good word for us, too, will yers?"

The Pacemakers started unloading their gear from the cavernous boot of the Humber, just as Rory Storm, Johnny Guitar, and Ringo Starr emerged from out of the fog humping the Hurricane's instruments and amplifiers.

"How in heck, did-did you get through with a car? The-the police have c-c-closed the c-c-car park entrance. They say, they c-c-can't cope with all the t-t-traffic. We had to-to leave our car b-back down the road."

"I just told 'em my uncle's a City copper, Rory," said Gerry, grinning.

"Is he re-really, Gerry? No-no k-kidding?"

"Course I am, you big dafty. But they wouldn't know that, would they?"

Spike slid up beside Sam. "Can I lend a hand, Sam?"

"Yeah, you can help me deal with all these mad sods. Here, take hold of one of Ringo's drums, while I carry his drumsticks."

"And wha-what's that lovely smell, I smell?" crooned Rory. "Oh, hot d-dogs, m-my favourite."

"Hey, and if our Sam's buying," shouted Gerry, "I'll have a Hamburger...in honour of my home away from home."

"All right, you scrounging lot," Sam shouted back. "As you managed to get yourselves through the fog, I'm buying. Just you sods remember me when you're rich and famous, that's all."

They made their way through the crowd to the food van parked opposite the entrance to the Tower Ballroom. Then they all stopped and did a double take. A midget, in black bowler hat and long grease-stained white coat, was jumping up and down outside the serving hatch, trying to roll down the shutter.

"Wotcher, Titch," Sam called out. "What's up?"

"Yer, yer not closing up are you? Only we-we was wanting some of yer lovely-smelling hot d-dogs, like," crooned Rory.

Sam and Rory stepped forward and helped the little man close the shutter. Surprised and pleased, he turned round and looked up at them and waved his hands up and down like a demented penguin.

"Thank you. Thank you, very much, lads, very decent of you. I'm sorry, though, but it's all gone. There's nothing left. Not a sausage. We've completely sold out...and in this fog, too. I tell yer, it's bloody unbelievable. I've never sold so many so fast in all my life. So, I'm off to get some more burgers and hot dogs. But I'll be back as soon as I can." The little man wiped his hands down his greasy white coat, climbed into his van and with a frantic wave of his tiny hand he drove off, yelling out the window, "Back as soon as I can. Promise."

"Foo-fook it," said Rory "I really f-f-fancied a hot-dog, too."

"Fook-its, right," sighed Gerry. "Sam was paying, an' all."

IT WAS LIKE a scene out of a painting that he could never forget by some mad bugger whose name he could never remember. It seemed as if everyone had gone completely bloody mad. The dance floor was one, jam-packed, seething mass of wriggling, writhing bodies. Everywhere, young girls were crying and sobbing or screaming and waving their arms. Less-fortunate latecomers stood atop tables and chairs at the back, waving hankies, headscarves or their high-heeled shoes. The boys just rocked where they stood, cheering and shouting, nodding their heads and stamping their feet in time to the beat.

The noise was almost unbearable and Sam had to cover his ears to hear himself shout, let alone think. He couldn't even hear what song The Beatles were playing. In a daze, and with the help of two members of the Mean Machine, he pushed his way along the edge of the crowd to the side of the stage. And what he saw made him stop and do another double take. The Tower's manager—the big, bluff Yorkshireman, Tom McCardle, dance-band smart in black bow tie and dinner jacket—stood, grinning inanely, tapping his feet and clapping his hands almost in time with the beat. Sam shook his head in disbelief. Good business aside, what was it about The Beatles and their music that made it so infectious, even to some old bugger that thought Joe Loss and his Orchestra were the cat's whiskers? McCardle saw him and smiled and pointed to the group and nodded and then joined in with all the riotous applause as Pete Best brought Carl Perkins' 'Matchbox' to a close. And as the four Beatles turned to snatch a quick breath before their final number, Sam grinned his biggest grin and gave them all two big thumbs-up in salute, and they all nodded and grinned back. "Thanks, fellas," he mouthed.

He glanced down at his watch. It was almost twenty past eight. Unbelievable. What a difference an hour had made to his life. How many heartbeats did it take to go from complete bloody failure to total success? "One," he said to himself. Then he thought better of it, counted his blessings, and settled on it being four.

"Thanks very much for your very kind welcome, Ladies and Gentlegerms. We'd like to finish our first set, now, with a song by Barrett Strong about something we all feel very strongly about...'Money'."

John Lennon struck the first jangling chord, locked into the beat of Pete Best's drums and Paul McCartney's bass, and the crowd went wild. And as impossible as it was for the already overloaded amplifiers to deliver any more power, the sound that emitted from them was louder than anything that'd come before; the sheer brute force of it hitting girls deep in the stomach and boys smack in the chest. And as John shouted out his demands and George and Paul echoed back their raw feelings of want, the merciless, thunderous beat seemed to drive everyone into a state of frenzy. The noise was indescribable, beyond incredible, and John's climaxing scream pushed at the very edges of reason.

Nothing else existed but the sound and the feeling of utter joy that flowed everywhere like a never-ending river and left the crowd rung-out, reeling, breathless, drained—and all too soon howling for more.

The Beatles nodded, grinned, and waved; totally taken aback at the scale of what they'd just wrought. They unplugged their guitars and staggered off stage, through a sea of glassy-eyed admirers. "Bloody hell, Sam," John panted. "That was soddin' great! We've never played to a crowd like that before. Never. It's got to be the best ever. Better than Hamburg at its bloody wildest. I can't wait to get back here, I can't. None of us can. So I'll tell you what, Leachy, we'll do three spots instead of two, if yer want. We'd play all bloody night for some more of that."

Sam felt as if his heart was about to burst out of his chest and he choked back the huge lump that seemed to have got stuck in his throat. All he could do was nod. He was as drained as everyone else in the Tower Ballroom, but utterly elated, and he patted John, George, Pete, and Paul each on the back as they made their way past him to the dressing room. Then he signalled to Terry McCann and Kenny Butcher that they should ready a few members of the Mean Machine to escort The Beatles back downstairs to their waiting van.

He hated to see The Beatles go. Hated the fact they had to go play another venue for a rival promoter. Really hated that that promoter was none other than Pete Best's mum, Mona—a woman who already thought of herself as The Beatles' unofficial manager. And he really, really didn't like the thought of that. But the hard truth was, 'Mo' already had The Beatles booked for the very same night as 'Operation Big Beat'. So he'd had no other choice but go see her on his bended knee, see if she'd release them. It'd been her idea that The Beatles play 'the Tower' first and then go play for her, afterwards. And, of course, he'd agreed, immediately, and been very grateful for it.

Even so, he knew the fans would riot if The Beatles failed to return for their second set, at midnight. Which of course was why, even as the crowd in the ballroom upstairs was dancing wildly to Rory Storm and The Hurricanes, his stomach began to twist itself into fist-sized knots of worry. Neil Aspinall had to drive The Beatles back through the fog, back through the Mersey Tunnel, on through a never-ending tangle of city streets, all the way out to Knotty Ash Village Hall.

And then the poor sod had to do it all again—coming back.

He followed The Beatles and the accompanying bouncers down the stairs and stood and watched until Neil's Bedford van had disappeared into the fog. Then he stood in the entrance hall and looked at the long line of people still queuing to get it. He strolled over and checked the number counter on the turnstile, again. Saw that it was two thousand, five hundred and seventy-three, and still counting. "Bloody hell," he said to himself, as he turned and walked towards the foot of the stairs. "If that many people rioted, I'd be a gonner, for sure. I'd never be able to get another venue this side of Garston graveyard."

How many heartbeats did it take to go from total success to complete failure? He didn't have to think about it. He knew the answer. It was five, if you counted Neil Aspinall, as well.

He started back up the stairs. Stopped halfway. Then shook his head and began to laugh. "You're only dead once, you stupid, Scouse git. So just stop bloody worrying and get on with it. I mean, what a way to go? Thrown off the top of 'the Tower' by thousands of rioting beat fans. And that, after having given them the best bloody night's rock 'n' roll of their entire bloody lives."

He sniffed, wiped his nose on the back of his hand, and awoke again to the frenzy all around him. Even he had to admit that all the things going on inside and outside the Tower Ball-room, that night, were completely out of the ordinary—potty in the extreme. And, as a constant stream of wildly excited young people continued to rush past him, up the stairs, he grinned and began poking himself in the chest.

"You did this. You. Sam Leach. You and rock 'n' roll togeth-er," he croaked, his voice thick with emotion. Then he laughed and whooped for joy and ran up the stairs with all the rest of the 'big beat' fans, waving his arms like a lunatic, his spirits lifting with his every step.

CHAPTER ELEVEN

Cutting The Mustard

"You know, them Beatles weren't too bad, Spikey. For a minute, I almost broke out in a sweat, myself."

Jimmy Molloy's big moon of a face beamed inches away from his own. It was close enough for the sharp-smelling aftershave to almost overpower him, but he had to admit even in all the heat generated by the crowd Jimmy Molloy still smelled as clean as he looked. It must be what being cool was all about, thought Spike. He grinned and shouted above the noise. "There's hope for you yet, Jimmy."

Jimmy continued to survey the scene. "Smart-arse. No. I take that back. Looking at you and your funny hair, Spikey, there's nothing smart about you, at all. Haven't you got any better threads at home, you scruffy art student, you? You'll never get anywhere with the girls looking like that."

"Can't afford them, either, Jimmy. But at least I can look."

"You can that, sunshine. There's some very tasty looking judies running about the place tonight." He flicked his eyes, left and right, seeing everything, missing nothing. "Thing is, you've got to look cool. Let the girls drool over you from a distance. They'll come round you like weak-kneed bees around honey then. Especially after their favourite group has been on and they think that you're something to do with the management. They don't mind, see, just so long as it gets them closer to whoever it is they're after. If they think you actually know someone in one of the groups, like, then you're in like Flynn." Jimmy turned, gave Spike a look. "Funny sort of behaviour, if you ask me, but there it is, it works every time. And who am I to look a gift horse in the mouth?" The face of the moon was suddenly eclipsed by shadow. "Oi, Spikey, you listening to me? Because this is the real gen, this is. It's taken years of careful study to accumulate."

"I'm listening to every word, Jimmy. Every single word."

Jimmy nodded. "Thing is not to try. Don't try to pull them. Don't even notice them. Don't say a word. Just be aloof and unavailable. And let 'em see the cut of your threads. Drives 'em wild, it does." Spike struggled to keep a straight face as Jimmy Molloy brushed his fingertips up and down the lapels of his light grey Italian-cut jacket to demonstrate his point.

"Excuse me, but isn't your name, Spike Jones?" Spike turned to see a ravishingly pretty girl. The girl smiled and patted the side of her beautifully teased-out beehive hair-do. "Only, I think I remember meeting you in Mr McCardle's office." She was a real stunner. As was her friend. Spike had to blink to convince himself he wasn't seeing things. "Mr McCardle...the manager of 'the Tower'? You brought round some tickets and posters?"

Spike, his tongue suddenly tied up in knots, ran a hand back through his hair. "Oh, yeah, er, what a great turn out tonight, all these hundreds of people, er, so nice to meet you again, er..."

"It's Thelma. And yes, Mr McCardle will be very pleased, I'm sure." The pretty girl smiled a sweet smile and waited. Her friend, though, seemed far more interested in the contents of her handbag.

Spike tried again. "Er, great, weren't they, The Beatles?"

"Yeah, they were fab. We both thought so, didn't we?" The girl called Thelma turned to her friend. The girl looked up at Spike with a cool appraising stare, smiled, and then went back to searching her handbag. "This is my best friend, Sandra. We just wanted to say hello, like. Ta-ra." And with that the two dark-haired, brown-eyed beauties turned on their stiletto heels and disappeared back into the crowd.

"Fuck me," said Jimmy Molloy, standing on tiptoe to keep track of the girls. "You actually know them? She was bleedin' lovely, she was.

"Yeah," gasped Spike, his tongue suddenly able to work again. "And her friend was a bit of alright, too, wasn't she?"

"Fook me, is right," he thought. How long does it take to go from dead to alive? A heartbeat. And his head filled with the Buddy Holly song and the face of an angel framed with long dark brown hair.

"There you both are." Sam Leach skidded up to them with a big grin on his face. "Been searching everywhere for you two layabouts." He poked Spike in the ribs. "Hey, guess what? Last time I checked the numbers, there were over two-and-a-half-thousand fans in here. It's bloody unbelievable. I tell you, when I called it 'Operation Big Beat' I had no idea it'd ever get that big. And the night's not half over yet." He turned to Jimmy. "You and the boys are doing a bang up job, tonight. Anything I need to hear about?"

"Not really, Mr Leach. A few girls fainting and a few scuffles, here and there, is all, but nothing serious. Somebody knocked over a table in one of the downstairs bars. We had to escort another kid out as he couldn't hold his drink, but he was harmless enough. No. The fog seems to have kept most of the toughest Teds away. It plays havoc with their haircuts. They can't stand it when their quiffs go all limp down their foreheads."

"Ah, Jimmy, lad. I've always said you and your brothers have got as big a gift of the gab, as you do with a punch-bag."

"Thanks, Mr Leach. I take that as a compliment."

"Here, tell you what. I got a real fancy for a hot dog. Only, after listening to Rory belting out 'What did I say' for twenty minutes, I'm so knackered I've only just realised how bloody hungry I am. Go see if that little fella and his food van are back, as I want to get one of them hot dogs down me neck before Rory and his Hurricanes dash down and scoff the lot. I'll treat the two of you, as well, if you like."

"Terrific. Yes. Thanks, Sam. I'll go get them. You and Jimmy stay and watch the Remo Four. Jimmy's getting with the beat, finally."

"Good lad," said Sam. "Here's a ten bob note. I'll have a hot dog with lashings of everything on it."

"Smart arse," Jimmy yelled, as Spike dashed down the stairs.

"GERROFF HIM, YER bastards. Pick on someone yer own size."

It was like being hit with a sledgehammer. Time stopped dead. He blinked and blinked. Tried to take in all he was seeing.

"Get a load of her. Who the hell does she think she is, then?"

"Interfering cow."

"Gerroff, I said, or I'll do yer, yer swines."

A gang of eight or nine Teddy Boys had hung the midget out the serving hatch of his food van and were pelting him with fried onions, hamburgers, and bread rolls. It looked a right bloody mess. He just hoped to God the red stains all over the midget's white coat were just tomato sauce. The gang leader, a dirty red bandana tied around his neck, had the midget's black bowler hat perched on top of his head and was conducting the mayhem with an empty beer bottle.

In the middle of it all was the brown-haired angel he'd met only moments before. Only now she was a red-eyed devil spitting fire. And as everyone else stood and jeered, and her friend Thelma screamed for her to come away, she was taking on the gang of Teddy Boys all by herself. Facing them down with a stiletto shoe in hand. Sweeping its three-inch, pencil-slim, stiletto heel, back and forth, in front of her.

"Gerroff him!" she screamed.

"Lemmedown! Lemmedown! You fookin' swines!" cried the midget. "You big cowards! You big fookin' cowards!"

"No, Sandra! No!" Thelma screamed.

"Fook off, out of it, yer stupid cows. Can't you see we're only having a bit of fun with him?"

Spike moved in fast and low.

"Gerroff him or I'll kill you, I will."

"Sandra! No!"

All Spike heard were the two girls screaming—all Spike saw was the Teddy Boy in the bowler hat and dirty red bandana. And he rushed forward and hit the Ted with a swinging right to the head. The gang leader staggered, dropped his beer bottle, and fell in a heap. Spike kicked him hard, twice, then spun round and went for the nearest gang member and felled the bloke with a flurry of punches. He gasped for air, re-balanced, and went for a third. The rest of the gang, momentarily stunned, stood and gaped, then attacked him from all sides.

The girls' screams grew even louder.

Spike dodged and ducked and twisted and turned and hit out as fast and as often as he could. A fourth and a fifth Ted went down. He felt a stinging punch to his left kidney, followed by a rain of blows to the back of his head. Then someone kicked the side of his right kneecap with a steel-tipped boot and he went down—hard.

"Gerroff! Gerroff him!"

Spike curled himself up into a ball the moment he hit the ground. Tucked tight to protect his head and his balls. The Teds closed-in fast, stood in a tight circle, and began to boot him into oblivion. All he heard were the jubilant shouts and cries of the gang. All he could feel was the unending fury of boots, brothel-creepers, beetle-crushers, and pointy-toed winkle pickers hitting every part of his body. He gasped for breath as the air was kicked out of him, but his lungs felt as if they'd been punctured by knives and had given up the ghost. He knew he was on the verge of blacking out. Knew for sure he was done for.

The sound of shouting grew suddenly louder and slowly he realised the kicking had stopped. But he stayed curled up on the ground, not daring to move, in case it invited more kicking. When a full count of ten had passed, without further hurt, he peered out from under the arm protecting his head and slowly rolled over. A grey shape whizzed by out of the corner of his eye. He heard a thud, a cry, a groan, but nothing hit him. He counted to ten, again, began to get up, but fell back, the car park spinning around him. When, at last, he came to, he saw a figure standing over him. But he couldn't make out who it was as the lights from 'the Tower' threw a foggy green halo around the person's head and cast the face in shadow. Then the figure laughed.

"You alright down there, sunshine? No don't get up for a minute. Just take your time. You're not Freddie Mills, you know."

Spike blinked, slowly moved his head, tried to move his body, but it was all too much of an effort. So he just lay on the concrete. Tried to come to terms with the massive beating he'd just taken.

Jimmy stayed standing over him as he continued to scan the car park. He glanced down at Spike. "Bloody lucky for you I changed my mind about having a hot dog and wanting a burger, instead. Because if me and my 'effin' brothers hadn't come along when we did, you'd have been a bloody piece of meat, yourself, by now. As it is, I think you'll live. From up here, it doesn't look like there're any bones broken, at least none of yours, that is. Okay to move, are you? Steady now, Spikey, up you come. Here give us yer hand, easy does it."

Jimmy Molloy chuckled as he helped Spike to his feet. "Look at you, you scruffy bugger. Come on. Let's get a stiff drink down your neck. I came running after you. But you'd vanished quicker than a dropped penny into a Scotsman's pocket. Thing being, if me brothers ever see me move fast, they don't ask no questions, they just follow. Dead quick. Which is how Tony, Timmy, and me arrived when we did. Feeling a bit better, now, are you?"

"Yeah. Yeah, I'll live. I'm one bloody big bruise, though. What about them girls?"

"What, that girl Thelma, and the other one? She's a real spit-fire that little one. She was giving one of the Teds a right bashing with the heel of her shoe when I arrived. Relentless, she was. She took a fist in the eye, though, the poor cow. Her friend Thelma took her to the First Aid station."

"She, okay?"

"She'll have a right shiner for a week or two, but she'll be okay. I hope she was worth it. You could've got yourself crippled, you daft sod. You never take on a gang like that, alone, whatever the provocation. You fuck off out of it, if you have to. Or you come get help. There's no shame in it, either way. Why do you think it is we always keep an eye out for one another? Fun? No. There's safety in numbers. So, don't ever be so stupid as to try it alone, again, okay? I might not be there to help you the next time."

"Yeah, I know, Jimmy. Only, it was about to get very nasty, so I had to do something."

"Okay, okay. So what do you want then? Scotch or hot dog?"

"What?"

"You heard, you prat. Slug of whisky or a hot dog?"

"The midget's okay then, is he?"

"Yeah, once we got him down and he found out you weren't

dead, he said to say, 'Ta very much' for what you did. Then he wiped all that food shit off himself, put on a clean white coat and got straight back to business. Plucky little bugger, he is. Anyway, can't you smell the onions and stuff?"

"Yeah, I can now, yeah."

"That's good, because he says you, me, and the girl can have free hot dogs anytime we want."

"Not feeling very hungry at the moment."

"That's alright, I already sent yours up to Sam. Oh, and just in case you're worried about them Teddy Boys. They took to their heels as fast as they could when we arrived. I don't think they'll be back in a hurry, either. At least not the ones being sent off to hospital in a taxi."

Spike tried to laugh, but it hurt. He coughed, instead, but that hurt, too. "I think I could do with that drink, about now," he croaked.

"Yeah, alright. Let's just walk you round a bit first. Get some fresh air into your lungs."

"Funny how everything can change in a single heartbeat, isn't it?" Spike said aloud, slowly moving his head from side to side.

"What you going on about, you daft sod? You're not going Doolally on me, are you?"

"No, no, Jimmy, it's nothing, really. Hey, thanks a million, like, for saving my skin back there. I thought I was a gonner, for sure."

Jimmy Molloy looked at him out of the corner of his eyes. "You know this makes us even, now, don't you? But I tell you what, Spikey, you can still count on Jimmy Molloy as your friend."

Jimmy smiled, satisfied, he'd repaid his debt in full. Then Tony or Timmy Molloy, Spike still couldn't tell which, came up with a steaming mug of something and handed it to Jimmy, who handed it to Spike.

"Thanks, Tone. Here, Spike, sit down inside the entrance foyer and sip this. It's Johnnie Walker, with hot coffee in it, our old dad's favourite tipple. One of us will pop down and see you in a bit, okay?"

Spike just nodded and stared off into space. Tony Molloy pulled Jimmy away and the two of them went back up the stairs to the ballroom, whistling and nodding to the beat that rolled down like a carpet from way up above. And he sat there, at the edge of his own fog, looking out across the car park, with his head thumping and his heart beating, and all he could think about was the girl and the words of the old Buddy Holly song, 'Heart-beat'. He didn't even know the girl. Had never even spoken to her. But his heart seemed to skip a beat even as he tried to picture her face again.

"Wo-aah!" Rory Storm and all The Hurricanes spilled past him, out into the car park, carrying their instruments, ready to dash back through the Mersey Tunnel and go play for Mona Best, at Knotty Ash Village Hall. Just like The Beatles had done. "Fabulous hot d-dogs," warbled Rory. "Hang on, fellas, we c-can t-take 'em with us in the c-car." Rory bounded over to the hot dog stand, blissfully unaware of the vicious fight that'd erupted in the car park not long before, and with arms waving and a cheeky smile plastered on his face he jumped to the front of the queue. "Hey, excuse us, please, everybody. Only we-we have to da-dash back over the other side and play Knot-Knotty Ash. So, Titch, I'll have one of yer lovely hot d-dogs with lashings of fr-fr-fried onions and t-t-tomato sauce, please, if I may?"

"Sorry," shouted the weary little man. "We're right out of tomato sauce and fried onions...will plain mustard do?"

SAM LEACH looked at his wristwatch for the hundredth time. "Fook it, Terry, I'm like a groom standing at the altar worrying that I haven't been jilted. You'd think I was married to rock 'n' roll or something."

"Yeah, well, you should go find yourself a proper girl, then, shouldn't you? Try some horizontal rock 'n' roll for a change. Do yourself some good."

"Alright, Errol Flynn, we don't all wave our swords around like you, you know."

The huge ballroom was packed solid. The Remo Four had pulled out all the stops to try and fill the void left by Rory Storm and The Hurricanes. Then 'Kingsize' Taylor and The Dominoes had rocked the place—Fats Waller style—for forty-five minutes of finger-popping rock 'n' roll. But there was no mistaking the buzz in the air for Gerry and The Pacemakers scheduled to come on at eleven and for the return of The Beatles come midnight.

A dulcet voice echoed around the ballroom and produced an expectant hush. "Ladies and Gentlemen, time now for one of Liverpool's most popular groups, Gerry and The Pacemakers. Starting their set tonight, with one of their very own numbers. 'What is the Number?'"

Freddie Marsden, the drummer, counted them in. Les Chadwick, Les Maguire and Gerry Marsden blasted out the opening chord on piano, bass, and guitar. Freddie double-kicked his bass drum. And Gerry and The Pacemakers were away and rocking. With Gerry delighting the crowd as much with his cheeky wit and cheeky smile, as his brilliant guitar playing and singing. Yet as much a fan as he was of the group, Sam's head was elsewhere. His heart in his mouth, his stomach in knots, all he could think about was the whereabouts of The Beatles. And he never once stopped pacing, back and forth, between the side of the stage and the dressing room all the bands were using. And, as he heard Gerry start to sing the final words to his big finishing number, 'You'll Never Walk Alone', he all but choked. "Well I'm bloody walkin' alone and about to get myself bloody crippled, into the bargain."

He peered into the dressing room for the umpteenth time, but there was still no sign of The Beatles. Not a whisper. Not a sausage. And he began to think the unthinkable. How in hell was he going to explain to the Tower's capacity crowd that The Beatles wouldn't be appearing? He couldn't just say they were stuck in Liverpool. Hadn't everyone braved the fog to get there? He couldn't think of a single soddin' excuse. The situation was worse than dreadful. It was the end. He was done for. They'd string him up as soon as look at him. What the crowd did to his poor bruised and battered body after that didn't bare thinking about. And he sat in the dressing room, his head in his hands.

That was when John Lennon dashed in.

"Wake up, Leachy. We're back and ready to give it all we've got. What a crowd, Sam, it looks even bigger than when we left. And in all this fog, too, it's bloody unbelievable."

For the second time that night Sam looked up at the ceiling and said a silent 'thank you'. Then, as an afterthought, he also asked if there was any way for 'Him' to grant Neil Aspinall sainthood when 'He' next happened to be in Liverpool, moving in mysterious ways, 'His' wonders to perform.

"Hey, are you listening to me, Leachy?"

The audience in the ballroom erupted as Gerry walked his song to its close, the sound of cheering and applause ringing to the rafters.

"Listening to every single wonderful word, John." And as he said it, Paul and George marched into the room carrying their guitars, followed by Pete carrying his snare drum. Sam opened his arms wide in welcome. "Now our Gerry's finished with them, out there, I tell you, there's no place else for them to go, now, but that topper-most of the popper-most you lads were going on about earlier. There's no other band, anywhere, let alone either side of the Mersey, who can take them there, but you Beatles. You lovely magical buggers you."

"Well, we all agree with you about that, Sam," trilled Paul.

"He's not as daft as he looks, is he?" quipped George.

"I wouldn't go that far," muttered John. "But what I will say is...let's go play some more bloody rock 'n' roll."

THE BEATLES blew the roof off 'the Tower' and then took the lead off the roof. The walls and floors dissolved, as did the massive fluted columns, the ceilings and stairways. Nothing else existed for the fans, but the beat and the sound and the rapturous feeling of being connected to every other single person there—everyone all one and the same.

"I tell you, Sam, I'm bloody worried and no mistake," said Tom McCardle. "I've worked for Mecca Ballrooms since I were a kid, like. And I've not seen anything like it in my entire bloody life. You've broken all records tonight. There's over four thousand in here. And they've all gone completely potty. The girls

THE ONE AFTER 9:09 115

are hysterical and the boys aren't that much better. The First Aid room is fair jammed with young girls fainting and I don't know where else to put them."

"I didn't know you had a First Aid room at 'the Tower', Tom, I'd have used it myself, earlier, if I'd known."

"When you said they'd pack the place out, Sam, I didn't want to believe yer, like. But I tell yer, with what I've seen tonight, I think the sky's the bloody limit with them Beatle lads, I do."

"You never said a truer word, Tom, but where do you put them once we top five thousand? This is one of the biggest ballrooms in the north of England, as it is? Where in hell do they go from here?"

When The Beatles ran off stage, a glassy-eyed Sam shook each one of them by the hand. "You're not just the best rock 'n' roll group on all of Merseyside, you know, fellas. For my money, you're the best rock 'n' rollers in all of Britain. You bloody well are, you know. You really are."

"Ta, Sam," said John, genuinely touched. "That was a night we'll always remember. Won't we, fellas?"

"Yeah, Sam," said Paul. "That was one of the all-time best. Really, really great."

George and Pete smiled, nodded their agreement.

"The best so far, lads, the best so far," croaked, a hoarse-voiced Sam. "There's nowhere you can't go. No height you can't reach. Here, here's your money. It was well earned. Thanks, fellas. Thanks."

Sam handed Pete the agreed fee of thirty quid, for two sessions, the most pay The Beatles had received to date, from anyone, anywhere. Then slipped them another 'tenner' on top.

John looked at him in surprise. "Hey, Sam, what're you giving us more for? Forty quid? You soft ha'porth. We said we'd have played for nothing, tonight, and we meant it."

"That's why, John. Look, earlier tonight, when it all looked like it was going down the karzey, you all stood by me. And I'll never forget that."

John smiled and nodded slowly. Then he turned and peered around the room as if seeing 'the Tower' and all of New Brighton, Wallasey, and Birkenhead—as if seeing out across the River

Mersey to all of Liverpool—as if seeing all of England and the whole wide world beyond. He stopped, looked at Sam. Smiled, almost bashfully. Said, very quietly, "We'll have some more of this, Mr Leach, if you please."

Sam, flush with the success, the money already burning a hole in his pocket, grinned. "Right then, me old Beatles. Let's do it two weeks from tonight. Same place, same line-up, same crew. It'll be fantastic. Sensational. Incredible."

"Bloody heck. There you go again, Sam," blurted Paul McCartney. "You're always overdoing things, you are, always trying to top yourself. It's great. And we love it. But give it a month, Sam. Any sooner than that and you'd end up losing all the money you've made tonight."

Sam took a deep breath. "Paul, me old mate, thank you for your concern, and I know you mean it, I do. But I saw what all of you did tonight. Twice. There's a real hunger, out there, for you, who you are, and what you do. I felt it myself. No kidding. Once, you start playing, no one moves, no one can take their eyes off you. The bars and toilets empty out. Even the girls that faint and get carted off immediately run back for more, as soon as they're on their feet again. It's bloody extraordinary. I tell you, even if you played here again tomorrow morning, the crowds would still come and they'd still be huge. You lads are pied pipers and before too long everyone's going to be following you wherever you go."

Paul glanced across the room at John, who gave a curt nod in reply. "Okay then, Sam," said Paul. "We'll be back here two weeks, from tonight."

"'Operation Big Beat. Number Two'," said Sam, his voice hoarse with emotion. "You've got to admit, it's got a really nice sound to it. A definite comeback beat."

CHAPTER TWELVE

Making Plans

Spike's head thumped like a drummer thudding out a four-four beat, which might've been bearable if it wasn't also for the bass-player double-thumbing every note. He rubbed his forehead. It'd been an amazing weekend. But it was a God-awful way to start a Monday.

When Jimmy Molloy had finally dropped him home some-time early Saturday morning, he'd swallowed a couple of aspirin and tried to sleep it off. Some hope. So he'd stayed up in his room all day pretending to be engrossed in a book and then slept most of the time. When he'd missed lunch and even gone without his tea, his mother had simply left sandwiches on a tray outside his bedroom door.

Come evening, he'd filled a bath with hot water, chucked in a handful of Radox bath-salts, and soaked his aching body. Suffer-ing all over again each and every kick he'd been given by the gang of Teds. Afterwards, he'd got dressed, slipped down the stairs, called out, "Won't be late," and was off out the front door before his mother even had a chance to reply. Then he'd gone to Sam Leach's big celebration party at the Iron Door.

He couldn't recall how he'd got home afterwards. All he could remember was lying fully clothed on his bed, again, his head spinning, endlessly, round and around the light-bulb hang-ing from the ceiling. Sunday had disappeared in a foggy haze of staggering to the toilet and throwing up or laying face down on his bed praying for it all to end. And when, at long last, his hangover had finally hung itself out to dry, and he'd fallen into a sleep of sorts, the alarm had gone off and his mother was outside his bedroom door, again, calling for him to get up.

Now here he stood, swaying in the drizzling rain, waiting for the bus into town. Eyes bloodshot. Everything a blur. His head-ache seeming to stretch every single sound like it was chewing gum. He looked down at all the excitement of the weekend dribbling away down the drain at his feet—and yawned. Tried to recall whether he'd remembered to brush his teeth or not. His mouth tasted like the bottom of a parrot's cage—and a long dead parrot, at that. His body was one big mass of purple and yellow bruises and he ached everywhere a body could ache. He'd done what he could, slathered on ointment he'd found in the medicine cabinet, and just hoped to high heaven it didn't stain his clothes too badly or make him smell too bad. As it was, it'd been touch-and-go getting in and out of the bathroom so his mother didn't see the welts and bruises all over his body. She'd have thrown a blue fit, if she'd seen the real state he was in.

He'd had to endure the usual barrage of nagging over the breakfast table. How he never seemed able to stick with anything. First, it'd been boxing. Then football. Then he'd wanted to be a printer, like his dad. Better still, an electrical engineer. Then—"Heaven's above!"—he wanted to be an artist. And after all that nonsense, he'd got this latest silly idea into his head about playing the guitar. "You'll never make a living with that thing, you know," she'd shout at him whenever he disappeared up into his bedroom. That morning though she'd gone on and on and on about him being out late, two nights running, and him being too sick to eat anything all-day Sunday. "The way you're going, Raymond Jones, you're going to end up a real nobody."

He knew the real reason for his mum's nagging was she didn't want him to be late for his appointment with Rex Makin. "Mr Makin's secretary said it wasn't anything to do with dad, Raymond. And he apologised for the short notice, but he'd be very grateful if you'd stop by at eleven o'clock this morning." So, loving son that he was, he'd done his best to look presentable. But his mother had put her foot down at his scruffy black roll-neck sweater and insisted he wear a jacket and a tie. It wasn't often the much-storied solicitor had occasion to contact them anymore, but when it happened his mother responded as if it was a message from God bloody almighty.

It'd been Rex Makin, that the NGA—the printers' trade union—had called on to help his mother collect damages from the

driver and haulage company held to be responsible for his father's death. As he'd later found out, the National Graphical
Association had a fierce reputation for litigation on behalf of its
members. They always hired the toughest solicitors. And as
young as he'd been, he'd realised that without Rex Makin's
skilled guidance and representation to council, he and his mother would've probably ended up out on the street and been left
with nothing more than their memories. The financial settle-
ment had meant his mum had been able to keep their house.
And that, supplemented by her job as a secretary at the Royal
Liver Insurance Company, meant they managed a modest living
of sorts.

For a quiet life, he'd gone back upstairs to change, only to
have his mother follow him and speak to him through the closed
bedroom door. "Now, Raymond, you won't be late, will you?
Remember, it's at eleven o'clock this morning." He hadn't replied, so she'd tried again. "Raymond Jones, are you listening to
me?" More silence. Then, like mothers everywhere, she'd given
in. "*Spike*...are you listening to me?" And he'd yelled back. "Yes,
I heard you the first time, mother."

SPIKE could barely keep his eyes open on the crowded double-
decker bus into town and much to the annoyance of the old lady
sitting next to him, he yawned long and loud and often. "Sod
this," he said, after the woman had clacked her false teeth at him
for the umpteenth time. So he made his way to the upper deck
and found a seat at the back, next to a roll-down window. Then,
with the cold air slapping at his face, he lit up a cigarette and
tried to get his wits into some kind of working order.

"Fook!" He'd missed The Beatles playing Hambleton Hall
that Sunday afternoon. The dance hall was right near where he
lived, too, and he tried never to miss them when they played
there. He took a long drag of his cigarette and blew the smoke
out through his nostrils. Then it hit him. Hard. He was in love.

He shook his head, but the feeling didn't diminish. So it was
real love. Had to be. It certainly wasn't like anything he'd felt
before. Not at all like when he'd gone out with girls at grammar
school and night school. That'd just been him fumbling with bra

straps, rubber corsets, and knicker elastic. Hoping and praying he got his end away before he died. He never had done, though, not properly. At the Art College, when the girls had all suddenly grown into women and one eventful night he'd had sex for the first time, he'd felt relieved and grateful, but not love. Even later, when he'd gone steady with a girl for six months and they'd got engaged, it'd been very pleasant and he'd loved the convenience of it all, but it hadn't felt like love, either. It struck him he'd never had to chase a girl before—not ever. Every other time had started with a girl showing a definite interest in him and he'd just gone along with it. Like some innocent, but very willing bystander guided as much by their knowing lips and soft hands, as by his own blind lust. Looking back, it seemed to him as if he'd just been sleepwalking through their dreams, not ever living his own.

This was different. It felt like a punch to the stomach and made his heart and dick ache like blazes. He loosened his tie, closed his eyes, and tried to conjure up the face of the brown-haired angel. Haunted by the image of the girl standing all alone against a whole gang of Teddy Boys with nothing but her stiletto shoe in her hand. He shivered and rolled up the window. "I'm in love," he whispered. And suddenly he was singing 'Heartbeat' again, accompanied by the relentless thumping inside his head.

It was walking up St. John Street, almost at Rex Makin's office, that he remembered the other incredible event of the weekend. Something he'd found out at Saturday night's big celebratory party at the Iron Door. Sam Leach was going to manage The Beatles.

SAM LEACH hadn't said a single word about it when they'd pinned up the banner on the wall behind the drinks table. 'THE SAM LEACH ORGANISATION. OPERATION BIG BEAT AT THE TOWER!!! RECORD ATTENDANCE 4,124 BIG BEAT FANS AND COUNTING!!!'

"Well done, Spike," was all he'd said, as he stood back and admired his young assistant's handiwork. "Your hand-lettering's a thing of rare beauty, something to behold. And who knows? Four certain people might even read between those lines. See what's really being said." Then Sam had smiled his most enigmatic smile and disappeared back off into his little cubbyhole of an office. Nothing more said.

The party had started up in earnest when The Beatles arrived straight from their performance at the Aintree Institute. And as the bottles had emptied, the jokes had got funnier and funnier and the songs and laughter longer and louder. Until, as with all good things, it all came to a sudden end. That's when Sam, his empty glass in need of one final refill, tapped George Harrison on the shoulder and pointed to the poster on the wall. "That, my Beatle friend, ish because of you." Then Sam twirled round, called to John and Paul and Pete, and raised his glass. "To the shenshashionalBeatlesh... Thish-ish-myparty... Butishtheirparty-toosh." Everyone clapped and cheered. The fellas all waved back, bowed in appreciation. And that's when Sam waved them into a huddle, off to one side. "John, George, Paul, Peeche. Fank you. Fank you very mush for everything," he whispered a little too loudly. "I just wanna shay...I wanna be your man..."

Only he never finished his sentence. He just slid down the wall and crumpled into a heap on the floor, a happy look plastered on his face. John, George, Paul, and Pete all laughed. "There, there, Leachy," John said, patting Sam on the head. "Just sleep it off, yer daft sod." "Thanks for another great party, Sam," Paul added. "Yeah, another towering achievement," said George. Then The Beatles just upped and disappeared off into the night, still laughing. So he and Terry had gone over to lift Sam up off the floor and put him in a chair. Sam had opened his eyes. Said straight out. "I'm gonna' manage them Beatlesh, I am, honesh. And you, Terry, dearesh old friend, and you, Shpike, my newish old friend, you're going come help me do it. And they'll all be rish and famoush. And we'll all just be rish." Then he'd pressed a finger to his lips. "But shoosh, now. Don't tell anyone. Or they'll all wanna be in on the act. Ishabig...shecret." Then Sam had winked, one last time, and passed clean out.

"I BLAME THAT, BILL HALEY. You juvenile delinquents were a nice obedient lot until he started his shake, rattle and roll. Want a coffee? You look like you could do with one."

Rex Makin wielded empathy as skilfully as a surgeon did a scalpel. It not only helped his clients take their minds off their current problems, it often led to them into revealing substantially more truth of the matter than they might otherwise have done. And with some people, there was no faster way into a problem than with a good old Liverpool put-down.

"It was never Bill Haley, Uncle Rex, it was Elvis changed the world. Yes, ta, a coffee would be great. And, er, I'm just getting over a cold, like."

"Elvis? Don't give me Elvis the Pelvis, he was just as bad." He pressed the intercom. "Hello, Marian, ask Mrs Ashby to bring in two coffees, please." He peered at Spike from over his spectacles. "Your mother told me you'd stopped going to classes at the Art College and you haven't done any drawing or picked up a sable brush in months. That's a real pity, you know, because you're very talented. We've still got that painting you gave us, up in the hallway, at home. And to think of all the strings I had to pull to help get you into the Art College. Your mum's worried sick you're going to turn into a right layabout."

"Well, I'm working just as hard at things these days, Uncle Rex. Honest, I am. Only, I'm learning to play the guitar, now."

"Oh, so it's a life on the music halls now, is it? And just how long is that going to last, Django Reinhardt? You said the same thing about wanting to be an artist. Where's all the money going to come from, your student-grant? No don't tell me. I don't want the responsibility."

"But isn't that what solicitors do, Uncle Rex? Help get people out of whatever mess they find themselves in?"

"I merely give advice, Raymond. I merely give advice."

"*To thine own self, be true.*"

"Why do you say that?"

"It's what's on the side of that little coffee mug you gave me that first birthday, after me dad died. You said it was a quote from Shakespeare's *Hamlet*. So, I'm only following the advice you gave me."

"Very funny, Raymond. I'm surprised you haven't suddenly got it into your head to become a Queen's Bench lawyer."

"No, just trying to be true to myself, Uncle Rex, as it can all be over and gone in a flash. Only, nobody ever wants to think about it. Not me mum. Not the teachers at school. I thought the tutors at the Art College would be different, but save for one really good bloke, everyone expected me to fit in to whatever hole they had handy. So when they told me all I'd ever amount to was an art teacher, I left. It wasn't true to what I feel inside. Not by a long chalk."

"Oh, so it's the truth you want now, is it? Well, you may be that proverbial square peg in that round hole, people go on about, but you're not a bad sort, Raymond, even though sometimes you might like to think you are. You come on like an angry young man, but I tell you I deal with real hard cases every day. And you might be a bit lost, but you're no lost cause, at least not yet. You're a bright lad, but a word to the wise. Out there in the big, bad, wide world, not everyone is as understanding as me. You'll find most of them are just too tangled up in their own hopes and dreams to have the time or energy to get involved with the likes of you and yours."

Spike nodded and got to his feet. "Sounds like where I came in, Uncle Rex. Think it's time, perhaps, I was going. Ta for the coffee."

"You're here, now, Raymond, so you might as well listen."

"It's just, Spike, now, Uncle Rex."

"Okay. Keep your hair on. I can't help it your dad's name was also Raymond. I'm sorry. So tell me, er, Spike, if the only thing you've got going on at the moment is you learning to play that guitar of yours, I was wondering if you might have some free time on your hands?"

"Very funny."

"No, I'm serious. When I remembered your mother telling me about you giving up the Art College to go play music, it gave me an idea. In fact, it's why I asked you to come see me. Thing is, I've got a little job I think you can help me with...something that should be right up your street."

"What street's that, Uncle Rex? Lonely Street? Spying on people cheating on their spouses at the Adelphi Hotel?"

"No, as it happens, Spike, I was thinking of that jazz club down Mathew Street, where they play that skiffle music you kids like so much."

"Skiffle's dead and gone, Uncle Rex. It's rock 'n' roll we dig now."

"Well, whatever it is they play, I can't go there and neither can my private investigator. He reeks of ex-copper, even with a clean shirt and a collar on. So what I'm looking for is someone who can go down inside the Cavern and places like it, and blend-in, no questions asked."

"The Cavern, Uncle Rex? How do you know about that?"

"You'd be surprised how much I know about what goes on in this town, Spike. But all I need to know from you, now, is whether you'd go visit some music clubs and venues for me? I'd pay you, of course."

"You're not serious?"

"Never more so, Spike, never more so. A very important client of mine is in dire danger, because someone he once helped put away in prison is about to be released. The man swore revenge. And even though I can have my client watched most of the time, I can't when he disappears down into one of these music cellars and clubs frequented by you young people. So I need someone who can follow him without it being too obvious."

"Sounds like you need *Danger Man* from off the telly, more than you need me, like. Who is it you want me to follow?"

"If you're in, Spike, I'll tell you. If you're not, I can't. Of course, you'd have to follow my man's instructions. But if you agree, I'd pay you five pounds a week while the job lasts. And cover out-of-pocket expenses, as long as they're reasonable."

"Blimey. Course, I'll do it. Who is it you want me to follow?"

"As I said, it's more a question of you going where my man, Harry Lightfoot can't. The person, in question, is a Mr Brian Epstein. His mother and father are neighbours of mine. He is, too. But I also act as their solicitor, so I'd like to keep it quiet and all in the family, so to speak. The Epsteins own NEMS Record and Music Stores."

"NEMS? 'The finest record selections in the North'. Yeah, I know NEMS. It's where everyone goes to listen to records. Great Charlotte Street, usually, as there's this terrific guy who gets American records in. 'Stateside'. 'London American'. The store in Whitechapel is good, too, but I can't say I've ever noticed anyone who acted like he was the owner. What was his name, again?"

"Brian Epstein."

Rex Makin took an eight by ten glossy photograph of Brian Epstein from a file and pushed it across his desk. "That's him."

Spike looked at the photo. "Oh, yeah, I recognise him, now. I think I might've even bumped into him, once or twice. So, let me get this straight, Uncle Rex. You want me keep a look out for this Mr Epstein when he goes down the Cavern, is that it?"

"No, I want you to do more than that, Spike. I want you to help me and my private investigator, Harry Lightfoot, make quite sure that Mr Brian Epstein doesn't go out and get himself murdered."

CHAPTER THIRTEEN

How Do You Do It?

The Beatles were coming to see him. Brian Epstein adjusted his tie for the umpteenth time and tried to stay calm. Over the last four weeks he'd seen 'the boys' perform many times at the Cavern. Had made a point of chatting to them on each and every occasion. Today was to be the first sit-down meeting at his office. He tried to work, but found himself fidgeting with excitement. So he went downstairs, into the store, aimlessly straightened a few things, then stood and looked out at a deserted Whitechapel. There was little foot traffic, but that was quite normal for an overcast Sunday afternoon. He did notice, though, that what passers-by there were stopped to admire the store's window-display, which was all very gratifying and a small thing, perhaps, but his own. He was shopkeeper enough to hope the interest shown would translate into Christmas sales. He consulted his wristwatch, winced, cleared his throat, shot his cuffs, blinked, and adjusted his tie again.

He'd toyed with the idea of wearing an open-necked shirt, silk cravat, and tweed sports-coat. All perfectly acceptable weekend wear. But as this could well be the beginning of a formal relationship with the group, he'd opted for workday business attire. It always paid to make the right impression. He looked at his watch again. They were now very late. He began to colour at the thought they might not come, at all, but as the flat grey December light slowly began to fade and the store darkened around him, he could do nothing but wait—and wait.

"Hey 'oop? Is anyone in there? Mister Epstein, sir? It's us."

The banging on the store's front door awoke him from his reverie and he quickly went to unlock it. There were only three Beatles standing there. He tried not to look too surprised.

"Hello. Thank you for coming. Let's go up to my office, shall we? I see Paul isn't with you. He's not ill or anything, is he?"

"No, he'll be along in a minute, Mr Epstein, sir," replied John Lennon. "He probably just forgot to wind his watch." The other Beatles nodded in agreement.

He nodded, and led the way upstairs, but even after half-an-hour of strained conversation there was still no sign of Paul McCartney. He tried to still his growing frustration and the creeping sense of dread his dream was already stillborn. Almost at his wit's end, he turned to the Beatle sitting nearest the door. "George, I wonder if you'd give Paul a ring...find out why he's so late. I'd hate to think it was something serious. You can use the phone in the outer office." The youngest Beatle raised his eyebrows in mock surprise, nodded, and left the room.

He smiled a thin-lipped smile at John Lennon and Pete Best, then turned and looked out of the window at the darkening Liverpool night. John pulled a face and retreated behind a handy copy of *Mersey Beat*. Pete did the same. And after more moments of pained silence, broken only by the murmuring from the outer office and the rustle of John's newspaper, George came back into the room. He gently closed the door behind him, turned, and said, very calmly, "Paul's just got up from having a nap. And he says he's now going to have a bath."

Brian Epstein was incredulous. "But this...this is disgraceful behaviour. It means he's going to be very, very late arriving."

George nodded. "He'll be very clean, though, won't he?" he said, eyes twinkling, a slow smile twisting into a lopsided toothy grin. John sniggered behind the now shaking pages of *Mersey Beat*. Pete turned away; bit his lip. Brian Epstein blinked and blinked and blinked and suddenly his irritation completely dissolved and he started to laugh, not realising he'd just taken his first real step into the strange new world of Beatles.

When Paul finally arrived, more than an hour later, Brian Epstein was already manager enough to realise a change of scenery was called for and he suggested they all decamp to a local milk bar. Once he'd paid for everyone's coffee and biscuits, there was little time left to beat about the bush. "Look, I don't really know too much about managing a group, such as yours, but with all the contacts I have with the major record companies, in London, I feel certain I can help you and be of real assistance in your future endeavours. And, if you were prepared to go along with me and give me a chance, I feel sure we can do something really special together."

The four Beatles listened intently to what Brian Epstein had to say. They appreciated his candour regarding his experience or, rather, the lack of it. They were already very wary of people who tooted their own horns too much. What really got to them was the magic word 'London'. That's where the real pot of gold was to be found—a recording contract with a major record label. It was, also, the very first time anyone had ever seriously asked about managing them. They'd be the first to admit they needed proper guidance if they were ever to achieve any real success. Still, they didn't want to be rushed into anything, by anybody, however honest and charming they might seem.

When Brian Epstein had finished, John glanced at Paul, George and Pete, then back at their would-be manager. "Well, that's all very nice, Mr Epstein, sir. We've all enjoyed the coffee and bikkies, and we definitely appreciate your interest in us. But you've given us a lot to chew over for one night. Plus, we've got to go play the Casbah Club, over in West Derby, before bedtime. So if it's alright with you, like, we'll just sleep on it."

"Of course, of course. I mean, I wasn't suggesting anything be resolved tonight." He stood up, his hands open, his heart on his sleeve. "Thank you for hearing me out. And in closing, may I say once again how very special I think you all are, as individuals, and as a group."

Paul nodded, smiled, and held out his hand. "Thank you, for your interest, Mr Epstein. We'll definitely think about it."

He grasped the opportunity. "Then perhaps we could all meet later in the week to discuss any further questions you might have?"

Paul glanced at John, who nodded back.

"Yeah, okay then, Mr Epstein. Later this week, it is."

"Would Wednesday afternoon be too soon? Only it's half-day, early closing at the store, and you're booked to play the Cavern that evening, so you could come over before that, couldn't you?"

He knew their schedule. That was flattering. It said a lot.

"We could," George drawled, "once we've all taken a bath, like."

"IT'S BRIAN EPSTEIN of NEMS Music Stores, Liverpool. Mr Tonkin, please. Yes, it is important. No, I don't mind waiting." He tapped his fingers up and down on his notepad. Scanned the list of record reps he'd called that morning. Everyone had been pleased to take his call. Everyone assuming it was merely the prelude to NEMS placing another large order for a consignment of records. However, once he'd steered the conversation away from the retail side of the business, all of his contacts had been of little help. So with this, his last call of the morning, he'd decided to dispense with pleasantries and get right to the point.

"Hello, Mr Tonkin? Brian Epstein of NEMS. Yes, thank you, we've received the advance copies of next month's record releases. Yes, I'm sure there are one or two Top Ten hits in there. Look, Mr Tonkin, I know you're busy, but given your knowledge of the record business I was wondering if I might ask you a few questions? No, there were no mistakes in last month's shipment. My questions? Yes. Firstly, how does one go about producing the music that gets recorded and released by companies such as Decca, EMI, and Pye? Also, how does one go about managing a group of musicians? What does one actually do? And supposing one wanted to become the manager of a pop group, what sort of contract would one need?" He listened for a few minutes, thanked the man for his time, and put the receiver back down in its cradle. He let out a long sigh.

The general opinion was the management side of popular music was full of dubious characters that all believed they'd found the new Tommy Steele or Cliff Richard. Failing that, they'd discovered some never-before-seen act destined to be the next show-biz sensation. Everyone had said he should just stick to selling records. On the other hand, if he did get involved with any singers or variety acts, he should make doubly sure he got a damn good solicitor to draw up a fool-proof contract, heavily weighted in his favour.

He drew a line through the last name on his list and tapped his fingers up and down on his desktop. He turned and stared out the window. It couldn't be that hard. But it seemed no one could or would tell him what to do or how to do it. All of which said he'd just have to follow his instincts and make it up as he went along. He pressed the intercom button. "Beryl, put in a call to Rex Makin, please. And make an appointment for me, for tomorrow, mid-afternoon, preferably. Thank you."

"THEY'RE TREMENDOUSLY GOOD, aren't they, Rita?"

"Yes, Mr Brian. All the girls in the store think they're fab."

"Yes, fabulous is right. Look, please don't think me too forward, but I'm going to the Cavern to see The Beatles this lunchtime. Would you care to join me?"

"You're not serious, Mr Brian?"

"I assure you, I'm very serious, Rita."

"I wouldn't want to be late back to work, Mr Brian."

"That's no problem, Rita. I'll inform Mr Taylor and Mr Brown that I've personally asked you to accompany me. It's okay. It's business."

"I'll go and get my coat, then, Mr Brian."

"Meet you upstairs by the front door in five minutes."

Rita Shaw shook her head in amazement. Mr Brian was usually such a stickler for correctness and now, here he was, acting like someone's slightly dotty elder brother, gushing with enthusiasm over The Beatles. She hurried to the Ladies toilet to check her hair and make-up. When you represented NEMS, everything had to be perfect.

A few minutes later she stood outside NEMS, her breath steaming in the cold air, excited at the prospect of seeing The Beatles play in the middle of her workday. She looked up and down Whitechapel, silently mouthing the words to 'My Bonnie', then turned to see her boss making his way through the store to the front door. She sighed, despite the odd rumours she'd heard about him, he really was a bit of a dish. He looked so very handsome in his dark blue tailored overcoat and silk spotted scarf. She put on her best smile and as Mr Brian exited the store, pulling on his leather gloves, he smiled warmly back at her. Then he glanced across the street and stopped dead.

As Rita Shaw would later tell her friends: "The colour completely drained from his face, like he'd seen a ghost or something, because he just turned and said, 'I'm sorry Rita, there's something I have to attend to, immediately. Please, resume your duties'. And without another word he just dashed across Whitechapel and disappeared."

REX MAKIN stared at the telephone handset, lost in thought. The buzzer sounded on his intercom. He replaced the telephone back in its cradle, glanced at his appointments book, and pressed a button. "Give me a few moments, Marian." He shook his head. "Never rains, but it bloody pours," he muttered to himself, his mind going ten-to-the-dozen. Harry Lightfoot had just called from the phone box at the corner of the street, having followed Brian Epstein all the way to the door of the solicitor's office. It seemed Brian Epstein's blackmailer had turned up on Whitechapel, across from NEMS, and had just stood there staring at the store. Worse, Brian Epstein had not only spotted the man, he'd dashed across the road in search of him. Only, by that time, the blackmailer had already disappeared back down into the tangle of small streets and alleyways.

He composed himself, put on a warm welcoming smile, and opened the door to his office. "Brian, how nice to see you. Do come in. Always a pleasure." He shook hands and gently ushered Brian Epstein into his office. He indicated a chair and then under the pretext of a sudden need to adjust the window blinds, he peered back at his guest with an intensity he usually reserved for criminals in the dock. "Is that all right, not too bright, is it?"

The unfiltered light lit up Brian Epstein's face, but revealed none of the lines of anguish he'd come to recognise over the years as clear evidence his client was in a state of extreme anxiety or despair. Instead, he saw that 'Queenie' Epstein's favourite son was looking positively radiant. "How very odd," he said to himself. "How very odd, indeed."

"The light's no bother, Rex. Thank you."

"Tea?"

"No, thank you. But thank you very much for fitting me into your busy schedule. The thing is, Rex, I have this marvellous idea, but I'm not at all sure how to go about it in a proper fashion."

"Some sympathy, then?" he said, pleasantly.

"I beg your pardon...Oh, yes, tea and sympathy, very droll. No, what I'm looking for, Rex, is some simple advice."

"Well, Brian, I've found, in this business, anything simple usually takes an awful lot of working out. But how can I help you?"

"I'm seriously thinking about managing an absolutely fabulous group of talented young musicians who all hail from Liverpool. And I want you to draw up an unbreakable contract for me."

"I'm not sure I heard you correctly, Brian."

"I'm going to manage them, Rex, these four young men who call themselves The Beatles. They're unique. They're going to be bigger than..."

"Brian. Brian. Brian, hold your horses, a moment. Please."

"I'm sorry, Rex, there I go again, my enthusiasm running away with me, but look, seriously, about this contract, I was thinking..."

His mind was going a mile a minute. Young Brian had just spotted the dreaded blackmailer who'd haunted his every waking moment, as well as his dreams, for the last three years. Yet he hadn't thought it worthy of a mention. All he wanted to talk about were these blessed Beetles, which in itself suggested Harry Lightfoot had been right about Brian's little visits to all those out-of-the-way clubs. The last thing Brian or his family needed was any further involvement with the City's Vice Squad.

"Let me interrupt you again, Brian, if I may. For a start, whatever anyone might have told you in the past, there's no such thing as an unbreakable contract. So please just put that right out of your head. Every contract that's ever been written has got a loophole in it, somewhere, big enough for any lawyer worth his salt to drive a coach and horses through."

"No, no, Rex, I didn't mean that. I don't want you to look at it just from my side. It has to be fair and equitable to both parties. It's for their protection, as well as mine. It's just that..."

"That's all very laudable of you, Brian. If you trust them and they trust you, that's all fine and dandy, but if in the end these Beetles go and welsh on the deal, you've had it, old chum."

He waited for his comments to sink in, then added, "But the real point is, Brian, I won't do it. Even from what little you've told me, it sounds just like all the other madcap schemes you've dreamed up in the past. And believe you, me, I've spent far too much time extricating you from them, as it is. Quite frankly, it's a preposterous idea. What on earth do you know about managing a pop group, anyway?" He shook his head, for once utterly unaware of the true impact of his words. "I don't want the responsibility, Brian. And I most certainly wouldn't want your mother and father thinking that I'd encouraged you in any way. They tell me you're doing great things with the store. Why not just be satisfied with what you've got? There are thousands of people out there that'd give their eye teeth to be in your place, with all your many advantages."

Brian Epstein sat in shock. Rex Makin's response wasn't at all what he'd expected. But he didn't blush or lose his temper. He simply nodded and got to his feet. "If that's your final answer, Rex, I have to say how very disappointed I am. And so I'll simply bid you, a very good day."

Rex Makin got up from his chair, came around from behind his desk, and followed Brian Epstein to the door. He held out his hand again, the look on his face one of genuine concern. "Look, Brian, no hard feelings. Please. I'm sorry, I really am, but there's nothing I can do or will do for you in this matter. I sincerely believe that if I did, I'd only be helping you to make a fool of yourself, all over again. And that I won't do."

Brian Epstein took the solicitor's proffered hand, more out of an ingrained sense of politeness, than past-friendship, but he was in a complete spin over the unexpected turn of events and his thoughts were desperately trying to focus elsewhere.

When his would-be client had gone, Rex Makin told his secretary to hold all calls and went back into his office. He stared out of the window for several minutes, seeing nothing, reviewing everything that'd just been said. "Damn. Damn. Damn."

Perhaps he had been a little too harsh in his response, even a little cruel, but someone had to stand up to young Brian and his madcap schemes, if only for his own sake. Something neither his mother, nor his father had ever seemed able to do in the past.

He shook his head. Even though he now knew what lay behind Brian's latest obsession—in all probability a harmless enough pursuit in itself—the remaining unknowns troubled him. Young Brian was still very much in danger from the blackmailer. The entry of these so-called Beetles into the picture only made the problem that much harder to manage and resolve. He shook his head again. "Damn the bloody Beetles. Damn them all to hell."

CHAPTER FOURTEEN

Queens Drive

Brian Epstein felt empty, lost, and alone, with no clear direction home, and he hated himself all the more for feeling as he did. If his dream could be dashed with a single 'No' what on earth did that say for any future chance of success? He'd walked aimlessly for hours. Gone to the Old Victoria, the Magic Clock, the Basnett, hoping for some small vestige of comfort, anything at all, but nothing and no one could diminish his sense of failure or growing sense of dread. And once the dam burst inside him, years of doubts and fears came flooding back. Mocking his attempts to restart his life anew. Draining him of all the newfound strength and determination he'd acquired since first discovering The Beatles.

He suddenly became aware of cold damp air slapping at him through an open slit of window and with a start realised he was driving at perilously high speed through dark, empty, rain-swept streets. He gazed through the fan of clear windscreen, out into the indifferent night. It appeared he was heading towards Edge Lane, a route he often took for a fast drive home to Childwall. It dawned on him then that it was also the road to West Derby. And in an instant, his deepest fear came rushing at him eager to be fed.

He'd experienced his darkest hour in West Derby. Now, as if by some unearthly magic, he was being propelled towards the same public toilets that'd witnessed his fall from grace. He saw again, his battered bleeding body curled up on filth-covered tiles, drenched in piss and vomit. And he cried aloud, fearing to see the monstrous shape of his tormentor emerging again from out of the pit of his living hell. His addled mind clutched at the very thinnest of straws. West Derby? There was something else about West Derby, something he'd heard recently, something that might yet save him, but what? What? What? He peered into the distance far beyond the moving wash of headlights and fixed upon a pinpoint of light. He pressed down hard on the accelerator and rushed towards it, hoping it would lead to revelation, but the light inexplicably split into two and the ominous black shape hidden behind the twin brilliances grew ever more massive. And for one horror-filled moment it seemed the very darkness itself was speeding to envelop and devour him.

His anguished cry dissolved into the incessant blare of a fast-approaching motor-horn. Time and road ran out. Points of light and waves of darkness merged into one. Blind instinct made him wrench the steering wheel hard left. The Zephyr Zodiac bucked, bounced, veered round, and spun slowly from out of the path of the unstoppable black mass of an oncoming heavy-goods lorry. He fought for control of the car with a strength he didn't know he had. And the Zephyr skidded, tyres shrieking, brakes screeching, through a suddenly crystal clear, eerily beautiful night—then the world and everything in it came to a dead stop.

He sat, a crumpled heap, his head pressed hard against the steering wheel, his body wracked by sobs. He heard an incessant banging that he couldn't immediately identify and only slowly realised he was pounding his fists on the dashboard. He shivered violently, pushed himself upright, wound-down the window, gulped in some cold damp air, and was immediately sick down the side of the car.

He pulled a handkerchief from his coat pocket, wiped his mouth, his brow, and sat and stared, unseeing, into the darkness. After an age, he took a deep breath, turned the key in the ignition, pressed the accelerator, and the engine roared into life. The sound through the open window startled him briefly, then he gave himself over to habit, put the car into gear, glanced in the rear-view mirror, and very cautiously drove off. After a couple of miles he came to a roundabout and his mind still out of gear, he went round and around in slow circles for several minutes. Which road should he take? Which road led to the past? Which road to the future?

The answer came to him like a brilliant ray of sunshine forcing its way through black storm clouds. West Derby was where 'the boys' had said they were performing, that last Sunday, a mere two nights and a thousand lifetimes ago. There it was—the new ready to rewrite the old. He gripped the steering wheel with a newfound determination. It was all too clear now that there was no other way forward. His only way out was with The Beatles and he knew it with a conviction that burned deeper than any past obsession.

Tomorrow he was to meet The Beatles, again, to discuss their future. So however dark his past, the sun would surely shine tomorrow, and shine on thereafter. He continued along the West Derby Road, but instead of going straight on—back into his past—he turned right and drove very carefully all the way down Queens Drive until he came to Childwall Fiveways and home. It was no time for silly accidents.

BRIAN EPSTEIN couldn't ever remember feeling so excited. How he'd managed to get through the morning without fainting clean away, he'd never know. He looked at the calendar and tried to imagine what he'd feel like once his meeting with The Beatles had been successfully concluded—how he'd feel in a year, in three, in ten. Today was the beginning of the rest of his life. A new life he was sure now would be free of darkness and full of hope. Last night had been a cleansing, a purging. He'd always taken pains to keep his duel lives apart—to separate the high from the low, the day from the night. Drawn, as he so often was, to seek out casual, anonymous sex with men he'd never knowingly meet again, he'd done everything humanly possible to separate seeming heterosexual from surreptitious homosexual. And if, on occasion, his need for 'Rough Trade'—as it was sometimes called—had caused him to suffer some small degree of humiliation, even a harsh beating or two, wasn't that punishment and payment enough? Didn't that absolve him of his sins? Balance the books, so to speak?

It took immense effort to accommodate everyone's needs as well as his own. To keep his family and the family business isolated from his private life. He knew it was slowly tearing him apart. That it was time to take control—to act. Time to move from the dark and out into the light. So he'd made his decision.

He'd manage The Beatles and, as their manager, their success would be his way out of Liverpool. And it was as much as he could do not to write the word Beatles in elegant script, over and over again, all over the pages of his desk diary. Instead, he willed himself to concentrate and reached for the order book.

It was half-day closing and so, even after everyone else had gone home, there were the rush of Christmas orders to catch up on. After a couple of hours diligent work he rubbed his eyes, stretched, and decided on some fresh air before The Beatles arrived. He had to be alert, have his wits sharp. So he went downstairs and without bothering to put on an overcoat he stood outside in the cold and scrutinized the store's window displays. In many ways, his turning point, in the family business—even perhaps his life.

It'd been simple enough. He'd had a clear vision of the sort of things people would want in their homes, in the future, and he'd fought hard to convince his father and grandfather that NEMS should offer its customers more up-to-date lines of furniture. His father had dismissed it as being just another madcap scheme, but to everyone's surprise the 'modern' department had proved very profitable. One window display he'd devised featured a dining room set with the chair-backs facing into the street. Four elegantly modern chairs positioned in a natural setting so that everything appeared more relevant, more visually arresting. Again, his father had initially been aghast at the idea, but a year later the orders for the dining room suite were still being filled and, in the end, the entire family had been delighted at his success. To him, it'd simply been a question of putting the right things together, in the right order, and in the right setting. But it wasn't just having a flair for design. The vision had to be right for the times, too, as only then was it powerful enough to withstand all the naysayers and sceptics. He went back inside and stood, for a time, lost in reverie.

"I tell you, the door's bloody well locked."

"That's because it's half-day closing, dafty."

"Well knock on it, then."

"You knock, you're nearest."

"Pete, you do it."

"Me hands are full."

"Well, use yer head, then."

"We could always use Bob as a battering ram, if we had to."

"We already are," growled John Lennon.

He opened the door and smiled a greeting as all four Beatles tried to push through as one. "This is me Dad," John said, pointing over his shoulder to the small dapper figure of Bob Wooler. The absurdity of it perplexed him for a moment. He'd fully expected the Beatles to come by themselves, his simple hope they'd all arrive together and on time. Now here they were with a stranger of sorts in tow and everyone smelling very strongly of beer. It was all suddenly so very awkward. The Cavern's disc jockey smiled at him, apologetically.

He knew very well who Bob Wooler was. And in many ways had every reason to be grateful to the man, as the DJ had been largely responsible for creating local demand for The Beatles' recording of 'My Bonnie'. So once he'd managed to get everybody sat down in his office, upstairs, he took Bob Wooler as his cue.

"Thanks to Mr Wooler's constant featuring of 'My Bonnie' in clubs and dancehalls around Liverpool, NEMS has sold over a hundred copies of your Polydor recording in the last week and a half, alone. Further, to which, I've already met with the London representatives of Deutsche Grammophon, the owners of the Polydor label, to ask them to release your record in the United Kingdom."

It was a good opening verse, but The Beatles were impatient to get to the chorus. That's why they'd brought Bob Wooler along. They liked and respected the DJ, because they knew he liked them and championed their music. He was also an adult, like Brian Epstein, and they wanted his opinion, because as eager as they were for business guidance, they were still very cagey about it all. When they'd all met up in the Grapes, prior to their appointment at NEMS, John Lennon had been his usual blunt self.

"This Epstein fella has no experience with rock 'n' roll other than selling pop records from his shops. From the look of him, he's probably more into Mantovani and his bloody Orchestra or, worse, bloody opera. So, the question is, Bob, as much as we need help, like, is this Epstein ever going to amount to anything? Or do you reckon he's all mouth and no trousers?"

As ever, Bob Wooler played it cautious and said he'd best hold his counsel until later. It was always the wiser course to rehearse your ad-libs before you ever gave voice to them, off the cuff, so to speak.

BRIAN EPSTEIN looked at each Beatle, in turn. "You don't currently have a manager, do you?" They slowly shook their heads. "So, I take it then," he added, cautiously, "that there's no one that negotiates your fees or that deals with your engagements on a regular basis?"

They shook their heads. After a lengthy silence, Bob Wooler made as if to speak, but it was Paul McCartney that spoke up. "As I said, last time, Brian, Pete sorts out our diary of engagements, usually. Helped of course by his mum, Mona. She owns the Casbah Club, like. But other than that, no, we don't have a proper manager. So we generally take whatever we can get."

"Yes, I see," said Brian Epstein.

"We take anything and everything we can get our bloody hands on, okay?" snapped John. "But we get lots of bloody work and we don't have to go bloody begging for it, either, if that's what you think."

"No, no, John, I'm not inferring anything. It's only that whatever you're getting from people, I think you're worth much, much more. And I think that all the promoters around Liverpool know that. That's why you're always in work, but really going nowhere at all."

The silence this time was like a blanket of fog. The truth of Brian Epstein's words hit hard, even though The Beatles had talked of little else for weeks. They were working harder and harder and becoming more and more popular every time they played, but were really just going round and round the same old circles. John, Paul, and George all shared a growing dread that, as big as The Beatles were around Merseyside, there was a very real danger that a proper recording contract, let alone greater fame and fortune, might elude them forever. Liverpool had very quickly and surprisingly turned into a dead end. And for once, drained of all their colourful banter, The Beatles stared back at the man who'd suddenly shone a bright light onto their deepest and darkest fear.

Brian Epstein smiled, almost bashfully. "As I told you, last Sunday, I don't have much experience of these sort of things, but I'd very much like to look after your affairs." He swallowed. "To put it simply, you do need a manager. The question is would you like me to do it?"

The Beatles sat as still as statues and just stared at him. He resisted the temptation to shoot his cuffs and instead re-read the points he'd written down on his notepad. He looked up. "If you did want me to manage you, I'd require fifteen per cent of your gross fees, on a weekly basis. In return, I would assume respon-sibility for arranging all of your bookings, which, let me stress, would be much better organised, far more prestigious, and would take you much further afield than all the venues you play here in Liverpool. I would also make it a point that you would never again play a date for less than £15, except for your Cavern lunchtime sessions, where I will renegotiate your current fee of £5, so that it's doubled to £10. With the number of people you attract to the club regularly, Ray McFall can more than afford it. Further, I will do my best to extricate you from the recording contract you signed with Mr Bert Kaempfert, in Hamburg. After which, I'll use my influence as one of the largest record retailers in the north-west to get you a proper recording contract with a major British recording company." He looked down, aligned his notepad with the edge of the leather-bound blotting pad and carefully and deliberately placed his hands flat on the desk. Summoning up all his theatrical training, he composed his face into one of quiet confidence. "So, would you like me to manage you?" He looked at each Beatle, in turn, again, purposefully ig-noring the ripples and currents in the silence.

John's eyes slid sideways and he wrinkled his nose. Paul and George both coughed so as to conceal the slight nod of their heads. Only Pete Best held Brian Epstein's gaze without regard to how his band-mates felt. This would dramatically change his role in the group and he wondered what his mother would think about it. After all, as she'd so often told him, it was really his group, wasn't it? Pete Best and The Beatles. He was the one the girls always screamed and shouted for. Everyone said so.

Bob Wooler did his best to fade further into the background. After all, he'd often been one of those greedy Liverpool promoters Brian Epstein had just spoken about. It was time to keep a very still tongue.

John's voice suddenly boomed out like a foghorn. "Right, then, Brian, you manage us. Where's the contract? On yer desk, is it? Give it us, here, then, and I'll sign it now."

"I don't have a contract for you to sign, John, because I didn't want you to think I was being presumptuous. However, I promise, I'll have one drawn up by the next time we meet."

"Will it make a difference to what we play, Brian?" Paul asked.

"No, Paul, not at all. I just want to help present you in the very best light possible, ensure you're always paid what you're worth, and given the proper respect that is your due."

This was the sort of stuff they wanted to hear. The Beatles nodded. At least three of them did. And so did Bob Wooler.

Bob Wooler was deep in thought. Even he'd underestimated the manager of NEMS. Brian Epstein's timing had been impeccable. If he'd had the courage or the vision or the money, he might've had a go at managing The Beatles himself. As it was, he had enough on his plate tending to his turntable, his ever-expanding record collection, and arranging for groups to play at the Cavern and elsewhere. One thing he knew for sure, though, this latest development would put a good few Liverpool noses out of joint.

George Harrison scratched his nose, absentmindedly. "I think I better go now, go relax in a bubble bath. I need to ponder what the word 'presumptuous' means when it's at home."

"I WOULDN'T TOUCH THE BEATLES with a fookin' barge pole, Brian." He winced, all but flinched. The Blue Angel wasn't

at all his sort of establishment. It advertised that it catered to ladies and gentlemen of taste, but to his eye the club's so-called
luxurious décor was gaudy and vulgar in the extreme. The club's
owner, a small, bearded Welshman, Allan Williams, handed him
a whisky. "Swollen-headed little shits, that's what they are. I
threatened to get the law on them for breach of contract and
blackball them in all the clubs and nightspots around Liverpool.
But me not being the vindictive type, I did nothing in the end."
He raised his glass. "Mud in your eye."

The man's high-pitched nasally whine was enough to give
anyone a headache. And as the Welshman went on and on and
on criticising The Beatles, spittle bubbled at the corners of his
mouth and it was difficult not to dismiss the vainglorious little
man outright. True, Williams had arranged bookings for The
Beatles around Merseyside, in the past. Williams had also got
them their first work in Hamburg. So if anyone in Liverpool had
any claim on The Beatles, like or not, it was Allan Williams.

Yet the thought of anyone else managing 'the boys' was already totally unacceptable and he gathered his wits, placed his
whisky, untouched, on the club's grand piano cum-cocktail bar
and raised an eyebrow.

"Really, Allan? But you helped the boys so much in the past, I
thought that perhaps you might still have..."

"They stiffed me out of my rightful commission, Brian.
They're an unscrupulous bunch and they only ever look out for
themselves. And to think of all I did for them, too. They
wouldn't have got anywhere, without me."

"Are you saying, Allan, that you no longer wish to be associated with them in any way?"

"Look, Brian, I heard you'd been asking all round town about
them, so let me make myself perfectly clear. I went out of my
way to get The Beatles an audition with Larry Parnes, famous
London pop impresario, and got them a tour of Scotland with
Johnny Gentle, one of his headliners. Then I not only arranged
for them to play in Hamburg, I personally drove the buggers all
the way there, myself. Then when they got themselves thrown
out of Germany, that first time, I spent weeks and weeks writing
letters and dealing with the authorities to get them visas and

proper work permits so they could go back. I even gave them work at my Jacaranda Club when there was nothing else, so they wouldn't starve. And what thanks did I get? A smack in the face with a wet fish, that's what. The moment my back was turned, the sneaky bastards went and contracted themselves to the same Hamburg club I'd been trying to get them into, then welshed on me by flatly refusing to pay me my proper agency fee."

"Yes, well, of course, I can see how that might upset you, Allan. But I really do believe in them and I'd like to manage them and push them as far as I can."

"I'd push the buggers off a cliff, given half the chance. The sods diddled me and I'm telling you, Brian, they'll diddle you. I want nothing more to do with them. Anyone can have them as far as I'm concerned. So if you do go and get yourself mixed up with them, just you make bloody sure you have someone draw up a contract tighter than a duck's arsehole."

Brian Epstein began to cough and choke. "I wonder if I might trouble you for a tonic water, Allan?" he whispered.

"Sure, Brian. Hold on." Williams reached for a soda siphon and splashed some soda water into a glass. "Look, don't get me wrong, they're nice enough lads, in their own way. Well, anyroad, sometimes they are. It's just that when it comes to money they're right bloody tightwads."

Brian Epstein sipped at his water and prayed he wouldn't start coughing again. "Yes, they are tight, Allan. But as I see it, it's that very tightness they have with one another, that makes them so very magnetic as a group. They're complete in themselves and don't seem to need anybody else, at all. The only thing they need is a little guidance and as improbable as it may seem, I've got this extraordinary feeling that with my help The Beatles can amount to something really big."

"Well bloody good luck to you, Brian, is all I can say."

Brian Epstein breathed a sigh of relief. At least, there'd be no competition now from this odious little man. He nodded and smiled. "Thank you, Allan. That's helped clear up the nasty little tickle I had. I think I'll have that whisky, now, if I may?"

SAM LEACH raised his whisky glass and twirled it around and around so it caught the light and twinkled like it was full of stars.

'Operation Big Beat II' had been a monster success. But then he'd left nothing to chance. Not a bloody thing. Not even with The Beatles heading the same line-up of top Liverpool groups.

He'd contacted all the local bus companies and organised special transport. He'd revisited the local constabulary and made another very generous donation to the Police Widows' Fund. He'd made good and sure the Mean Machine was oiled and ready. And just as well as there'd been a minor dust-up with a gang of Teddy Boys, which the Machine had soon sorted out. And despite Paul McCartney's fears that people wouldn't turn up, more than four and half thousand beat fans had converged on the New Brighton Tower from all over Merseyside. Smashing the attendance record he'd set two week's earlier.

All weekend, people had been coming up to him, or telephoning him, to congratulate him. Suddenly, 'the Tower' was the place to play and the place to be seen. 'The rocking city' now had a new and even bigger beating heart and it was all down to him, Sam Leach. And he'd counted his profits and his blessings and, that very morning, had succeeded in booking 'the Tower' for every Friday night in December.

Even more importantly, with all the extra cash now promising to flow in he could make good on one of his most cherished dreams. He could afford to manage The Beatles. All he had to do was get them down to London—then get all the top agents and record companies to sit up and take proper notice.

After which it'd be 'Bob's yer uncle and Nellie's yer aunt'.

The first order of business though was to find a suitable London venue to showcase the group. And with Terry McCann knowing the London scene like the back of his proverbial hand, how difficult could that be?

Sam Leach
Manager of The Beatles
The Leach Organisation
Liverpool & London

He could already see it printed on a business card.

CHAPTER FIFTEEN

Ticket To Ride

"As I'm sure you're very well aware, Peter, presentation is of paramount importance. So I was thinking that perhaps we could place a vase or two of fresh-cut flowers in the window…" He stopped in mid-sentence, his gaze suddenly fixed on the far side of the street.

Peter Brown, his new assistant, stopped taking notes and stared at him, a look of concern on his face. "Is everything all right, Mr Brian?"

"Yes, yes, of course, Peter…look, there's something I must do," he said. "Do, excuse me." He dashed out of the store.

Peter Brown hurried to the window and looked on in astonishment as his boss wove his way through the streams of morning traffic. It put him in mind of the matador in the bull-fighting poster on the wall in his boss's office. Then, as the sound of disgruntled car-horns drifted in from outside, someone with a big black umbrella walked past the store window and Mr Brian was lost from sight.

SPIKE drained his coffee and banged the cup down on the table. Half an hour was long enough to wait for anyone. Mr Harry soddin' Lightfoot had failed to show up for his very own meeting. And after all his blather over the phone about not being late, too. "Typical, bloody grown-up." He zipped up his leather jacket. "Sod this for a game of soldiers," he said and made his way between the crowded tables of the Kardomah Coffee House. He stepped out onto the corner of Whitechapel and Stanley Street, sniffed a runny nose into submission, and pulled his collar up around his ears. Look in on Hessy's? Or make his way to the bus station? Catch a No.75 home, get the back seat, upstairs, have a smoke? He rubbed his face. It felt like it was starting to drizzle. "Bugger," he said. The sound of horns honking and tyres screeching made him look up. Some idiot in a dark suit was hurrying across Whitechapel, weaving in and out of the traffic, looking to get himself killed. "Bloody 'eejit," Spike yelled. He looked again. It looked like that Epstein bloke Rex Makin had talked about. He glanced across the street towards NEMS. It had to be him. "In for a penny, in for a pound," he muttered, and sprinted off in pursuit.

He slowed to walk when he got to Button Street and turned down towards Rainford Gardens. That's when he saw Brian Epstein speaking to some bloke outside the White Star pub. It was pretty clear Epstein was doing most of the talking, but he wasn't close enough to hear what was being said. It was an odd sight, though. Epstein in smart suit and tie and the other bloke, about as rough as you'd find this side of the docks, in donkey jacket, dirty jeans and work boots. The greasy-haired bloke held himself like a real hard man, too, and just stood, there, fists bunched, glaring at Brian Epstein.

He began to walk nonchalantly down the alleyway and a hand came out the shadows, gripped his shoulder, and almost lifted him off his feet. He opened his mouth to yell, but a face appeared with a finger pressed to its lips. Not a sound, not a bloody peep. His body tensed under the steel grip, then his mind caught up with the rest of him and he forced himself to relax. Soon as he did, so did the hold on him. A voice whispered in his ear. "Nip back round to the top of John Street. If you see the bloke in the donkey jacket, let him pass, then follow him, and don't you dare lose him. If he catches a bus at the bus station, you hop on board, too. I won't be far behind. Now go."

He slipped and almost lost his balance as was pushed back into the alleyway. Out of the corner of his eye he saw the bloke in the donkey jacket turn and peer at him. So, as casually as he could, he coughed up some phlegm, spat on the cobblestones, and bent down to tie his non-existent shoelaces. It wasn't much of a performance, but it seemed to satisfy the bloke, who returned to scowling at Brian Epstein. He turned and walked back into Whitechapel, never once looking at the figure of Harry Lightfoot still standing hidden in the shadow of a doorway.

HARRY LIGHTFOOT shook his head. "Bloody fool could've have ballsed everything up," he muttered. Then again, young Jones had caught on pretty quick, so maybe he wasn't a complete loss. A bit older than the photo Rex Makin had shown him, same funny hair though. He leaned forward. They were still at it. Only now the bloke in the donkey jacket was nodding his head up and down like a bloody donkey and whatever it was, Mr Brian bloody Epstein was saying to the blackmailer hadn't got him killed yet.

"Very interesting," he whispered, as he slipped back into the shadows. A moment later Brian Epstein walked past. Even in the drizzling rain and without a raincoat, the manager of NEMS looked as neat as a new pin. What was perhaps more remarkable, the man's face was devoid of fear. No look of desperation, either, only determination. "Doubly interesting," he thought. He felt the tension drain out of him. He'd been ready to intervene at the first sight or sound of real trouble, but in the end nothing had happened. He inched forward and saw the blackmailer turn and walk away. He followed him until he was sure the man turned down into Mathew Street, heading towards John Street. Then he turned and quickly made his way back to Whitechapel and the NEMS store. He peered in through the window, as if admiring the display, and was relieved to see Brian Epstein safe and sound, inside, talking to two very smartly dressed young men. "Good. Now you just stay in the store, like a nice gentleman, and let me get on with doing what Mr Makin is paying me for." He sniffed up the cold in his nose, turned, and strode up Whitechapel, the other pedestrians quickly making way for him.

SPIKE was sat upstairs on the No.75 bus he'd usually take home to Huyton, the only trouble, so was the bloke in the donkey jacket. He lit a cigarette and tried to look inconspicuous by reading a newspaper he'd pulled out of a litterbin. What a turn up? He'd caught sight of the man at the corner of Lord Street and followed him all the way to the bus station, only to end up on the very bus he'd been making for in the first place. He suddenly started coughing like a bloody novice as cigarette smoke went down the wrong hole and he prayed the bloke wouldn't turn around to see what all the fuss was about. He took a deep breath, held it in, and ended up coughing and spluttering all the more. A fine bloody private eye, he made; more like a public dick. He coughed and so did the bloke standing right in front of him.

"Where to?"

It was the bus conductor.

He had no idea how far his quarry was going, so he said the first thing that came into his head. "Er, Page Moss, please." Close enough to home, the stop he'd take for Hambleton Hall, but what if the bloke went on any further? He'd cross that bridge when he came to it. He began coughing again.

"Page Moss? You're sure now? Only it's a long walk back."

"No, I know. I mean, yeah. Ta."

The bus conductor rolled his eyes and held out his hand for the fare, then after checking to see he'd been given the right coins, he adjusted his ticket machine, wound the handle, and printed off a ticket. The conductor went off, down the aisle, collecting fares, and stopped by the bloke in the donkey jacket.

He leaned forward, but couldn't hear what the man asked for, which meant he'd really have to keep his wits about him. He felt the engine shudder into life and the bus set off. It was only as the streets of the city centre began to slip by that he thought of Harry Lightfoot. He was a big enough sod and not exactly someone you'd miss in a crowd, but he hadn't seen him anywhere in the street or noticed him getting on the bus. "Bloody typical," he muttered. "Don't do as I do, just do as I bloody well say." The bus soon made its first stop and he looked down at the people in the queue waiting to get on, hoping he might see Harry Lightfoot, but there was still no sign of him. He took a drag of his cigarette, but even the thought of the money Rex Makin had promised him, gave little comfort. Then for some reason he started thinking of a dark-haired little angel called Sandra and it was hard for him to stop breaking out into a smile.

"MR ALISTAIR AND MR PETER, I wonder if I could see you both in my office, please. Thank you." He touched his tie and went up the stairs to his office, where he hastened to the window to look down into the street, but of the blackmailer there was no sign. He wasn't sure whether that pleased him or not. How very odd? He noticed his dark suit glistened where the drizzle had settled on it. And while he waited, he gently patted his face and hair dry with a crisply folded white handkerchief and then blotted his shoulders and lapels. He had to admit he felt cleansed, which in light of recent events was a rather wonderful sensation. There was a knock on his office door. "Come in," he said. His two personal assistants entered. It was clear from their faces, that neither of them knew what to expect.

It was, Peter Brown, the young man he'd recently hired away from Lewis's department store, who spoke first. "Is everything all right, Brian?"

He allowed both men to be a little less formal when in private and out of earshot of the other staff. "Yes, yes, it is. Thank you, Peter."

"Well thank goodness for that," exclaimed Alistair Taylor. "When Peter came and told me how you'd just broken off in the middle of a sentence, Brian, and then dashed out of the store, we thought it so peculiar we both put on our coats and came out looking for you."

"How very thoughtful of you both, thank you, but there was no need. I had everything under control."

They stood looking at him in respectful silence. Then Peter Brown could contain himself no longer. "What on earth was it, Brian?"

He paused for but a moment. "It's to do with that dreadful occurrence a few years ago. The one I told you both about in the very strictest of confidence. You see, the man who beat me up and who then attempted to blackmail me and threatened to kill me is being released from prison and, of course, I've been terribly concerned and not a little frightened about it. Only, the thing is, you see, that's all changed now, because I decided I should start to take control of my life. So when I saw the man, just standing there, on the other side of Whitechapel, staring at the store, I had no choice, I simply had to rush across the street and confront him."

"You didn't actually go up and speak to him, Brian?"

"I did, Peter. I told him I'd give him money and help him get work in Manchester or Bolton or Nottingham, anywhere, just so long as he agreed to stay away and never bother me or threaten me again. I told him that it really wouldn't do for him to get into trouble again. I suggested that we both be sensible about every-thing and that if he agreed to my proposal, I'd even put something in writing for him, so he could be assured I'd keep my part of the bargain. And he agreed to it."

His two assistants looked at him, speechless. And he could do nothing but smile, a serene look of triumph upon his face.

HARRY LIGHTFOOT hummed quietly to himself as he followed the bus, taking care to ensure there were never more than three or four cars between his little black Morris Minor and the dou-ble-decker. The bus turned up Edge Lane. He did the same, reducing speed as the bus pulled in at a bus stop. "I wonder?" he said aloud. He nodded as he saw the blackmailer jump off and make for an alleyway. "Thought so. The same old flies on the same old shit." He quickly checked his rear-view mirror and prepared to stop. Then just as the bus began to move off, he saw young Spike Jones jump from the rear passenger platform and go up to the nearest shop window and stand, looking at whatev-er was on display. As he drove by, he saw the young man turn and follow in the steps of the blackmailer. "Good lad, you're not a complete loss." He parked, got out, locked the car door, then crossed the road and went into a telephone box. Was met by an old-style coin-box. No matter. He always carried lots of change. And keeping his eyes on the alleyway, he put four pennies in the slot, dialled a number from memory, and waited to press Button 'B' when someone answered.

"Mr Makin, please. Tell him it's Mr Lightfoot and it's urgent."

He hummed to himself as he waited. "Hello, Mr Makin, sir. Yes, just as we expected. The bugger turned up again right across the road from NEMS. And, just as before, Mr Epstein eventually spotted him, because he rushed out the store and ran across the street towards him. So, of course, the bloke turned and scarpered. Only, this time, your Mr Epstein followed him down into the alleyways and marched right up to him and tapped him on the shoulder. I thought there was going to be some real trouble then, but he just started talking, all matter of fact, like. Not shouting or anything. No, Mr Makin, I have no idea what was said, but the blackmailer just stood there scowling for a good five minutes or more, then he just started nodding. After which your Mr Epstein simply turned and walked back down the alley, as calm as can be. What's that? No, as I said, I couldn't hear a thing. A promise of money, I shouldn't wonder. I tell you this, though, judging by the look on his face, your Mr Epstein looked as if he could've taken on a whole army of blackmailers, all by himself, too, and no messing."

There was a noise at the other end of the phone that might've been a cough or a snigger, he couldn't tell, so he just sniffed up the cold in his nose and carried on with his report.

"And as for your young Mister Jones. What with me seeing the blackmailer standing as bold as brass on Whitechapel, I had to forgo our meeting at the Kardomah, so I could keep an eye on things. Bit later, when Jones appears out the blue, on Button Street, I put a flea in his ear, but he caught on quick. No, I had the lad follow the blackmailer and he's in Joker's place, now." This time there was no mistaking the meaning of Rex Makin's response. "I know, it wasn't quite the sort of club you had in mind, Mr Makin, sir. And given what happened, it's probably the worst place in all of Liverpool, he could've ended up in, but there it is, I'll just have to deal with it." He nodded as he listened to Rex Makin. "Yeah, I'll watch myself, and him, too. Right, then, Mr Makin, best be off."

SPIKE shook his head. Of all the clubs in all of Liverpool it would have to be The Joker's. He'd had a bad feeling about it the moment the bloke in the donkey jacket had jumped off the bus. Sam and Terry had taken him there, very late one night, a million years before. The Joker's was the one place you could get a drink out of hours without too many questions being asked. All the local crooks went there, a lot of local businessmen, too, even the non-crooked ones. At some point Sam had whispered in his ear about the club also being a favoured haunt of the city's CID and pointed out a number of plainclothes police officers noisily enjoying themselves, but he couldn't tell whether Sam had been pulling his leg or not.

Sam had told him the club took its name from its owner, a huge black man who must've weighed well over twenty stone. With his shaved head, mustard coloured eyes, and skin so black it looked purple in the club's lights, the man was a massively intimidating figure. And although everyone knew him only as Joker, the only time the club owner was ever known to smile was when a fight broke out. Then with a slow nod of his head, the big metal front door would be locked shut until sufficient blood had been spilled on the floor and people needed to be carried out and dumped in the alley outside.

Rumour said Joker had used a red-hot carving knife on the club's previous owner, until the man had agreed to sign over the club's legal deed and title. Then he'd cut the bloke's fingers off so he couldn't go back on the deal. True or not, it set the tone of the place, as did the roaring fire in the club's main room. Regardless of the weather outside, Joker always sat close to the flames, in a huge leather armchair, the undisputed lord and master of all he surveyed.

The place gave Spike the soddin' creeps.

CHAPTER SIXTEEN

The Joker

Spike stood in front of the big black metal door, pressed the bell push, and waited for the cover of the spyhole to slide back.

"What da' fook you wan' man?"

"Want a drink, is all."

"Who fookin' said?"

"Er, Sam, Sam Leach said I could, like."

Spike looked dead ahead, a blank look on his face, wiped the cold from his nose with the back of his hand, and waited.

"You one dem fookin' musicians, man?"

"Yeah, play the guitar, like."

The peephole slid shut. Spike heard a bolt being drawn back.

"Okay. In."

"Ta."

He pushed aside a heavy velvet curtain and entered the dark interior of the club. Stood for a moment to let his eyes get accustomed to the dim light, then made his way to the bar. No one looked at him. Although by the time he'd ordered a pint of Bass and taken a sip, he was pretty sure he'd been checked-out by everyone inside the club. All he had to do now was keep his head down and not attract any more attention. After a few minutes staring at the bottles on the shelves, he turned round slowly, nonchalantly, one elbow on the bar, and looked over the rim of his beer glass. The man in the donkey jacket was over by the fire, talking to Joker, the big boss surrounded by his motley crew of hangers-on. The flickering shadows playing across the sea of dark faces reminded Spike of a painting by Goya, but he quickly blinked the image away.

'Donkey jacket' was doing all the talking. Spike couldn't hear what was being said, but knew it wouldn't be wise to try getting any closer to the fire. He turned to face the bar and quietly sipped his drink. Heard a glass crash to the floor, but didn't look round. It was none of his business. It made him realise, though, Harry Lightfoot or no, he'd already had enough of the place. He drained his glass and just as suddenly had to pee. He nodded to the barman, pointed in the direction of the toilets, made his way through to the back of the club, and overheard Joker talking. It didn't sound like he was telling a joke.

"You go away, now, man. You know I don't make no habit of frowin' good money after bad. Isn'dat right, boys?"

"Dat's right, boss," hissed Joker's gang of hoods.

"You know my business. I lend you. You give back. Today, you give me double. If not, den next week you give me three times what you owe me. After 'dat, who knows, I may not be so understandin' and I cut your balls off. Isn'dat right, boys?"

"Dat's right, boss," chorused the chorus.

Spike didn't look to see how hard donkey jacket man was taking it. Just kept his head down, made straight for the toilets.

When he got back to his spot at the bar, the barman had already refilled his beer glass. He nodded, felt around in his pocket, and pulled out half-a-crown. He looked at it, forlornly, he hadn't been given any change the first time and it was all he had left. Not wanting trouble, he pushed the coin across the bar, nodded his thanks, and took a sip of beer. He turned and bumped into donkey jacket man, knocking his elbow, spilling his drink. Fook. "Er, sorry, there, la'," he muttered.

The man spun round. "What's your fookin' problem?"

Spike kept his head down. "Sorry. Didn't see you, like."

"Too fookin' right, you long-haired fooker."

The man peered at him. Sneered. Spike just hoped the bloke didn't remember him from earlier. "Sorry," he said, again, slowly turning away and reaching for his drink.

"Don't you turn away from me, fook-face."

The bloke was taller and heavier than Spike, so he knew he must look like easy game. Plus, the bastard would still be smarting from the tongue-lashing he'd just got from Joker and would be looking for something or someone to punch. He fit the bill exactly. The bloke prodded him, hard. "Oi, I'm talkin' to you, you pansy-arsed queer."

Spike didn't reply, just moved further along the bar. And as the man stepped forward to prod him again, he turned, head down, chin tucked in, in a classic boxer's stance, and threw a punch that hit the man smack on the nose. Completely taken off-guard, the man stumbled back and all but fell on the floor, only managing to keep upright by grabbing hold of the bar. "You fooker," he yelled, blood streaming from his nose. The man righted himself, snatched up a beer bottle and smashed it against the bar. Then, rolling his shoulders, he stepped towards Spike, waving the jagged edge in front of him. "I'm going to cut your fookin' balls off...stuff 'em down yer fookin' gob."

Joker's boys closed in on the action like a pack of hungry wolves. But Joker gave a grunt and one-by-one they fell back into line, save for one, who moved to lock the big front door. The rest of the club fell silent. The only noise, the scraping of tables and chairs as people moved to get a better view. The only movement, the flickering flames of the fire and the odd-shaped shadows dancing on the walls.

A thunderous hammering on the big metal front door shattered the silence. "Open up! Police!" a voice shouted. The doorbell began ringing non-stop. And as pandemonium broke out in the club, the man in the donkey jacket lunged at Spike with the broken bottle.

HARRY LIGHTFOOT kept banging on the front door with a brick. The moment the bolt was drawn back, he shoved hard, slammed the door back and pushed through the velvet curtain. Everyone still inside the club froze. "Alright, Gunga Din, back off. It's not you I'm after," he growled as someone stepped in his path. He headed straight for the bar—a 'don't-even-think-of-fucking-with-me' look on his face. "Alright, calm down everyone. Nobody's going to get hurt, unless they're seriously looking to get their head smashed in. Just a few questions, is all. And as long as nobody's under age or smoking weed in my face, you can all go home in a little bit." With that the club lapsed into a sullen silence, pregnant with violence. He ignored it, slowly looked around, and then made his way over to where Joker was sitting.

"Just looking for someone, Joker," he said, without edge or rancour, "but I can see he's not here. Sorry, if it costs you business."

"Not as sorry as he'll be, Harry, whoever he is."

"Yeah, just like the Mounties, I always get my man."

"And me my pound of flesh." The big black man chuckled, his eyes narrowing to slits. "Been long time. Drink?"

"No, thanks, Joker. I don't drink as much as I used to. Only, I've got to watch my health, like."

"Yes. We all got do dat, Harry. You stay healthy, now, man."

"That, I will, Joker. That, I will."

HARRY LIGHTFOOT glanced over at Spike Jones sitting all hunched up in the passenger seat of his little Morris Minor. One of the boy's eyes was badly bruised and swollen. There was also a nasty gash along the collar of the lad's leather jacket, as if someone had swiped at him with a broken bottle. "Bet I know who did that, an' all," he muttered. It meant he'd arrived only just in time and he was angry with himself for having put the boy at risk. He noticed Spike was starting to shiver, the adrenaline having run its course. He turned the ignition key. "Here, young 'un, what say we go and get ourselves a good nosh, somewhere? Plate of egg and chips would go down a treat, about now. Let's try Joe's Cafe, in Duke Street. Nick, the owner's a friend. He'll look after us." He flicked a switch. And as the little orange indicator arm slid out the side of the door pillar, he checked his rear and side mirrors and slipped out into the traffic. Humming tunelessly, he drove back into the city centre a good deal faster than was normal for him.

When they got to the cafe, he took Spike through to the kitchen, gabbed a clean dishtowel, soaked it in warm water, and used it clean the blood off the boy's face. Then he took another towel and emptied half a tray of ice cubes into it. "Here, hold this on your eye," he said softly. Then with a grim smile and nod to Nick, hovering nearby, he steered Spike to an empty corner table, sat him down, and returned a few moments later with two steaming mugs of hot sweet tea.

"How you feeling, now?"

"Better, thanks," Spike said. "Reckon I'll live."

"That, you will," said Harry Lightfoot. "Here, drink this."

"Just very thankful you came along when you did, Mr Lightfoot. It was about to get a bit nasty. That's all people seem to be doing these days; stepping in, to save me from getting a serious hiding. Thanks."

"No thanks, necessary, young Spike. I'm only sorry it happened. It was my fault you were there and you shouldn't have been."

"No, I said I'd help. I can't blame you for me slipping and banging my face on a barstool. It's me that should've been more careful."

He stared at the young man. "No," he thought, "this one's not a complete waste of time like so many kids nowadays. Got some spunk to him." So maybe Rex Makin was right, there was more to young Spike Jones than met the eye. "I've ordered the mixed grill for both of us," he said, "the liver and bacon will do you good. More tea?"

Spike nodded. "If you don't mind me asking, Mr Lightfoot, how did you know it was me, back there, in the alley?"

"Easy enough, I looked in on the Kardomah earlier. Scanned the faces. Reckoned you was you, from an old photo Mr Makin showed me." He paused. "As for what happened at The Joker's, even though I saw you had blood on you, I had to pretend not to notice. I couldn't just barge in and go straight for the ruddy blackmailer, either. It had to look like I was there on other business or the bugger would've twigged. The bastard slipped out the secret door at the back while I was talking to Joker."

"But wasn't that the whole idea, to follow him?" Spike asked.

"Yeah, but not for him to know we were doing it. He'll pop up again, though. His sort always does."

"What about Joker? His whole gang looked ready to rumble."

"They don't want any trouble with the police. They just want to be left alone to do their business. Sell women. Deal drugs."

"But wouldn't they have known, like, that you're an ex-copper?"

"Joker does, but he's a cool customer, that one. Always bides his time and waits until the tide turns to his advantage. He doesn't lose face, then. And he would've, you see, if it ever got round his club got turned over by a mere civilian. Anyway, me and him go way back to when we were raggedy-arsed nippers, on Parliament Street." He leaned forward, peered at the damage. "That cut over your eye looks a lot worse than it is," he said. "You'll have a bit of a shiner for a few days, but no real damage."

Spike gingerly touched the area around his eye and winced.

So did Harry Lightfoot. "No, don't touch it, just keep them ice cubes on it. And put some more ice on when you get home, okay?"

"You know the Joker, then?" Spike asked.

"Joker? Yeah, from way back. Liverpool born and bred, he is, despite what people might think. Like that fire, he always sits next to. It's supposed to remind him of the climate back in Africa. Although I know for a fact the bugger's never once set foot there. He's a dangerous sod, but he's always known who to pay off and who to cut in. You'd be surprised at who he's got in his pocket. But as long as his boys don't slice up too many of the wrong people, by which I mean white people, the City constabulary mostly turns a blind eye to his drugs, gambling, and strings of prostitutes." Spike looked askance. Harry Lightfoot chuckled. "Ciggy?" he said, pushing a nearly full pack of Player's Navy Cut across the table. "Here, you have them," he said. He struck a match and lit both cigarettes. Then he settled back in his chair and blew out two long streams of smoke. "Tell me, Spike," he asked, "are those Beatle fellas, Mr Epstein's so interested in, are they any good, like? Only it sounds like jungle music to me. I like big bands myself. Not Ted Heath or that oily Joe Loss. More, Count Basie and Duke Ellington, proper music, like. Have you heard any of them?"

Spike nodded. "Heard the names, like, Mr Lightfoot, but I can't say..."

"Call me, Harry. Okay? Just, plain old Harry."

"Yeah, okay, Harry. Er, me dad liked Frank Sinatra."

"Lovely voice, that one. Especially when he was with Tommy Dorsey. But his newer, Nelson Riddle stuff, isn't too bad."

Spike was on solid ground, now, and perhaps for the first time since meeting the ex-copper. "But as for The Beatles, Harry? Yeah, they're dead good," he said. "I mean, there's hundreds of bands round Liverpool, but there's just something about The Beatles that makes them different. Lots of people say so. There's this guy I work for, now and then, name of Sam Leach. Used to run the Casanova Club, now puts on big shows at 'the Tower' over in New Brighton. He just can't stop raving about them. Says they're the best things since Elvis. And, now, as you say, this Mr Epstein is interested in them, too, and he owns NEMS record stores. So all that must say something about them."

Harry Lightfoot nodded. "Was only wondering, like. I will say this, though, they certainly had a lot of energy the time I saw them. One of them had quite a nice voice, too, very melodic, he was when he sang a ballad."

"You must mean Paul McCartney," Spike said, chuckling. "Yeah, he's got a great voice, but he can also really belt out a song if he has to."

"Want another cuppa?" Harry Lightfoot asked.

"Er, no thanks, Harry, I'm full to bursting, as is."

"Well, I'll just have one more of them cigarettes, if I may?"

Spike held out the packet of Player's. "They're yours."

"Nay, lad, I gave them to you, I just want the one." He took a cigarette, lit it, and as the match flared looked closely at Spike, pleased the lad already seemed to be on the mend. "You probably had to pay for a beer or two, back at Joker's. And at them prices, too." He produced his wallet, slid a ten-shilling note across the table. "That should cover it. Call it your first expenses." He took a swig of tea. "Another question for you?" Spike nodded. "You still up for all this, Spike? Because if you're not, like, I'd understand perfectly you wanting to drop it."

"No, I'm okay with it, Mr Lightfoot, I mean, Harry."

"Okay. In which case, there's something I need tell you. There'd have been no reason to, if all this Joker malarkey hadn't happened, but as it has, like, you might end up hearing a few things about me one day that might cause you to wonder. So I best tell you myself."

Spike nodded, lit a cigarette, eyes glued on Harry Lightfoot's sombre face.

"To begin at the beginning, then. Back when I was a Detective Inspector, my somewhat overdeveloped sense of duty made me a fly in certain people's ointment. In that I put at risk certain long-standing financial arrangements that existed between various parties in the Liverpool underworld and a number of, my then, brother officers. My continued refusal to accept bribes caused a few of my former colleagues to feel nervous enough to question my loyalties, as well as my motives. Then one bright sunny morning I was found, passed-out, dead-drunk, in charge of a motorcar reportedly belonging to a certain infamous Liverpool 'Madam'. An incident made all the more damaging, because the car ended up demolishing a good part of a posh ladies' dress shop in Elliot Street. I was suspended from duty and the whole incident might've been ended there were it not for a number of brown-paper envelopes, full of hard cash, allegedly also found in my possession. None of which, I could satisfactorily account for. A departmental investigation later amassed a busload of uncorroborated reports from various Underworld informants that I'd made a long habit of extorting money from clubs and brothels and such. I protested my innocence. It was bloody obvious to me, of course, I'd been framed, but nobody listened or cared. The powers-that-be then decided that, given my otherwise exemplary record, it'd be better for the Force if I took early retirement. That way, everything could be swept back under the carpet and everything return to normal. To make a long story short, my once promising career was cut horribly short and I ended up a private investigator for the odd firm of solicitors."

He signalled to the waitress for the bill, but Nick, the owner, came over to the table and shook his head. "That's alright, Harry. This is on the house. Your young friend, okay, now, is he?"

"Yeah, thanks, Nick. Walked into a lamp post, is all."

"Yeah, well, there's a lot of them around Liverpool," said Nick, "but the shifty buggers will keep up and moving about."

Harry Lightfoot turned his mouth up into a smile. "But as to our dinners, thanks, Nick, but we're here on business, tonight. So I'll pay, if it's all the same to you?"

He slipped a pound note from his wallet.

"Yeah, sure, Harry. You want a receipt, then?"

"Please. And thanks for the loan of the towels."

"Think nothing of it. Did the same for me once, remember?"

"Yeah, well, thanks, anyway, Nick."

"You go safe, now, Harry, and the young lad, too. Okay?"

Harry Lightfoot nodded and turned back to Spike "I think we've done enough looking after Mr Brian Epstein, for one day. So, I'll drop you off home, if you'd like. Over Huyton way, isn't it? I'll just go for a pee. Then we'll be off. Okay?"

Spike nodded, smiled a weary smile. He stared at the ten-bob note in his hand. He was up five shillings. "This'll only end up going back to NEMS," he muttered to himself. Then he pocketed the money and began dabbing at his bruised and blackened eye with the icy wet dishtowel.

BRIAN EPSTEIN smiled. "It's going to be alright, now, Joe, I know it is. You needn't worry about me, anymore. I've taken care of things."

"Well I hope so, Brian. For your sake."

"I simply thought of it as a business proposition and it became so much easier." He paused, sipped his gin and tonic. "The thing is, Joe, if he's paid his debt to society, then he's also paid his debt to me. So the money I offered him is simply to help him get back on his feet."

Joe Flannery put both hands flat on the Basnett Bar's marble countertop, as if for added support. "But Brian, he'll only come back asking for more when the money's gone. That's what always happens. Blackmailers never let go or give up."

"Well, he gave me his word that he would. So I'll just make the one payment, just the one time, then it's over and finished with."

"But why on earth would you trust him, Brian, after what he did to you?"

"For the simple reason, he's got more to lose, now, than I have. If convicted again, he goes back to prison for a very, very long time."

"But he threatened to kill you, Brian."

He turned to his friend, his eyes distant. "That time before, I...I almost wished I was dead, I was going nowhere, I was lost, but it's different now, Joe, I have a destiny to fulfil."

Joe Flannery stared at his friend, Brian Epstein, very much alive in his brave new world, and he sighed, inwardly. He admired Brian. He loved Brian. Now was not the time to argue his case. So he smiled and raised his glass. "I know it's been a terrible burden for you, these last few months, Brian. So let's both raise a glass to the future, because as foolish as I think it was for you to do it, I'm immensely proud of you for facing up to that dreadful man. It's as if there's a whole new you, standing there. And I couldn't be more delighted for you, old friend. Cheers, Brian."

"Thank you, Joe, you dear, dear friend, you."

Joe Flannery had spoken the truth. He *was* like a new man. Nothing must ever be allowed to come between him and his beloved Beatles. And nothing now would stop him from making them a huge success. In fact, he'd already convinced an A&R man from Decca Records, in London, to come see The Beatles play at the Cavern, the very next week. And what a wonderful surprise that'd be for 'the boys'—his wonderfully talented, beautiful boys.

"Could anything be more important than this?" he said, his eyes seeming to sparkle in the mirror on the other side of the Basnett Bar.

CHAPTER SEVENTEEN

Teddy Boys

Brian Epstein parked the Zephyr Zodiac, got out, looked around to get his bearings, but failed to notice the little black Morris Minor that'd just pulled into the kerb some distance behind him. He turned his coat-collar up against the chill sea air, walked across the empty car park and around the base of 'the Tower'. He tried to imagine the tower that'd once stood atop the four-story, Victorian-style, redbrick building. Saw it very much in the style of the tower at Blackpool. Prosaic. Dull. Uninspired. Having none of the open, curved elegance of the base of the Eiffel Tower. Even so, 'the Tower' had apparently been hugely popular in its early days. And again during the big band craze in the Thirties and Forties. Or so he'd read that morning. The big question now was whether 'the Tower', being so distant from the city centre and so long absent from people's hearts, could really be a regular attraction for the beat-crazed youth of Liverpool.

Posters advertising that Friday night's 'Big Beat Session' had been on display at NEMS for the past week and tickets had sold so rapidly it'd greatly peaked his interest. When he'd asked Rita, in the record department, about 'the Tower' she'd simply raved about it. "It's really huge, Mr Brian, and dead posh. Not grotty, like some places I could mention. It's got a real ballroom, with a stage and a proper dance floor, and there's dance competitions and everything. Thousands of people will be going, I'm sure."

Which was why, early that evening, he'd driven over to New Brighton so he could witness events for himself. He'd watched from a distance as The Beatles arrived in their battered old van and made a mental note to improve their mode of transport. A second group had driven up in what appeared to be a butcher's delivery van and he'd chuckled at that. This wasn't the Philharmonic Hall that was for sure. Soon after, another band arrived in a splendid old motorcar well past its prime, the incongruity of it only adding to the growing magic of the affair. He drifted on. Saw whole fleets of buses and coaches arrive. Saw the first trickle of beat fans steadily grow into a torrent. Listened with increasing delight to all the banter about The Beatles and the other groups—the air abuzz with excitement and expectation. And for an hour or so, buoyed by what he'd seen and heard, and oblivious to the cold or the quizzical looks, he'd sailed on a ferry of dreams, back and forth across a never-ending river of fans, feeling as happy and as free as ever he'd done in all his life.

Sam Leach's 'Big Beat Session' was the first event he'd witnessed that even came close to matching the scale of his own vision for The Beatles. A long line of fans queuing up outside the Cavern was all very well and good, but the club itself was far too small, too limiting—like so much in Liverpool. This was different. This was popular music on a grand scale. And he nodded a silent salute to Sam Leach. If The Beatles could attract such huge crowds to 'the Tower'—and he was in no doubt it was The Beatles everyone had come to see—they could do so in the rest of the country and the entire world, too.

Lost in dreams, he returned to the Zodiac and was about to turn the ignition key, when there was a sudden eruption of noise outside the motorcar. And in a split second he was thrust into a dark and different world. A gang of youths in leather jackets and tight trousers dashed between the lines of parked cars, hooting and hollering, all of them converging on 'the Tower' as if intent on storming the very ramparts. One of the yobbos stopped, leered at him through the windscreen, banged the bonnet of the car with his fist and shouted, "Fook you, you wanker." The youth's badly pockmarked face, framed by lank, greasy hair and a dirty red bandana tied crudely around his neck.

The unexpectedness of the violence shook him to his very core and he began to shiver uncontrollably. And with eyes squeezed tight shut he slid further down into the driver's seat and curled into a ball. Afraid now, not just for himself, but for his 'boys'—his beloved Beatles—trapped in 'the Tower'. He was helpless and could do nothing at all to protect them. And he hated himself for being so weak. He was worse than pathetic. He'd failed The Beatles before they'd even set out together on the long and winding road to success. And he cried out in torment as the dark shadow he thought had been vanquished forever, rose from out of the pit and slouched menacingly towards him.

A motorcar horn sounded, again and again and again, echoing around the car park. A cacophony of urgent notes meant to attract someone's attention, though he had no idea whose or why. But the barrage of sound was enough to stop his nightmare in its tracks. And he blinked and blinked and the dark shadow that'd threatened to engulf him only moments before faded away to nothing and was gone. He wiped his brow with the back of his hand, swallowed, straightened his tie, and stared at 'the Tower' through the motorcar's windscreen. "Take care of my boys for me, Mr Leach," he said quietly. "Without them I'd be forever in misery." He turned the ignition key. The Zephyr's engine roared into life. And he drove back through the Mersey Tunnel to Childwall. Again, failing to notice he was followed all the way home by a little black Morris Minor motorcar.

SAM LEACH was good and mad as he hurried down the long staircase. His first 'Big Beat Session' at 'the Tower' had hardly started and there was already big trouble. A gang of Teddy Boys had set upon two young fans down in the car park and kicked them unconscious. Good job he'd decided to have some of the Mean Machine always on patrol outside 'the Tower', otherwise the poor sods would've been dead, not simply out for the count. The gang had scattered at the first sight of the bouncers, apparently. But not before one of the younger Molloy brothers had brought down the gang's leader with a flying tackle worthy of Billy Two Rivers, the wrestler on TV. The Teddy Boy was now being held, all trussed up, until 'the boss' arrived.

Spike quickly pulled him aside when he finally reached the car park. "We were dead lucky, Sam. This car-horn going off nonstop alerted us. Otherwise we might not have stopped them in time." He pointed out the dirty red bandana tied around the gang leader's neck "It's the bastard that did the midget at 'Operation Big Beat'. Let me have him, Sam. I'll murder him, I will."

"Back off, Spike. This needs handling the Liverpool way.

Anyway, you don't need another black eye." He'd have dearly loved to beat the pimply-faced Teddy Boy into a pulp, too, but he restrained himself, even if only just. He knew full well if he didn't deal with the gang problem, once and for all, future attendance at 'the Tower' would greatly suffer. And that'd hit him where it really hurt—in his pocket.

He nodded to the bouncers holding the Teddy Boy. "Let him go. I want a word." Sam—a dangerous, almost sleepy look on his face—leaned forward. "Listen, gobshite, you and your gang of coffee-bar cowboys think you're so fookin' hard. What was it this time, twenty or thirty of you kicking the daylights out of two youngsters? You cowardly bastards have been terrorising dances round here for as long as I can remember. Yet, you run away at the first sign of any real trouble. You're no better than a bunch of schoolgirls. I bet you're all queer, anyway. You and your pansy-arsed girlfriends should come back, sometime, face some real men. Next week, if you like, if you're not all busy putting curlers in your hair. So, just, fook off! Before I forget myself and let these boys here have you for fookin' breakfast."

He nodded to Jimmy Molloy, who stepped in and slapped the Teddy Boy, hard and fast, on both cheeks. "You heard what nice Mr Leach said, miss. Fuck-the-fuckety-fuck-off. Now."

The Ted rubbed his face and stared blankly at Jimmy, Sam, and Spike, tried to sneer, thought better of it, and slunk off into the night.

"Reckon he'll be back, Sam?" asked Jimmy Molloy.

"I'm counting on it, Jimmy. After what I just said to him, he'll be back next time with all his mates. Together with as many other fook-wets as he can round up...the whole lot of them baying for revenge." He looked at the ring of faces. "Thanks, guys. Hot dogs, all round, and an extra quid in each of your pockets. Kenny, Jimmy, a word in your cauliflower ears."

SAM LEACH couldn't take his eyes off the tastiest bit of crumpet he'd seen in weeks. Her sexy way with The Twist had nailed him to the floor, made his throat dry. "Lovely little mover, isn't she?"

"Yeah," said Spike, mesmerised. "She's really smashing."

"The one dancing with her is not too bad, either. You could do worse, you know. They're sisters, apparently."

"No, they're not, Sam, they're just good friends. I've met them."

"Like heck, you have. I saw them first and I have it on very good authority that those two lovely little blondes are sisters."

"No, not the girls in black, Sam. I'm talking about those two brunettes dancing next to them. I fancy the little one in the pink dress."

"Just as well then, sunshine," Sam growled. "That could've very easily been the beginning of the end of a once beautiful friendship."

Terry McCann stuck his head between his two love-struck friends and whispered loudly, "Their names are Joan and Vera, Sam. And I've just had a premonition they're going to win to-night's 'Miss Twist Contest' hands down. What do you think?"

"That's called cheating, that is," laughed Spike.

"No, it's not," croaked Sam. "It's called, true love. And any-way, just you always remember, all's fair in lust and war. Which reminds me, Spike. Shouldn't you be outside with the two younger Molloys, about now?" The look on his face said he wasn't joking.

"Just going, Sam. And honest, it's the one in the pink I fancy."

SPIKE JONES wolfed down his hot dog, wiped his mouth, and then threw the greasy paper into an open oil drum. It was cold and damp outside and half an hour was quite long enough to be standing out in the car park. He pushed his way through the big glass doors, vaulted over the turnstiles, and pounded up the stairs to the main bar. Looking flushed, his blood circulating properly again, he walked through to the far end of the bar, nodding his head in time to the beat thudding through the walls. He signalled to one of the other bouncers to let him know he was free to return to the ballroom. Then he stood, his back against the bar, and looked out at the sea of sweaty, thirsty faces.

"Who do you think you are? Ronald Shiner?" He turned

round and saw a vision in a pink dress. "Hello. Your name's Spike, isn't it? I'm Sandra. We met once. Only I wanted to say, thank you, in person."

The thought of being likened to an out-dated comedy actor and a titchy one, at that, suddenly seemed to be the most wonderful thing anyone had ever said to him. The brown-haired, brown-eyed angel had appeared, right out of the blue, and spoken words of love. And while his tongue was busy tying itself in knots, his heart beat so loudly in his ears it completely drowned out the thud of bass and drums rolling down from the ballroom.

The girl looked up into his face and he felt 'the Tower' shake on its foundations. He stopped breathing. He could feel her eyes combing through his hair, examining his face, gently touching his still badly bruised eye. Then the vision giggled and turned away for a moment and dug into her handbag. He swallowed, unsure of what to expect. Then a clean white handkerchief with a little pink letter 'S' embroidered on it appeared in her hand. She touched it to her mouth, moistened it with her tongue, then leaned forward and wiped away the little red smear of tomato sauce on his cheek. "I thought, for one awful moment, you'd been fighting, again," she said.

Her dark eyes sparkled, mischievously, as she stepped back to examine her handiwork and he felt his knees turn to Mersey mud. He struggled to say her name, "Sa...Sa...Sandra. Yes, I remember, I..."

"I met you here with my friend, Thelma. That night you..." Her hand went up to her own eye. "I had a bit of a shiner myself, for days and days, afterwards. My dad was furious, but it's gone now...mostly."

'Sandra'. The word filled his mind with fluffy pink clouds. He swallowed, desperate for his tongue to start working properly. "Yeah, I looked for you afterwards, like. You were terrific...very brave."

"Terrifically foolish, more like."

"I...I just saw you and your friend Thelma, dancing. "

She bit her lip. "You did? Well, we didn't win or anything, but it was a real lark, doing The Twist."

"You...you were t'rrific."

"Yes, you said that." She said, softly, her eyelashes fluttering.

"I mean it. Can I...er...buy you a drink later, perhaps? Or a cup of coffee, somewhere, sometime, only I'm meant to be..."

"Yeah, that'd be really nice. Only I'm just waiting for Thelma to come back from the Ladies, like. And when I saw you, I thought well...you know. I just wanted to say, hello."

"Yeah, good, er, great, um..."

"I wrote my number at work down on a piece of paper. I work at Lewis's in the city and I could meet you one lunchtime, if you like?"

"Yeah, yeah, that'd be great."

"Just ask for Sandra Dudley. That's me."

He took the piece of paper and studied it like it was a new guitar chord. "Sandra Dudley," he said, looking up. "I'm Spike Jones."

Yes," Sandra said, looking into his eyes. "I know."

SAM LEACH approached the following week's 'Big Beat Session' as if it was a military campaign. He hired sixty additional bouncers and issued each temporary member of the Mean Machine with a steward's badge. He paid yet another visit to the local constabulary, explained his problem, what he planned to do about it, and made another donation to the Police Widows' Fund. He also suggested that, perhaps, the police Z-car could turn left instead of right on its way to make its regular, late evening check up at 'the Tower'. And the 'boys in blue', knowing the true cost of policing, were only too pleased to oblige.

Sam had thirty of his new faces loiter in small groups in the car park, laughing and smoking, as if waiting for mates or girlfriends, or simply queuing for burgers and hotdogs. Always one to know when a good idea was worth stealing, he'd arranged for one of the outside crew to signal 'the off' with three longs beeps of a car horn. Then he'd placed the rest of the Mean Machine up the stairs, out of sight. Then everyone waited.

He'd seen enough war films to know the power of ambush. But the real reason he'd made a point of telling everybody to allow all the Teds to go through the turnstiles without confronting them, however many turned up, was that he wanted to get their admission money in the till before he had them flung them out on their ears. As he explained it, "The sods have to pay to get in, just like everyone else. It's costing me a bloody fortune to lay on all the extra muscle, so it's only right the cost of it comes out of their hides."

Spike even offered to go stand by the ticket counter until the gang arrived, so when they caught sight of him, he could act scared and run for the stairs. "It'll be like showing a rabbit to a pack of slavering dogs, Sam."

Sam agreed. "Worked once, should again. So I'll stand next to you, look prosperous, and we'll wave two red rags at the sods."

The gangs of Teddy Boys came early for their revenge and stood around in small groups, laughing and shouting, oblivious to everyone else. Their numbers swelled until there were at least a hundred of them. Then, moving as one, they suddenly turned and surged through the front doors into the vestibule. The gang leader pushed his way to the front, rattled a turnstile and rapped a handful of coins on the ticket counter. "Shop!" he cried and the rest of his gang took up the cry, the noise ricocheting around the entrance foyer. And suddenly the gang leader was through, flexing his muscles, and he stood, legs apart, waiting imperiously for his drape-jacketed minions to surround him. The King Ted, his pockmarked face, impossibly white in the glare of the overhead lights, happened to look up as he retied his newly-washed red bandana around his neck. He spotted Spike, shook his fist, and yelled. "Oi, you, fook-face. You're fookin' mine, you are." Spike looked startled and turned away and that was when the Ted caught sight of Sam, resplendent in bowtie and tuxedo. "And you," the Teddy Boy shouted, as he produced a flick-knife from out of nowhere and pointed it at Sam. "You're fookin' dead, as well, you are...you big-mouthed fooker."

Sam and Spike exchanged worried glances, worthy of Laurel and Hardy, turned on their heels and fled up the stairs. And the whole mob of Teddy Boys chased after them, brandishing empty coke bottles, knives, bicycle chains and wooden chair-legs, all of them howling at the top of their lungs, each and every one of them intent on doing some very serious damage.

Meanwhile, the two decoys pounded up the stairs, Sam moving surprisingly quickly for a dedicated smoker. But the Teds started gaining on them. "Bloody hell," panted Sam as he fumbled for a police whistle he had on a lanyard around his neck. He tried blowing it, but nothing happened. "I'm out of puff, you blow the bloody thing." He thrust the whistle at Spike, who grabbed it and give it a good blow. The sound of the whistle pierced the air. And as the two friends dashed around the final bend of the staircase, Kenny Butcher, Jimmy Molloy, and the rest of the Mean Machine, streamed past them like water churning in a millrace.

"Excuse us, gentlemen," Kenny grunted, as he sped past. "We have some rather urgent business to attend to, downstairs."

"Too right," snarled Jimmy Molloy. "My kind of business."

Sam skidded to a stop and grabbed hold of Spike's arm. "Are you coming back down, then? Only, you'll be able to tell your grandchildren you saw this." Then he laughed. "Honest to God, now I think of it, I'm sure that pimply-faced Ted was wearing blue suede shoes."

"Well he's going to get them trodden on, good and hard, isn't he?" yelled Spike, laughing, as the two of them raced back down the stairs.

SPIKE JONES banged his empty beer glass down on the bar. An after-hours drinking session was just one of the many great perks of working for Sam Leach. "I needed that, Sam. Bashing heads is thirsty business. That was, hands down, the best punch up I've ever been in. The bastards never saw it coming. Never knew what hit them."

"All down to military planning and, of course, the Mean Machine being the best and biggest team of bouncers anywhere this side of London. I got the idea from a piece I saw, in the *Sunday Pictorial,* about Field Marshal Montgomery's tank battle, at El Alamein. He trapped old Erwin Rommel's Afrika Korps between a big pair of pincers and cut their bloody balls clean off."

"Well those Teds certainly got given the full Monty...and no mistake. Though I have to say. Sam, it was the furniture van you had on hand to take all the wounded to hospital that was truly inspired."

"True. That was my idea. But that's me, isn't it? Always thinking of the punters' needs. Another drink? How's your love life, these days?"

"I'm in love, Sam."

"Really?"

"Yes. I just saw her standing there. And bang…I was in love."

"Exact same, happened to me, sunshine," Sam grinned. Then, just as suddenly, the grin faded. "Here, her name wouldn't be Joan, by any chance?" he said very quietly.

"No, no, no. She's called Sandra. I can't stop bloody well thinking about her. It's driving me crazy, it is."

"Sandra? Yeah, nice name that. Not as nice as, Joan, mind you, but nice." Satisfied, Sam let loose another grin. "Well, lucky you, but it's about time, isn't it? I was getting worried there for a minute. I mean, when you've reached my level of sophistication and discernment you can afford to be choosy. At your tender age, though, you should be out there every night, with the rest of them, howling and sniffing at anything that moves."

"But you always said you believed in quality over quantity, Sam."

"You got cloth ears as well as a puffy eye? What I said was, always go for quality *and* quantity. What the heck do think I'm doing with all these 'Big Beat Sessions'? I'm not just giving the fans one great band, for their money, I'm giving them six, as well as throwing in a dance contest, with real prize money, every week. You can never have too much of a good thing, Spike. Not when it comes to giving value for money. Or even love for that matter. That's why I'm going to manage The Beatles. No other band in Liverpool gives out as much as they do. They could play every night for a year and they'd still have the fans coming back, begging for more. That's why we're all off to London, tomorrow morning. The Beatles are already too big for Liverpool. So I'm going to help them conquer the nation's capital, then the rest of Great Britain. Who knows, after that, maybe the world? Yeah, I'll help them take over the whole bloody world and why not?"

"Well if anyone can get them there, Sam, you can."

"Yeah. And not only can I get them there, sunshine, I'll bloody well do it with style, too. Real Liverpool style." Sam punched the air.

"Er, I heard there's this other bloke got the exact same idea."

Sam stopped dead, while his heart beat boldly on into the future. "Yeah? Really? And just who might that be, when he's at home?"

"Bloke called Brian Epstein, Sam. Owns NEMS Music Stores. Only, I know someone who knows him, like, and he heard."

"I thought you might mean him. Terry heard the same thing." Sam sniffed and wiped his sweaty forehead on the back of his sleeve. "Do you think he's serious? Only, I met him once and he's a right snotty git, if you ask me. I can't really see him doing any real rockin'."

"Apparently, he goes round all the clubs and halls to see The Beatles, any and every chance he can get, like."

"Well, I tell you one place you won't be seeing the bugger and that's Aldershot, down in London, where The Beatles will be tomorrow night. I've arranged a big 'Battle of the Bands...Liverpool versus London'. Only, I've got a very funny feeling about who's going to win. And guess who's going to be standing right there, holding the crown over their little Beatle heads when they do? And when the lads see what I can do for them in London, the war will be over and done with before the battle has even begun. Then it's good night and good riddance to Mr soddin' bloody Epstein."

"He'll never know what hit him," Spike grinned, suddenly very taken by the idea.

"Yeah," nodded Sam. "Never let the bugger see you coming. Just knock him right out of the ring before he even steps foot into it."

"Only fair, Sam, considering all you've done for The Beatles."

Sam Leach nodded, a faraway look in his eyes. "Everything's fair, Spike, when you're in a knockdown fight for something or someone you really, really love."

CHAPTER EIGHTEEN

Misery

Sam Leach rammed a last piece of toast into his mouth. "And as well as inviting a whole bus-load of London agents to come see you lads play tonight, I've arranged to see the famous impresario, Tito Burns."

The Beatles, sat warming themselves in the tiny kitchen of Sam's mother's house and still bleary-eyed because of the ungodly hour, all slowly nodded and raised their steaming mugs of tea in silent salute.

He thought it best not to mention he'd already had his meeting with Burns. Or that he'd been thrown out on his ear. "London's got quite enough guitar groups, thank you, Mr Leach. Please don't call back."

But as he'd reasoned to himself countless times since the failed meeting, it could all be put to rights once The Beatles had had a chance to knock the stuffing out of the music scene down south. Aldershot was but the opening shot of the battle.

Not wanting to trust such precious cargo to Neil Aspinall's clapped-out Commer van, he'd hired a posh new van with proper seats for The Beatles, and a car and driver for himself. "No offence to Nelly, lads, but there's a lot riding on this. Anyroad, the poor sod could do with a lie in, given all the late hours he's had ferrying you lot around."

"He'll only get into mischief, Sam. The devil always makes work for idle hands. You should know that, if anyone should."

"Alright, Reverend Lennon, that's quite enough from you. You lot just get in the van and take your seats."

John's eyes widened. "Oooh, look lads, new seats. Where should we take them to, Sam? Or can we just rip 'em up, like?"

"Leave off. I paid extra cash money to have them installed, so you'd all be comfy on the journey, south." He turned to Spike. "Got all the stuff me mum made up for these ungrateful swines?"

"Yeah, Sam," said Spike. "All the sandwiches and the…"

"Hey, Spike," interrupted Paul, "shouldn't that be, 'Aye, aye, Sam'?"

"Oh, yeah. Eye, eye, is right," Spike said, pointing to his black eye. "Still a bit of a shiner, isn't it?"

"Ah, the mark of the Liverpool kiss," whispered John.

Spike laughed. "You should see the other bloke. Anyroad, there's loads of sarnies, lashings of tea, and tons of biscuits."

"Oooh…bikkies," crooned John. "Luvverly bikkies."

"Never any expense spared in getting you lot to the top of your poppermost," said Sam, smoothly. "And with Terry driving, you're in safe hands. His driving licence is as valid down south as it is up here."

"Do they drive on the same side of the road down there, then?" asked Paul, in mock astonishment.

"Yeah," said Pete. "They've got road signs in English, too."

"There's posh." John turned to Terry McCann sitting patiently in the driver's seat. "Can you read signs in English, Terry?"

"I must be off my bleedin' rocker agreeing to drive you gang of Teddy Boys all the way down to London."

"Bon voyage, lads," shouted Sam, banging the side of the van with the flat his hand. "I'll be following behind in the other car."

"Do we have to cross the sea to get to London?" asked George.

"No, there's only the frontier once we get the other side of Birmingham," said John, helpfully. "After that, who bloody knows?"

Three or so hours later, Terry McCann pulled into a petrol station on the outskirts of Birmingham and while he refuelled the van, Spike and Pete got out to stretch their legs and go for a pee. John yawned long and loudly and rubbed his eyes. "I'll be bloody glad when I've had enough of this," he said. Paul yawned. "Me, too, and we're not even half way there. But, I've been thinking, John. We haven't really signed anything official with Brian Epstein, yet, have we? So what do you think, then? Sam Leach could be good for us, couldn't he? At least, he knows the business."

John looked out of the van window and saw Sam's car pull into the garage forecourt. "Yeah, he does that, Pauly. He's a good 'un, too. He's been good to us, lots of times, so I know he'd never fiddle us, like. So, no, it wouldn't hurt to give him a chance, but let's not promise anything, yet. Not until we see how things go down in London."

"In Aldershot, you mean," said George, yawning. "Al-der-shot. Wherever the hell, that is. Because the real question, my fellow Beatles, is whether or not Sam's the one who's going to get us to where we're going."

"Got a good point, there, young George," said Paul.

"As per, bloody usual," laughed John. "Let's go have a piss."

SAM LEACH told his driver, Dave, to stop outside the lone newsagents shop and he got out to buy a copy of *The Aldershot News*. He couldn't but notice that Aldershot looked completely dead, even though there were a good two hours yet before the shops closed. The van carrying the four very stiff and weary Beatles and a peacefully sleeping Spike pulled into the kerb. He marched right up to it, newspaper in hand, and rapped on the passenger-side window.

John wound down the window. "We was wondering, like, do they have real live people down here in London, Sam, or have they heard we're coming and decided to go into hiding?"

Sam smiled. "Don't you worry your little head, John, they're probably all at home getting ready for tonight's 'Battle of the Bands'. Anyway, cop a load of that, I know it from memory." He thrust the newspaper through the window and stood back, arms spread wide, his voice like that of a sports announcer on the telly. "'Liverpool versus London. 'Liverpool's Number One Rock Outfit' direct from their German Tour'. How about that for some rockin' publicity, then?"

John rifled through the newspaper then thrust it out the window. "What bloody publicity, Leachy? There's sod all about us, in this."

Sam picked up the paper from off the pavement and hurriedly began leafing through it, oblivious to the loud groans coming from inside the van. Terry McCann, seeing the growing look of despair on Sam's face, hopped out. "There's fookin' nothin' in it, Terry," Sam shouted, his voice hoarse. "There's nothing, no full-page advertisement, no half-page advertisement, not even a classified ad. There's sweet fook-all."

"Nothing? But I saw you hand them the cheque."

"I even remembered to sign it, too. Where's that soddin' newspaper office? News? I'll give 'em news. I'll have their guts for garters."

They drove around the town. "There it is!" Terry shouted. "See the sign? *Aldershot News and Military Gazette*."

"Miserable gits, more like it," Sam yelled back. "Right, I'll soon sort this out." He stormed into the newspaper's tiny reception room followed by The Beatles, Terry, and Spike. He slapped the Saturday paper down on the counter and rapped angrily on the frosted-glass window.

After a little while a dark shape appeared and the window was drawn back. "And we'll have less of that, if you please. You could break it, doing that, you know." The snotty voice belonged to a frosty-faced, middle-aged woman in pointy-rimmed glasses, her hair up in a tight bun. She narrowed her eyes at the sight of the wild-eyed Sam Leach and simply looked askance at the gang of uncouth Teddy Boys surrounding him. She quickly began to slide the window shut.

"Here, hold on, missus," Sam shouted, blocking the window with the offending newspaper. "What happened to my advertisement?"

"I don't know," she said. "I'm not a mind reader, you know."

"Well, all the beat fans in Aldershot are gonna' have to be. You took my bloody money. So where's the advert I paid for?"

"You don't need to talk to me like that, you know."

"I know. I just need the practice. So what about my ad?" Sam waved an arm behind him. "These boys are the best rock 'n' roll band in Britain. Thanks to you lot no one knows they're here."

The receptionist looked over her glasses at the grim-faced Teddy Boys messing up her very tidy reception area. She glared at Sam. "I'll take a look, but we're not in the habit of making mistakes, you know."

The woman returned with a brown cardboard file. "It shows here, you paid by cheque and it's our policy with new customers not to run any advertisements until the cheque has cleared. So your advert will go in next week's newspaper. Good day." She slid the glass window shut with a bang.

"Careful," shouted John Lennon. "You could break it, doing that, you know." He pushed past Sam and tapped politely on the window.

The receptionist pulled back the glass and stared in surprise at the Teddy Boy standing there, smiling sweetly. She narrowed her eyes again. "Yes?" she said. "What do you want now?"

"Excuse me, Miss Bun," said John, politely, "but we can't come back next week, like. We're already booked to play Knotty Ash Hall."

"Then good riddance to the lot of you," she snapped, slamming the glass partition shut and noisily locking it from the other side.

"Sod off to you, 'an all," said George, making for the door.

Outside, Sam thought quick and hard. When in doubt do something, anything. "I tell you what lads, never say die, we'll drive round the town, pin up posters on every hoarding or telegraph pole we see. That done, we'll drop off your instruments and equipment at the Palais Ballroom, then I'll take everyone for a quick bite to eat at the little cafe opposite. How's that sound?"

For once, The Beatles were stone cold silent.

After grabbing something to eat, they all split up and scoured the town for prospective punters. Handing out handbills to everyone they met. They visited every pub and coffee bar and dropped word about the fabulous group playing that night, at the Palais. But the good people of Aldershot weren't interested, even when, in utter desperation, Sam played his final card and told any and everyone that'd listen that admission was free.

"Aldershot's not ready for rock 'n' roll or The Beatles," Sam said, dejectedly, lighting up another cigarette.

"Aldershot's so crap, they're not even ready for inside bloody toilets," snapped John. "But as we're already bloody here, let's all just sod off down to Soho, in London, and get ourselves royally pissed."

"Hey, come on, John," pleaded Paul. "We've got to give it a try, even if we only play for five minutes. Eh, oop, kid, what do you say?"

"No, they can all go and get buggered...the dozy sods."

Paul put his head on one side and started to sing 'There's no business like show business'. He smiled inanely and waved his hands in the air as if they were tambourines. "Hey, come on, John." He kicked a foot out like a Kentucky minstrel and started prancing up the street. "Hey, Johnny, you know the show's always gotta go on."

"Ah, sod it," snapped John. "Where the fook are we going to, fellas?"

"To the top, Johnny," they all chorused back.

"And which fookin' top is that, fellas?"

"To the top of the fookin' poppermost, Johnny," they all yelled.

"Okay, fellow Beatles, we fookin' well play. The show goes on."

Everyone cheered then, even Dave, Sam's driver.

SAM LEACH opened the doors of the Palais Ballroom at half-past seven on the dot, as advertised, but the only thing he was met with was a face-full of swirling snowflakes. He closed the door quickly. "God's holy trousers, whatever did I do in my past life to deserve this?" He shook his head. "No business, like no business? Sod that, let's have a ball, anyway." He sauntered into the ballroom. "They'll all be along in a minute, lads, so why don't you get started. Just think of it being like your early days in Hamburg. You know, those times you told me about, when it was the sound of your music alone that had to grab the punters by the scruff of the neck and drag 'em in, off the street. What was it called, now? The Punjabi?"

"No!" The Beatles all shouted back. "The fookin' Indra."

"That's what I meant," said Sam. "Do some fookin' Indra. If anything will bring the buggers in, it'll be a bit of that."

"Yeah," sniffed George. "*Mach* some more bloody *schau*."

"*Mach schau! Mach schau!*" yelled John into the microphone.

"Okay," shouted Paul, vamping a run of notes on his bass. "Pete, count us in." Pete hit his sticks together. *Tik-a-Tik-a-Tik-a-Tik-a.* Paul hit a single bass note and launched straight into 'Long Tall Sally'. That done, fully energised by the music, The Beatles shot themselves full of rhythm-and-blues and ripped it up and rocked it up for three finger-blistering, pick-scraping hours. They pounded out the beat as if they were playing 'the Tower' in front of four thousand screaming fans, not the eighteen or so people dancing and jiving at the Palais Ballroom. And Sam, Terry, Spike, and the van driver, Dave, could do nothing but lose themselves in the magic of it all. Swinging and swaying, clapping their hands, popping their fingers, and tapping their feet to the relentless rockin' Mersey beat.

And then with John's final scream that all he ever wanted from life was 'Money', The Beatles rolled up the night with one last long chiming chord. Everyone clapped and cheered, jumped up and down, and shouted for more. And all four Beatles up on the stage, their hearts thumping in their chests, sweat pouring from them, looked out from under the spell they'd just cast and saw that as tiny as the crowd was, the cry for more was as urgent and as heartfelt as any audience they'd ever played to.

John sighed and nodded at Paul. Paul nodded at George. Paul, his voice hoarse, whispered, "Roll Over Beethoven." John, George and Pete each nodded back. George picked out the opening notes of the Chuck Berry rocker, each note as sharp and bright as the glass in the mirror ball hanging from the ceiling. The girls spun. The boys jived. And The Beatles rocked it, two by two, for ten glorious minutes and everyone dug to the rhythm-and-blues until 'Liverpool's Number One Rock Outfit' brought their first rocking visit to the south to a close.

Roll over Aldershot and go tell London the news.

Sam stood at the foot of the stage, beaming. "That, fellas, was bloody marvellous. You did yourselves and all of Liverpool proud. So, what say, we celebrate? I've asked the local judies if they'd like to stay on for a bit and, believe it or not, they all said yes. I wonder why? So I had our Spike go and get in two crates of Watneys Brown Ale and a box of Smith's crisps from the pub over the road. So, if you're up for it, like, I'll go crank up the record player, put on a swinging platter or two, and we can all have ourselves a proper party."

John didn't bother looking at Paul or George. He already had his eye fixed on something blonde standing in the middle of the dance floor. "Oooh, yes, please, Mr Sam, I could do with a bit o' hanky-panky about now. I need to exercise me evil ways."

They all took turns dancing with the girls, everyone doing their version of The Twist. John, impatient for his next turn at dancing waltzed with George, then Paul. Pete sat that one out. They played 'Bingo' using beer bottle-tops as counters. Played football with Ping-Pong balls. The rest of the time they just played the fool. John, his back hunched, his face distorted, staggering around the ballroom yelling, "The bells. The bells. It's the bells."

Sam handed Spike a camera. "Here, Spike, take some more photographs. I want to remember this. They're certifiable, the lot of them."

"Yeah," said Spike, "certifiably brilliant."

There was a sudden loud hammering on the front door.

"Come on in, if you're coming," shouted Paul.

"Bugger off!" yelled John.

Terry went to investigate and quickly reappeared, his arms waving from side to side, in a frenzied hand-jive. He snatched the needle arm from off the turntable, spun round, and mouthed the word, "Police."

The effect was instantaneous. John began giggling and was soon doubled up with laughter. Paul sniggered. George grinned. Pete bit his lip. Sam, madly signalling for quiet, bounced his hands up and down in front of him as if trying to push the sound to the floor, but it did no good, the giggling and laughter just grew louder, as did the knocking.

Sam sighed, burped, belched; went to deal with 'the bizzies'.

"What the bloody hell do you think you're doing?" yelled an authoritative voice. "Do you know what bloody time, it is?"

Sam peered out into the gloom. In the pale yellow light of the street lamps were four police vans, two police motorbikes, a mounted policeman, and a very big, sour-faced police sergeant.

"Er...um...we were just finishing, like, constable."

"And about bloody time, too. It's gone bloody midnight. And you lot are creating a very serious disturbance of the peace."

Sam blinked and blinked and tried desperately to sober up. "Er...we...er...were just going, officer."

"Now, wouldn't be soon enough," barked the police sergeant. "You bloody shower have got fifteen minutes to get out of Aldershot, do you hear me? On yer bikes, the lot of you, and don't you ever come back."

"You and Aldershot can fook off, too," George muttered under his breath. "Never would be far too soon for us ever to come back here."

BRIAN EPSTEIN buried his head in his hands. Had they already left him for another? The very thought of it was too much to bear. They'd told him in that off-handed manner he'd quickly come to realise was their way of dealing with potentially embarrassing issues, that Sam Leach had arranged for them to go down to London, to play in a place called Aldershot. Aldershot? That wasn't London. That was a dreary suburban wasteland, some thirty-five miles southwest of the city, known only for its dreadful Army camp. He shivered at the thought. What sort of fool would think of taking The Beatles there? Sam Leach had and the man was no fool, as was attested by his many successes around Merseyside. Even if his ideas were a little grandiose for someone so uneducated, they obviously worked and were very profitable. He might even learn a thing or two from this Mr Leach. Just as long, as the man hadn't already stolen The Beatles away from him.

What was Sam Leach's game? Was he really angling to become their manager? He sighed. For in his heart of hearts, he knew the local promoter with the tousled hair and rude manners was the only person capable of taking 'the boys' away from him.

He sighed again and reached for another pile of record company invoices, tried to keep his mind on his work, but his thoughts kept on returning to Aldershot.

Was it already over, before it'd ever really begun?

He looked out of his office window at the grey clouds lowering over Liverpool, his mind a complete fog. Over the course of the day, the 'not-knowing' had become so intolerable that, at one time or another, he'd yelled at almost everyone in the store. He'd even shouted at Alistair and Peter over something so trivial he couldn't remember now even what it was about. What was worse, they'd looked at him with their pitying, all-knowing eyes. The two of them, no doubt, thinking he was worrying about the blackmailer again. All of which had only served to make him all the more irritable.

Only, it wasn't his past that haunted him now. It was the uncertainty about his future. And the dark shape that confronted him no longer bore the face of the horrible, odious blackmailer; it now wore the face of Sam Leach.

Oh, that he'd never met the loathsome little man—the one person in all of Liverpool that could reduce his cherished dream of managing The Beatles to ashes. "Oh," he muttered to himself, over and over again, "could anything be more miserable than this?"

CHAPTER NINETEEN

Momentum

"Bollocks and buggeration."

Bob Wooler was not a happy man. The Beatles were late, very late, damnably late, damagingly late, disastrously late. They'd never been so late. Late for a special, one-off, Sunday show he'd advertised in the *Liverpool Echo* as 'Big Beat Beatle Boppin'!!!' no less. And despite all five support groups having played their socks off and him having spun all the latest discs from his collection, as well as filling the spaces in between with his trademark mellifluous patter, with no sign at all of The Beatles, the fans at the Hambleton Hall 'Hive of Jive' were getting restless, very restless, indeed.

"Buggering...bastardly...buggeration," he muttered, his hands opening and closing around imaginary Beatle throats. This could turn serious in a veritable heartbeat. Even with the bands agreeing to go on twice, there could well be demands for refunds. "What's their buggering game?"

"Should I, perhaps, address you as, Mr Lennon, Senior?"

Bob Wooler spun round. It was Brian Epstein. What on earth was he doing at Hambleton Hall? He was the very last person you'd expect to see way out in the Liverpool suburbs, late on a Sunday afternoon. Shouldn't he be off, singing in a synagogue or something? No, of course, not, that's what they did on Saturdays, wasn't it? He smiled his best 'I'm a busy, busy person' smile. "Hello, Mr Epstein. Er, yes, John's little joke. Please just call me, Bob. What on earth brings you out here, of a Sunday?"

"I've come to see The Beatles perform. You see, I'm…"

"Haven't we all," he snapped. "But as Liverpool's finest haven't yet bothered to grace us with their presence, we're both bang out of luck. And after all I've done for them, too. It's totally unprofessional."

He could tell by the look on the younger man's face that he'd hit a nerve. Good, another Bob Wooler bulls-eye. Posh Mr Epstein would have to learn to put up with a lot more than that if he was going to get his manicured fingers dirty in the Liverpool music scene, let alone manage The Beatles. Serve him bloody right for turning up, out of the blue, unexpected and unannounced. He'd heard the would-be Beatles manager had been asking around town about him—all no doubt because the boys had dragged him along to NEMS. So, if nothing else, Mr upstart Epstein would've heard from everyone that it was Bob Wooler who was largely responsible for the Merseyside beat boom. And was, therefore, not someone to be messed with, even if you did happen to own the biggest group of record stores in Liverpool.

"I'm sure, The Beatles really appreciate what you've done for them, Bob," Brian Epstein said, smiling his most-winning smile. "They were only telling me recently how they consider you their biggest supporter. I mean, that wonderful piece you did on them in *Mersey Beat*. What was it you called them, 'Rhythmic revolutionaries'? And what was it you said? 'The Beatles are the hottest local property any rock promoter is likely to encounter'. Well, I have to say, Bob, you're absolutely spot on, of course."

It's always flattering for a writer to have his words quoted back at him. And the young businessman's obvious warmth and enthusiasm for The Beatles reminded him of his own true feelings for the group. "I meant every word, Brian. I don't think we'll ever see the likes of them come bursting onto the scene again. Er…what was it you were saying, earlier?"

"I was just about to say, Bob. I think I'm on the verge of signing a contract with The Beatles. And if I do become their manager, this tardiness of theirs is just the sort of thing I would attend to, immediately. It's completely unprofessional. And not just when they're dealing with a true professional, such as yourself, but with absolutely anyone at all."

He knew The Beatles were still mulling over Brian Epstein's proposal, despite the fact the man knew bugger all about the entertainment business. However, if all the rumours about Sam Leach also throwing his cap into the ring were true, it could go either way. He hated the very thought of having to deal with

Leach every time he wanted to book The Beatles. That'd be a constant bloody torment that would. Bloody Leach. Bloody bothersome, buggering Sam Leach.

Then it was as if Brian Epstein had been reading his mind. "I do believe the boys were playing for Sam Leach, last night, Bob. Somewhere down in London. It would've been such a long day for them. I can only hope they haven't got themselves into any sort of trouble."

"Leach?" He almost exploded. "Leach? It would have to be him behind all this. He's a royal pain in the backside, that one."

"Quite," said Brian Epstein looking at his wristwatch.

A door crashed open in the tiny room next to the stage and they both looked around to see Pete Best carrying in his drum cases.

"About bloody buggering time, too," muttered Bob Wooler.

TERRY AND SPIKE finished unloading The Beatles' equipment from the van. "Think that's everything," said Terry. John Lennon, cigarette in one hand, guitar-case in the other, peered at him. "We'll take it from here, Terence. You must be right knackered driving all that way from London. You just sod off home for your tea." Terry McCann, a little taken aback by John's unusual display of concern, nodded wearily and climbed back into the driver's seat. "I'll be off, then. See you, lads. See you, Spike. Thanks for all the help. Sam'll settle up with you, in the week, okay?" Spike nodded and saluted with a microphone stand. And with one last tired wave to one and all, Terry drove off. Spike turned, picked up the black tom-tom carry-case and a cymbal stand and made for the side door into the hall. "Seems you're the road manager, Spike, until Neil shows up with his van," said Pete, on his way out. "Put those inside, then let's do the amps."

Paul waited until Pete and Spike had disappeared back inside the hall and then turned to John. "I've got a feeling our Sam isn't going to be the one that's going to get us where we're going to, is he, John?"

"Did once, Pauly, not now. Not after what didn't happen in London. I'd say Mr Sam Leach just shot himself in the foot."

"He Al-der-shot himself in the foot, you mean," interjected George, stubbing out his cigarette with a twist of a winklepicker. "In my humble opinion, like, that was a gold-plated bloody disaster from start to finish. And with us arriving so late for his 'Big Beat Beatle Boppin' session, I just know our little friend, Mr Bob-a-job Wooler, is going to be hoppin' good and mad."

"He'll look that much taller, then, won't he?" suggested Paul.

"Yeah," said George, "he'll definitely loom larger, like."

"We'll have done him a bloody favour then, won't we?" snapped John. "What the hell's he got to complain about? Let's go in."

Bob Wooler glared at them, as angry as ever they'd seen him. "I'm certainly not spinning the overture to *William Tell* as I normally do to announce your entry on stage. There's less than twenty minutes left for you to perform, as it is. What do you think I'm running here, a bloody holiday camp? This sort of behaviour could ruin your reputation with the fans. Mine, too, if you keep this sort of thing up." He scowled at John Lennon, who for once bit his tongue and just nodded.

Paul jumped in. "Sorry, Bob, it was out of our control, but it won't happen again...promise." That's when the two Beatles both saw Brian Epstein looking at them through the open doorway into the dancehall.

John's face reddened, then darkened. "Right then. Left, right, left, right, on we bloody go with the show, 'Private Jock Lennon's bone-weary youth-club band'." He gripped the neck of his guitar, and stormed onto the stage followed by the rest of The Beatles.

Bob Wooler almost lost his temper when Pete stuck his hand out and asked for full payment after The Beatles' all too brief performance, but for once he, too, bit down hard on his tongue. He knew all too well The Beatles true drawing power around Liverpool and the one thing he wanted to avoid was any bad blood between him and the band. That'd be disastrous. He slowly counted out fifteen one-pound notes and handed them over, consoling himself by muttering all manner of curses against the real villain of the piece, Sam Leach. He patted Pete Best on the shoulder. "As always, you lads were great, thanks. Let's just hope we can hear a bit more of you next time, okay?" Pete nodded, smiled, but said nothing.

Wooler turned and went over to join John, Paul and George who were talking to Brian Epstein. He smiled his most forgiving smile. "Excuse me for butting in, lads, but even as short as it was, that was great. I've paid Pete your full fee, just to show you how much I appreciate you finally turning up. And, oh, yes, Brian, here, was telling me you're about to sign that management contract with him. Great idea. Wonderful idea. He's definitely your man. He's successful, he's smart, and he's got big plans for you. He'll get you where you want to go. I just know he will. Anyway, that's what I think. See you all at the Cavern, tomorrow lunchtime." And with that, he went over to the record player, gathered up all his discs and started placing them into the travelling case he'd had specially made. He smiled to himself. That was brilliant, like all his best ad-libs. He'd given a black eye to Sam Leach and his management plans and made a friend of Brian Epstein, all in one go. And if that wasn't worth fifteen bloody quid, what was?

SPIKE was on his second trip out to Neil Aspinall's van, this time carrying George's Gibson amplifier, when he caught sight of a thickset man standing across the road. Even in the fast-fading light, he knew it was definitely the blackmailer. He hefted the amplifier up into the van. "Here, Neil, got three pennies for a threepenny bit? Only I've got to telephone home, quick, like. Tell them I'm safe back."

"A likely story. But I often use that one across the road, myself, so I've always got some pennies on hand." Neil dug inside his trouser pocket, pulled out a handful of change. "Yes, here you are, Spikey. Just don't go spending it all on one little judy, it 'aint worth it. Or so John keeps on telling me."

"Chance'd be a fine thing. Thanks, Neil. Won't be a mo'."

He ambled nonchalantly out through the gates and along the street to the telephone box. Pulled open the door, wrinkled his nose at the smell of stale piss, and went inside. He lifted the handset, dropped four pennies into the slot, and began to dial

Harry Lightfoot's number. Someone started tapping the outside of the phone box and he all but jumped with fright. He turned to see a leather gloved fist waving a finger at him through one of the missing panes of glass. "If you're calling me, lad, there's no need. And if you're calling anyone else, now's really not the time," a voice said, very quietly.

"Harry?" Spike whispered.

"The self-same, old son, who else would it be? The black-mailer? Listen, you just pop back into the hall and keep your eyes open. I'll watch from here. Then, if Mr Epstein leaves with them Beatle lads, I'll run you home, afterwards, okay? Off you go. And Spike?"

"Yes, Harry?"

"Remember to press Button 'B', lad, and get your pennies back."

BRIAN EPSTEIN drove John, George, and Paul back into the city. Pete and Neil, all the Beatles' equipment now safely stowed away in the back of the van, made ready to drive off to Pete's home, in Hayman's Green.

"Hey, Spike, you want a lift up to Huyton?"

"No thanks, Neil. After all the time spent locked up in a van these last two days, I think I'd rather walk. It isn't far. Thanks. See you."

"You go safe, Spike," yelled Pete. "Thanks, again, for your help."

He waved, goodbye, and walked up St David's Road, past the phone box, until he saw the little black Morris Minor parked in a side street. He nodded to the shadowy figure sitting behind the wheel, opened the passenger door, and got in. "Hello, Harry."

"Evening, Mr Jones. Here, let me move those things off the seat." He gathered up his thermos flask, a sandwich tin, and camera and flash attachment from off the front-passenger seat, reached over, and placed them in the back. "Had a fun time, have you?"

Spike nodded to all the cigarette ash on the front of Harry Lightfoot's raincoat. "Not as much fun as you by the look of it."

"Touché, young Spike. Touché." Harry Lightfoot chuckled, coughed; offered Spike a cigarette. "Here." He lit both cigarettes with a lighter. "Our nasty little friend hoofed it when he saw Mr Epstein come out surrounded by them Beatle fellas. Probably thought he'd picked up a gang of toughs or something. Anyway, Mr Makin reckons that now the blackmailer's got a smell there's real cash in the offing, the bastard will try more violence, just to squeeze out as much money as he can, like."

"I can keep an eye out at the Cavern, tomorrow, Harry, and Wednesday, Friday lunchtimes, too, as I know 'Eppy' will be..."

"Who?"

"Oh, sorry, I mean, er, Mr Epstein. 'Eppy' is what The Beatles call him now they're saying he's definitely going to be their manager."

"Is he, now? Interesting. Mr Makin will be surprised."

"Anyway, I heard 'Eppy' say he might not get to those lunchtimes, but he'd definitely be there on Wednesday night. And, of course, The Beatles will be at 'the Tower', again, on Friday, so he's bound to be there, as well."

Harry Lightfoot turned the ignition key, looked in his rearview mirror, put the car in gear, let go the handbrake, and drove off. "Interesting place, that New Brighton Tower. Who is it you work for there, again?"

"Fella called, Sam Leach," Spike said, rolling down the window and flicking his cigarette ash outside.

"You've mentioned him, before. Good sort, is he?"

"The best. Sharp as a tack, but funny with it and as genuine as the day is long. I like him lots. Pity is, he wanted to manage The Beatles, too."

"Well, whether he does or doesn't, happen he should go far. I haven't seen crowds like that around 'the Tower' since the days of Joe Loss and his Orchestra." The Morris Minor pulled into the kerb outside Spike's home. "Oh, I nearly forgot, here's some money from Mr Makin." He leaned across and handed Spike a sealed envelope. "You go safe now, because in them clothes and with that hair you could be taken for a right hooligan."

"Thanks, Harry. And to think I was going say, you were a good sort, too. For an ex-copper, that is."

"Cheeky monkey. Night, night."

"Night, Harry. Thanks for the lift."

Harry Lightfoot made to drive off, then stopped. "Spike."

"Yes, Harry?"

"That black eye of yours looks like it's clearing up, nicely."

SAM LEACH slept through most of Monday. Come Tuesday, he put on a clean shirt, clean tie, his third-best suit, and went to the Grapes for a lunchtime pie and a pint. When he'd paid his money and taken his first sip of beer, the barman remembered to tell him that his musician friends, John something and Paul somebody, had left a message for him to meet them at the Kardomah Coffee House, anytime that afternoon. "Thanks," Sam said, pocketing his change. "I'll finish me lunch, then pop round. I could do with a coffee."

Sometime later, feeling more at one with the world, Sam burped loudly, and pushed open the door of the Kardomah. "Hello, lads. Another coffee for you both?" John Lennon and Paul McCartney looked at him, their faces a mixture of relief and concern.

"Er, yeah, another coffee would be great thanks, Sam," said Paul.

"Better make it a big, black one, Sam," said John.

Sam brought over a tray of coffees, sat down, took an almost full pack of cigarettes out of his pocket and placed it, open, on the table.

"About your money for last Saturday, if we could just hold on that till next Friday, at 'the Tower', you'd be doing me a real, big favour."

"Er, sure," said Paul, "considering what happened, an' all."

John reached for a cigarette, avoiding Sam's eyes. "Yeah, sure, Sam, sure. It's the least we can do, considering."

"Good one. So, you both recovered, yet?"

"We're still recovering," said Paul. "We played Hambleton Hall, Sunday afternoon, and were so late getting there, we were met by a very unhappy and disgruntled Bob Wooler..."

Sam coughed; chuckled. "The weekend wasn't a dead loss then, was it?" He picked a piece of tobacco from his teeth.

Paul continued on. "We played the Cavern, yesterday lunchtime."

"You boys are the hardest working rock 'n' roll band in Liverpool," offered Sam. "You should be right bloody proud of your..."

"Well, we're not," snapped John. "We're like bloody rats on a treadmill, we are, and we're going bloody nowhere, very bloody fast."

Sam Leach was jolted out of his after-lunch reverie. He and John Lennon had a business relationship that verged on being a proper friendship. He knew John usually held his barbs in check where he was concerned, even when they were trading insult for insult. He put down his cup. "Woah, John where did that come from?"

"It gets to me, sometimes, Sam, that's all," said John, his voice thick with emotion. "You work your bollocks off. You have dreams. You make plans. And it doesn't amount to a soddin' thing."

"So, we've been thinking, like, Sam, and we've got a real, big favour to ask of you, an' all," Paul said, quietly.

Sam, suddenly very awake and very alert, slowly relaxed back into his seat. They knew they needed help and they were about to ask him to manage them. He swallowed and reached for another cigarette.

Paul cleared his throat. "Thing is, Sam, there's this rich fella that wants to manage us and we know he doesn't know the business, half as well as you do. And we know you said you'd like to manage us and we said wouldn't that be fun and we'd do a record together and stuff, but, well, the thing is, Sam, this fella's a bloody millionaire. And he can get us to..."

"He can get us to the toppermost of the bloody poppermost, Sam," croaked John. "And, if he has to, he can buy us all the way there, too."

Sam could hardly breathe. And suddenly he was coughing and spluttering like a novice nun—the cigarette smoke having gone down the wrong hole—and Paul McCartney was slapping him on the back like he was a baby. And all he wanted to do was cry, cry like a baby. They weren't talking about him, but someone else. Some rich sod, with money to burn. 'God giveth. And then God taketh away'. How very cruel, life could be.

"Gerrof, gerrof. I'm okay, really. Went down the wrong hole, is all. So what are we talking about, here? Some millionaire has tripped over you and fallen for you, is that it? Well, that's great, that is."

Paul jumped in with both feet. "Well, Sam, there's this millionaire, 'Eppy', owns a chain of shops, comes from a rich family, and he's got this real flash car, and he wants to manage us. And we thought, well, with you knowing what you know about everything, you could check him out for us. See if he's really kosher, like. See if he can get us…"

John piped in. "See if can get us to where we're going to, Sam."

" 'Eppy'? Is that his name, then?" asked Sam, hurriedly sniffing air up into his addled brain. "From round Liverpool way, is he?"

"Well, that's what we call him, like," Paul said brightly. "And, yeah, he owns NEMS record stores."

The penny finally dropped as the bottom finally fell out of his world. They were talking about Brian Epstein. 'Eppy'—short for Epstein. God, but he could be thick sometimes. They wanted him to go meet the toffee-nosed git, then give them his blessing, to boot. 'God giveth, and God boot-eth you in the arse'. Suddenly, he didn't feel like believing in anything or anyone, anymore. "Let me get this straight, you want me to go over to this Brian Epstein's office, check him out, and see if he's on the level, is that it?"

"Yes," John and Paul said in perfect harmony, "That's it, exactly, Sam."

SAM LEACH had hold of the silly, little sherry glass so tightly he was afraid he'd snap the stem. It didn't matter the Sherry was much too dry—that it had all the appeal of paint stripper—the simple fact the glass gave him something solid to hold onto, was enough. He'd dreaded making the phone call to NEMS. Dreaded having to make an actual appointment. Dreaded even more having to dress up for it. Clean shirts didn't grow on trees. He'd brushed his teeth, brushed his hair. Damn it, he'd even brushed his Hush Puppies. Done everything he could think of to make himself look respectable and business-like. But he was outclassed the moment he stepped into Brian Epstein's office.

Then, to cap it all, the bloody man had totally disarmed him by speaking to him as one might to a parent or guardian, warmly and with obvious shared concern. And he'd seen all too clearly that beneath all the public-school polish Epstein had a determination and a drive to succeed that wouldn't admit to failure. And despite himself, despite his misgivings and increasingly heavy heart, sitting there, silly glass in hand, he'd been utterly transported and transfixed by his rival's future vision for The Beatles. More importantly, the man had the money and connections to make his vision real. Sam shook his head. He couldn't see Tito Burns, the London impresario, throwing Mr Brian Epstein out on his bloody ear.

What hit home the hardest was that despite all his own grandiose plans, he'd never once seen the really big picture. Couldn't have seen it, even if he'd stood atop the New Brighton bloody Tower. The Beatles' would-be manager was pointing to a new and different horizon, a world away from Liverpool. And then suddenly the meeting was over. They'd shaken hands, smiled, and he'd exited stage bloody left. Then, still in a daze, he'd crossed over Whitechapel, walked round to Mathew Street, and so to the Grapes. All the way, wrestling with the demons on each shoulder. Why in hell should he tell John and Paul that this bloody 'Eppy' of theirs was the man they were looking for? They'd bloody walked out on him. All but shat on him from a great height. What in hell did he owe them?

"Buy you a drink, Sam?" Paul called out when he entered the pub.

He nodded. "A whisky, Mr McCartney, and you better make it a double." He removed his coat, sat down, and just stared off into space. John, meanwhile, could hardly contain himself and sat grinning and pulling faces. The minutes dragged on and then with a rush and chink of glasses, Paul returned with two half-pints of black velvet and a double whisky.

"Well, Sam, how did it go? What do you think of our 'Eppy'?"

"Sam?" John added, staring at him intently. "Our 'Eppy'?"

He took a deep breath and slowly nodded his head. "He's definitely the one to take you where you want to go, lads." He downed the whisky in one, to drown the taste of the Sherry. "He'll take you all the bloody way to the toppermost of your poppermost, if you'll let him."

The two Beatles looked at one another and nodded. 'Eppy' had passed the final test. 'Eppy' was their man. They nodded and touched glasses. Now all they had to do was get 'Eppy' to meet their families.

"Just, remember to remember me when you get there, fellas," Sam said, softly.

John turned and looked at him. "Don't be daft, Sam, you'll always be with us, you will. We've got places to play and records to make. 'Eppy' can manage us. You just keep on putting on them great shows of yours. We'll all win, then, and there's nothing can stop us."

"Cheers, Sam," said Paul. "And thanks a million, like."

"I'd say ten million, at least," he said, staring ruefully into the bottom of his now empty whisky glass. "Chin-chin."

BRIAN EPSTEIN smiled a contended smile. He hoped his little 'command performance' had done the trick. Not that he'd been acting. Everything he'd said about The Beatles was true. It was just there were other, far more important people that needed convincing. Even so, his chat with Sam Leach had been good practice. First, though, he needed to call Bert Kaempfert, in Hamburg. Find out how to get 'the boys' released from the recording contract they'd signed when they'd played as Tony Sheridan's backing group. Then he'd attend to the final, most important hurdles—the boys' families.

His telephone call to Polydor Records completed, he consulted the list of names and addresses he'd carefully written down in his desk diary. First call was to John's legal guardian, his Aunt Mimi. The second call, to Pete's mother, Mona Best. It was likely that both women would be home during the day. He'd call Paul's father, Jim McCartney, then George's mother and father, Harry and Louise Harrison, later, when both men would've returned home from work. He ran his finger down to 251 Menlove Avenue, pressed the intercom, and gave his secretary the telephone number to call.

Given the enthusiastic smiles he received from all four Beatles, following his visits to their families, he'd been a great success. But he had yet one more trump card to play. He'd both shocked and thrilled the boys, at the Wednesday night session at the Cavern, by producing a real live Decca Records executive from out of his hat. Mike Smith, one of Decca's senior A&R men, had travelled up from London by train just to see and hear them play. The all-important first step to a recording contract with a major label.

"Where's our 'Eppy' taking us to, fellas?" shouted John over his shoulder as he led The Beatles out onto the Cavern stage to the urgent sounds of Rossini's *William Tell Overture.*

"To the toppermost, Johnny," they all chorused, giddily.

"And what rockin' top is that, fellas?"

"To the toppermost of the rockin' poppermost, Johnny."

"Yeah, yeah, yeah. And don't it feel just bloody marvellous?"

TERRY McCANN stared at his friend. "Blimey, Sam, you look like you just lost a five pound note and found a sixpence."

"It's much worse, Tel. I've not only gone and lost The Beatles, I think I've gone and lost that lovely girl, Joan, you introduced me to, as well."

"What do you mean lost The Beatles, you stupid git? How could you lose them? You never had them in the first place. Anyway, there're loads of groups around Liverpool, but you losing that Joan, that's different. You need your head examining there, my old son. What the fuck happened?"

Sam pulled at his face with both hands. "She overheard Johnny Guitar, of The Hurricanes, remark about some flash new blonde only going out with me because I had a few bob. She was so offended, she told me she never wanted to see me again."

Terry shook his head. "I'll string Johnny's balls up by his guitar strings, I will. He's talking out of his arse and you know it."

"Yeah, but why get tied down to anyone? Just play the field, eh?"

Terry exploded. "Not when you've found a girl like Joan, you don't, you stupid sod. Now go call her and tell her you mean business."

He turned. "But I'm not ready for a serious relationship, Tel."

"Everyone is, Sam, if and when they find the right one."

BRIAN EPSTEIN smiled. It'd been another long and exhausting week trying to balance the needs of NEMS with the demands of The Beatles. But Sunday would see it all pay off. There were only the details of the management contract to go over—then he'd officially become The Beatles' manager. And feeling happier than he could ever remember, that Saturday night, he'd gone to see 'the boys' play the Cavern. Afterwards, they'd even invited him to join them at a party that six student-nurses were throwing in their honour. He'd laughed, glad at last to be taken as one of the boys, but had excused himself. Said he should get off home, as tomorrow was going to be a big day. Then he'd driven away, in his car, feeling simply elated. And so much so, that on reflection, the week did perhaps call for a special ending, something to help release all the tension inside. And soon he'd found himself at Feather's, one of Liverpool's more discreet private clubs. Yet try as he might to lose himself in all the gay chatter and laughter, he found his heart really wasn't in it. And when he felt the club's owner was being even more patronising than usual, he decided to call it a night. And so he paid his bill, put on his coat and, and with just the right amount of boredom on his face, made for the door.

Outside, he pulled on his gloves against the cold and let his eyes adjust to the dark. A voice said, "Hello, love. What brings you out on a cold night like this?" He looked up and smiled and someone punched him in the face. He staggered and lurched away from the horror that'd suddenly taken shape to rob him of life at the very moment he'd never had so much to live for. He cried out, in numb terror. But the dark man was soon on him again, punching and kicking at him, mercilessly.

A blinding white light suddenly split apart the darkness and he and his attacker were etched against the black of night like exotic butterflies pinned to a collector's table. The attacker, fist raised to strike, looked round, startled, and was caught by a second flash of light. He could only imagine what his own face must look like. Full of surprise, pale with fear, trickles of blood pouring from his nose and mouth—not at all acceptable. And, sobbing, uncontrollably, he fell to his knees, then fell forward and curled up into a ball on the ground, whimpering.

Then everything went black.

HARRY LIGHTFOOT ran from out of the shadows and hit Brian Epstein's attacker with a flurry of well-aimed punches. He kneed the man in the balls, threw a wicked kidney punch, and when the attacker went down, he kicked and kicked until the man's body lay motionless. The door of Feather's opened and someone looked out and squealed in horror, then slammed the door shut. The ex-copper didn't even bother to turn his head or move the boot he had pressed down hard on the blackmailer's throat. He waited until the body convulsed and started coughing and only then did he look down. "If you stop struggling, matey, you'll have just enough air. Otherwise, I'll just press down all the harder. Got it?" There was a short gurgling noise that could've been a 'yes'. "Now, before I kick you senseless, again, I want you to listen very, very carefully. Got it?" He released his foot a fraction until he heard the gurgling noise again. He leaned forward. "You've been a bit of a bully, you have, preying on helpless, little boys. Only, it's going stop, right here and now. Have you got that? Thing is, you see, I've got photographs of you attacking that nice, harmless gentleman over there. And what with your criminal record and all the threats you've made, if they ever got shown to the right authorities, they'd put you away for life. As under English Law, it'd be seen as clear evidence of attempted murder. So you'd get life in prison, you would. Life. You got that in your head, have you?"

The gurgling noise erupted again, though with a lot less force.

"You're sure now? Only, I wouldn't want to think you didn't fully understand, like." The sound of air bubbling through blood and spit increased. "Good, because this, now, is Liverpool Law. One more report about you, anywhere, round here, and it'll be your legs I crush first, then your fingers on your hands. By which I mean you'd never be able to hold your dick ever again. And that's only if you hadn't already been found floating in the River Mersey. Do I make myself clear?" Noise gurgled up from below, again, as the man pissed himself. "Good, I think I might be getting through to you, at last."

For several minutes, Harry Lightfoot kicked the man with the sort of finesse and expertise that only comes from years of playing rugby. And only when he was completely sure he'd kicked the man truly senseless, did he sniff up the cold in his nose and go over and help Brian Epstein to his feet. "It's alright, Mr Epstein, sir. I don't think that nasty man will be bothering you, anymore, not ever. And that's a promise. Come on, now, let's get you cleaned up and get you home."

SAM LEACH just couldn't stop thinking about the luscious little blonde, named Joan. Beatles be blowed, this was real love, and no mistake. So that Saturday, rather than journey back down to Aldershot, with Terry McCann, and Rory Storm and The Hurricanes, for a second 'Battle of the Bands', he handed over enough money to cover expenses and stayed home. Then he'd put on a clean shirt and his very best suit, brushed his hair and his shoes, and with a big bunch of fresh-cut flowers clutched in his hand, had gone round to Joan's house.

He pressed the bell and stood waiting at her front door, as nervous as ever he'd been in his life. Then when he saw her standing there, surrounded by a nimbus of light—a real blonde haired angel in the living flesh—he handed her the bouquet and told her, straight out, there was no truth at all in Johnny Guitar's silly, spiteful remark. That he'd already had words with the guitarist about it. Who'd as good as admitted he'd only said it, in the first place, because he'd been so dead jealous.

So he'd asked her, right then and there, if she'd go out with him and could they start over again, please, that very night.

At first, she'd said 'No', she couldn't. She'd promised to go dancing with her girlfriends. And, honest to God, his heart had immediately broken in two. But then, after only a moment's hesitation, she'd smiled at him and said, "Sunday night would be just fine." Then added that she was already looking forward to it. And his not so wooden heart had started beating again.

And as he walked home, through a bitterly cold Liverpool night, a huge smile plastered all over his face, all he could do, all the way, was sing Elvis's latest hit and remind himself, again and again, that if you treated people nice, treated people good, treated them like you really should...then sometimes, just sometimes...'God not only giveth...He also let you keepeth'.

"Thank you, God," he said, over and over again, his eyes lifting up to heaven with his every other step.

CHAPTER TWENTY

No Negatives

"Bloody hell, 'Eppy'." John Lennon's concern was very real. Now he'd made up his mind Brian Epstein was the one who could actually help The Beatles succeed, an attack on 'Eppy' was an attack on himself. "Who did it to you? I'll fookin' kill the bastards."

George and Paul looked shocked, mumbled their concerns. Pete came in with a tray of Cokes, saw the condition of Brian's face, and stopped dead. "Bloody heck, Brian, you look like you got knocked down by a bus. What happened?"

"Er, nothing, Pete," said Brian, his hand brushing over the bruised welts on his face. "I tripped in the dark and fell down some stairs, that's all. Look, there's no need to fuss, really. It was an unfortunate accident. It could have happened to anyone."

"Well, you're not just anyone, anymore, 'Eppy', you're one of us, now," said John, glancing pointedly at the others for agreement. "So, just you be a lot more careful in future. Okay?"

Brian Epstein nodded, smiled, and felt utterly tongue-tied.

"Coke, Brian?" asked Pete, offering the tray.

Grateful for the diversion Brian took a bottle of Coke, and for a few minutes the only sounds in the empty Casbah Club were 'Eppy' and the four Beatles sipping Coca-Cola, the creaking of the Beatles' leather jackets and the scrape of cowboy boots on the stone floor.

John stifled a burp. "Right then, 'Eppy', it's your show. What do you want to talk to us about?"

Brian Epstein put down his Coke and reached inside his briefcase. "I simply wanted to take a few moments to go over the first draft of the contract with you."

"I'd say you've got things off to a flying start, 'Eppy', what with you arranging for that Decca fella, Mike Smith, to come up and see us at the Cavern. I can't see as we'd have too much to add, especially since you tell us Mr Smith's already invited us down to London to audition on New Year's Day. So, as for the contract, I'm sure it's all fair and above board. Don't you, fellas?"

"Yeah, brilliant move with Decca, Brian," said Paul, grandly. "That was the deal we had. You get us a recording contract and you get to manage us."

"I'd like to hear what else you're thinking, though," said George, very matter-of-factly.

"Yeah, I would, too," said Pete.

"Of course," said Brian, smiling at each Beatle in turn. He held up the contract. "It's very much as we discussed earlier. The contract is to be effective for a five-year period from 1st February 1962. I'll use my business contacts to get you a recording contract with a major London company. I'll handle all your bookings and make sure you get to play better venues. I'll also ensure you get better paid at each venue...nothing less than fifteen pounds, a time. For which, I will take ten per cent of your gross annual income up to £1,500, rising to fifteen per cent once your earnings go beyond that. The remainder to be computed weekly and divided equally between you, after all your expenses have been deducted. Then, as it's almost certain you'll get the Decca recording contract, I'll continue my talks with Bert Kaempfert, at Polydor, to get you released from the contract you have with him. My task then will be to get you on the radio and on to television as soon as I possibly can."

"Is that bloody all? On the bloody telly? I'll put my cross on the contract now," said John, rubbing his hands with glee.

"After me," shouted Paul, giving it a big thumbs-up.

"Sounds all very satisfactory," said George, grinning.

"About time, too," said Pete. "After all we've all been through."

Brian Epstein beamed. "Well, if we're all in agreement, then, I'll have everything ready for you to sign in the New Year. I'll get off a press release about your Decca audition to Tony Barrow, who writes the 'Off The Record' column in the *Liverpool Echo*. One other thing, I've arranged for a professional photographer to take some new publicity pictures of you."

"That's very nice of you, 'Eppy', but we've already got some great photos that our friend Astrid took of us, in Hamburg. We could use those. Save a bit on expenses, eh?" suggested John.

"Bill Harry's got hold of them at the moment," added Paul, helpfully. "So he can use them in *Mersey Beat* whenever he wants."

"I don't suppose we could use these, then," said George, pulling an envelope from out of his coat pocket. He smiled, wickedly. "Only, they're the ones from that wonderful night in Al-der-shot." He handed round the photographs, one by one. The first showed John and George dancing, arm in arm.

Brian Epstein tried desperately not to blush. There were circles, he frequented in Liverpool, where such a photo could all too easily be misconstrued. The second picture was almost as bad. It showed John with his face and body contorted into an ugly caricature of a hunchback. It was silly, even juvenile, but it could cause offense. A third picture showed John, George, and Paul, drinking from beer bottles and looking glassy-eyed and drunk. Sam Leach looked very much the same in another photo. The stupid man obviously had no idea just how damaging such pictures could be if they ever fell into the wrong hands. He handed the photographs on and tried to still his growing irritation. The Beatles, oblivious to his concerns, continued looking at the photos and howling with laughter.

"Aldershot?" Brian said, primly. "From that Saturday night? With Sam Leach?" He took a moment to compose himself. "No, they're definitely not the sort of pictures, I have in mind." He forced a chuckle and tried to make light of it all, but that was dampened by George's next comment.

"Oh, these are nothing, Brian. You should see the ones Bill Harry has of us. They're much worse, especially the ones of our John."

Brian Epstein looked as if he'd had a sudden attack of heartburn. He turned to face John. "In what way is that, John?"

John blinked, owlishly, and did his best to look innocent.

"Do you think our George is talking about the one with you standing round with a pig on a leash, there, John?" inquired Paul.

"You remember, the one where you're only in your socks and underpants, wearing a posh Tyrolean hat," added George, helpfully.

"No, that's the one of John standing in the street, reading a newspaper. There's definitely no pig in that one," offered Pete.

"Hey, John, I'd never tell anyone about that photograph of you wearing a toilet seat around your neck, on stage, honest, you have my word," said Paul, soothingly.

"And I'll never speak of the photo of you with that toilet plunger on your head and the roll of toilet paper on your guitar," added George. "My lips are forever sealed."

Brian Epstein looked dazed, unsure of what he'd unleashed, missing the humour completely. John Lennon, his instincts alerted, glowered back at his fellow Beatles. "Shurrup, fellas, that's enough." He turned to Brian. "They're quite harmless, 'Eppy'. A bit of fun, like. Nothing more."

Brian Epstein didn't turn a hair, he just said, very quietly, "Fun can sometimes come back to haunt you, John."

"Look, 'Eppy', if it'll make you happier, I'll go round and see Bill Harry, tomorrow, and get them all back, okay?"

"If you would, John." Brian forced a smile. "But don't get me wrong. It's only that I want the best for you all. You deserve no less."

"But what about them photos of Astrid's?" George asked, politely.

"Yeah, Brian, they're really brilliant, they are," added Paul.

"Yes, they are, but they show who you were then, not who you are today or who you might be tomorrow." Brian looked at each of them in turn. "Look, I know it's still early days between us, but if you want to play the sort of venues and clubs that'll pay you a lot more money than you've been getting, then you'll have to smarten up a little."

They looked at him through narrowed eyes. He'd got their full attention, now. The thought of more money meant more to them than any talk of percentages. Lots of money, that's what they each wanted—and a recording contract. If they had to smarten up a little, then so be it. It was no time to rock the boat.

Brian Epstein felt the same. "I really don't want you to lose your individuality or for you to look square or anything, but you'd never get past the door of a good place looking like that." The Beatles fidgeted in their leather gear, but said nothing. And at last feeling on more comfortable ground, he continued on with his litany of change. "The jeans you wear aren't particularly smart and don't project the right sort of image. We should also think about you not eating or drinking when you're on stage. And for you not to swear or shout back at the fans." He paused. "Perhaps you could all be a little more punctual," he added, reasonably, his gaze coming to rest on Paul. "It's just that if we smooth out the edges, a little, here and there, there'll be no limits to the heights we can scale together."

John Lennon leaned forward, his chin cradled on his fists. "I could listen to you going on like this, all night, 'Eppy'." He sniffed, contentedly. He turned to his fellow Beatles. "So, where are we going to, then, fellas?"

"The toppermost, Johnny," they chorused back.

"And which toppermost is that, fellas?"

"The toppermost of the poppermost," they yelled, patting each other on the back. Then they all raised their Cokes to their 'Eppy'.

HARRY LIGHTFOOT poured sugar into his coffee, stirred it, then let the spoon clatter back into the saucer. "Excuse the gloves, Mr Makin. They make me a mite clumsy, at times." He sniffed up the cold in his nose. "Anyroad, since we last spoke, I've got a definite feeling that blackmailer won't be troubling your Mr Epstein, anymore." He sipped his coffee; looked over the rim of his cup. "I heard as how the bugger met with some sort of unfortunate accident that put him in hospital. Fell down some steps or got set-upon by darkies or some such." Rex Makin stirred his coffee and glanced down at a large buff-coloured envelope lying on the tabletop. The private detective tapped it with a gloved finger then pushed it across the table. "Funny thing, Mr Makin, there may or may not be something in there that could shed light upon the matter. There could even be photographic evidence of some crime being committed. Certainly enough stuff, like, as could put someone away for a very, very long time. There could even be a negative or two in there. Hard to tell, if it was left unopened and kept under lock and key in a very safe place by someone who'd know what to do should circumstances ever demand it."

Rex Makin nodded, pulled a handkerchief from his coat pocket and used it to pull the sealed envelope closer. Across the front, in block letters, were the words: TO WHOM IT MAY CONCERN. There was no name, no address, and no date. Nothing at all to suggest what was inside, who'd sent it or where it'd come from. He nodded, slid the envelope from off the table and into folds of his briefcase, on the floor, by his feet. He snapped the case shut. "Let's hope that's an end to it then, Harry. Thank you. Submit your expenses and I'll put them through. I'll settle up with young Raymond, myself. I'm only too glad the lad worked out, so well. I'll also let the client know a little Christmas box is in order for you."

"Thank you, Mr Makin, that little hobby of mine costs a bob or two to keep up. Cameras and film, flash bulbs, and the like." He drained his coffee. "Been trying me hand at a bit of night photography recently. Pictures of buildings, the city centre, down by the river, people in the street, that sort of thing. Some nice shots, even if I say so myself."

"Very handy, that you also do your own developing and printing."

"I find I always get much clearer results that way."

"Couldn't see you popping down the chemists with them, Harry."

"I only ever need go there for my cough medicine or a tin of throat lozenges, Mr Makin, sir."

BILL HARRY heard the sound of boots clumping up the stairs. Then the door burst open and John Lennon came dashing in.

"Hey, Bill, give us back all them Hamburg photos, will yer, or I'm in the shitter."

Bill Harry stood and came round from behind his desk, careful not to knock anything onto the floor. "What the bloody heck you on about, John? What about, 'Good morning, Bill?' 'How are you, Bill?' 'How's Virginia, Bill?' Seeing as I haven't seen hide nor hair of you for weeks." He glared at his visitor. "I'm fine, by the way, John. How the bloody hell, are you? And how's our lovely Cynthia? Still putting up with you, is she?" He snatched a pile of large-sized envelopes that John had picked up at random from off one of the tables. "Careful, yer daft sod, I've got them all piled-up in order."

"Bloody hell, Bill, all I want is me bloody photies back. The ones I gave you from when we was last out in Hamburg."

"What, the ones of you in your underpants playing silly sods? Or the ones with you and the pig and the lavatory brush?" Bill Harry scratched his head with both hands, shedding irritations by the handful. "Alright, pray tell me how can I be of assistance, Mr Lennon?"

"That's more like it, you bugger. Who do you think you are, the proprietor of some posh bloody newspaper or something?"

"Do you want your poems back, as well, then? And all yer other scribblings, too? Is that it, John? Time to destroy all the evidence, is it? What about that 'On the dubious origins of The Beatles'? If anyone hears you heard it from 'a man on a Flaming Pie', they'll lock you up, for sure. Pity, we already published it in *Mersey Beat* six months ago. Hang on, I'll go check, see if the paddy wagons are waiting outside."

"Bloody hell, Bill. All I did was ask for me photies back. Anyroad, it's not me getting on about it, it's our 'Eppy'."

"You've signed with him, then?"

"Course, we have, dafty. He's the best offer we've had. Truth is, he's the only real offer we've had that has any chance of taking us anywhere."

"Fancy a cup of tea, do you, John?"

"I will, if you'll be mother."

Bill Harry filled the electric kettle from a tap in the toilets on the floor below and made a pot of tea. Then the two old friends sat and poured over the black and white photos of John and the other Beatles from their wild times on Hamburg's Reeperbahn.

"Look at them through 'Eppy's eyes and he's got a point."

"Well, Astrid's lovely photos aside, John, I'd say it's a toss up between the picture of you and George being hugged by them transvestites in that Roxy Bar place you told me about. Or the one of the both of you and our Paul, on your knees, begging like mad dogs in front of a bowl of Prellies."

"They're only slimming tablets for women, for fook sake."

"Over in Germany, John, but not here. Preludin's prescription only, over here. Proper drugs. But as for keeping your weight in check, you could always take up football."

"I'll boot you to death, meself, any more lip from you."

"Might make a good headline, John. But would that be before or after The Beatles have won the next *Mersey Beat* Popularity Poll?"

SPIKE stared into Sandra's eyes. Sandra stared into his. The ever-repeating bass notes of the mainline diesel engines, the staccato clatter of the local trains, the constant chatter of people; everything and everyone, coming and going; all dissolved into some far-distant ethereal music. Even the tinny echoing voice of the station announcer sounded like someone reading a poem. Liverpool's Lime Street railway station was never, could never, be as magical as it was at that moment.

"It was nice going to the pictures with you tonight, Spike. Thank you."

"Yeah, the film was good, too. *The Frightened City*. The film's theme tune played by none other than The Shadows."

"I've gone off them and Cliff. They just don't move me, anymore."

"Hank Marvin's still a dead good guitarist, though."

"What was that actor called, the cat burglar one?"

"Something Connery, I think. Never noticed him before."

"You look a bit like him, you know."

"Getaway, do I 'eck."

"No, you do. Well, perhaps not your hair or your clothes, but in your face, you do."

"Hang on, I'll just go steal some jewels for you, shall I?"

"My hero." Sandra twirled away, then suddenly stopped. "You know, I always meet my sister, Maureen, here, when she comes and visits from London. It's where I see her off from, as well."

"Well, it would be, wouldn't it?"

"It would be, what?"

The Tannoy system sparked into life again. "*The train arriving at Platform Seven is the nine-ten from Manchester...*"

Spike tipped a finger to his forehead and imitated a London copper. "I think it's what's called a railway station, Miss."

She smiled. "I love train stations; they're dead special. Even now, just waiting for a local train, home. It's like when I was little and saw them big ships going down the Mersey and out to the sea, off somewhere, far away. That's what this station is for me, it's where my future will start, one day."

"What, by simply taking a train to Manchester or Birmingham?"

"No, dafty, London, America, the world, I don't know. Anywhere. I don't care. Just so long as it's away from…"

"Me?"

"No, you're the best reason there is to stay. Only, I always promised myself I'd leave when I was eighteen, like my sister did. Just go off to London, get away from here. Be by myself. Try to find myself."

"But I'm here, now, and I've found you." Spike said.

"Yeah, you did." She squeezed his hand. "And it's lovely, it is."

"Fancy a quick cup of tea or a Coke or something, before you go home?"

"That'd be nice, Spike. Thank you."

In no time at all, they sat drinking coffee in the station cafe.

Spike looked up from stirring his cup. "What you said, San, about always wanting to get away to London." His voice turned dramatic. "To *The Frightened City*." Then soft. "What's that all about, then?"

Sandra smiled. "I'll tell you when you're twenty-one."

Spike leaned towards her. "I get given the key then, do I?"

"The key to me, anyway." She smiled again. "And that's a promise, that is."

"All right, that's a date." He nodded. "It's funny, though."

"What? What's funny?"

"You can't wait to go off and find something, somewhere. And here's me, trying to find that same missing something, somewhere inside." He paused. "I suppose I've always been looking, too. Always wanting to be something else...a boxer, pilot, electrical engineer. Then when I finally got into the Art College to study art, be an artist, I thought that was it. Only I didn't fit-in. So now it's me making music, playing the guitar. And I love it, I really do."

While he'd been talking, Spike had been doodling on a paper napkin with a ballpoint pen. It was a picture of Sandra's face.

"Ooh, let's have a look." Sandra reached forward, brushing Spike's hand. She swivelled the napkin round on the tabletop.

"It's nothing, really," he said, softly.

"It's...it's me, isn't it? That's really lovely, that is, Spike. You're so very talented."

"If only I could play the guitar, half-as-well."

"Why is that the grass is always greener, elsewhere?" she said wistfully.

Spike sniffed up the cold in his nose. "I suppose, it's so you keep on searching." He glanced up at the wall clock. "Can I see you again, Sandra?" She bit her lip and nodded. "At 'the Tower'? Boxing Night?" She nodded again and smiled. "Great," he said. "Let's go catch your train."

They left the warmth of the cafe and went out onto the station concourse. Even late on a Sunday, Lime Street Station still bustled with people. Spike looked over towards the ticket gates. Then he turned and noticed the instant photo-booth. "Hey, come on, San, let's have something else to remember tonight by. Four poses for two bob."

Sandra looked to see what Spike was pointing at. "Instant photos? Oh, yeah, let's. Just let me just brush me hair, first."

The booth was empty, the curtains drawn-back on both sides. Spike pulled a two-shilling piece from out of his pocket, held it ready, and stood in front of the mirror and did his best to brush his hair into place with his other hand. Sandra came up and stood beside him and quickly brushed her hair. She looked at him in the mirror. "I can do that for you, if you like."

"No, it's okay, thanks. I've done it."

"No, dafty, I mean, properly. Cut it. Style it. Do it like your friends, The Beatles, have done theirs. You said you liked the way they looked."

"What? Like John and Paul and George's hair? Really?"

"I told you my sister, Maureen, works in a posh hairdresser's down in London. She showed me how. You can trust me. I'd do it properly."

"Really? Yeah, okay. That'd be great. I'd like that."

They sat down on the stool inside the booth and looked into the glass in front of the camera lens. "It's much too low," said Spike, taking charge. "Hold on, I'll spin the seat round and raise it up. Try it again." They sat side-by-side and leaned in close towards one another. "Perfect."

"Now what do we do?" Sandra asked, quickly rubbing her tongue across her teeth and her lips, before breaking into a fit of giggles.

"First we compose ourselves," said Spike, laughing. "Then I put the coin in and we wait for the flash to go off. Four times."

"All right, this is serious," said Sandra, immediately giggling again. "Sorry. Sorry."

"Sandra, behave yourself."

"Okay, okay. Here, we go now. I'm ready. Put the money in."

Spike leaned forward and put the coin into the slot and leaned back and smiled and tried to hold it, but he began to grimace. Then the flash went off. "I had me eyes half-closed," giggled Sandra. That set them both laughing. The flash went off a second time. He pulled a funny face. So did Sandra. And the flash went off a third time. Then he turned and pulled Sandra close to him and then he kissed her.

The flash went off a fourth time and Sandra's world changed in that instant. She'd never been so thrilled by a kiss in all her life. Spike held her tight and then he kissed her again and her lips moved, but no words came out. She just tingled all over and her body felt warm and alive and wonderful. And Spike felt like he could drown forever in the dark silky waves of Sandra's hair.

"The train about to depart from Platform Five is the ten-forty, local train calling at..."

"That's...that's my train," Sandra said, her face flushed, her eyes sparkling. "Will them photos take long, like?"

"Says three minutes on the sign," said Spike. "Not too long."

They stood outside the booth, holding onto one another, not saying a word, just waiting for things to develop. The moments and the minutes ticked by. So slowly, so quickly, so slowly, until their faces suddenly fell into view. Neither of them moved. Then Spike reached forward, pulled the little strip of black and white photos out from between the polished metal guides and handed it to Sandra. She held the photo-strip up for them both to see. It was there, caught forever, amidst a sea of giggles and laughter and funny faces, their very first kiss. "It's the best Christmas present, ever," she whispered. "Thank you, thank you." She turned, her eyes flashing, and went up on her toes, and kissed him, again. Then she ran for her train.

"HEY 'OOP, 'EPPY'. Look at you. Who'd you think you look like, then?"

"Well, you did say I was one of you, now, John. So, seeing as you all insisted you wear your leather jackets and trousers for today's photo session, I thought I'd show some support."

"Well, thank you for your support, Brian. I'll always be sure and wear it." He waited for the groans to subside. "But you, in a leather jacket. There's hidden depths to you, 'Eppy'."

"Er, yes, I suppose there are, John," said Brian, softly.

"It looks good on you though, Brian. It does," added Paul.

"It's the drainies and the winklepickers," suggested George.

"But he's not wearing any," countered Paul.

"That's what I mean, it's the drainies and the winklepickers...they're missing. But I wouldn't go in for them, Brian. Not if I was you. Better you just stick to the leather jacket and polo-neck sweater...they're dead gear."

"Shall we begin, then, Mr Epstein?" It was Albert Marrion, the photographer. He normally specialised in weddings, kids, and family groups. Scruffy-looking beatnik groups weren't at all his cup of tea. So this was most definitely going to be a one-off.

"Pete? Neil? How are we doing?" Brian called.

"Almost ready, Brian," Pete Best yelled over his shoulder.

"Just another minute or so, Mr Epstein," echoed Neil Aspinall. "Just setting-up Pete's snare drum, now."

"Where would you like 'the boys' to stand, Mr Marrion?"

"Over there, against the wall, on that little stage, guitars in hand, if you please. Then I'll just snap off a roll or two."

"Well, boys," beamed Brian, "let's hope we see the fruit of today's labours gracing the front pages of next week's issue of *Mersey Beat*."

"Well, I filled-in all my voting forms. How about you, Pauly?"

"Another lot tonight, John. Then I'll have them all finished."

"Vote early and often, that's the ticket. At least, that's the way it is in Liddypool. Democracy, I think they call it elsewhere." John fluttered his eyelids.

"But we still have to watch out for all them other groups cheating, you know," added George, thoughtfully. "They're all untrustworthy swines, the whole lot of them, especially that Rory and his hundreds of Hurricanes. And I know for a fact, Gerry's got every single one of his Pacemakers, and all their families and friends, all filling-in forms like mad. We'll be bloody lucky even to get a look in, we will."

"He never bloody walks alone, that one, does he?" sniffed Paul.

"Does he, heck. But you are, all, of course, all forgetting that the saintly Bill Harry is one of my oldest and closest and dearest friends. I say no more," said John, smiling, serenely.

"Gentlemen, if you're ready. You. John, is it? Over there, please. Thank you. And you. Paul, is it? What sort of guitar is that, then?"

"It's a bass guitar, mister. A Hofner I bought in Germany."

"Looks more like a violin, if you ask me." The photographer carried on fussing around Paul with his light meter. "Okay. Good. Excellent."

"Mine's a Rickenbacker," drawled John, narrowing his eyes.

"Excuse me?" said Albert Marrion, suddenly caused to refocus upon the Beatle that was giving the most trouble. "A what?"

"A Rick-en-back-er...made from an old German biplane."

"Clever people, those Jerries," sniffed the photographer. "Made marvellous cameras before the war. Good. Hold it up then. Thank you. That's the ticket."

"George?" Brian asked, quietly.

"Yes, 'Eppy'?"

"Tell me, what does 'gear' mean?"

CHAPTER TWENTY-ONE

In From The Cold

"How much? You must be off your head, Mr Epstein." Tony Sheridan was shouting. The negotiations, he'd thought would be no more than a formality, were going nowhere. "Five hundred Deutsche Marks per person, per week? Even I won't be getting that much. And, however much you think The Beatles might've improved, they're not worth that."

"They are to me, Mr Sheridan, and to all the promoters in Liverpool. They're the biggest attraction of their kind in north-west England, fans line up for hours to see them. I'm certain they'd prove a very sound investment for Herr Eckhorn."

Peter Eckhorn, owner of Hamburg's famed Top Ten Club, understood English perfectly, but he preferred that Tony Sheridan, his club's resident singer and his partner on this expedition to hire the best Liverpool groups available, did all the negotiating with the Britishers.

Tony Sheridan repeated the amount his boss was prepared to pay for The Beatles to play a six-week season at the Top Ten Club. "Four hundred Deutsche Marks, a week, is our final offer, Mr Epstein."

Brian Epstein moved his desk diary a fraction, but said nothing. Tony Sheridan glanced at his boss. "Okay, four hundred and fifty." Brian Epstein still didn't respond. "No? So you're going to pass up a contract at the best beat club in Hamburg for a lousy fifty Marks per soddin' Beatle?"

"No, Mr Sheridan, but it appears you are."

Peter Eckhorn coughed. "Entschuldigen Sie mich, bitte, Herr Epstein. Please. In the past, Tony, here, was very good for The Beatles. And now, proudly you tell me Polydor are to release, here in England, the record Tony and The Beatles, in Hamburg, recorded. The Top Ten Club was also very good for The Beatles. I, also, was very good for The Beatles. I made sure for them to keep out of trouble. At one time, I even used my name for Peter und Paul to be released from the police station. We're both businessmen, Herr Epstein. We know how the world turns round. I have offered you more than I planned. Will you now reconsider, please, and let The Beatles come to Hamburg?"

"I'd be glad to, Herr Eckhorn, for two thousand Deutsche Marks, a week."

Tony Sheridan butted in. "When the lads told me they had a new manager and we should deal with you, I was glad for them. It meant they were going places, but this is nothing but daylight robbery."

"It would be, Mr Sheridan, if I let them play for less. And as you weren't convinced of that at last night's 'Boxing Night Ball', please let me invite you to be my guests tonight at 'The Beatles' Christmas Party' at the Cavern. Maybe that'll help you decide."

Tony Sheridan looked fit to burst. He turned to Peter Eckhorn, but his boss simply shook his head. "Es hat keinen Zweck, weiter darüber zu diskutieren," he said, under his breath. The singer nodded, stood up, and buttoned his coat. He glared at The Beatles' manager. "Thanks, but no thanks, Mr Epstein. And do remember it says: 'Tony Sheridan *and* The Beatles' on the record label, not 'The Beatles'. So please excuse me when I say, fuck The Beatles' Christmas party. Fuck the Cavern. And fuck you."

"Danke schön, Herr Epstein." Peter Eckhorn said, getting up from his chair. "Obwohl es nichts zu danken gibt. Guten Tag!"

"OH, DIRTY MAGGIE Mae, they have taken her away and she won't walk down snowy Lime Street anymore. Oh, the judge he..."

"Shurrup, John," yelled Neil Aspinall. "I'm trying to concentrate up front, here. It's like trying to see through a bloody blizzard, it is."

"That's because it is a blizzard, Neil," yelled George Harrison. "It's bloody f-f-freezin' back here, it is. Isn't there any more heat?"

"Just cuddle up and shurrup, will you. I'm doing me best."

"Oh, driver Nelly Mae, he has lost his bleedin' way and he won't get down to London, New Year's Day..."

"Bloody shurrup, will yer, John. Or you drive," Neil shouted.

"Is that with or without his glasses on?" asked Paul.

"Where the fook we going to fellas?" yelled John.

"To London, Johnny, for our audition with Decca."

"Whose turn is it to lie on top?"

"Mine, you bugger. Shove over."

"I'll be glad when I've had enough of this."

"Me and all. It's all right for some, though, isn't it? 'Eppy' went by train. Probably had his breakfast and dinner on it, too, lucky swine."

"Want another one of me cheese butties, Johnny?"

"No, ta, George. It was good of yer mum to make them up for us. I'd have starved otherwise. Got a spare ciggy, have yer?"

"How long, now, Neil?" called out Pete.

"In all this snow, I don't bloody know, but we're just coming up to a place called Watford. So, an hour or two, maybe."

"Ten bloody hours of freezin' me bloody balls off. We better get a warm reception tomorrow or I'll start a bloody revolution, I will."

"I think I'd just settle for a hot of cup of tea, at the moment."

"Strike us a match will yer, I want to warm me hands up before I have another look at the Christmas card 'Eppy' sent me."

John pulled a crumpled envelope out of his coat pocket and eased out the card. "There's a bloody snow scene on this, as well. He must've known." He read the card out aloud in a posh voice, not unlike Brian Epstein's. " 'John'...hand-written in ink, mind you...'With all Good Wishes for Christmas and the New Year'. Then, in brackets, 'Especially January 1st. Brian Epstein, 197 Queens Drive, Liverpool 15'." He paused. "It's lovely, just like a poem by a man named Lear."

"We all got one," drawled George. "Mine's still on the mantelpiece, at home."

"Ah," said John, "but I bet you didn't get any kisses on yours."

BRIAN EPSTEIN was working himself up into a red-faced fit for the benefit of The Beatles. "This is intolerable behaviour. We shouldn't have to put up with this sort of thing. It's highly un-professional and an obvious slight, because we come from Liverpool." He had to do something about the nerves inside the little waiting room at Decca's West Hampstead recording studio. Losing his temper was as good a solution as any. He consulted his wristwatch, again, but it still stubbornly pointed to the fact that Mike Smith, the young A&R man who'd be supervising the audition, was very, very late. "And to think that I treated him so very well when he came up to see us."

"Sorry I'm late. I was out all-night at a New Year's Eve party." Mike Smith tumbled into the room, looking very much the worse for wear. "I hope someone's been looking after you, but I've got to get an Alka-Seltzer or I'll die. Back in a minute, then we can get started. Why don't you take yourselves and your equipment into Studio Number Three, I'll be right in."

Brian Epstein was about to say something withering, but by the time he'd marshalled his thoughts, the door to the main studio corridor had closed on Mike Smith. So he did what he always did at such moments, he shot his cuffs and put his best foot forward. "Right, gentlemen, let's all go in, shall we?' He picked up his briefcase and led the way. The recording studio was much larger than they'd expected and they stood for a moment, look-ing around, silently, as if in a church. Then the guitars and drums came out of their carrying cases and the rubber covers came off the amplifiers.

Mike Smith came into the studio, took one look at the bat-tered state of the Beatles' amplifiers. "Blimey, they look almost as bad as I feel. Do they work? I'm not sure we can use them. I'll have to get an engineer in to have a look. Won't be a minute."

"Happy New Year, to you and all," said George, annoyed. "What does he mean we can't use them? What the bloody heck does he think we've been using for the last many years, tea chests and biscuit tins?"

"Let's just tune our guitars, fellas, and leave Doctor Franken-stein to his headache. Nel, go give Pete a hand, why don't you."

"Certainly, John, which one?"

"Very funny, if only you could drive half as well as you tell jokes, you might still have a job."

They waited and waited and waited. Then a technician in a white lab-coat finally arrived and took a quick look inside the back of their amplifiers. The man took off his spectacles, wiped them, took another look, shook his head, made a 'tutting' sound, and disappeared.

Brian Epstein did his best to fill the vacuum. "While we're waiting, boys. Let me say, just once again, that the songs I've selected for you today are designed to demonstrate every facet of your talent to the people at Decca. Your singing, your playing, and of course, your song-writing ability. I'd like to think I've specifically chosen those…"

He was cut short by a voice from the control room. "Hello. Hello, in there. We're going to have to ask you to plug your guitars directly into a set of studio speakers. Your amplifiers are unusable for recording purposes. They probably need new valves and the speakers may be blown. Won't be a minute. Then we'll be recording live to tape."

It was almost eleven o'clock by the time the engineers were satisfied with the arrangements for recording onto Decca's state-of-the-art, two-track, mono tape machines. Mike Smith pressed the talkback microphone button on his control panel. "Okay, gentlemen, those levels will have to do for now. We'll record, as many songs as we can do in the time we have left, which, will be, approximately, one hour. Red light on, please. Thank you. Tape rolling."

Paul McCartney took a deep breath and prepared to sing a song he'd written with John, called, 'Like Dreamers Do'. He swallowed his nerves, nodded, and George Harrison slid straight into the song's two-bar intro. A slick sequence of four pairs of chords, rising chromatically to the point where Paul would normally lean into the microphone and sing that he'd just seen the girl of his dreams. But the only sound that came from out of Paul's mouth was a strangled croak. He coughed and massaged his throat. "Er, sorry there, Mr Engineer, sir, can I…can I, er, start again?"

"Don't strangle yourself, Pauly," John muttered. "It's hard enough as it is to find a good bass player."

"Just, carry on, please," Mike Smith's voice boomed-out from the studio speakers. "We'll tell you when you to stop."

"Er, Sorry, there, fellas. Okay, George, let's try it again."

George, his eyes glued to the neck of his guitar, nodded and launched straight into the complex run of opening chords. Paul hit his bass guitar strings, sharply and confidently, nerves all gone now, and sang as sweetly and as imploringly as ever he'd done, his voice rising and falling theatrically like a seasoned professional singer. Pete tapped out all eight beats on the ride cymbal, snapped a simple repeat pattern on the snare. John, eyes narrowed in concentration, smoothed and filled the spaces in between with the characteristic bright-sounding chords of his beloved Rickenbacker. Until at last George repeated the run of chords he'd opened the song with, topped off by his favourite 'Jim Gretty' chord.

"Right, thank you. Let's move straight on to the next one."

The Beatles looked at one another. There was no applause, no shouts or screams, nothing but the echoing silence from the control room and a sudden, "Tape rolling" from out of nowhere. Welcome to the big time.

John Lennon took a deep breath, stepped up to the microphone, and he and the other Beatles threw themselves into 'Money'. The pace was a little faster than usual, but they were starting to rock now, eager to throw off their nerves and show Decca Records just what they could do if given half the chance.

"Okay. A little fast, let's just move on to the next one."

John stepped back, yielded the microphone to Paul, and almost immediately heard, "Tape rolling." His heart still beating fast, he nodded to Paul and George, then at Pete, and they all counted-in together.

Up in the control room, Brian Epstein heard the first notes of 'Till There Was You', a particular song favourite of his from *The Music Man*, and he began to relax. It was all starting to go rather well. He waved his finger in what he imagined was the correct tempo and very quietly tapped his feet as Paul took a breather and George went into the guitar solo. "Bloody hell," Neil whispered, as he heard George's fingers slow and seem to stick.

Down in the studio, George grimaced and began to sweat as his usually sweet little solo soured and fell apart. Paul's eyes fluttered in anguish, John swallowed hard, Pete kept tapping away, and somehow The Beatles managed to get through to the end.

"Thank you. Next. Tape rolling."

Brian Epstein consulted his list. Next up was a novelty number to be sung by George Harrison, 'The Sheik of Araby'. A song made popular by another one of his favourites, the Cockney singer, Joe Brown. He'd spent considerable time working out the exact order of the first four audition numbers. First, a Lennon-McCartney original composition, then an up-tempo rock and roll number, followed by a popular show tune, and then a novelty number. The people at Decca couldn't help but be impressed by the group's versatility as all-round entertainers. The remaining ten or eleven songs in the audition would merely add to that first, successful impression. "Yes," he said to himself, "things were beginning to come together nicely." Smiling, he glanced across at Neil Aspinall and was disconcerted to see that The Beatles' road manager was looking very worried.

"They're as nervous as hell in there, Brian," whispered Neil. "I've never ever seen them like this before. I'm sure that red light thingy in there must be bothering them, couldn't they just switch it off or something?"

Mike Smith, overhearing the conversation, turned and looked over his shoulder and said, curtly, "No, we can't. The red light is there to stop people from entering the studio while a recording session is in progress. It's standard procedure throughout the entire industry."

Brian Epstein didn't like being chastised, at the best of times, but he nodded graciously and mouthed the words, 'thank you'. But once Mike Smith had turned back to his mixing console, he glared pointedly at Neil Aspinall and shook his head for him to be silent. When The Beatles had completed the next couple of songs with what even he had increasingly begun to feel was less than their usual confidence and vibrancy, he cleared his throat and spoke up. He was, after all, the manager and managers should at least attempt to manage during times of difficulty.

"Excuse me, Mike, could I possibly speak to them, in there?"

"Certainly, if you think it'll help. Just press the talkback button, there, and speak clearly into that microphone."

"John?" Brian Epstein's voice boomed around the studio walls. All the Beatles looked up in surprise. "John, you seemed just a little breathless on 'Memphis, Tennessee'. Perhaps you should just take a moment and take some deep breaths before you start the next song."

John Lennon exploded. "When I want your advice on how to sing a song, Brian, I'll bloody well ask for it. Now, if you don't mind, I've got an audition to do. So just shurrup, will yer." John turned his back on the control room and picked out random notes and chords that he pulled into a twanging discord with his guitar's 'Bigsby' vibrato arm. "Right, fellas, time for some rock-a-throwing rock-a-billy."

Brian Epstein, embarrassed beyond belief, ran from the control room, his face red, tears pricking at his eyes. The Beatles began bopping their way through Carl Perkins' 'Sure To Fall', John, quite indifferent to any pain he'd caused. And by the time Brian had regained enough composure to return, half-an-hour later, the audition was all but at an end. The boys had just finished 'Besame Mucho' and were about to launch into their final number, 'Searchin'. "Tape rolling." And suddenly it was all over.

Mike Smith switched off the red light over the studio door and called everyone up into the control room to listen to the playback. Dazed, they all sat where they could, or leaned against something, and listened to the audition in its entirety on the big control room speakers. It didn't sound too bad, at all. Fifteen songs recorded in little more than an hour. Even Mike Smith, fingers tapping up and down on the control desk, seemed pleased with the results. Playback over, the young Decca A&R man thanked them all, profusely, for coming down to London. Then he quickly ushered everyone out into the lobby, apologising that he was running way behind schedule and had to set up for another audition. He shook everyone's hand—even Neil's— and assured everyone that it'd been a fine audition, one of the very best. Then he shook Brian's hand again and said that he should expect to hear from Decca in the very near future.

Then The Beatles found themselves, back out in the cold.

"Well, what do yer think?"

"I think we did alright, don't you? It sounded OK."

"I messed me damn solos up, more than once. Sorry, there, fellas."

"Well, it sounded great from back where I was sitting."

"Neil, what'd you think?"

"A good session, John, but a little bit, er, sticky, here and there."

"Well, I think you all did marvellously," Brian interjected, effusively. "I think it's all now a mere formality. It'll probably take a few days for everything to go through all the proper channels at Decca, so we should have an official offer from them in a week or two, at the most."

"We could've all done much better than we did, Brian," said John, pointedly. "Me, especially, but maybe you're right and it wasn't too bad, and I'm worrying too much, and it'll all come out right in the wash. It bloody better, anyway."

"THREEPENCE, PLEASE."

"No, I want three copies, please, mister. If you can possibly spare them, that is. We want one each."

"Alright, then, ninepence, altogether."

"Look at that bloody headline, fellas. 'Beatles Top Poll!'"

"We'll have none of that sort of talk, in here, if you please."

John Lennon looked at the other two Beatles, then back at the newsagent who was glaring at him from behind the safety of his shop counter. John grinned, sweetly. "We're The Beatles, mister, and we've just come top of the *Mersey Beat* Popularity Poll. See. It says so, there, in big black letters, 'Beatles Top Poll!'"

"I don't care who the bloomin' heck you are or what it says in that rag of a paper, we'll have none of that dirty talk in my shop, thank you."

"You're bloody lucky we paid you for the papers, you silly old sod. We usually just pinch them."

"Right. That's it. Gerroff out of it, the lot of yers, before I call the police."

"Hey, come on, John. There's never any winning with his sort. He thinks he owns the news and it's his job to guard the public's morals."

"Yeah. And I bet he's the first one to look for all the dirty bits in the *News of the World*, on a Sunday."

"Oh, bloody hell, Bill Harry's only gone and spelt my name wrong again. Look at it. 'Paul McArtrey'. What's wrong with him?"

"Hey, stop complaining, you. We came top of the poll, didn't we? And that picture of us looks pretty good."

"It's the only name I got," sniffed Paul. "But, yeah, you're right. That Albert Marrion did all right for us, didn't he?"

"Our guitars have come out nice," said George, holding his copy of *Mersey Beat* up so he could examine the details more closely. "They're very different looking, like, but they go together quite well in the photo. Means they must look good on stage, too. Never thought of that before."

"Yeah," said Paul. "Funny though, isn't it, the way the photo's come out on the front cover? The three of us on one side and Pete over on the other, all by himself."

"I think his drumming let us down badly, at Decca," said John, tersely. "It was all over the place. Either too bloody slow or too bloody fast. I didn't know whether I was coming or going, half the time."

"Yeah," said George, slowly. "I'm not blaming him for everything, like, but I didn't feel too good about what he was doing back there."

"Him and bloody 'Eppy', it's a wonder we got through it, at all. I don't want 'Eppy' picking our bloody music for us, ever again, that's for sure. I'll listen to the rest of it, because I still think he can help get us to where we're going, but I'll be watching him a lot more closely, in future."

"Yeah," said George. "I think we should watch both of them, more closely, from now on. Musically speaking, that is."

"HEY 'OOP, SAM, I've just had this Jerry fella on the telephone asking to speak to The Leach Organisation. He read the name on one of your posters, like, which is how he came to call me here at 'the Tower'. Hold on a minute." Tom McCardle, manager of the New Brighton Tower, took a big white handkerchief out of his trouser pocket and blew his nose; long and loudly. "Sorry about that, Sam. Hope I didn't blow your bloody ear off. Anyroad, this bloke...Fisher, I think he said his name was...says he wants to talk to someone about hiring The Beatles for this club of his, back in Hamburg, Germany. I don't know anything about your dealings with the lads, like, but I told him you'd be here tonight. So, him and this mate of his are going to pop in and see you and The Beatles, at the show. Okay?"

"Right, thanks, Tom. But it's nothing to do with me. They've gone and got themselves a new manager. Fella, called Epstein, who owns all them NEMS record shops in Liverpool."

"Jewish, is he then? Clever lads. It always helps having one of them sort looking after your money. I mean, look at Mecca Ballrooms and all their success. See you tonight then, Sam. Bye."

Sam Leach put the phone down. Should he call Brian Epstein and tell him there were a couple of Germans, in town, looking for him? No, best let everything run its own course. After all, he wasn't in the running anymore, was he? He'd help out when he could, like, but Brian Epstein could do his own managing from now on. He poured himself another cup of tea and waited for Terry McCann to arrive and drive him over to 'the Tower'.

"A COUPLE OF JERRIES, you say? All right, Sam. I'll have Jimmy look out for them and I'll let you know when they arrive. We'll probably hear the soddin' Panzers coming from a mile off, anyway."

It was a little after eight o'clock when a big white Cadillac bounced into the car park. Two blond-haired men in long black leather coats got out. They didn't wait in the queue, but marched straight into 'the Tower'.

"*Achtung! Achtung!*" shouted Jimmy Molloy. "It's the bleedin' Gestapo. And what the fuck's that they were driving?"

The two Germans entered the foyer. Terry and Jimmy, standing side by side, at the foot of the stairs, nodded an acknowledgement, and waited to be approached. "Careful," said

Terry, out the side of his mouth. "Watch out for the little one, looks like he could be a bit handy, moves like a boxer."

"Gotcha," sniffed Jimmy, having made much the same appraisal, himself. "Not a good time to remind them we won the War, then, eh?"

The taller one, of the two Germans, spoke first. "Good evening, gentlemen. Is one of you, by any chance, Mr Sam Leach?"

"You're not a bleedin' Jerry," spluttered Jimmy Molloy.

"Nein, but I am," said the smaller one. "My namen ist Horst Fascher. So pleased, to be meeting you. A very interesting place, for a club, you have, with this grosse Tower, Herr Leach."

"No, Mr Leach is upstairs, Mr Fascher. My name's Terry McCann. This is my associate, Jimmy Molly. We work for Mr Leach. Very pleased to meet you." Terry smiled, but stood his ground, and waited.

"I'm Roy Young," the tall one said. "We're here to find the best talent in Liverpool. Get them to come play at the new Star-Club, that's opening in Hamburg. I spoke to a Mr McCardle about it, earlier."

"Yes, I know," said Terry McCann. "Follow me, please."

"NICE TO MEET YOU, Mr Fascher, but I'm not the one you need to talk to. Look, The Beatles will be along in a bit, why don't you both have a drink on me and watch the other groups until they arrive."

"Thank you, Herr Leach. Yes, I think we will wait for them."

The Beatles arrived an hour later.

"Horst! Bloody hell...what a surprise. What're you doing here? Hey, fellas, it's Horst Fascher, come to see us. How you doing?"

"Sehr gut, my friends. Very good." Horst Fascher beamed and stood up and embraced each Beatle in turn, looking at their faces, staring deep into their eyes as he did so.

Paul stood and awaited his hug, a big smile on his face. The friendship went all the way back to their very first visit to Hamburg. Horst Fascher, one of the most-feared men along the entire length of the Reeperbahn, had been chief bouncer for Bruno Koschmeider, owner of the Kaiserkeller club. An exfeatherweight boxer of fearsome renown, it was rumoured he'd once been convicted of manslaughter after killing a sailor in a street fight. The Beatles had all met up with him again, on their second visit, when Horst, having changed allegiance and clubs, had gone to work for Peter Eckhorn at the Top Ten Club. Horst Fascher was very definitely the one man every musician visiting Hamburg needed to call, friend. The dangers were just too great, otherwise. Paul didn't even want to think about how many times Horst had saved him and John and George and Pete from being duffed up—and in all likelihood from a lot worse, besides.

"Also, let me please introduce to you my friend, Roy Young. He is to play the piano at the new club that I, with my good friend, Herr Manfred Weissleder, on the Grosse Freiheit, in Hamburg, will soon make open. The Star-Club, it is to be called. And we are here today because we wish you to come and play for us, on the very first night that this club is opening...und for afterwards, also. It will make for us some very good fun and be like good old times, yes?"

"The Star-Club?" said Paul. "That's great, Horst. But we, er, have a proper manager, now. So, you've got to go talk to him about it."

"Yeah, Horst," said George. "We don't decide things, anymore."

"George's right, Horst," added John. "It's no longer up to us."

Horst Fascher smiled. "But we need not any manager between us. We shake hands, like always. Horst Fascher's word is good, yes?"

"Solid," said Paul, very quickly. "But, er, there won't be a problem, it's just a formality. You can go see him, tomorrow, if you like."

"I'M AFRAID it's completely out of the question, Herr Fascher. I must tell you, in all fairness, that I'm still in negotiations with Herr Eckhorn. 'The boys' have all but given their word they'll play for him, at the Top Ten Club, when they return to Hamburg." Brian Epstein clasped his hands together and smiled, his face one of regret.

The man in the leather coat and close-cropped blond hair nodded, slowly, turned his head, and burst into a torrent of German, which had the other visitor, an English musician by all accounts, exiting the room without even a by-your-leave. The German turned to him, again, and smiled. And all of a sudden he was enormously glad there was a large desk standing between him and his rather un-gentlemanly guest.

"Herr Epstein, maybe you not understand my not so good English. Excuse me, please. But if I may say now to you the same as I would to someone in Hamburg speak?" He paused. Smiled again. "There will be no Top Ten Club...if The Beatles do not come for to play in the Star-Club. You understand? There will be no place where The Beatles can play...live. I hope this is now made so clear?"

Brian Epstein understood all too clearly. Or thought he did.

"Perhaps I should talk to The Beatles about this, Herr Fascher." He consulted his diary, looked up, and tried hard not to swallow. "Could you make another meeting on Monday? Say, at eleven o'clock?"

When Herr Horst Fascher returned two days later, at eleven o'clock, on the dot, he was met at the front door of NEMS, by Beryl Adams, Brian's personal secretary, and ushered very, very quickly through the store and up the stairs to her boss's office.

"Herr Fascher, how very good of you to come. Is it too early for a Sherry? Some Schnapps to help keep out the cold? Or better yet, a malt whisky? Beryl, please be so good as to take Herr Fascher's coat. Good. Thank you. And no interruptions, please."

He poured a large measure of single malt for his guest and a small Sherry for himself—all the while trying to keep his hand from shaking. He handed the cut-glass tumbler to the German and sat down.

"I spoke to 'the boys', who say, 'Hello, again', by the way, and they all tell me that when Horst Fascher says something will happen, it most definitely does. Which means we can all be assured that the Star-Club, your new venture with Herr Manfred Weissleder, will be a huge success when it opens this coming April." He sipped his Sherry, looked up, and smiled. "And so as I've yet to receive a firm offer from Herr Eckhorn and the Top

Ten Club, I feel it's in the best interests of The Beatles and all concerned for me to now open discussions with you."

Horst Fascher took a sip of his malt whisky and nodded his approval. "I understand that you asked a fee of 500DM for each Beatle. A total of two thousand Deutsche Marks for each week they play."

Brian Epstein was shocked Horst Fascher knew the exact figures. He hadn't even discussed the numbers with The Beatles. But he was catching on to Hamburg ways, very quickly. So he simply smiled and gave a short curt nod.

"This is acceptable to us," said Horst Fascher, nodding agreement. "And I am also, to give you this, from Herr Weissleder, so we do not misunderstand each other, ever again." He took a white envelope from his inside coat pocket, leaned forward, and placed it on top of Brian Epstein's desk diary. Brian Epstein looked at it, unsure of quite what to do. Horst Fascher nodded. "It is, how you say, behind the table?"

"I think you must mean 'under the table', Herr Fascher," Brian Epstein said, very matter-of-factly. "But look, please, this sort of thing is totally unnecessary." He tentatively pulled the envelope towards him and slowly opened it. Inside, was a single, one thousand Deutsche Mark note. He looked up, the barest hint of surprise upon his face.

Horst Fascher raised his glass in salute. "For this one time, Herr Epstein. Just between good friends. To say, thank you."

"Yes, I think we're beginning to understand one another, perfectly, Herr Fascher," said Brian Epstein, raising his glass. "Danke schön."

"OKAY, 'EPPY', where do I sign then?"

"There, John, across the postage stamp at the bottom of the contract," said Brian Epstein. "Where it says, 'SIGNED by the said JOHN WINSTON LENNON in the presence of'. Then, Alistair, acting as witness to the contract, will add his signature next to yours."

"A six-penny stamp doesn't seem quite important enough, though, does it?" said George, getting ready to sign.

"Better than getting a four-penny one, any day of the week," said John. "But it's the bit that says, 'IN WITNESS whereof the parties hereto have hereunto set their hands this day and year first before written' that gets me. I've read it hundreds of times and I still don't understand a bloody word. Is it all like that, 'Eppy'? Or is any of it written in English?"

"It doesn't seem right to be putting your signature across Her Majesty's face, does it?" said Paul. "But if it makes it official?"

"It does, Paul," offered Alistair Taylor. "Once you've appended your signature over the postage stamp, the contract will stand up in any court of law."

"There you are then," said Paul, signing with a well-practised flourish, 'James Paul McCartney'. "

"And last, but not least. Pete, if you please," purred Alistair Taylor, sliding the contract across the meeting-room table. "Just there, where it says, 'the said PETER RANDOLPH BEST'."

Pete Best finished signing. Alistair Taylor gathered up the contract and handed it to Brian Epstein for his signature. Brian demurred. "You just go ahead and witness mine, as well, Alistair. I'll do it later. I think now's the perfect time for champagne."

Brian turned to the room, "Gentlemen," he said, raising his glass. "Could there be anything more important than this? We have signed *our* contract. And while we still await word from Decca, about *your* recording contract with *them*, I'm sure it's all simply a question of red tape and it will all be agreeably settled within a few more days. You are *Mersey Beat* Poll Winners. 'My Bonnie' by Tony Sheridan *and* The Beatles has had its official British release on the Polydor label. We have an audition lined up for you, with BBC Radio, on the 12th of February. We also have a signed contract for you to be the stars...at a substantially increased fee, I may add...at the opening of the fabulous, new Star-Club, in Hamburg. Where, I am reliably informed, by Herr Horst Fascher, they are also looking to book such recording luminaries as Gene Vincent, Ray Charles, and Little Richard."

"Gene Vincent? Fookin' hell. Oh, excuse me, 'Eppy'. But, I mean to say, we're talking, Gene bloody Vincent, here."

"Ray Charles? That's dead good, an' all, that is."

"And Little Richard? *Aaaah-wop...bop-aah-wop! Whooooooo!*"

BRIAN EPSTEIN placed both hands flat on top of his desk and stared at the envelope lying on the leather-edged blotter.

Postmarked London SE1. The company's name and address printed in raised ink—thermography, he remembered it was called—all very impressive and appropriate. The letter was one of the most important of his life—the herald of so many good things yet to come. It was most certainly the precursor to everyone's dreams coming true and, as such, was most definitely a moment to savour.

He noted the date of the postmark. Saw it had taken two days for the letter to get to Liverpool—the delay obviously due to the atrocious weather. But now the long days and even longer weeks of waiting were finally over. There was no need for him to worry any further.

He reached for the letter-opener on his desk, gently inserted it under the sealed flap, and carefully sliced open the top of the envelope. He removed the single sheet from inside, the crack of the bonded paper sounding preternaturally loud. He glanced at The Decca Record Company Limited logo—also printed in raised ink—smiled, and read the letter. Then he read it through again—the hand holding the letter starting to shake.

He simply couldn't believe his eyes. But there it was in black and white. A letter dictated to, and typed by, the wretched man's secretary. All very formal and short and to the point, 'Dear Mr Epstein, Mr Rowe regrets to inform you that...'

He stood up, his throat suddenly very, very dry, and he went over to the credenza and poured himself a large glass of water and drank it all. Then he poured himself a second glass and drank that down, too. After which, he sat down at his desk again and dutifully recorded the event in his desk diary—*Wednesday, January 31, 1962. Decca Record Co. Ltd. officially rejects The Beatles*—the heavy snow falling silently outside the window only adding to the growing chill in his heart.

CHAPTER TWENTY-TWO

Dancing in The Street

"Don't know about all this snow, but attendance is so bad Sam's thinking of cutting back. The only time people bother to get their arses across the Mersey is when them Beatle friends of yours are playing."

Spike blew on his hands to keep warm. "They're not exactly what I call friends, Jimmy. I know them enough to say 'hello', like, because of that time I helped Sam down in London. Other than that, they keep very much to themselves."

"Yeah, they are a bit like a gang, aren't they...safer that way, I suppose." He stamped his feet. "Alright, let's get back inside. I'll buy you a whisky." Jimmy Molloy suddenly laughed. "Here, who'd have thought it, you and me off to see *South Pacific*?"

"Yeah, thanks a bunch, there, Jimmy."

"I know, I can't stand all that bleedin' 'happy-happy-talk' either, but if it makes Thelma go all soft and teary-eyed and I get a bit of a cuddle out of it, afterwards, then, me, I'm happy to happy-talk all night long, I am."

"So just because you don't want to go see it on your own, you get Thelma to ask her best friend, Sandra, which means, I've got to go, as well."

"Well, I'd feel dead soppy going, by myself, wouldn't I? I know Thelma and me are a bit more serious about courting than you and Sandra, but there are limits. Anyway, it'll be more of a lark with the four of us."

"*South Pacific*? Couldn't you have picked something else?"

"It's what the girls want, Spikey. They're fed up with all the snow, too, you know. So a couple of hours on a tropical island will do them a world of good. Anyway, sunshine, if you're coming with us you'll have to smarten up a bit. Can't have you turning up in that grotty leather jacket of yours. You'd put the mockers on the evening before it even started. Now, I know you're stashing all your dosh away to buy a new guitar, so I've got something for you, next time I see you."

"What's that, Jimmy? The piano score to *South Pacific*, so I can sing along while the girls wash us right out of their hair?"

"You'll see, Spikey. Talking of which, that new haircut of yours looks a lot better, I must say. It's still a bit weird, mind you. You look just like one of them Beatles. I suppose your Sandra did it for you, did she? She told my Thelma, she loves you. And that can't be too bad, now, can it, Spikey? Your Sandra says she loves you."

JOHN LENNON stuck another throat lozenge into his mouth. "These Zubes play bloody havoc with the taste of the beer, but I can't do without them when I get all hoarse. They helped get me through tonight, though, I'm glad to say."

"We could've always got Rory Shtorm to fill in for you, again, like he did Thurshday night," Paul chuckled into his beer glass.

"I'll fill you in, any more of that," snapped John. "That was the first time I've had laryngitis. First time I ever missed a date."

"A week of firsts," said Sam Leach, stepping in quickly. He raised his glass. "To the opening of the first 'Beatle Club' in West Kirkby; to your first club-date in Manchester, last night; and to Brian, here, for earning his first commissions as official manager of The Beatles."

"Yeah, here's to our 'Eppy'."

"Yeah, sheers there, Brian."

"How does it feel, Brian?" asked Sam, cheerily, keeping everyone's attention on the flushed, but happy face of Brian Epstein.

"I love it, I do, if that's not too strong a word. And I really couldn't have done it all, without all your helpful advice. Thank you, Sam."

Brian Epstein raised his glass in salute. The celebratory 'pub crawl' was yet another first, another rite of passage, another sign he'd been accepted into the world of Beatles. They'd started at the Grapes, gone on to the White Star, then, as 'the boys' were still banned from Allan Williams' Blue Angel Club, had ended up at the 'Phil'. If nothing else, the camaraderie and constant banter had helped push Decca's rejection to the back of his mind. It still deeply hurt, but the drink helped dull the pain and for that brief respite he was grateful.

"Yesh," said Paul, swaying. "You're a good man, Sham Leash. You've been helping our friend, Horsh, too, haven't you?"

"Helped find him a ballroom for his Star-Club auditions, is all. I'm not daft, you know. I knew right away I'd rather have that bugger as friend, than as an enemy."

"Even zo you von ze War," sniggered John, throwing his hand up in a mock-Nazi salute. "Ve huf ways uf making you our frendz. Or ve shoot you dead."

"You…" Paul tried to poke Sam's shoulder, but swayed and missed. "You…you're always helping shum-one, you are, Sham." Paul's head went in one direction, while his eyes went the other.

"And I think I best help you into a taxi, Mr McCartney. Get you home," said Sam steering him gently towards the pub door.

"Then the real men can get on with some serious drinking," shouted John, popping another Zube lozenge into his mouth.

When Sam Leach returned, John was telling Brian about Ringo Starr, The Hurricane's drummer. "He flew out to Hamburg, to back Tony Sheridan, at the Top Ten, for Peter Eckhorn, back in December, but he's come straight back home. He couldn't put up with Sheridan, apparently, even for thirty quid a week, a free flat, and a car. He says Tony Sheridan's a real nutcase, which is the same as what you said, 'Eppy'. It's pleased, our Rory, no end, Ringo re-joining the group."

"That's right," agreed Sam, downing his whisky. "Rory and The Hurricanes just don't sound the same, without our own little Richard banging up a storm on his drums."

"Ha-ha-ha," John, deadpanned. "A joke. Sam said, a joke."

"I've got another one for you," said Sam. "That is, if you real men are still serious about doing some real serious drinking?"

"Us men are still very serious about it, aren't we, 'Eppy'?" said John, saluting like an army private. Brian, still not wanting to be left out of anything, smiled and nodded enthusiastically.

"Right then, we're off to The Joker's," said Sam, smiling evilly. "I trust you're still in a fit state to drive, Mr Epstein?"

Brian Epstein blinked, unsure if Sam was being serious or not. "I'll have you know, I can drive as well as you, Sam Leach."

"That's what he's worried about," scoffed John. "He can't drive."

They all clambered into Brian's Zephyr Zodiac and drove over to Edge Lane—John, doing non-stop 'Goon' impressions, all the way.

"Tell me, Sam," said Brian, on his third brandy and starting to slur his words ever so slightly. "It's way past midnight; almost one-thirty. So, why do the police allow the club to serve drinks, so late?"

Sam Leach grinned, leaned over to a group of people on the next table, tapped one of them on the arm, and introduced Brian to several senior Liverpool police detectives. Once Brian had regained his composure, Sam pointed to the shadowy figure in the far corner of the club. "And that big black gentleman sitting over there by the fire, surrounded by all those other big black gentlemen, is the other reason." Sam leaned in close. "That's Joker, himself, in the flesh, so to speak. Holds cards on half of Liverpool, he does, and when he plays he doesn't ever play to lose."

"How fascinating," said Brian, "I had no idea there was such a dark side to Liverpool."

Sam Leach bit his tongue, hard, ordered another round of drinks, and after another hour or so of aimless gossip and dedicated drinking, Brian's head began to drop and he rested his eyes for minutes at a time. John swirled his brandy around in his glass. "You know, Sam, I could kill him, sometimes, but he's alright, is our 'Eppy'. His heart's, definitely, in the right place."

"His wallet is, too," Sam chuckled.

John pulled a face. "No. He just wants the best for us. He's even had this little Jewish tailor of his, over in Birkenhead, measure us up for some posh new suits. And I know I'm going to feel like a bloody performing-seal, dressed in a grey-tweed suit, like, but if 'Eppy' thinks it'll help get us into better places then I'm all for it, as are the others."

"Well, when you're rich and famous, and faraway from here, don't ever say I didn't take you to all the best places, John."

"Aldershot? The Joker's? How could I ever forget, Sam?"

"If you're not careful, Lennon, I'll make you pay. Anyway, you just rouse sleeping beauty, here, and I'll go settle the bill."

John gently shook Brian Epstein awake. "Come on, 'Eppy', it's time to go home. It's almost three o'clock. Wakey-wakey."

Brian started awake. Looked around in confusion, for a moment, then remembered where he was. He rubbed his eyes.

"Off to London again, next week, then, 'Eppy'?" asked John.

"Yes, John, I am," Brian said, yawning. "Tuesday's early morning train from Lime Street Station. The appointment's all been arranged."

"Right," said John, his nostrils flaring. "Just remember to give them buggers at Decca, a right good kick up the arse, from me."

BRIAN EPSTEIN was determined not to take 'No' for an answer, this time. It'd been less than a week since Decca had rejected The Beatles and now he was travelling down to London for a meeting he'd arranged with executives at the record company. He was utterly convinced they'd change their minds if only he had a chance to tell them all about the wild and ecstatic scenes he witnessed every time The Beatles played, in Liverpool.

He arrived at Decca's headquarters exactly at noon and was met by Dick Rowe, Decca's head of singles and A&R, and Sidney Beecher-Stevens, their sales manager. The two executives greeted him warmly and took him up to the seventh-floor of the building, to the company's very own executive club, 'the Albert Embankment'. He knew Decca was all too aware of the importance of NEMS to their record sales in the North. He knew, too, they'd probably try to handle him with kid gloves and soft soap. He didn't mind that. All he wanted was another chance.

And after a long, leisurely lunch, where the conversation touched upon everything but The Beatles, Dick Rowe ordered coffee and brandy for everyone and, at last, got down to business. Cigar in hand, he turned, and smiled. "Now about your boys. Not to mince words, Mr Epstein, but we don't like their sound. Groups are out. And four-piece groups, with guitarists, particularly, are finished. Save for The Shadows, of course, but they're already so very well established."

He couldn't believe what he was hearing or the fact they'd rejected him before he'd even had a chance to plead his case. "But...but in Liverpool, fans queue up for hours hoping to see The Beatles perform."

"Guitar groups are on their way out, Mr Epstein." Dick Rowe let the ash from his cigar drop into an oversize glass ashtray. "You'd be better off, by far, just sticking to what you do so very, very well."

He couldn't contain himself any longer. He pushed back his chair, felt his face flush, but this was no longer just about him, it was about 'the boys'. "Believe me, you're so very, very wrong. These boys are going to explode once they appear on television. They'll be bigger than The Shadows. One day they'll be bigger even than Elvis Presley."

Dick Rowe smiled. Why, he wondered, did people always reach for the impossible when searching for superlatives? He glanced across at Sidney Beecher-Stevens, raised an eyebrow, and waited while the young Liverpool businessman took some cooling sips of water. Then, as kindly as he could, he said, "Your boys just won't go, Mr Epstein. Believe me, we know about these things. You have a very nice record business in Liverpool, why not just stick to that and leave this side of the business to us?"

JIMMY MOLLOY gave Thelma a little nudge "That was my kind of film, that was," he said. "Much, much better than I expected."

Spike glanced at the traces of lipstick smears on Jimmy's cheek. "Yeah, what you saw of it, like." He looked up London Road, towards Sampson and Barlow's ballroom, site of Sam Leach's old Cassanova Club, and pulled up the collar of his jacket. He'd have much rather spent the evening listening to some real live beat music.

As if reading his mind, Jimmy leaned in towards him. "Now, now, Spikey, it's just one night out, for the girls." And with a big grin, he stuck out his chin so Thelma could use her handkerchief to wipe away all evidence of their kissing session. Job done, he clapped his hands. "Right, then, let's the four of us nip round the Lord Nelson for a quick drink, then it's Thelma and me off to

James Street for a slow train home."

With Sandra and Thelma sat at a table in the corner of the lounge, Spike and Jimmy ordered drinks from the bar. Jimmy turned to Spike. "You never know, Spikey, I might get lucky, tonight, play my cards right." He moved his eyebrows, up and down. "Know, what I mean?"

Spike shook his head, laughed, and reached for his drinks.

Jimmy laughed, too. "Here, another thing, that old black tweed jacket of mine looks so good on you, you might as well keep it."

Spike almost spilled his beer. "What? You don't mean that?"

"Course, I do. I'm yer mate, aren't I? Anyway, it doesn't fit any of me brothers, so it's yours." Jimmy Molly looked at him, hard. "For when the four of us are all out together, like, okay?"

Later that night, as they made their way to Lime Street Station, Sandra put her arm through Spike's and gently brushed her hand up and down the sleeve of his 'new' jacket. "Looks really good on you."

"Still can't believe Jimmy gave it me," said Spike. "Says I need to make the right impression when we all go out on a date, like."

Sandra nodded. "Well, he's right. It's important to us girls our fellas look smart. It makes us feel good, too." She giggled. "Oh, sorry, I didn't mean for it to come out sounding like that."

"Like what?"

"To suggest you normally look very scruffy, like."

"Cheeky monkey."

Sandra giggled and looked up at her Spike, her eyes sparkling. "You look really lovely, you do. I thought so the very first time I saw you. And I like the way you look. Lots. And I like you, too. Lots. It's just you look gear, now, as well. It's nice."

A tingling feeling welled up inside him and Spike felt fit to burst. This girl was wonderful every single moment. And before he knew it, he'd pulled her towards him and kissed her on the lips. And she kissed him, back, tentatively, at first, and then with real passion. Then she pulled away and looked up at him, her face radiant, shining.

Sandra felt so happy she could've danced in the street. When Spike stopped and kissed her, it was as if her whole body had quivered in response. She wanted to tell him right then and there how much she really loved him, but she just sighed and hugged him. And the two young lovers walked down Lime Street holding on to each other as if for dear life, lost to Liverpool, lost to the world.

They'd been walking arm-in-arm for but a few minutes, when a gang of Teds appeared out of nowhere and pushed past—one of them purposefully bumping into Spike. Sensing trouble, Sandra pulled Spike closer, kept her head down, and carried on walking. "Come on, Spike," she said, as calmly as she could, "or I'll miss my train."

Spike felt the tap on his shoulder and he let go of Sandra's arm and stepped forward and sideways, ducking down and away. He turned, his fists already coming up, but the Ted had moved back, out of reach, and stood taunting him. The other members of the gang, all milling around, further up the street, laughing and egging him on.

"Oh, fancy yourself as a bit of a boxer, do yers?" the Ted sneered. "What do yers think yer look like with that silly fookin' haircut?"

Spike, up on the balls of his feet, ready for anything, peered intently at the Ted. Fixing on the yob's greasy hair, pimply face, and dirty red bandana tied around his neck. "What's your trouble?" he snarled.

"You!" The Teddy Boy thrust out a finger at him. "Don't like yer fookin' hair." It was the Ted from 'the Tower' car park, the one who'd attacked the midget and gone for Sandra. The Ted hadn't recognised either of them, but it was all too much of a performance for the pimply sod just to be toying with them. The gang was out for blood.

"Come away, Spike," Sandra said, firmly. "Let it be."

"Ooh, yeah, let it be, Spike. Run away, run," taunted the Ted. And right on cue his gang took up the chant. "Run. Run. Run."

Spike turned to go and that's when the Ted ran at him. But he was ready for it and he threw his weight onto his right foot, swivelled back, left arm ready to block, right arm swinging up and round, and he hit the Ted, hard, on the chin, and knocked him clean off his feet. "Run!" he shouted to Sandra, but she'd already taken off her stiletto shoes to come to his aid. "Oh, hell," he said, gasping for breath. And he caught hold of her and propelled her down Lime Street in her stocking-feet. The angry chorus of howls and shouts behind them, giving wings to their heels.

They fled down the street, past St George's Hall, towards the station entrance. "I can't go on," cried Sandra. "I'm all out of puff." Then, like a knight in shining armour, a policeman in a black pointy helmet and raincoat stepped into view, up ahead. The Teds saw the policeman and skidded to a halt, milled around for a moment, and then slunk back into the night, yelling obscenities over their shoulders.

"You two young 'uns, all right, are you?" sniffed the copper. "Them louts giving you trouble, were they?"

"Yeah," said Spike, out of breath.

"Lucky, I came along, then," the policeman said, nodding.

"Very lucky," said Sandra, panting. "Thank you, officer."

"Evening," said the copper. "You two go safe, now." Then he walked off.

Spike looked at Sandra, then down at the ladders in both her nylons and her now very dusty and dirty feet. "Are you alright, San? Shall I carry you?"

"No, I'm okay," she said, quietly. "It's not the first time I've had to run for it. And knowing Liverpool it won't be the last."

"Come on," said Spike. "Let's see if the Punch and Judy is still open. A hot cup of tea would do us both good."

They ended up at Joe's Cafe. As they entered, Spike thought back to the time he was there with Harry Lightfoot. He shivered, looked round, and was startled to see three of The Beatles sitting at one of the far tables with Brian Epstein. "Funny, how lives overlap," he thought. They looked to be deep in conversation, but his eyes met with John Lennon's for an instant. John looked straight at him and turned away. John just cut him dead. The touch of Sandra's hand, on his, startled him, a second time.

"You alright, Spike?" she asked.

"Yeah, yeah, yeah. Thanks," he said, shaking his head. "It's just that...oh, never mind. Hey, I should be asking you that."

"Don't your friends want to know, then?" Sandra said softly.

"The Beatles, you mean?" Spike said, a little downcast.

"Yeah," Sandra said. "I saw them when we came in, but I don't think they saw you. They were too busy talking. Don't take it to heart. They may have troubles of their own. They didn't look too happy."

Spike chanced another look. It was true. John, Paul and George didn't look at all happy. Brian Epstein just looked miserable. Spike turned and looked at Sandra. Even after all she'd just been through, she still looked way beyond compare, really fab. He realised, right at that moment, he'd do anything for her, and always would. It must be real love, he said to himself. And he'd always thought love was just for squares. How very wrong he'd been. How very lucky he was.

He lit two cigarettes and handed one to her. "You know, when my dad died, I got so very angry with the world and everyone in it. I felt totally alone. At first, I tried to lose myself in electrical diagrams, technical stuff. Then when that didn't work out, I went in the opposite direction with fine art, drawing, painting." He looked down at his bruised knuckles—it was as if they belonged to somebody else. "I was searching for something, without ever knowing what it was I was searching for." He felt Sandra's hand in his and held onto it as if it were a lifeline. He looked into her eyes. "This music thing. Trying to play rock 'n' roll and rhythm-and-blues and stuff. I've never felt so alive or free, or so at home. It's as if I can do anything, go anywhere. Kansas City, Memphis, Tennessee...anywhere. All the anger just fades away."

"That's just how I feel when I'm dancing," Sandra said softly. "Free as a bird, without worries. That everything's going to be alright and I'll never get old, and that no one will ever hurt me ever again."

"They never will, if I'm with you, San."

"I know," she said, squeezing his hand.

" 'EPPY', you should try using that charm of yours to get us back into the Blue Angel, again. The bloody little Welshman's ban on us going there is playing hell with our social life. I love Joe's Cafe, but there's only so many times I can sit here or at the Punch and bloody Judy, waiting for you to come back from London. I need a proper place to drown me sorrows in."

"Yes, okay, John. I'll talk with Allan Williams for you."

"For us, 'Eppy', for all of us," John said, flatly.

"Yeah, Brian, it's where all the groups go after playing a gig," added Paul.

"So how did it go with Decca, Brian?" George asked, quietly.

Three pairs of eyes swivelled towards Brian Epstein like weathervanes catching the wind. "I'm afraid it's a flat, 'No', George."

"Oh, bloody hell, 'Eppy'," groaned John. "I thought you said…"

"But they did give me two reel-to-reel tapes of your audition to use as we see fit," Brian added quickly. "So I took them to Pye Records."

"And what did they say at Pye Records, Brian?" asked Paul.

"They said, 'No', Paul. Pye weren't interested. 'Old hat', they said." All three Beatles groaned. "So I went to Oriole Records."

"And?" John asked, curtly.

"I'm afraid they also said, 'No'. I'm so very sorry."

"Well, that's it, then, 'Eppy', isn't it? We're completely bloody buggered. EMI has turned us down, twice, already. So who the hell's left?" John groaned and buried his head in his hands. Then he looked up, amazed at the answer, it was so obvious. "I know, 'Eppy'," he said in a strangled voice. "You could try Woolworth's 'Embassy' label. We could always be the bloody bargain basement group people listen to on the cheap."

Everyone laughed and groaned. It was just too dreadful to contemplate.

"There is someone else." Brian said, taking a deep breath. "Next Tuesday, I'm going to see George Martin, head of EMI's Parlophone label. A music-publishing friend of his, Sid Colman, recommended me to him. Mr Colman's very interested in publishing your songs."

John Lennon and Paul McCartney's ears perked up at that; someone was actually interested in publishing their songs. That sounded good. Music publishing wasn't the same as recording, but it was a start. There had to be money in it, somewhere.

"Tell us more, 'Eppy'. Tell us more," said John.

"I haven't spoken to George Martin, yet, but his secretary sounded awfully nice." Brian Epstein smiled and, like a stage-magician pulling rabbits out of a hat, produced two 78-rpm acetate discs from the folds of his briefcase. He held up the two plain cardboard record sleeves. "I had them made from the audition tapes at the HMV record store on Oxford Street. Anyone can walk in and do it. The engineer, there, really liked your sound and he sent me up to the music publishers, Ardmore and Beechwood. Suddenly, it was as if I was in the right place at the right time, with people that would actually listen to your music for once. It was wonderful." He let out a sigh and smiled. "I've got a really good feeling about this one, boys. Really, I have."

"Well done, 'Eppy'," said John. "Parlophone, is it?"

"Parlophone?" said Paul. "But who's heard of them?"

"The man that buys the records for Woolworth's, probably," said George. And everyone laughed and rattled their spoons around the rims of their cups—anything, at all, to help relieve all the pent-up stress from all the waiting and waiting.

"You know, one day, those people at Decca will kick themselves for turning us down," said Paul, nodding, sagely.

"Yeah," agreed John. "I hope they all kick themselves to death." He pushed his chair back and stood up. "Excuse me, Gentlegerms. I'm off to the little boys room to make me mark."

On the way to the toilets John bumped into Spike making his way back to his table. "Hello, Spikey, lad. Didn't recognise you there for a moment without my glasses on. It must be that funny haircut of yours. Odd, but it somehow reminds me of me and George and Paul. I think I'm flattered." He grinned and peered at Spike a little more closely. "You all right, are you? Only you look a bit flushed, like."

"Yeah, okay, thanks, John. Only, Sandra and me just got jumped by a gang of Teds after coming out the pictures."

"You both, okay, are you?" John looked over at Sandra sitting patiently at the table. He smiled and gave her a little wave. "Nice looking little judy, you've got there, Spikey. Looks a bit like my Cyn, till she went and dyed her hair blonde."

"Yeah, we're okay, now, thanks, John. And you? Only I heard all the clattering and banging, like?"

"Oh, that. Our manager just did something right, for once. But as for you, you Welsh Goon, you take more care of yourself. See yer."

When John got back to his table, he said something to the others, and both Paul and George turned and waved at Spike and Sandra. Brian Epstein looked round, too, and smiled in their direction, not quite sure who he was smiling at or why, then he turned back to the three Beatles and they were all of them soon lost in conversation again.

THE LITTLE BLACK MORRIS MINOR trundled past the front of the Adelphi Hotel. Harry Lightfoot threw it a look, he'd been watching the place for days, but that 'watching' job was now all but over, thank God. He turned up Lime Street towards the station and had just reached London Road, when a rowdy gang of youngsters, Teddy Boys by the looks of them, ran out into the street in front of him. He cursed and swerved around them. "Bloody idiots." He'd just mow the buggers down next time.

He was tired. It was always that way after days and days of him 'watching', especially when the parties involved hardly ever showed themselves. He looked forward to the weekend. With a bit of luck, if the weather held, he could take his camera out to the docks and out along the estuary. He wanted to capture it before it was all gone, forever—allowed to rust and fall away to nothing—all in the name of progress. He reflected on the new two-and-a-quarter Rolleiflex camera he was thinking of buying. Not a Hasselblad, admittedly, but a bloody good camera, all the same.

Knowing how tired he was, he was extra careful with his driving. Last thing he wanted was to be pulled over by a patrolling Z-car or waved down by a copper with a torch. There were lots of his old friends on the Force that might find that funny, but there were a good few that wouldn't. He turned into his street. From the looks of it, there were only a few people, still up—watching the telly, probably. He pulled into the kerb, parked, and got out. Then he locked the car and, keys in hand, made for his front door.

"Hell's bells." He'd left his camera and flashgun in the boot. He turned and that's when he saw them closing in on him. Four or five darkies, all of them carrying something in their hands—chair-legs, coshes, lead-pipes, he couldn't be sure. Then he saw the glint of metal in the light of the street lamp and he knew they really meant business.

All he had on him were his keys and a ballpoint pen, in his pocket. He felt for the plastic cap, flicked it off, and slipped the barrel of the pen into his hand. Then he turned and ran along the street, banging and hammering on front doors. But it was late and, as he ran, he even noticed one or two lit windows suddenly switching to black.

They followed silently. There were no calls, no taunts, just the quiet pad of thick rubber-soled shoes and the hiss and rasp of their breathing. Suddenly, he turned and went for his two nearest attackers and punched one, hard in the face, raking his keys up and across the man's cheeks, then he kicked the other, hard in the shin. He heard a footfall, behind him, and jerked his elbow backwards, smashing something. Then he pumped his arm forward and stabbed the point of the Biro into another attacker's cheek.

He shifted balance, to try and kick out again, but he was hit low from behind and he felt himself start to fall. Someone hit him on the side of the head, just as his other leg was kicked out from under him, and he fell heavily to the ground. And for a full minute or two, the black-faced shapes blurred over him, beating at him again and again with their wooden clubs, like flies swarming around a bloody carcass.

A single word from out the darkness, little more than a grunt, made them all stop and step back. A tall thin black man stepped forward and shone a torch down onto the body curled-up on the ground. There was no expression on the man's face. He could've been a council inspector examining the drains. He leaned down, something flashing in the dim streetlight, and he waved whatever he had in his hand close to Harry Lightfoot's face. And as the bottle of smelling salts rudely pulled the private detective back to consciousness, the tall black man grunted again and one of his men rolled Harry Lightfoot over onto his back—the blood streaming from ex-copper's head and face, pooling black on the pavement.

Harry Lightfoot coughed, spluttered, groaned; the harsh gurgling noises in his throat sounding like a man about to drown in his own vomit. The tall black man leaned over, scoured his throat, and very carefully spat a yellow gob of spit down onto the ex-copper's face.

"Boss, he say, you no mess wid his business, not ever. 'Special wid people dat owe him money. You got dat, now, man?"

The message-bearer kicked Harry Lightfoot back into oblivion, flicked open a knife, leaned down and cut all the buttons from off the big man's raincoat—the blade drawing jagged shapes in the fabric. He sliced through the raincoat's belt and flicked open what remained of the coat. Then he cut the buttons from off the tweed jacket beneath, before slicing through the pullover, the shirt and tie, and the cotton vest underneath. Then he slowly dragged the knifepoint up across the now bared chest and neck until it hovered above one of Harry Lightfoot's eyes. The knife blade flashed in the night, leaving a fish-hook-shaped gash in the ex-copper's cheek. A cut to the bone that when it healed and scarred-over would always resemble a letter 'J'.

Battle Of The Bands

Brian Epstein arrived five minutes early for his appointment at the Manchester Square offices of EMI, Britain's biggest recording company. For once, he wasn't kept waiting, and was immediately shown to the office of Parlophone's head of Artists and Repertoire.

George Martin smiled, came round from behind his desk, and held out a hand. "Mr Epstein, I presume." Tall, elegant, distinguished looking, the man made a very positive first impression.

"Thank you for seeing me, Mr Martin. It's so very good of you to give up some of your valuable time."

"Sid Coleman suggested that I should. He's rather taken with one or two of the songs you played him." George Martin was very well spoken, his accent as polished and precise as Brian Epstein's own. He was educated, intelligent, and urbane, and quite unlike anyone The Beatles' manger had met in the music business—save for himself. George Martin smiled warmly. "The Beatles, isn't it? Why don't you tell me a little about them...and then let's have a listen, shall we?"

Brian Epstein thought it best not to mention that EMI's two other record divisions had already rejected The Beatles and he slipped effortlessly into his sales pitch. "The Beatles are a simply marvellous group, Mr Martin, and so very talented. They're absolutely huge in Liverpool. So I wouldn't be at all surprised if you told me you'd already heard of them." When George Martin demurred and gently shook his head, he continued on without missing a beat. "Well, I must say, that does surprise me."

It was a cheeky thing to say, but George Martin let it pass. It was common wisdom that nothing of any importance ever came out of the provinces—especially anything from 'up North'. So he steepled his fingers, leaned back in his chair, and waited to be won over.

"The boys are in demand all over Merseyside. Fans queue up for hours to see them at the Cavern Club, in Liverpool. At one venue, across the River Mersey, literally thousands of young people turn up, every Friday, to jive to their music. Yesterday, the group auditioned successfully for a BBC radio show, in Manchester, which will be recorded and broadcast in early March. So, as you can tell, even before hearing them, The Beatles really are beginning to go places."

Manchester? Yes, mused, George Martin. There was the famed Hallé Orchestra, as well as a fine radio orchestra, but like Liverpool it was about as far away from the centre of popular music as one could get. He smiled, noncommittally, as Brian Epstein handed him the acetates of The Beatles' Decca audition. He placed one of the discs on the turntable, set the playing arm, sat back, and waited to be charmed.

Brian Epstein leaned forward. "The recording could be better, of course. The boys don't come across fully, but they're a terrific group of individuals; bright, funny, and full of life. And it's not until you meet them, that you can really appreciate them for who they are."

George Martin listened, politely, to both discs and all fifteen songs, making comments at the end of each one, but in truth he wasn't too impressed. It was old stuff, mostly, with a few show tunes thrown in for good measure, plus one or two pleasant-sounding songs the group had purportedly written themselves. He did note that more than one group member sang lead vocal, which was unusual. They harmonised well and that was interesting. It was all a bit raw, but had a rather gritty quality, too. And that did intrigue him. He commented favourably on George's guitar playing, thought John's original song, 'Hello Little Girl' was catchy, and liked Paul's voice on 'Till There Was You'.

He glanced over at his secretary, Judy Lockhart-Smith, who he'd invited to sit in for the music portion of the meeting. She nodded and raised her eyebrows in appreciation. He smiled, but said nothing. It might be worth seeing these Beatles, at that. He didn't have anything to lose. Plus, he was looking for a pop singer or pop group to do at Parlophone what Norrie Paramour, Columbia's head of A&R, had done with Cliff Richard and The

Shadows. "Okay, Mr Epstein," he said, nodding his head slowly. "Bring these Beatles of yours down to London and I'll give them a recording test."

Brian Epstein groaned inwardly, Decca had given him the exact same response and it had got The Beatles exactly, nowhere. But as he already knew all too well, beggars in the music business had to choose their words very carefully. So he put on his very best smile. "Thank you, Mr Martin. Thank you. I know you won't be disappointed."

George Martin smiled and offered his hand, again. "I'll have my secretary check my diary, Mr Epstein. She'll call and let you know when I'm available."

THE KARDOMAH COFFEE HOUSE was packed, as it'd been every Friday afternoon in living memory, and John, Paul, and George, having just finished a lunchtime session at the Cavern, sat toying with their second cups of coffee and their half-empty packets of fags. Neil Aspinall and Pete Best had already gone off, in the van, and it wouldn't be long before they, too, would get off home for a quick kip and a bath prior to getting themselves ready to go do a gig at the New Brighton Tower. The only novelty; this week they were going to try squeeze-in an additional half-hour set at the Birkenhead Technical College between their two scheduled performances for Sam Leach, at 'the Tower'. They were working harder than ever, yet they were still no nearer to the all-elusive recording contract.

"Brian's charm worked well enough on Allan Williams," said George. "He got him to let us back inside the Blue Angel."

"Yeah, but it's not the little Welsh gnome we have to worry about, now, is it? It's George Martin. It's been more than two weeks since he gave 'Eppy' the nod and we still haven't heard a single bloody peep out of him or Parlophone. That's where 'Eppy' has to use that famous bloody charm of his...getting us inside EMI."

"Yeah, it's not even as if they're offering us a contract, it's another bloody audition. All we want is for them to set a date," muttered Paul.

"Fook, but I hate all this waiting," John groaned.

"Well, we passed the audition in Manchester, didn't we?"

"Yeah, George, and I'd like to just say thank you on behalf of the group and myself for the vote of confidence. And, yeah, we'll be on the radio, just like good, old 'Eppy' promised us. And, yeah, the week after next, *Teenagers' Turn*, here we bloody come. But it's still not the big time, is it? And there's no soddin' way of us ever getting to the toppermost of anything, without us having a proper bloody recording contract."

"Ah, but we'll be on the show with Mr Bernard Herrmann and The Northern Dance Orchestra, won't we? That's big time, that is," said, Paul, helpfully.

"Ah, it's only me, Pauly," sniffed John, wiping his glasses on his black pullover. "Just me having me daily bloody grumble."

"If you want something to grumble about, Johnny," chuckled George, "Brian says he wants us to wear our posh new suits on the radio. If they're ready, by then, that is. He says he wants us to make the right impression, even though no one will be able to see us, like."

"Well as long as 'Eppy' keeps his hands off of what music we play, I couldn't care bloody less," snapped John. "I'd wear bloody balloons if it'd help get us a recording contract."

"Yeah, well, then, why don't we talk about drumming?" suggested Paul. "Because, I've got to say, I quite liked it when Ringo Starr sat in with us, that time Pete was ill. It felt okay, like. Like he really fit in."

"Yeah," said George, reaching for a cigarette. "I'd have to agree. I like the way Ringo bashes his skins and does his little rolls and fills. He's a good thumper, dead solid, but his backbeat is real subtle, like, and he can really drive them Hurricanes when he has to. Not that he's happy about everything, otherwise he wouldn't have gone off to Hamburg to play for Tony Sheridan, then turned right round and come back again. So, I reckon, like, that little Ritchie's got itchy feet."

George looked at his two closest friends, expecting them to comment, but they just stared back at him. It wasn't often they let him get a word in, edgewise. So he held off lighting another cigarette and continued on with his line of thought. "I like him.

He's dead dry. Once, just being silly, like, I asked him, 'Why should Ringo Starr?' Quick-as-a-flash, he said, 'Because he wouldn't let Tommy Steele'. So I said, 'You're not talking about the things that made Marty Wilde?' He shot back: 'No, the other stuff that turned Johnny Gentle'. And, look, I know that sounds dead daft. But that's the point...it was fun. He's not as good with words, as you are, John, but he's got wit. Even when he's slow, he's quick. It's just like Paul said. Not only is Ringo one of the best drummers in all of Liverpool, he fit in with us really well."

"Yeah, he's a real good lad, he is," added Paul. "A little flash, with his rings, his beard, his sharp clothes and stuff, but he's all right with it, he is. Pete's okay, too, don't get me wrong, he can play, but, er, the funny thing is, like, I've never really felt he's been a real Beatle."

John put his coffee cup down on the tabletop, very slowly. "Thank you Professors Sigmund Harrison and Gustav McCartney. Look, I dig Ringo, too, I do, but we shouldn't upset the apple cart while we're so close to getting an audition with Parlophone. I know, after we did Decca, I said Pete doesn't always get it right. And that sometimes it's as if he's not even there. I know he doesn't always spark. Damn it, there's times he doesn't even speak for weeks, let alone days. But he's okay, he is, and he's done okay for us these last two years. So he'll do for us now. I think we've got much bigger things to worry about."

George and Paul bit their tongues and nodded. They'd said their piece. They'd let it be, for now, which was just as well, for at that exact moment someone came up and cast a shadow over their table.

"Hi, John. Hi, guys. Heard you got yourselves a record out and a proper manager, too. That's great. Who is it? Sam Leach or Ray McFall?"

It was, Ian Sharp, an old friend of John's from the Art College, who now worked as a set designer at the Playhouse Theatre. He stood, smiling, coffee cup in hand, waiting to be asked to sit down.

"Hello, Sharpie. No, it's not Leachy or McFall. But it'll cost you another coffee, all round, to sit down."

"Scrounging buggers. Hold on. I'll be back in a tick." Ian Sharp went up to the counter, brought back a tray of coffees, and sat down. "There's some bikkies, 'an all. So who's the mysterious new manager, then?"

"He's a millionaire businessman. Drives a big car and owns lots of record stores," said Paul, proudly.

Ian Sharp's eyebrows shot up. "What? It's not somebody called Epstein, is it? The one with the record store across the road...NEMS?"

"Yeah, it is, why?" said John, his eyes narrowing.

"Which one of you is he after, then?" Ian Sharp rolled his eyes, theatrically, and nodded, but the three Beatles looked at him, blankly. He stared at each of them, in turn. "You do all know he's dead queer, don't you?"

"What the hell you talking about, Sharpie?" John spluttered.

"He's as bent as three-pound note, John. Known as Mr 'X' around certain Liverpool theatrical circles. Likes it a bit rough, too, apparently, if you know what I mean? God, you didn't know, did you? None of you did."

"No. He's never one of them, is he?" John gasped. Ian Sharp fluttered his eyelids and nodded. John shook his head. "Well, we sort of guessed it, like." His face suddenly hardened. "But he's always been nothing but proper with us. So it doesn't matter what the hell he does in private. It's his business. All that matters is what he does for us."

"Good for you, John, but my advice is don't ever bend down to pick up your contract." Ian Sharp sniggered, flourished his little pinkie, and very gingerly placed his cup down onto the tabletop. "Good seeing you, fellas, but must dash. As ever, Dame Theatre calls." The three Beatles sat in stunned silence, their cups of coffee untouched.

SANDRA KISSED SPIKE on the cheek and slipped off her coat. Spike took hold of it with a theatrical flourish and hung it up.

"Welcome, milady. It's wonderful you could get away."

"I told them at work I had a headache and had to go home. Only I didn't tell them whose home." She smiled, mischievously. "I got a train and here I am. When will yer mam be home?"

"A couple of hours, yet. The Beatles are on at five. So we've got time for some tea and crumpets, if you like?"

"Yeah, great, I could do with a cup of tea. It's nice, here, isn't it? You're dead lucky living in a house, like this."

"Yeah. Probably for not much longer, though."

"Oh, really? Where are you going to, then, Marco Polo?"

"Don't know yet. Everyone leaves home, eventually, don't they?"

"If they're me, they do. I've got to get out and down to London, like me sister, Maureen, and soon, or I swear I'll go potty. It's like I'm dying, here, in Liverpool, even before I've ever had a chance to live."

"You're a right little rebel without a cause, you are, San."

"That must make you one of them angry young men that people are always going on about, then," sniffed Sandra. "Me? I'm a right little Liverpool raver, just raring to go."

Spike touched her cheek and smiled. Then he poured the tea and buttered the crumpets, and the two young lovers sat round the kitchen table simply enjoying the moment and each other.

"How's that friend of yours doing in hospital?" asked Sandra, sipping her tea. "The one you said was once a policeman."

"Harry Lightfoot, you mean?"

"Yeah. It must really be odd having one of them as a friend."

"No, he's a good bloke. Reminds me of me dad. Got his own set of rules and sod what anyone else thinks, if he believes he's in the right."

"Will he get better, like? You said they beat him up, pretty badly."

"Yeah, hope so. When I went to see him, he said it all looked much worse than it was and not to worry, it'd mend. He was just very glad nothing got punctured, even though they broke lots of ribs, a couple of his fingers and really cut his face up bad. He said, considering the blokes that did it to him, like, it could've been an awful lot worse."

"Darkies, wasn't it?"

"Yeah. A gang of them jumped him, late one night, outside his house. One of his neighbours called for the ambulance."

"Bloody nig-nogs. They're savages, they are. You can't trust any of them. It's the same when they come into the store."

"Sandra! That's not like you to say things like that."

"Well, it's true. The way they go on, sometimes, it's frightening. They should all go back to the jungle and leave us be."

"That's just the sort of thing you said your dad would say. But haven't you ever thought, like, that all that music we like, all the songs you love to dance to and I love to play, it's all by black people? I mean, just think. Chuck Berry, Ray Charles, Little Richard, The Coasters, The Shirelles, 'Smokey' Robinson. They're all darkies and every one of them dead brilliant. You love all those Tamla Motown records. And we're all the same people in the end, aren't we? Whether we come from Liverpool or America or Africa."

Sandra sat silent, her half-eaten crumpet growing cold in her hand. "No, I've never thought of it like that, before. Not ever."

"I didn't think of it meself, like, until I heard The Beatles talking about it, that time I went down to London with them, in the back of the van. They were saying there never would have been rock 'n' roll...or Elvis...or even Buddy Holly, if it wasn't for Negro music."

"I feel real bad, now." She put the remains of her crumpet down on the plate and stared at the kitchen floor. "You've gone and made me feel dead miserable, you have."

"No, San, I'm not having a go at you, honest. But it's never just a case of black and white, there's good and bad in all of us, that's all I'm saying."

"Now you sound just like a know-all, bloody priest, you do. "

"No, it's what Harry Lightfoot once said, that made me think. Just take look at me and how I present myself to the world. I look like a Teddy Boy the way I dress. Leather jacket, drainies, boots...but I'm an 'okay' bloke. And yet who's to know that if they don't know me?"

"I hate Teddy Boys. Always causing trouble, they are."

"I bloody hate them, too, Sandra. And, look, I'm sorry about all this. So, let's just talk about us and sod everybody else, okay? Hey, for a start, we've been invited to Sam Leach's engagement party, a week Saturday. Knowing Sam, it'll probably go on all night. So will that be okay with your mum and your dad?"

Sandra nodded. "I'll just tell them that I'm staying over at Thelma's. And if she and Jimmy end up going, she'll tell her mam, she's staying with me." She looked up and smiled. "I'm okay, now, Spike. Honest."

"Good. But there's more. Right before the party, Sam's going to put on a special show at Knotty Ash Hall with Rory Storm and The Hurricanes, and…The Beatles…and guess what…we're going to be there."

"Oh, that'll be fab," she said, hugging his arm. "But look at the time, The Beatles will be on the radio soon."

"Into the front-room. I'll switch on the radiogram. It's their first time on the Light Programme. People were saying in Hessy's that The Beatles recorded all their songs yesterday, in Manchester. I tell you, I couldn't be more excited if it was me on the radio."

"Ladies and Gentlemen, boys and girls, it's '*Teenagers Turn…Here We Go*'. And this week, on the show, along with Bernard Herrman and The Northern Dance Orchestra, we present Brad Newman, The Trad Lads, and The Beatles pop group. So teenagers, everywhere, it's your turn, now. And so, here…we…go!"

Sandra and Spike sat, ears glued to the radio for the next half-hour. Sat patiently through the dance orchestra, the ballad singer, and the Trad-jazz band—everything so boring and old-fashioned. And then suddenly they heard The Beatles singing 'Dream Baby', 'Memphis Tennessee', and 'Please Mister Postman'. And they imagined the lads in the radio studio and sang along with their every word. Dreaming sweet dreams. Pleading for long distance information to connect them to a number in Tennessee. Imploring Mister Postman to please, please, wait—wait for just one more minute.

Then it was all over. And as all the cheering and clapping of the teenagers in the studio audience washed over them, the two young lovers sat staring into each other's eyes. Smiling. Knowing. Happy together, because without even saying a single word they both knew something very important had just happened between them. Hearing The Beatles on the BBC, like that, some-how marked the start of a new future for them, too. 'Liverpool Resurgent', no less, and in their lifetimes. Sandra toyed with her hair, looked away. "Spike, if we were ever parted for a long time, would you write me a letter everyday?"

"Course, I would, San. Only, I'm not the one always going on about getting away to London, am I? That's you."

"Yeah, well, I've got my reasons and the only reason I'm still here, Spike Jones, is because of you."

"Well, in that case," said Spike. "You better stay for tea and meet me mam. She's dying to meet you."

Sandra turned and bit her lip and pulled him to her and gen-tly kissed him. And they stood, arms locked around one another, kissing, passionately, for ten minutes or more, before they slow-ly descended to the sofa and then to the living room carpet.

RINGO STARR hit the snare with a crack. Rory Storm threw his arm out, pointed at the audience, held a finger up to heaven, and stepped into 'Blue Suede Shoes'. He rolled his shoulders, thrust out two fingers, and Ringo cracked the snare a second time. On three, Rory shook his arm and snapped his head from side to side. On four, he swivelled his pelvis, stiffened his legs, and spun round. The cat now well and truly out of the bag, he trembled all over, slowly rolled his head, shook his curly blond locks, dipped and dropped, jumped and jived, spun round again, told everyone they could do whatever they wanted to. Then he suddenly stopped, snarled, curled his lip, looked mean, magnificent—real cool, man, cool—and growled that everyone better lay off Sam's Hush Puppy suede shoes. He paused for the very briefest of moments—let the moment crackle in the air—then Rory Storm and The Hurricanes set about blowing the roof off.

The full rocking force of Liverpool's 'Mr Showmanship' swept up everything before it. This was 'the Storm' everyone loved— Rory leaping and writhing, his shocking canary-yellow suit a never-ending blur. The Hurricanes in matching sky-blue suits and ties, forever dipping and diving behind him. Rory whirling the microphone stand around his head. Rory trembling like he'd been electrocuted. Rory prancing. Rory dancing. Rory jumping.

Rory strutting. Rory twisting. Rory twirling. Owning the stage, owning the night. Unstoppable. Unbeatable. Unsurpassable.

It was Battle of the Bands—Liverpool-style.

"Bloody hell, Sam, will you look at that," shouted John Lennon. "He's out to bloody bury us, he is."

"Well, he always did in Hamburg...always does at 'the Tower'," George Harrison, piped in. "So, I can't see as how our Rory would be any different, tonight, given even half a chance, like."

"I bet the swine swipes all our best rock 'n' roll numbers, too," moaned Paul. "We'll just have to make up our song-list as we go. See what he leaves us. If he leaves us anything, that is."

Sam Leach laughed. "Well, it's a rockin' good way to start off my engagement party, lads. Just you remember, all those punters out there are paying for all the food and booze you'll be scoffing down, later."

"Well, in that case, Sam," sniffed John, narrowing his eyes. "We'll just have to go blow all those Rory Storm clouds away, won't we?"

Rory lit into 'Be-Bop-A-Lula'.

"That's my bloody song," John exploded. "Gene Vincent's and mine. I'll do Rory, He knows that's my favourite number."

For the next hour, Rory Storm and The Hurricanes grabbed the best songs in the rock 'n' roll cupboard. He took Elvis's Top Ten rockers and then stole Eddie Cochran's very best songs, including Sam's all-time favourite, 'Summertime Blues'. Then he made off with Buddy Holly's catchiest riffs, before reaching for Carl Perkins' 'Lend Me Your Comb'. He swiped 'Cathy's Clown' and 'Claudette' from the Everly Brothers. Took 'I got a Woman' from Ray Charles. Then turned up the gas even higher still with Jerry Lee Lewis's 'Great Balls of Fire'.

Everyone's nerves and brains utterly rattled, he smiled his million-watt smile, pointed to each Hurricane, in turn, smiled at the crowd, combed his curly golden locks with his giant plastic comb for one last time. He did the splits, rebounded, stood to attention, bowed from the waist, swivelled his pelvis, spun round and around and was gone.

"Sweet Lord," muttered George. "We have to follow that?"

"What with?" Paul sighed.

"Let's bloody hit them with 'Johnny B Goode'," snarled John.

"Righto, Johnno," shouted Paul. "I'll blow their ear drums to smithereens with me Hofner bass." He turned to the other Beatles. "Pete. You hit them with your 'atomic' beat. And George?"

"Yeah, Pauly?"

"Go ring that bloody bell, why don't yer."

John strode onto the stage and grabbed hold of the mike. "This is a number by Chuck Berry...a Liverpool-born schoolteacher with bad teeth and no humour." George hit straight into the opening riff and he and his fellow Beatles lit into 'School Day', as if possessed. And for the next hour-and-a-half The Beatles kept up a blistering pace, not letting up for an instant. They followed their opening number with even more of Chuck Berry's best. Then ripped through Little Richard's repertoire with Paul taking the lead on 'Long Tall Sally', 'Tutti-Frutti', and 'Kansas City'. John kept things spinning with Larry William's 'Dizzy, Miss Lizzy' and Carl Perkins' 'Honey Don't'. George took a turn with Tommy Roe's 'Sheila', Bobby Vee's 'Take Good Care of My Baby', and The Coasters' 'Youngblood'.

To give his band-mates' voices a break, Pete opened up Carl Perkins' 'Matchbox' and followed that with The Shirelles' hit 'Boys'. Paul went 'Searchin' for The Coasters again. John gave people another hit of Arthur Alexander's 'A Shot of Rhythm and Blues', reintroduced them to 'Anna', before grabbing everyone by the throat with Smokey Robinson's 'You Really Got a Hold on Me'. Then he capped everything off with Barrett Strong's 'Money'. After which, the place exploded into one long roar of cheers, whistling, stamping, and thunderous applause.

Sam Leach ran onto the stage, as wrung-out as if he'd been up there playing the music himself. He clapped, cheered, took hold of the microphone, and waved everyone to silence. "Blimey O'Riley! I've never seen or heard anything as spectacular as what happened here at tonight's 'Battle of the Bands' and I doubt if any of us will ever see the likes of it again, however long we live." Everyone clapped and cheered for their favourite band. Sam patted the air with his hands—waited for all the noise to die down. "So listen...what can I say? There can be no winners tonight other than all of you and me...and all of Liverpool...for being home to such fabulous entertainers as...Rory Storm and The Hurricanes! And The Beatles!"

He turned, applauded both bands again, asked the audience to show their appreciation again, and then left the stage. The hall exploded into another riot of clapping, stamping, cheering, and whistling. After it showed no sign of abating, Sam ran back on, took up the microphone and held it between his hands as if in prayer. "What do you say, fellas? Ray Charles' 'What'd I Say?' to bring the night to a proper close? Send everyone off home, drained but deliriously happy?"

Sam spun round and cocked his head and raised his eyebrows—in mute question—and the three hundred or so beat fans roared, cheered and stamped their feet in response. John Lennon and Rory Storm glanced at one another, nodded. The two drummers settled back behind their drum kits. Guitars got replugged into amplifiers. And the two bands came together as one. Then Rory and John and Paul took turns in stretching their final song's call and response to its very limits. And for a good twenty minutes or more Knotty Ash Hall rocked on its very foundations and Sam Leach's 'St. Patrick's Night Rock Gala' rolled into local legend as the one night of rock 'n' roll no beat fan alive should ever have missed.

SPIKE sipped his beer, scanned the crowd. It meant a lot that he'd been invited to Sam and Joan's engagement party. If nothing else it meant he really was part of the local beat-music scene. Helping out behind the scenes was all very well, but now he was rubbing shoulders with all the musicians. If not exactly as an equal then as a known face. The Beatles were all there with their girlfriends. George, the lone wolf for the night. He saw Brian Epstein chatting-up Joan's pretty blonde sister, Vera. And Bob Wooler chatting away ten-to-the-dozen to everybody that mattered—people like Gerry Marsden, Rory Storm, Ringo Starr, Johnny Guitar, and 'Kingsize' Taylor. Terry McCann was there, of course. It was Terry who pointed Bill Harry out to him.

"That intense looking bloke over there is the editor of *Mersey*

Beat, Spike. You should go and introduce yourself, to him, Spike, do yourself some good."

He sipped his beer and thought he was seeing double when he saw two Sandras standing in front of him. "Spike, this is Rory's sister, Iris. She's going out with Beatle Paul. Only as you can see, we both have the same red dress from Lewis's." Spike smiled, said "Hello," and shook Iris's hand. "Yeah," said Iris. "And if we see a third girl in the same red-dress we're not going to scratch her eyes out, are we Sandra? We're going to start an all-girl singing group, like The Shirelles." The two girls raised their glasses of Babycham, in salute, and went off, arm-in-arm, laughing, to search for a girl with the red dress on.

"I'll be your manager, if you do." Spike called after them. Then he looked down at his empty glass and went in search of another beer. He pushed in next to Ringo Starr who was standing by the drinks table talking to a couple of lads in brown suede jackets. "Nah. Didn't get on with Tony Sheridan. I know they all call him 'The Teacher', like. But the only thing he tried to teach me was how to curse in three different languages. And with me coming from Liverpool, I can swear in at least five of them, as it is. So I came back home."

The two guys dressed in brown suede laughed and that's when Spike realised they were his old mates from school, Dave Brown and Fraser Britton.

"Hey, Fras! Dave! How you doing? Didn't recognise you."

"Bloody hell, is that you, Spike? Sod me, but you look different, too. It's your hair...you look just like one of them..."

"Like one of them hairy Beatles," said Ringo, a drink in each hand. "Looks daft, if you ask me, but leave alone and let live, I say. Anyroad, excuse me, lads, I have some ladies to attend to."

"You look gear, Spike," said Fras, beaming. "What have you been doing with yourself? Can you play that bloody guitar of yours, yet?"

"Yeah, a bit. Jim Gretty's very pleased at how I've come on, like."

"You've been going to Hessy's for his Monday night lessons?" Dave did an imitation of Jim Gretty. "Okay, lads, let's all try to play 'Singing The Blues'." And without a word being spoken, the three of them began singing, and as Fras and Dave harmonised with one another in thirds and fourths, Spike sang, effortlessly, in fifths.

Then in a spontaneous tribute to Jim Gretty and all he'd done for hundreds of young aspiring guitarists across Merseyside, everyone at the party, who knew of the sacred Monday night ritual at Hessy's, joined in with singing 'Singing The Blues'. It was magical, heartfelt, and as the last notes of the song's plaintive final plea drew to a close, there was a burst of cheers and applause and scattered individual toasts to Jim Gretty. Then Gerry Marsden shouted, "Three cheers for our Grim Jetty," and everyone cheered again.

Sam Leach yelled out, "Who's soddin' engagement party is this, then?" And Gerry giggled and shouted, "And three cheers for our Leachy and our Joanie, an' all." And everyone clapped and cheered, and the whole house rocked and the party rolled on into the night and well into the following morning.

"You sounded dead good there, Spike," said Fras, looking thoughtful. "What you doing tomorrow? You want to come over to me mum's place and sit in while we practice? Only, one of our guys left to go join another group and we're looking for someone to replace him."

"Yeah, great," said Spike, trying not to show how excited he was. "So the group's going well, is it? Where you been playing?"

"Hamburg," said Dave Brown. "That's how we know Ringo."

"Hamburg? You're bloody kidding? That's dead gear, that is."

"Yeah, we're going back there next week to play the Top Ten Club, again."

CHAPTER TWENTY-FOUR

Die Grosse Freiheit

"Garston six-nine-double-two."

Spike quickly cleared his throat. "Can I speak to Paul, please?"

"Is that you, Neil?" said a voice.

"No. Me name's, Spike Jones. I, er, know Paul, like, from when The Beatles play 'the Tower'. And I went to London with them, when they did that gig for Sam Leach. Only, I've got a question for him."

"Okay, Spike Jones, is it? Hang on a mo."

Spike heard a muffled voice shouting something, then a few moments later, another voice answering back, "Thanks, there, Mike." Then a voice, as clear as a bell, said, "Hello, this is Paul."

"Er, Paul, this is Spike, a friend of Sam Leach's. You may not remember me, but…"

"Course I do, Spike. You helped us with our amps, once. Then there was that unforgettable trip to Aldershot. What can I do you for?"

"It's, er, about playing bass guitar. Only I've been asked to join a group and play bass for them, in Hamburg, but I know sod all about it. And you're so bloody great at playing it, I thought I'd ask you."

"Got yourself lumbered, have you?" chuckled Paul. "Lucky you. I only play the bass myself, like, because John and George flatly refused to do so, but if you're looking for lessons, I don't…"

"No, no, just a chat. I'll have a bash at it, anyway, but I couldn't think of anyone better to ask. I mean you're dead brilliant at it."

"Well, there's no need to take the lead of the roof," laughed Paul.

"Just half hour with you, Paul, and I'd be well on me way."

"Well, look, Spike, I'm very busy, and I'd like to, and that, but...Hey, hang on a mo, weren't you at Sam and Joan's engagement party last weekend? And wasn't that your girlfriend who was with my Iris? The little dark-haired girl in the red dress, just like the one my Iris was wearing?"

"Yeah, it was, yeah. Why?"

"Well, why didn't you say so, dafty? They were as thick as thieves all night. Iris said your girlfriend was real gear. Look, I'll tell you what, I'll stay on, for a bit, after tomorrow's lunchtime session at the Cav and we can talk then, okay? Bring your bass guitar. Hey, and come early, if you like. I'll tell Paddy, on the door, to let you in."

"Yeah, thanks, there, Paul. That's terrific. Great. See you."

Next morning, Spike was at Hessy's Music Store when it opened. Then he hung out in the Kardomah, hardly able to contain his excitement, until eleven-thirty, when he all but ran round to the Cavern. When the girls standing in the queue saw him walk by—in leather jacket and jeans, carrying a couple of guitar cases, shoulders all hunched up, hair combed down over his forehead—there was a sudden wave of murmurs and squeals. But the sound just as quickly broke and shattered against the cobblestones as the girls all realised it wasn't one of their lovely Beatles.

Paddy Delaney, the Cavern's doorman, smiled, nodded, and waved him into the club. "Never mind, lad. One day, eh? Paul said to go straight on down. They're in the back, setting up." The doorman turned to a big blond-haired kid standing next to him, another of the Cavern's many bouncers. "Mal, give him a hand down the steps with his guitars. There's a good lad."

Spike stood by the stage watching Paul's right hand move up and down the neck of the bass. He concentrated that hard, he could hardly think, and the lunchtime session just flew by. And suddenly it was all over. The club emptying, his bottle of Pepsi still almost full, and Paul calling him into the cubbyhole that doubled as the band room.

"Hello, what brings young Spike Jones here, then?" asked George.

"The Welsh Goon's going to join a group in Hamburg. Aren't you, Spikey?" John tut-tutted and shook his head in wonder. "Anyroad, we'll leave you in Paul's capable hands. We're off round the Grapes for a quick one."

Paul turned to Spike. "See what I'm giving up? Come on. Bring your gear out to the stage. Let's get started."

Spike picked up his guitar cases and followed. When Paul saw the red Rosetti Solid 7 being lifted out of its case, he laughed. "Bloody hell, Spike, for one awful moment I thought my old guitar had come back to haunt me. What a piece of shite those are. If you can play that, believe me you can play anything. In the end, I just stuck some piano strings on mine and used it as a bass guitar. Then, thank God, I bought myself this." Paul plugged in his violin-shaped Hofner bass, plucked at a string, and a loud bass sound boomed round the empty Cavern. "What you got in the other case?"

Spike lifted up a big-shouldered, blonde Hofner bass. "I, er, got this, this morning. I told Jim Gretty you were helping me and he let me borrow it. It's second-hand, like, but what do you think, is it worth me buying?"

Paul smiled. "Oh, yeah, much better. That's gear, that is. Stu had a brunette one. It's got a good sound. So, great, yes, buy it on the never-never. Now first you listen. Then I'll plug you in and we'll see how you do. Okay?"

Spike nodded and tried to work some saliva back into his throat.

"Now...as to being the bass player. Your job is to fit in and add to whatever the other instruments are doing. Whether it's the guitars playing chords or lead, or the drums banging out fours or doing fills, it's the bass that holds things together, underpins it all, and gives the music depth and drive." Spike nodded, worried nothing would go in, but in the end took confidence from Paul's easy-going manner. "Hey, don't worry, there, Spike. You'll soon pick it up. Just remember, the most important thing is to listen. Because the guitars tell you the notes you can play and the drum pattern gives you your beat." Paul began to play, his fingers moving slowly up and down the neck of his guitar, his plectrum plucking the strings.

'Du du-du, du du-du, du du-du-du'. The notes from the big 15-inch speaker in Paul's specially-built 'coffin' bass amp went booming back and forth through the Cavern's three vaulted, brick arches, causing little flecks of dried whitewash to flutter down from the ceiling and onto the floor.

"Okay, that's what I'd play for a twelve-bar blues in C. So, you plug-in the Rosetti and play the chords C, F and G7 and I'll play the bass notes underneath. Good. Listen. Hear how simple it is? When that gets a bit boring, we can do this." Paul's hand flew down the neck of his guitar to hit the same note an octave higher. "Hear it? Sounds good, doesn't it? It's the same note, an octave above. So throw one of those in, occasionally. Just always remember to follow the pattern laid down by the bass drum and the snare. Okay, then, now we're really starting to go places."

Spike was on cloud nine. Suddenly, it was as if he could not only hear the bass, he could actually hear how it fit in with the other instruments and what it could do to make a song come alive.

"Now. The simplest bass line uses what they call the root notes of whatever chords are being played on the other guitars. Okay. Play the same three chords again and listen as I take the basic notes from each chord. The first, the third, and the fifth...and play those. So, as you play the chord of C, then I can play the notes C...E...G. Hear them? Good. Now play the chords through, again. Yeah. Yeah. Good. So, as you play the F chord, I play the notes F...A...C. And as you move to G7, so I can play G...B...D. Then it's really up to you whether or not you play the F to match the chord's seventh note. The bloody amazing thing is that it works the same for major or minor chords. Okay, now Spike, I'll play that bloody Rosetti guitar of yours. You play your 333. And let's hear you thump out some rhythm-and-blues."

JOHN, GEORGE, PAUL and PETE sat in the Punch and Judy cafe, opposite Lime Street Station, waiting for Brian Epstein's train to arrive from Euston. At times, it seemed as if they'd been waiting for 'Eppy' forever. Yelling, "break-a-leg 'Eppy'" or "knock-em-dead 'Eppy'" every time he'd left Lime Street and gone off, again, down to London. Each time, hoping against hope, that this time he'd bring back the news he'd secured a recording contract for them at long bloody last.

"He's due in, anytime now," sniffed John, looking at his watch.

"I just hope they don't change it to Central at the last minute. They're always digging up the railway line, somewhere," said Paul. "Especially as they're switching to electric-powered, now."

"There must be a notice, over there, somewhere, then, telling whether the train's going to arrive on time or not," said George.

"See yer, when you get back, George," said John, with no intention of moving himself. "Hey 'oop, no matter, here he is."

The Beatles had long since given up trying to read their manager. And they all waited patiently while he bought them yet another round of coffees.

"Any luck?" John asked, the moment Brian Epstein sat down. "Has Parlophone given us a date? Or signed us, yet, 'Eppy'?"

"No. No, I'm afraid they haven't, John. And to try and keep things moving, I went along to Philips Records, as well. But I'm afraid the people there, have also said, 'No'. I'm sorry."

"Bugger, bugger, bugger," said George, reaching for a cigarette.

"Sod it, 'Eppy', even the bloody Seniors have gone and got themselves a recording contract." John covered his face with his hands and groaned. He slowly opened his hands and peered out from between his fingers. "That's it, then, isn't it?" he said, his voice muffled. "It's really going to have to be Woolworth's Embassy label then, isn't it, because there's no one bloody left." This time nobody laughed.

SANDRA stirred her coffee and tried hard not to cry. The sights and sounds of Lime Street Station filled her with sadness now—all the hustle and bustle no longer signalling freedom and adventure, but loneliness. She looked at Spike, so full of excitement over his coming trip to Hamburg, and saw that even though she was still very much in his heart, in his mind he was already away in Germany, playing his bass guitar. He looked up from his cup of coffee and smiled.

"Will you be going over to 'the Tower', on Friday, then?"

"Yeah," said Sandra, putting on a brave face. "And there's a special Beatles Fan Club night at the Cav, Thursday. So, I'll be going there with Thelma, 'an all."

"Yeah, well I just asked Jimmy to keep an eye on you, like."

"Why? Don't you trust me or something?"

"No. No, of course not, San. It's just, er, it's just about them Teds or anyone trying to bother you. I just wanted him to…"

"That's all right, then. He's nice, is Jimmy; a good friend."

"It won't be long, you know, till I come back home to you, San. It's only six weeks."

"Sounds like forever, to me," said Sandra, quietly.

"I'll write you every day, you know."

"Yeah," she said, her voice flat.

"What's that supposed to mean?"

"I said, yeah, good," she sniffed. "I'll be singing 'Please Mister Postman' everyday, won't I?" She sipped her coffee and looked away.

"Oh, sod it, if you're going to be like that, I won't go. Okay?"

She blinked away a tear. Looked at him. "Of course, you will, you big dafty. You've got to go. I'd go if it were me, honest, I would."

Spike gently squeezed her hand. "Yeah."

Sandra sniffed again and reached for a handkerchief from her handbag. She touched it quickly to her eyes and nose, then replaced it and snapped the bag shut. "Thing is, while you're away, Spike, I'm thinking of going down to London, to stay with my sister, for a week or two. Only, it's going to seem so very lonely here without you."

"So this London thing's about me, then, is it?"

"No, it's not about you, it's me. I've got to get away. Different reasons, maybe, but it's the same in the end. We both want to be free of something. I just need time to think some things through, that's all."

"But what? I want to understand, San, I really do, but you're always so damn mysterious about it all. What's so special in London?"

"Look, nothing, okay, nothing, just me sister. Alright?"

Spike reached for a brown-paper parcel leaning against his suitcase. He gave it to her. "I hope you think this is special, San."

She looked at him, surprised. "What's this, then?"

"You can open it now or just take it home. I did it for you."

Sandra stroked the little parcel wrapped in brown paper and tied-up with string. She carefully undid the knots and un-wrapped the parcel, to reveal a framed canvas. Printed neatly, across the back, in black wax crayon, were the words: 'TO MY SANDRA, WITH LOVE, FROM ME TO YOU - SPIKE'. She turned it over and gasped. It was a painting of the two of them, as they'd been captured in one of the instant photos, that first night at Lime Street Station. She looked up and pressed her lips together hard and tried to keep from crying again. She sniffled. Swallowed. Smiled. Looked into his eyes and back at the painting showing the two of them, looking so very happy and in love. "Oh, my God, Spike, it's beautiful, it is. It's really fab."

"It's you and me, San. That night I first kissed you."

"I know, dafty," she said, touching her handkerchief to her eyes again. "In the photo booth." She reached inside her hand-bag and drew out a little red purse and produced two little black and white photos. In one, Sandra had her eyes half-closed and Spike was grimacing. In the other one, the two of them were de-liberately pulling funny faces. "I look at them whenever I'm feeling sad and they make me laugh."

Spike nodded, smiled. "I've got number three, where's the other one?"

Sandra opened her purse to reveal the picture of the two of them kissing, framed in a little window die-cut into the red leatherette and protected forever by a clear sheet of celluloid. "I keep the kiss, special, like," she said, looking into his eyes. Then she bit her lip and sniffled and said, in a tiny, quavering voice. "And I will, forever, because, I love you, Spike."

Then she started to cry—with happiness.

SAM LEACH pushed open the door of the Kardomah Coffee House, hoping he'd arrived first and that Brian Epstein wasn't already sitting there, waiting for him. But there he was, all immaculate and polished, looking as if he owned the bloody place. Making notes with his posh bloody fountain pen in a small, black leather-bound notebook; a cup of coffee sitting in front of him like an obedient little lap-dog.

Paul McCartney had gone to the Grapes, looking for Sam, earlier, to give him the message that Brian Epstein wanted to chat to him on some important business and could Sam pop round to NEMS as soon as possible, like. Sam, bristling at the very thought of being at anyone's beck and call, had replied, tersely, "Yeah, sure. Okay. Only, it'll have to be in my office, this time. In the Kardomah, the table on the far left, by the window, around three o'clock, if that's suitable."

"Hello, there, Brian; how's tricks? No, it's okay, I'll get me own coffee and biscuits, thanks." Brian Epstein nodded and smiled and went on making notes. Once he'd got his coffee, Sam took a seat opposite, pulled out a packet of cigarettes and lit up. He tapped his matchbox up and down on the table. "The lads back off to Hamburg, next Wednesday, then, are they? Well it's about time, they started working for your living, isn't it, Brian? And what about our George, then? Is he feeling, any better? Must be a right sod, him going down with German measles, like that; but at least they won't need to quarantine him, will they? I mean, he'll only be re-exporting them back into the country where they came from in the first place, won't he?"

Brian Epstein all but winced at Sam's quick-fire humour, but he smiled. After all, they were there to discuss a very serious business matter. Sam, seeing Brian's somewhat nervous de-meanour, realised something really important must be up and he began to ready himself for whatever was coming. He bit into a digestive biscuit and drank his coffee. Brian had already stolen The Beatles away, right from under his bloody nose, so what more could he bloody well want from him?

Sam didn't have to wait long to find out. After a few minutes small talk, Brian Epstein cleared his throat and said, matter-of-factly, that he was looking for a share in Sam's Friday night shows at 'the Tower'. "The Friday night franchise is now the single, most successful, large-scale musical venue on Merseyside." Brian looked down at his notes. "It regularly attracts audiences of between two and three thousand, occasionally bringing in as many as four thousand." He looked up. "And as such, the Friday shows represent the best possible on-going showcase for The Beatles." He paused, took a sip coffee, and gently placed the cup back down in the saucer.

Sam Leach could hardly breathe, let alone believe his ears. He knew Brian Epstein had some nerve, but this was way beyond bloody ridiculous. All too often, in the past, he'd had to suffer jealous promoters trying to do the dirty on him, but this took the bloody biscuit tin as well as the bloody biscuits. It was little more than brass-faced, bloody daylight robbery. And, of course, it would be Brian Epstein, one of God's chosen few, that was attempting to do it. How bloody typical was that?

But Brian Epstein read Sam's continued silence as interest. "You see, Sam, my plan is to present big-name British recording artists at 'the Tower', with The Beatles always positioned as second on the bill. My idea being, that it would not only provide the boys valuable experience of being on stage with some really big names from the 'Hit Parade', it would also give them some very valuable added exposure. A double-win."

Sam's mind got into top gear very, very quickly. Book the biggest names in rock 'n' roll? Yeah. Why ever not? And why not American artists, too, while we're at it? After all, Buddy Holly had once played the Liverpool Empire. And Allan Williams had once booked Gene Vincent and Eddie Cochran to play at the old boxing stadium, before poor old Eddie died in a car-crash and the arena had been shuttered for good. It could be a very good business, with lots of profit for both parties. What's more, if Brian Epstein, with all his money, financed the shows, what was to say he wouldn't also finance Sam's dream of starting his own record label.

He heard himself saying, "Another coffee, Brian?" Brian Epstein shook his head. So he smiled and continued on, trying to contain his growing excitement. "You know, that's not a bad idea, Brian. I think 'the Tower' could attract some really big names, at that. Yeah. Okay, then. Why don't we give it a try? You put up the money. I'll do the promoting. Then we can split the profits, fifty-fifty. Okay? Sounds very good to me. I think I'll get us some fresh coffee, anyway, so we can celebrate." Sam pushed his chair back, but stopped suddenly when he saw Brian Epstein shaking his head. "What's up, Brian? What?"

"No, I'm afraid that's not what I had in mind, Sam," Brian Epstein said, shaking his head again. "That won't do, at all. I simply couldn't agree to it. You see, my brother, Clive, and I have just formed a new company called NEMS Enterprises and we're partners, which means it would have to be a three-way cut...and so you'd get a third."

Sam Leach held onto the table and sat down with a bump, his face and knuckles getting whiter with each passing second. "Sorry, Brian, I thought I just heard you say that I'd only get a third of the deal."

Brian Epstein nodded.

Sam was dumbfounded. Brian Epstein was not only trying to push his way, scot-free, into a franchise that'd taken months to build up. Soddin' years, if you took into account all the other clubs. But on top of that, he was only offering him a third of the profits. "Fook me," thought Sam, I must be dreaming, I can't bloody believe this." He grimaced, as if hit by a sudden attack of heartburn. "In that case, Brian, me old cock...no deal. Trouble is, you see, I've got too many partners of my own to consider. I mean; there's my future wife for a start and my as yet unborn children. Added to which there's my mother-in-law. Plus, I've got a dog and a cat. So, by my calculations, that means there's only an eighth left over for you or a sixteenth if you include your soddin' brother. I would've thought any proper business-man would be able to see that, even a nancy, fookin' Jew-boy."

Time stopped for both men—all bridges suddenly burned.

Brian Epstein blushed bright red, utterly taken aback by Sam Leach's unbelievably rude and obnoxious response. He stood up, his eyes blinking repeatedly. Seeing nothing, saying nothing. Deeply puzzled as well as shocked at what had just occurred. He slowly held out his hand, which Sam shook, very begrudgingly. Only then did he seem fully present and he blinked again and shook his head. It'd been a singularly unpleasant experience, to-

tally unforgivable, and as he buttoned his overcoat he stared at
Sam across the expanse of red Formica tabletop—now grown as
wide as the River Mersey.

"You've just made a dreadful mistake, Sam," he said, shaking
his head, slowly. "Why? I don't know. But it's one that I think
will come back to haunt you for the rest of your life."

"Right, then," sniffed Sam. "I'll just have to go take refuge in
me big golden Tower then, won't I? Bye, Brian. Have a nice life."

SPIKE had never known a journey be so long or boring. Whoever it was said, 'Life's a journey, not a destination', had obviously
never had to travel to Hamburg.

He'd taken the early train down to Euston, a taxi across London to Liverpool Street Station, another train up to Harwich,
and then boarded the night ferry to the Hook of Holland. And
after all that—all the interminable stop, go, stop, go—he'd had to
sit through another long, dreary train ride, before arriving,
bleary-eyed and very grumpy at Hamburg-Hauptbahnhof. Then,
after another unbelievably long wait, he'd at last managed to get
a taxi to St. Pauli, 136 Reeperbahn—The Top Ten Club.

It didn't exactly look or feel like newfound freedom. In the
flat grey light, St. Pauli was seedy, shabby, dirty, foul-smelling,
and just plain depressing. Much like Liverpool on a cold, rainy
day. At first he thought he'd got the address wrong, the place
looked like it was out of 'Hänsel und Gretel'. Then he thought of
the Casbah Club, in the basement of Pete Best's mum's house,
and just accepted it for what it was.

Fras met him and took him upstairs to a tiny room at the
very top of the building that acted as a dormitory for groups
booked to play the club. It was cramped, to say the least. "This is
where we all sleep." Fras pointed to an empty camp bed by the
far wall. "That's your bunk, over there. Dump your case and
come back down."

They had a quick run through the set he was expected to
play, after which he was allowed a few minutes shut-eye. But before he knew it, he was on stage for real—another real eye-
opener. It was less a dream come true, more a real fookin'
nightmare. His mind went a complete blank. His fingers froze

on the fret board and refused to move. He even forgot how to breathe. All he could hear was his heart banging in his chest and the blood coursing through his ears. Then a wall of sound fell on him. The boom of the single bass note he'd been hitting over and over and over again crashing down around him. Then as the words to 'Dizzy, Miss Lizzy' drew him back into the world it was as if he'd been reborn. He blinked, gasped for air, and heard Fras shouting at him through a curtain of brilliant white light. "Yeah. Yeah. Yeah. Go, Spikey, go." And suddenly he was moving his fingers up and down the neck of the guitar. Sliding, pressing, gripping, releasing—as if he was pumping his very life-blood back into his stunned body and disbelieving mind.

"Just feel it," Paul McCartney had told him. "Once you got the basics, the rest will come. So just enjoy it and don't get your knickers in a twist over whether you're playing properly or not. The main thing is the sound. Get it good and loud. And if you ever lose your way just bang out four beats to the bar and try lock in with the bass drum. Give it some thump, give it some feel, because if you're enjoying it, rocking it, your mates in the group will pick up on it and so will the fans. Just like tuning forks...they'll all feel what you're feeling and get in the groove with you."

Spike played and sang backup until he couldn't play or sing another note. Someone handed him a bottle of something that all but snapped his head off. And when it kicked in for real, he played on and on without stop. Then he heard the wave of shouting, whistling and applause that marked the end of his first multi-hour set and left the stage feeling utterly washed-out, but about ten-foot tall. The last thing he remembered, after he was sure he'd lost his voice forever and before he lost what little was left of his mind, was the little old lady attendant who sat inside the doorway to the Gents toilets. He'd gone up to her, just as Fras had told him to do, pointed to his throat and croaked, "Danke, Mutti."

The little old lady had nodded at him, made a clucking sound, and chided him in a squeaky little voice. "Ach, ist die Kehle nach Hamburg. Die 'Hamburg throat' that I think you must be having.

Ist das Bier, Liebchen. Das Bier ist, in Hamburg, much more different than your Bier in your England ist. Here, take now,
please, two of these." And from out of her voluminous old
handbag she'd produced a tube of Preludin tablets, which she'd
handed to him with a curt nod and a pat on the hand. He'd
thanked her, thrust the German banknotes Fras had given him
into her hands, and washed the pills down with Coca-Cola.

During the final set, he'd played bass like a wild-eyed demon
and sung like a blinded nightingale in a cage. Then he'd just
crashed. Or it might've been the following night he did that, or
the one after, he couldn't tell. Days and nights just bled into one
another. The first week was a total blur.

He'd catch himself staring at the blackened, swollen fingers
and thumb on his right hand, the dried blood on the callused
fingertips on his left, and just shake his head. "How in hell?" But
he couldn't remember much of anything; not eating; not wash-
ing; not even sleeping. When not playing with the band, he lay
on his camp bed, just gazing into the dark or at the cracks in the
walls and ceiling. Waiting for the car-horns to start blaring so he
had reason to get up or waiting for Fras to yell that he was needed down on stage.

Once he'd proved he could hold his own, stay the course, the
guys showed him their 'secret' Hamburg. The strip-tease clubs,
peep-show arcades, sex-shops, and the 'kerb-swallows' walking
up and down every street. They took him to the 'Street of Windows' that ran the length of the Herbertstrasse to see the
prostitutes on open display.

He hadn't been able to believe his soddin' eyes.

There were women of all shapes, sizes and colours, in all
forms of dress and undress. Women in leather, women in lace,
women in starched white uniforms and in shiny black rubber,
women with nothing more on than a few pasted-on sequins and
artfully draped feathers.

In one open window, there was a blonde-haired giantess in a
black corset and black leather boots. And as she'd coolly cracked
her whip at the parade of people passing by her window, he'd
just stood and stared, eyes like Catherine wheels, mouth opening and closing like a fish on a marble slab. "Fookin' hell," he'd

said, over and over, unable to stop gabbing. "Will you just look at the tits on that? They can't be real, either of them, they're as big as fookin' footballs."

They took him to 'The Armoury', a shop at the far end of the Reeperbahn, full of coshes, knuckledusters, gas guns, flick-knives, pistols, rifles, and sub-machine guns. Once he'd got over that, they took him to a number of St. Pauli's more interesting clubs and bars. The Hippo Bar, where he saw women wrestling in mud. Then to the Telefon Bar, where a telephone call to one of the elegant hostesses sitting at the tables could've had him in a room upstairs with his trousers down around his ankles before the bell had stopped ringing. Then they'd stopped by clubs where women did things with other women and clubs where women did things you could never have imagined with snakes, dogs, and donkeys. The sort of things that once you'd seen the once, you never really ever needed to see again, like, unless you were a bit sick and twisted to begin with.

To finish the night off, the guys dragged him to the Roxy Bar and, over funny-coloured drinks, had introduced him, to 'The Duchess'. His only real memory of the place being that it'd seemed full of very tall, glamorous women with very deep voices. Not that he'd been in any condition, by that time, to know the truth of anything.

Next night at the Top Ten, one of the 'ladies-of-the-night', in the audience, had taken a particular shine to him and given him the universal sign for wanting a fuck. Smacking a hand into the fold of her elbow, bringing her arm up like an erection, shouting 'Gazunka!' and sending a bottle of champagne up to him. Fras and Dave had laughed themselves silly, at that, as it meant he was definitely set up for the night. Highly flattered and high again on pills and beer, he'd enjoyed a brief dalliance in the corridor behind the stage during the rest-period. Then, as day follows night, he'd gone back to the girl's flat after the show—a willing lamb to the slaughter—and woken up in her bed, sometime the following day, feeling like a new man. All so very different to the girls back in Liverpool and the never-ending fumbling with bra-straps and girdles and trying to get your hand up their skirts and inside their knickers—like a Christmas present with far too many knots to untie. He'd had a hard-on for hours, sometimes, and not been able to do soddin' thing about it.

But this German girl had gone and opened up a whole, new world. He'd felt awkward, at first, which he'd put down to all the beer and champagne, but given the proper guidance and encouragement he'd been agreeably surprised at just how quickly he'd got the hang of things. At the start, it was like playing bass; matching the beat to the rhythm. After that, it was as easy as riding a bike, even if he had fallen off once or twice.

It wasn't until later, back at the Top Ten, still in a euphoric daze, that he'd thought of Sandra, and his cheeks began to burn horribly. Fook. He'd completely blanked her out of his mind. What did that mean? He didn't want to lose her—he loved her. But this wasn't really about her, was it? It was Hamburg.

And suddenly he knew why there was so little talk of Hamburg among the musicians, back in Liverpool.

No one had wanted to give the game away.

So who could blame him? The way everyone went on and on about shagging, all the time, it was only natural for a bloke to be more experienced—nothing to feel guilty about. Even so, he decided to write more letters to Sandra to tell her how much he loved and missed her. After all, that's where the real world was—back home in Liverpool.

But that was Hamburg for you.

At night, when the never-ending neon lights held back the shadows and the dark, it was, Spike thought, just this side of paradise—a non-stop riot of new sights, sounds, and sensations.

Dave told him all the bands really, really hated the place for the first few weeks. Then, they loved it forever. "You always take home much, much more from Hamburg than you ever arrive with," he said.

Fras pulled him aside then. "You might have been born in Liverpool, Spike," he said, "but Hamburg's the place where you grow up...and grow up real fast."

Then Fras and Dave told him they'd finished with the Top Ten Club and that The Persuaders were going to play the fabulous new Star-Club that was opening around the corner.

TONY SHERIDAN was spitting mad when he learned The Persuaders were leaving the Top Ten to go play the Star-Club with Roy-fucking-Young. "You scheming bastards. You might've fucking told us."

"What the fuck would you have done, then, Tone?" Dave Brown shouted back, balling his fists.

"I'd have fucking kicked your arses out of here, you ungrateful fucking swines," yelled the Top Ten Club's resident top attraction.

Chin down, fists up, Spike moved in, to take him out.

"Leave it, Spike," growled Fras. "Look, Tone, we're only going where the work is. And it's not as if we went looking. Someone saw us play and offered us work; that's all. We'd have been right prats, to say 'No', and you know it. There aren't too many people still breathing, let alone alive, in Hamburg who've ever said 'no' to Horst Fascher or Manfred Weissleder."

Tony Sheridan blinked and went silent. It was true. You always had to watch out for yourself. And you always went where the work was. You and the music were the only things you ever really had any loyalty to. Anyway, he was slated to play the Star-Club, himself, the following month. So he just sighed and nodded his head. "Yeah, well, just fuck off out of it, then, before Peter Eckhorn gets back and thinks of doing something really nasty to each one of you."

"Yeah, thanks, Tone," they'd all mumbled. "See you round, eh?"

Then they'd removed their gear from out the Top Ten Club as fast as was humanly possible, whizzed down the stairs, and gone whooping up the Reeperbahn. Glad to have got away without everyone getting a very serious hiding.

CHAPTER TWENTY-FIVE

Cry For A Shadow

John Lennon was flying high, enjoying life at long last, and loving every bloody minute of it. Back in bloody Hamburg and The Beatles cocks of the bloody walk, the star bloody act at the Star-Club, the 'toppermost' bloody club in St. Pauli. What was it 'Eppy' was always saying? 'Could anything be better than this?'

"Hey, 'oop, look, fellas. It's Klaus and Astrid. Yoo-hoo. Hello-ee. It's us. Hello-ee." All but bursting with happiness, humming loudly, arms stuck out from his sides like wings, he ran down the airport concourse like an aeroplane in full flight, just as he'd done back in the schoolyard at Dovedale Primary School. Okay, it was silly, but sod it, if you couldn't stick your head in the clouds, occasionally, what good was life? As he got closer to Astrid Kirchherr, he throttled back and got ready to land a big kiss on her cheek. He scanned the waiting area, looking for his best friend, Stu Sutcliffe, but could see no sign of him. "Typical bloody artist," he said to himself, "always bloody late."

"Hey, Astrid. What a lovely surprise to see you and our Klaus. How did you know we were meeting George and Brian off the plane? Where's our Stu? Can't drag him away from his painting, is that it?"

Then he saw the look on Astrid's face and his heart faltered and his mind started to go into free-fall.

"Stuart's gone, John."

"Gone where, love?"

"No, John. Stuart ist tot...he is dead. There was very much bleeding inside his brain. He died yesterday on the way to hospital. He's dead, John. Gone. And we wait now here to meet his poor mother, also, from the plane."

He couldn't breathe. His face froze into a mask as his guts turned to ice and suddenly he was back again—being told his mother, Julia, had just been knocked down and killed by a car.

He'd died that time, too. Just like he was dying now—dying to the world. The same cold, cruel world that'd gone and taken away the only other person he'd ever loved with all his heart.

"You've always got to be true to your passion, Johnny," Stu had told him countless times, in letters and conversations. "That's the only thing that'll never ever lie to you."

Now Stu was dead and gone, too.

What'd he done to deserve such hurt? Why take his mother from him? Why take his closest friend? What on God's green earth had either of them ever done to hurt anyone? Julia had always been so full of life and fun. Stu was always so open, honest and alive. Why take them when there were so many other miserable sods in the world no one would ever miss? What did it all fookin' mean? What? He'd just been given his answer, in spades, hadn't he? It meant nothing. It was all just shite—the whole fookin' lot of it—just shite.

He knew in that instant he had to harden his mind and cover over his heart or one day he'd look and see that someone else he loved had gone and died and it'd break him forever. You had to decide. You either lived or you died. There was no standing in the middle. And somewhere, deep down inside him, in the place where he'd crashed and burned only moments before, he howled in pain—a primal scream for his mother, for his friend, and for himself being born again into a world of hurt and anger and unrelenting pain. He pushed through a curtain of white light and found himself sitting, huddled on a bench, rocking backwards and forwards. Shivering. Shaking. Babbling. Crying. No, he was laughing. No, he was crying. Fook! What did it matter, laughing or crying, he was the one who was still alive, even though he'd almost died. From now on though he'd love by his own rules. Only ever open his heart to the love he made himself—the love you took with you when you died—the only love that would never ever leave you or betray you.

He looked up to see Paul trying to comfort Astrid, arm around her, his face white. And Pete, sitting alone, staring off into space, crying his eyes out. Then suddenly there was George and 'Eppy', both ashen-faced and silent, already knowing the worst. And Millie Sutcliffe, Stu's grief-stricken mum, utterly lost and bewildered, still unable to believe her lovely Stu was dead. Minutes stretched into eternities and then with not even enough emotion left for anyone to say goodbye, Klaus Voorman gently ushered Astrid and Mrs Sutcliffe away. And suddenly there he was again, alone in the world, even as 'Eppy', George, Paul, and Pete tried to comfort him, but there was no comfort now and certainly not for him, he was a real nowhere man.

SPIKE hit a single bass note—rapidly, repeatedly—eight-to-the-bar—sending a shock wave of sound pulsing out into the club. He stopped, stilled the string. Cliff Lewis hit the snare. And Roy Young yelled *"Aaaah-wop...bop-aah-wop!"* and began hammering his piano and hollering out the words to 'Tutti-Frutti'. The Star-Club's yellow PVC curtains swished open and the crowd roared its approval. Out of the corner of his eye, Spike caught the stage lights reflecting on Fras's glasses, as he nodded to keep time. Saw the high-hat, snapping up and down. He locked onto the beat and became one with the bass drum. And for the rest of the set, he was gone, man, gone. Carried along by Cliff Lewis's frantic drumming, Fras and Dave's rocking guitars, and Roy Young's great voice and boogie-woogie-style piano.

"Aaaah-wop...bop-aah-wop...bop-aah...Whoooooo!"

Next, Roy Young belted out 'The Girl Can't Help It' and then he called for everyone to 'Keep A Knockin' because 'Oh, My Soul' they just might get to meet 'Lucille' and 'Baby Face'. At the end, as the crowd roared for more, the Roy Young Combo reprised one last blistering throat-shredding chorus of 'Tutti-Frutti' and a final *"Yipee-yi-ye...Aaaah-lop-bam-boom!"*

Afterwards, laughing, clowning, Little Richard's songs coursing through their veins like speed, they made their way back to the dressing rooms. They passed a line of Star-Club posters stuck up on the corridor walls, just like the ones that'd been plastered up all over St. Pauli for weeks. Spike waved at one. "Been meaning to ask, like, what the hell does that mean?"

Dave Brown, ever eager to show off his History and German 'A' level exam successes, struck a jangling chord on his guitar and said, in the voice of a pompous teacher. "Taken, literally, it says, 'THE TIME IS AT HAND. GERMAN FARMERS' MUSIC IS OVER. LONG LIVE ROCK AND ROLL'." He laughed. "But what it says to me, like, is that the kids around here have all had quite enough of this Fatherland business...und zey vont to tell all ze boring old farts who've been running ze place and trying to fook up ze world, das rock 'n' roll ist here to stay, und it's high time for zem all to pack-up zer old kitbags and go."

"No more fookin' up the world, is right," yelled Spike. "Roll over Herr Hitler and tell Comrade Stalin the news."

THE AIR inside the all-new Star-Club already felt old and stale. Clouds of cigarette smoke mixed with the smell of cheap perfume, rivers of sweat, and spilled beer. The atmosphere was electric though and the seething mass of a thousand or so people stamped and cheered and roared in anticipation. And, as the opening, bass-laden chords of Ritchie Barrett's rocker 'Some Other Guy' throbbed and pushed from behind the yellow PVC curtains, the roar of the crowd reached a new crescendo.

The curtains slowly swished back to reveal The Beatles. John and Paul, at the microphones, strumming and thumbing their guitars. George bent over his guitar, concentrating on his run of chords. Pete hitting the ride cymbal, kicking out the beat for all he was worth. Yet, even with all that, the welcoming roar of the crowd faltered and dipped. There were murmurs of confusion, even whistles of dissatisfaction. It was The Beatles—had to be. It just didn't look like them. Gone was their all-rocking leather gear. Instead they were all smartly dressed in matching dark grey suits, white shirts, and black narrow knitted ties—the New York skyscrapers painted on the stage backdrop only adding to the odd sense of dislocation—even disassociation.

It didn't sound at all like The Beatles, either.

The wild and thundering beat had been savagely tamed. Though it was the club's fault this time, not Brian Epstein's new vision. The place had been built as a cinema and the acoustics were all wrong. Sound from the stage immediately bounced back from the balcony, leaving the bass notes to die, and the song flat and utterly lost of its drive. The Beatles, their sensitivities ever attuned to their audience, all felt the drop in response and reacted.

Paul hit his bass strings even harder. John and George adjusted the controls on their guitars. John turned round to Pete, shouted for him to bloody well thump harder. And slowly, slowly the sound lifted from off the floor and reclaimed the lost bass notes and by the time The Beatles had brought 'Some Other Guy' to a finish, they'd been forced to drive themselves and their sound to a whole new level.

"Fookin' hell," groaned John. "That was almost a total bloody disaster." They'd really have to work hard for their money in this place. Manfred Weissleder would demand it of them, anyway. So for the next hour he urged The Beatles on and on and on and they beat and bashed and sweated and sang their way through to the end of the first set. He bowed, along with George and Paul, in response to the rapturous applause—another 'Eppy' touch. "And to think there's another seven bloody weeks of this hour-on-hour-off, daily-grind to go yet." As posh as the new club was, even with the better class of digs they'd been given across the street, it already felt like a bloody prison. And even with all the extra effort, where was the bloody recording contract they'd been promised? That was the only thing that'd get them off the never-ending bloody roundabout of club dates—the only real hope of them ever getting a one-way ticket out of bloody Hamburg.

Glad of the break, he downed a beer, grabbed a bottle of Coke, and went for a piss. The old-lady washroom attendant greeted him like a long-lost son and he gave her a big hug, a kiss on the cheek, and scored a tube of Prellies. Then he washed down a couple of pills with a mouthful of Coke. "Willkommen nach bloody Hamburg," he muttered, making his way back to the table reserved for The Beatles. He plopped himself down and took a long sip of beer. "So when's it going to start happening, like you promised, 'Eppy'? Fookin' when?" The startled look on Brian Epstein's face said it all. The stupid bugger had probably thought it'd been a good start to the night and not the near fookin' disaster that it almost was. As per bloody usual the ignorant sod had missed the point, completely.

"Soon, John, soon. It's all going to work out, I promise. One day, you'll all be bigger than Elvis Presley, I just know you will."

"Bigger than Elvis? My arse, Brian," he growled. "Gene Vincent's gammy leg is bigger than we are." He banged down his empty beer glass. Stuck out his chin. "If you want my opinion, 'Eppy', old boy. I'd say it's high time you pulled your bloody finger out. And I don't mean out of some bloke's trousers, neither." The victim of his assault, hurt beyond measure, coloured and turned away. He fixed his gaze on the back of Brian Epstein's neck, narrowed his eyes, and said, "Where we going to, fellas?"

"To...the...er...to the..."

"I said, where we fookin' going to, fellas?"

"To the top, Johnny?"

"And which fookin' top is that, fellas?"

"To the toppermost of the poppermost."

"We make the music, Brian. We sing the songs. We sweat our bloody guts out, Brian. We do our bloody job. So when are you going to start bloody doing yours?"

"I'm trying, John, I am." Brian Epstein spun round, his voice rising in pitch with every word. "My parents think I'm mad. My friends think I've gone completely round the twist. But I'm doing everything I possibly can...and more. Why can't you just be a little more reasonable, yourself, for once?"

"Well, I can't say I'm feeling too reasonable at the moment, Mr Epstein. The truth is, like, I'm starting to lose my patience. As I think we all are. So, whatever it is you think you're doing, it's not good enough. You've got to do more. Your job is to get us a recording contract. So my advice is that you stop all your faggoty-arsed day-dreaming, for once, Brian, and just go do it."

"Oh, leave off, John," snapped George. "You're always having a go at him, you are."

"And you can shurrup, too, Georgie Porgie. When I want your opinion, I'll bloody well ask for it."

But George didn't back down. "Someone's got to tell you. You're becoming a real drag, John. Me, I agree with, Brian. I know we can make it, but we never will if we've got to fight you and everyone else, besides."

"I can't be Johnny-be-good all the time just to bloody please you and everybody soddin' else, George. So, if you don't like it, you can fook off, too."

"I bloody well will, an' all. And you can fook off, too, you sod."

"Right, lads," said Paul, cheerily. "Who's up for another little sing-song, up on stage, then?"

"Fook off, you, an' all."

"Yeah, I heard you the first time, John, but if I fook off, then all that'll be left of The Beatles will be Pete banging away on his drums."

"Why don't you all just shut it?" Pete shouted. "You lot are always bloody bickering, you are. Just leave me out of it, okay?" He pushed back his chair. "I'm bloody well going out for some fresh air, I am."

"Not like our Pete to have a little outburst, like that, is it?" said George, quietly.

"It must be something in the air," said Paul.

"It's Friday the fookin' 13th, that's what it is," snapped John.

"I wonder which one of us is going to be extra unlucky, to-night, then," whispered George.

That was when Horst Fascher approached their table.

HORST FASCHER closed the door of Manfred Weissleder's of-fice—a room that'd once served as the projection booth when the Star-Club had been a porno cinema—and hurried back down to the main floor. The undisputed crime boss of all of St. Pauli was about to make one of his rare visits to the netherworld and everybody needed to be warned. Be extra alert. The club's open-ing night had gone very well, so far, but there was still no room for mistakes. None. *Niemals.* A dissatisfied Herr Weissleder was just too unthinkable to even think about. Hamburg's reigning porno king trusted few men and it was he, Horst Fascher, who'd recommended that his boss hire the one and only Beatles for the grand opening of the Star-Club.

Und, Gott sei Dank, sein Chef war sehr zufrieden mit Den Beatles.

So pleased, in fact, his boss wanted to mark the occasion by presenting each Beatle with a heavy gold identity bracelet. And once Horst Fascher had managed to gather Brian Epstein and the boys backstage—all very muted, for some reason—Herr Weissleder made his presentation in his best halting English. Then ascended back up to his office at the top of the building to attend to the rest of his ever-growing pleasure empire.

The gold bracelets—the name of each Beatle engraved on one side, the words 'Star-Club' on the other—were not only an expression of Manfred Weissleder's pleasure, they were also a sign of his protection. Lesser people, he wished to favour, received a gold star to wear on their lapels or were given a star-shaped sticker to put on their car or guitar case. It was a symbol—known throughout all of Hamburg—that signalled the wearer should be left totally unmolested and unharmed. And in no way taken advantage of by any members of the underworld—or even the police.

Horst Fascher touched the little star-shaped pin in his own lapel—not that he needed to wear it—his fearsome reputation was protection enough. But him also wearing a gold star gave the pin added status, which was very useful when dealing with so many gullible and, all too often, completely irresponsible Britisher rock 'n' roll musicians.

Manfred Weissleder had decreed there be no trouble at the opening night of the Star-Club and that retribution against troublemakers, be swift and dire. And word had duly gone out. The many outsiders and foreigners that flocked to St. Pauli, each and every night, who knew little of the language, and even less of Hamburg's unwritten laws, were only to be expected. But there'd been rumours, floating around for days, that certain rival club owners had paid various Hamburg gangs to disrupt the Star-Club's all-important first night. Which was why Horst Fascher had instructed every one of his trusted lieutenants to be on constant lookout for any sign of trouble. No fights, brawls, or arguments were to be permitted. None. Not even by one single, solitary, drunken sailor. Any and all trouble was to be dealt with instantly and all evidence of it immediately removed.

PAUL McCARTNEY shook his head. "Bloody hell, I thought those waiters were going to kill that poor bloody sailor. His head was split open like a coconut. There was blood and brains all over the place."

"Just like the Garston Baths," sniffed John Lennon, minutely examining his new gold bracelet, but otherwise quite unimpressed. "Do you remember the night that young kid almost got booted to death, in front of us? Now that was bloody horrible to watch, that was."

"Well, you've all come a long way since then," said Brian Epstein. "I'm sure, tonight's episode was just a single, unfortunate incident."

"Did you see the size of those truncheons they were hitting the poor lad with," said Paul. "They were huge."

"Better those truncheons than those gas guns they've all got," said George. "Those things could make you go blind."

"No, it's playing with yourself that makes you go blind, George," said John, batting his eyelids. "No. The worst things are the spring-loaded coshes Horst and his crew use. They're dead nasty, they are. Knock you out faster than a Lime Street whore's handbag."

"That shop, down the way, that sells all them knuckledusters, coshes and knives and things," said George, thoughtfully. "Do you reckon we're now able to afford that big bazooka they've got in the window?"

"No, that's gone, there's a machine gun there, now," said John, banging down his empty rum and coke glass.

"Hey, do you remember that time we were at the Kaiserkeller?" said Paul, lighting a cigarette. "That night we went down that little club, with Allan Williams, and that big gangster-looking fella walked right up to the table we were sitting at and pulled a big bloody gun out of his coat and shot that bloke, sitting with us, right in the face?"

"Course, I remember, you daft twat. There was blood and guts and bits of brain all over me new leather trousers. Scared me shitless, for weeks, it did. I thought I was a right fookin' gonner, too, I did."

"John, please. That's quite enough. That sort of language is quite inappropriate, even here. Do remember, please, you are out in public."

"Well, why don't you remember it for me, Brian," John shot back. "That's what you get your percentage for, isn't it? Bloody hell, if I can't enjoy a bloody drink while I'm up there, knackering myself on stage, every bloody night, till bloody four in the morning, what the fookin' hell am I doing here, Brian? For that matter, what the fook are any of us doing here? Explain that to me, if you can, you stuck-up, pansy-arsed Jew. You're like all the other snotty upper-class bastards who think the rest of us should just shut-up and do as we're told. Well, fook that, Brian. And fook you, 'an all."

Brian Epstein, mortified by John's outburst, flushed crimson. "Look, John, I...I...I didn't mean to upset you. I just meant to...oh, damn...damn." He crossed his arms and turned away, again.

"Oh, bloody hell, here we go, again. Look, Brian, we're wearing your bloody monkey-suits and we've promised not to eat chip butties, belch, fart, or swear on stage. What more do you bloody want?"

Brian Epstein didn't respond. He couldn't respond.

"Look, 'Eppy', I'm sorry," mumbled John. "I didn't mean it. Okay? It's just with Stu dying, an' all, I'm all wound-up tighter than a bloody alarm clock. It's as if he'll walk in here any minute and we'll all get up on stage and be together, again. Only, the only trouble is, now, he never will, will he?"

When Brian Epstein still didn't respond, John pulled a face and reached for one of Paul's cigarettes. "Give us a light, will yer, Paul?"

"Er, Brian, where's Stu's Mum staying? In a hotel, is she?"

Brian Epstein turned, still very hurt. "No, George. She's staying with Astrid's family. She's...look I'm so, so very sorry about Stuart, really I am. It's awful. It can't be easy losing one's dearest, closest friend."

"Oh, please don't start again, 'Eppy'," snapped John. "A rich queer like you could never bloody know. So just leave it alone, will yer."

Brian Epstein, all but in tears, turned away, again.

John Lennon, his face set in stone, sat staring at the stage.

Paul looked over at John and Brian, the two of them, worlds apart, again. Damn and blast it, what a bloody awful night it was turning out to be. Friday the fookin' 13th was right.

HOW COULD JOHN have been so spiteful, so hurtful, so damnably beastly? John's remarks had pushed him deep, deep down inside and he stared out into the dimly lit, smoke-filled club, seeing nothing, hearing nothing. His entire world narrowed to a dark, shadowy tunnel where only hurt, anger, and he lived. And he sat there, alone in the crowd, feeling more hurt than he could ever remember.

It was the first time John had made such a derogatory remark to his face about him being a Jew. He'd had to put up with that all his life, but he'd never once been ashamed of being Jewish. But John had also called him a pansy and a queer and that was another matter entirely. But as with any accusation of homosexuality, it was always simply better to deny it and go on, as normal. That, after all, was how he'd dealt with such incidents, in the past.

This constant bickering between he and John was getting everybody down. It'd started with that first, awful outburst at the audition with Decca. Then continued with John's bitter response to Decca's rejection, when John had told him, in no uncertain terms, that he better keep his 'bloody bastard' hands off their music in future.

Things had gone steadily downhill ever since, but he was baffled as to why. It couldn't be the new suits he'd had them wear on stage or the rules he'd drawn up concerning their behaviour. They'd all agreed to do that. No, it had to be the recording contract or, rather, the lack of it.

Or perhaps John's real fear was that The Beatles simply weren't good enough and they'd never amount to anything. But that was patently ridiculous. They were brilliant originals and as he kept telling them one day they'd be bigger than Elvis Presley.

Stuart Sutcliffe's death had come as a crushing blow—he understood that—but it'd only served to bring to the surface all the fears and frustrations that must've been gnawing away inside John for weeks, if not months. That was it. John was under intolerable pressure to succeed and everything that'd been bottled-up inside was bursting out. The anger hadn't been directed at him. John had been lashing out at his own hurt. It was John that needed comforting, not him. He saw that clearly now.

He was startled by a sudden noise and looked round and saw dark shadows twisting and swirling as if to take monstrous form. He tried to move, put out a hand, cry out, but he could do none of these things. All he could do was watch in growing horror. Then his heart simply stopped dead. It was the dark stranger—come from out of the shadows—from out of his nightmares—to haunt him, hurt him, kill him. Oh, no, no. Dear God. No. It couldn't be happening again, not now, not here in Hamburg. No. No. No.

He tried to cry out again, but couldn't. And as the tall faceless shadow pushed towards him, through the crowds on the dance floor, the interplay of dark and light resolved into no one he recognised. He started to shiver uncontrollably as the spectral figure loomed over him, pointed towards him, and then addressed him in a voice of doom. "Sind Sie, Die Beatles?"

Everything around him slowed to a standstill. His only focus the silver automatic pistol in the man's hand that was pointed at him and all four Beatles. The only real question now—whether he was capable of throwing himself in front of the bullet? Could he pay the ultimate sacrifice for his dream? Would he willingly die to save John? Paul? George? Or Pete? Even, as angry and upset as he'd been, only moments before? Could he do it? Could he give his life for The Beatles?

"Bist Du John Lennon? Ist Ihr Namen, John Lennon?"

Dear God, it *was* John that the gunman was after.

"Are you, John Lennon? Is your name, John Lennon?"

No, that would never happen. Not while there was still breath in his body. He felt the heat rise in him, not as a blush of shame or humiliation, but as righteous anger. He started to get up, to throw himself across John. He could do it. He would do it. My God, he was doing it. It was the right thing to do, the honourable thing to do. After all, he was their manager and they'd put their trust in him. It was as if a huge flashgun had gone off in his mind, everything now as clear as day. This was his destiny— to create and then save The Beatles for the entire world.

As he looked up, the moment etched forever into his brain, he saw another face, not his own, but a face that was John and Paul and George and Pete, all one and the same, but that was none of them. It was young and fresh-faced, like them, with the same pale, English skin that always threw the beard's blue-black shadow into relief. The same tousled, dark Beatle hair, the same black leather jacket and blue jeans. It was 'his boys' as he'd first seen them in Astrid Kirchherr's photographs, in Bill Harry's of-fice—just as they'd appeared that first lunchtime session at the Cavern.

He saw the boy in the black leather jacket lunge for the gun-man's arm. Heard screams and shouts and a sound like a crack of a drumstick against snare drum. There was a single scream. And then the pistol fell, slowly, oh-so-very-very-slowly onto the floor, and all he could hear was the heavy pounding *boom—boom—boom—boom* of bass guitar and bass drums and the endless crashing of cymbals.

Brian Epstein felt the earth tilt beneath him. The gunman and the leather-jacketed boy were lost in moving walls of people. Covered by swirling curtains of darkness. He heard no more shots. No sudden cries of death. There were only shouts and laughter and the sounds of crashing glass—all of it echoing as if caught in a long dark tunnel.

He tried to recover both his balance and his senses. And he turned to look at 'the boys'—his dear, dear boys—as the full ca-cophony of sound rushed in and engulfed him. And the music from the band up on stage washed over him in repeated waves and the thundering *boom—boom—boom—boom* of the bass drum caught and meshed with the high-hat rasp of his own short snatched breaths and he was drowning all over again. And no way out of it—only more darkness.

JOHN LENNON made his displeasure known. "Bloody hell. You come off stage, hoping for a bit of peace and quiet, a pleasant drink with yer mates, and all you get is these rowdy-arsed, Nazi bastards who can't hold their bloody drink, knocking over tables and messing things up for everyone. I tell you it's getting worse than Garston Baths, on a Saturday night. If I wasn't feeling so bloody knackered and 'Eppy' here didn't need the money, I'd tell them all to go fook themselves." He tilted back his head and shouted, "Hey, Horst, do yer job. '*Mach*, some bloody *schau!*' We've got some serious drinking to do, here, before we do our next set."

He turned and saw Brian Epstein's ashen-white face. "Bloody hellfire, 'Eppy', you look like you've just seen a ghost or something. You, all right, are you? Here, drink your brandy. George, give him your rum and coke. God, you must find all this a bit too rough. But don't you worry, none, 'Eppy', noisy disturbances like that are normal here in Hamburg. It's normal, most places back in Liverpool, come to that, but it doesn't bother us, any, we've seen it all a million times before."

"Are you all right, there, Brian?"

"Yes. Yes, thank you, Paul. I'm all right, really, I am. Only I...I thought for one awful moment that...Oh, it was horrible."

John was truly taken aback when he saw 'Eppy' bury his face in his hands. He reached over and gently touched him on the arm. "Hey, 'Eppy', look I'm sorry what I said before. You know I didn't mean it. It's just that with Stu being dead, I'm all worked up. He was my best friend. I already miss him something terrible. I know I can be a right bastard, sometimes, but I don't mean it. Honest. Just ask the fellas."

"Don't believe him, Brian, he's a complete and utter swine."

"Yeah, a big swine with big bloody brass knobs on."

John narrowed his eyes and scowled. "Thank you, Messrs Paul Ramone and Carl Harrison, I know I can always count on you two."

Paul and George just looked back at him, smiled sweetly.

'Eppy' turned to face them all. "John...John...about what you said just then. Thank you. Thank you. Only, it means a lot, it does. More than you could ever know. And thank you, each one of you, for trusting, in me. I promise, I won't ever let you down.

I'll help get you all, all the way to the top, even if I die in the attempt, really I will. You have my word on it."

"Well, don't die on us, 'Eppy'. We'd all be well and truly buggered, if you ever went and did that. So we'll take you at your word, for now. You just go and do what you said you'd do for us, okay?"

"Yeah, Brian," nodded Paul, enthusiastically. "Then we'll all end up millionaires, together."

"Yeah, and I can buy myself lots of nice new guitars," laughed George, taking a very long drag on his cigarette.

"I fancy a nice new set of Ludwig drums and a car, myself," said Pete. "Just to be going on with, that is."

John nodded, narrowed his eyes, and smiled. He looked at the group he'd forged and, clapping his hands together and rubbing them for luck, he shouted, "Right then, fellas, where we going to?"

"To the top, Johnny," yelled the other Beatles. 'Eppy' did too.

"And which top is that, fellas?"

"The very top, Johnny."

"And where's that, fellas?"

"The toppermost of the poppermost."

"Yeah. Yeah. Yeah," he cried, committing the moment to memory.

SPIKE blinked awake, but when he tried to lift his head it thumped like hell and the room spun round. He tried to push himself up, but couldn't. A strong hand was very firmly holding him down.

"Nein, beweg' dich nicht. Do not move."

He looked up into the face of Horst Fascher.

"Horst...did you see? There was a man...a man who was going to shoot John Lennon. I tried to stop him, I did, but I..."

"Ja, I saw this man, also," said Horst Fascher, quietly. "It is good, now. Nothing bad here tonight has happened. It is over now and it is finished with for good."

"But he had a pistol, Horst. I saw him raise it...point it. I shouted."

"Ja. I also saw und heard this. So quickly I stopped this man."

"Then you...*you* saved John's life, Horst."

"Ach, it is nothing. They do not understand how often in the past I have had to do this thing for all of them...for Paul, und Pete, und George, und John, also. St. Pauli is full of not so good people. Und so always I must take care about them. Und, now, slowly you must sit up for Horst und then you must this drink."

Horst held up a small glass tumbler. Spike took it in both hands and sipped at the clear liquid expecting it to be water, but it was neat Schnapps. He spluttered, choked, and erupted into a fit of coughing.

"See? Now, you live. Und soon you will feel much more better. Yes?" Horst laughed and banged Spike on the back several times. "Gut. Good. Now this I give you. Und, in Hamburg, this always you must wear. Verstand? Everyone will know this pin. It says you are under Herr Weissleder's protection. Und under mine, also, now, forever." He pinned a tiny gold star onto the lapel of Spike's jacket. "You verstand this, Spike? Horst und his brothers, Uwe und Freddie, also, of course, will take care about you, forever. You, in unserer Familie, now are. Und so, now, no one will hurt you ever again. Nie und nimmer. This, I promise you in my life."

CHAPTER TWENTY-SIX

Nowhere Man

Brian Epstein had lived the stuff of nightmare for far too long to doubt there were more things in heaven and earth than ever he could dream of, but the incident in the Star-Club had driven his deepest darkest fears to the surface and him to the very brink of madness.

Every time he looked at John, it thrust him back to the horrific moment when he thought he'd lost the hateful, hurtful, cruel, capricious, mean, moody, magnificent, irrepressible, irreplaceable, one-of-a-kind, wonderful John Lennon, forever. Every stranger's face seemed full of threat, every shadow pregnant with some new horror. All he could do now was try to outrun whatever peril might still be lurking in the shadows. At the very least he had to get out of Hamburg, back to Liverpool, back to London—and fast. Otherwise, he really would go mad. So he told 'the boys' he had pressing family business at home and left for England the very next day.

John's words had hit him hard. The Beatles *were* going nowhere and, in his heart of hearts, he knew he was to blame and he had no choice but to redouble his efforts. He immediately re-established his punishing schedule of twice-weekly trips to London. Calling upon the same people, at the same record companies, even without an appointment, in the vague hope that something might have changed since his last visit. He hated being told, 'No', over and over again, but it was the indignity of being left to cool his heals in waiting rooms for hours on end that he found really insufferable.

Things were also getting very difficult at home. His father was becoming increasingly angry at his neglect of the family business and had told him, to his face, he was mad to go gallivanting off to London on behalf of "those *nudnik* Beatles." Yet even that didn't deter him.

His one abiding concern was how to get George Martin to respond. He gave serious thought to withdrawing all of NEMS' business from EMI. Threaten to no longer stock discs from their Columbia, HMV or Parlophone labels. Calculating that the loss of revenue would be too much even for the giant company to bear. It would be easy enough to accomplish. He could special-order any record he needed from other retailers. And if the 'stick' didn't work, he could always offer EMI the 'carrot' that NEMS would guarantee to buy three thousand copies of any single recorded by The Beatles. Damn it, he'd buy ten thousand copies, if it helped bring in a recording contract.

The only thing he had any real control over was The Beatles. He could never allow anyone to wrest them from his grip or cause them to ever question their allegiance to him. And to that end he wrote several names on a notepad and drew circles around those of Bob Wooler and Ray McFall. He put a tick by both names. The Cavern needed The Beatles almost as much as The Beatles needed the Cavern, which meant he should establish a stronger business relationship with both men.

He put another tick next to Bill Harry's name. John's close friendship with the man, plus, his own fortnightly record column, meant The Beatles could always count on the *Mersey Beat*'s editor for support.

Allan Williams, The Beatles' so-called ex-manager, was still very critical of 'the boys' and his unbridled sarcasm could all too easily damage the group's reputation around Liverpool. Even so, Allan Williams could still be of help, so that earned the man a question mark.

Next was Mona Best, Pete's mother, who had the irritating habit of always referring to The Beatles as "Pete's group." It was true, she owned the Casbah Club, promoted dances at Knotty Ash Hall, and in the past both she and Pete had acted as de-facto managers of the group—making bookings, collecting money, that sort of thing. Even so, that didn't entitle either of them a say in the group's future or how it was managed. The Beatles were *his* boys, *his* group. He put a second question mark next to Mona Best's name.

He crossed out Sam Leach's name. Then drew a circle around the names of Tom McCardle and Terry McCann. He'd often seen both men at 'the Tower' and had been impressed with their organisational abilities. Yes, distinct possibilities there. His thoughts strayed back to Sam Leach and the hold the man had on all-important Friday-night franchise at 'the Tower'. He was livid at the thought of being permanently locked out of the deal and he knew he had no other option, but to storm 'the Tower' and lay siege to it.

He shook his head. What had possessed the insufferable little man to act as he did? The very fact that he, Brian Epstein, had wanted to go into business with Sam Leach must've shown he fully acknowledged the man's past success as a promoter. Why else would he have offered a third of NEMS Enterprises in return for the two of them jointly promoting the Friday night shows. He'd as much said so to The Beatles and they'd been delighted at the prospect. Only the foolish, pathetic, ridiculously stupid little man had turned him down flat. For heaven's sake, why? Couldn't the man see he was being offered a chance of a lifetime? On top of which, Leach had then been unforgivably rude. Well, then, good riddance to bad rubbish.

"DO YOU REALLY love him, Sandra?"

Maureen stopped cutting Sandra's hair and looked at her younger sister in the mirror. They were in the little bedroom she kept specially for Sandra in the house she and her husband, Jack, had recently moved into, just off World's End, the unfashionable end of the King's Road. It was more Fulham, than Chelsea, but Sandra thought it was heaven.

"Do I love him? Yeah, I do, Morr, lots."

Maureen nodded. "Are you sure? Even though he's still over in Hamburg. Getting up to God knows what?"

Sandra nodded, careful not to move in case Maureen cut off an ear. "Yeah, I do. I trust him. Loads. Anyroad, it's not for too much longer. He writes me letters almost every day and says he misses me madly." She turned, looked up at her sister "You saw the painting he did of us? That's real love, that is."

Maureen raised an eyebrow and smiled, knowingly.

"No, he's fab, Morr, he is. I know he acts all cool on the outside. Like he doesn't really care about things. But he does care, Morr, he does. Inside, he's loving and kind and he cares about me. And I know he feels the same way I do about getting out of Liverpool. So, yeah, I really love him. I do."

"Have you, you know, let him shag you yet, then?"

"Maureen!" cried Sandra, twisting away from Maureen's scissors. "What an awful thing to ask." She sat and scowled.

Maureen shook her head, tried not to smile, and very tentatively started snipping away again. "Does he use anything, like?"

"What do you mean?" Sandra said, quietly.

"A contraceptive, dafty. 'French letter'? 'Rubber Johnny'?"

Sandra blushed bright red. "Er, no. No. I don't know."

Maureen stopped cutting. "Well he should or you could end up pregnant. There's never any telling what a fella will do. He may marry you or he may just bugger off. So you've got to think about it, love. And if I don't tell you to, who will? Because if you ended up alone you'd have little choice but to live at home and you wouldn't want to bring a baby up anywhere near our dad, would you?"

Sandra winced, shivered, the joyful feelings of a moment before, falling away like so many pieces of newly cut hair.

They'd both suffered from the unwelcome attentions of their father. He was the real reason Maureen had left home and why Sandra couldn't wait to get out.

Neither of them had ever said anything to their mother about their ordeals. Both sisters believing that it was their fault and that it was up to them to save their mam from all the shame and hurt of knowing. So they'd each suffered and endured in silence—at first all alone—and then together. Dreading, ever being left alone in the house with their father. Hoping that some day he might be run over by a bus or that, one day, at work, he'd just fall in the Mersey and drown. That was the terrible dark secret the two sisters had shared for so long—the stark fear of the all-too-familiar shape looming in the doorway of their bedroom, limned in light from the passageway beyond. A dark confusing presence coming ever nearer to block out thought and mind. To smother them with beery breath and rip apart their sleep with rough callused fingers and hands. And worse things still.

"How's he been since I've been gone?" Maureen said, as she snipped away again with her scissors. "Have you been okay?"

Sandra nodded. "The last time he tried was just after you left and I told him I'd kill him if he tried it again. Said I'd push a knitting needle in his ear when he was sleeping or poke his bloody eyes out. And that when he was dead, I'd tell our mam, and all his friends down the docks where he works...the whole bloody world...what a dirty old sod he was. He shouted at me, threatened to hit me, but he didn't. I told him I'd scream the place down if he did. He hit mam, though, a good few times and did a lot of shouting, but he's left me alone since. There's been awful atmospheres round the house, but I always keep the bedroom door locked and push the chest of drawers in front of it, each night. And whenever I can, like, I stay over at Thelma's."

Maureen stood back, looked at her little sister in the mirror, and tried to stop from crying. Then she gently rubbed Sandra's shoulders. "You're a bloody little marvel, you are, Sandra. I always felt like killing him, myself, but I never told him. I was always too frightened of what he might do to you or our mam."

Sandra looked up at Maureen and sighed. "I know. I thought I'd die the day you left home. I'd always felt that...that you..."

"I had to get out, Sandra. Or maybe I really would've killed him. Does your, Spike, know about it? Have you told him?"

"No. No, I haven't said anything, to anybody, not ever, not even Thelma. I'd be too embarrassed. And I could never tell, Spike. I'd just die." She paused. "Does...does your Jack, know?"

Maureen sighed and put her scissors down on top of the dressing table. "Yeah, he does. Everything. When I just couldn't stop crying after each time we, you know, we did it...intercourse, like. He kept on asking what was wrong and one time I just broke down and told him."

"What did he say?"

"He said that he'd kill our dad if he ever met him again."

"Is that why he never comes up with you, when you come visit our mam?"

"Yeah. That's why he says you can come live here, anytime, you like." Maureen paused, rubbed her little sister's shoulders again. "And you should, you know. London's great. There're loads of things to do, places to go. The Hammersmith Palais is up the road." She smiled. "All right, you. Shut your eyes." She plugged in the hair-dryer and began brushing out Sandra's hair. After a time, she said, "Okay, you can look, now."

"Ooh, it's fabulous, Morr." Sandra looked in the mirror and turned her head, left and right, and her hair swung, elegantly, like a dark silk curtain, and then resumed its original shape. "Oh, you're so clever."

"No, it's my boss, Mr Vidal. He's the clever one. It's fantastic what he does with hair. I had to learn a whole new way of cutting before I could work in his salon in Bond Street."

Sandra moved her head. "I love it, Morr. I absolutely, love it."

"You deserve it, love. It's not only that Spike of yours that can have a new haircut. All the fellas will be chasing you, now."

"Don't matter, if they do. Spike's the one I love, Morr," Sandra shook her head and took refuge behind the wings of her new hairstyle. "But it's not like we've really done anything, yet...Spike and me...we haven't. We snog lots, like, and it's lovely. He's a dead good kisser. And...and I've let him, you know, feel me and...and touch me." She pointed to her lap. "And he's put it between me legs, like. But I've not been able to...to go any further. I just go stiff. Then I shake and start to cry and he stops, even though I know he really wants to do it. He's a bit funny for a while, then. But he's never ever been nasty. I want to do it, though, Morr, I do, because I love him. Only I'm frightened, because I don't want to get pregnant, but I also don't want to lose him, either." Tears began to trickle down her face.

"Hey, I didn't mean to get you all upset," whispered Maureen. "I just wanted to make you look even prettier than you already are."

"Thank you," Sandra said, meekly. "I don't know where I'd be without you, Morr."

"Look, just in case, I'm going to give you a couple of Durex contraceptives that Jack...that we use. You can roll them up in a hanky; keep them in the bottom of your handbag. Then if you ever get to the point...well...at least, you'll have something handy when, you know, when you and your Spike do it, like." She gently nudged her sister.

"Oh, Morr, give over," Sandra tried hard not to blush again.

"Come on, you, Lady Muck, help me clean up this mess."

"Does it, does it hurt, Morr?" Sandra said, quietly.

"Does what hurt?"

"You know, when...when you and Jack do...have intercourse?"

"It does a little, the first time, always, but then after that, if you love the fella, it's really lovely and there's no better feeling in the whole world."

"Oh, Morr. You're so lucky having, Jack. He's a lovely fella."

"I am, and he is, but I'd never have found him if I hadn't left home and come down to London. So you should really think about it."

"I'd love to live in London, Morr, I really would, but I couldn't leave Raymond, it'd have to be the two of us."

"So who's this Raymond fella when he's at home? I thought you said your boyfriend was called Spike."

"He is, Morr. Spike's the nickname his dad gave him. His proper name's Raymond, like his dad. Only, after his dad died, he...well, he says he didn't want to be called that, anymore." Sandra looked up at Maureen, hoping she'd understand. "It's just that when I think of the two of us...well, you know...maybe one day getting married...well, in my mind, I always say, 'I do, Raymond' and not, 'I do, Spike'. "

Maureen shook her head. "You duck egg. There's never ever telling what goes on in that little head of yours, sometimes."

"That's what Raymond says...I mean, that's what Spike says to me, too." Sandra giggled. "Thanks for everything, Morr. I don't know where I'd be without you. Yes, I do. I'd be bloody nowhere."

BRIAN EPSTEIN knew he could always count on his adoring mother. That's why he'd invited her to afternoon tea at the Adelphi Hotel. The very last thing he needed now was for his father to insist he give up all his 'madcap' schemes and return to managing the record stores full-time. His mother was the only person in the world who could intercede for him. And over cucumber sandwiches, cream cakes, and Earl Grey tea, she listened patiently to her favourite son as he spoke of his many current frustrations. Especially, as regards George Martin not returning his calls.

She patted his hand, told him she had every confidence in his ability to succeed and told him not to worry. She poured them both another cup of the hotel's excellent tea. Then said, a little mysteriously, "At least, now, Brian, one thing's for certain. You'll never have to worry ever again about being bothered by that horrid loathsome creature from your past." When he raised an eyebrow, in question, she simply smiled—Mona Lisa to the life—passed him the lemon slices and would say nothing more on the matter.

Reassured there'd be no more trouble on the home front, he began to marshal his forces for his assault on 'the Tower'. Even though The Beatles were contracted to be in Hamburg for another month, he needed to start laying the foundation for their return and he saw 'the Tower' as the key to their future success. The first thing he did was to persuade Bob Wooler to act as his front man. He offered the disc jockey-compère-cum-music promoter a percentage of the profits from any shows they presented jointly and clinched the deal by promising that any such event would be billed as 'A Bob Wooler Show'. And as he also needed someone with strong links to the promoters in London, he made a similar deal with Allan Williams.

Confident he now had both men securely in his camp, he invited them to his office so he could outline his plan to wrest the Friday-night franchise at 'the Tower' away from Sam Leach. "What I intend to do, gentlemen, is bring in a top-line draw to rival any star that's ever performed in Liverpool...someone, say, as big as Buddy Holly or Eddie Cochran were in their prime." He paused. "I refer to none other than the great American rock 'n' roll legend, Jerry Lee Lewis."

"Bloody hell," cried Allan Williams, his eyes going from side to side as he worked out all the many ways he could profit from such an event. "That's a spectacular idea."

But it was Bob Wooler's stunned response that pleased him the most. He'd rendered Liverpool's authority on all-things-musical, momentarily speechless. "Think about it, Bob," he said, smiling. "What better way to attack 'the Tower' than with great balls of fire?"

However, Bob Wooler was already way ahead of him. The wordplay, though obvious, was worthy of a grin, but the idea behind it all called for true acclaim. "It's brilliant, Brian. No venue or promoter could ever resist such a headliner. The profits from drink sales, alone, would be huge. And with Liverpool now losing many of its top groups to the Star-Club, for two and three months at a time, it'd be harder than ever for Sam Leach to put together line-ups that can draw large enough crowds to his Friday night shows. The management at 'the Tower' will jump at the chance to have Jerry Lee Lewis perform there."

"Jump at it? They'd jump off the top of 'the Tower', if it was still bloody standing. I get chills just thinking about it, Brian. I mean, Jerry Lee-bloody-Lewis? How much better can you get than that?"

"I'm so glad you both think it's a good move. I just have one or two tiny details to attend to first. Then, together, we can go storm 'the Tower'."

As one of his favourite architects and furniture designers once said, 'God is in the details'. And he rather hoped his close attention to his first problem would help put pay to the second. His dealings with the local dancehalls and club-owners were proving especially irksome. Most of the people concerned were simply obnoxious. Worse, the time he spent arguing with them kept him from attending to the all-important issue of securing 'the boys' a recording contact in London. He knew though he had to keep The Beatles engagement diary full to the brim. Have them playing seven nights a week and as many lunchtimes as possible. So he needed someone to take the burden of Liverpool off his hands, as it were. As luck would have it, he'd heard on the grapevine that his old friend, Joe Flannery, had not only become a manager of a local beat group, but had also managed to establish a good rapport with most everyone on the local beat scene. All he had to do was engineer a chance meeting with Joe, at the Basnett Bar, and manage the evening's events to their logical conclusion. And once his friend had offered to help—as of course he undoubtedly would—he'd ask Joe to get in touch with Terry McCann, on his behalf, to help set up a meeting.

His plan was to march straight into the lion's den. Meet with McCann and offer the man the job of organising the security staff for all future NEMS promotions. He'd offer to double whatever Sam Leach was paying. Then seal the deal, on the spot, with a hundred pounds, cash bonus. A little inducement the Londoner would surely jump at. The tiny details then all dealt with, he'd telephone 'the Tower' and make an appointment to see the manager, Tom McCardle.

TOM McCARDLE'S young secretary proved to be a rather pretty girl and she gave both he and Bob Wooler a most radiant smile as she showed them into her boss's office. It was, thought Brian Epstein, a very auspicious start.

"Come in, gentlemen. Thank you, Thelma. You don't have to wait. I don't think we'll be needing any tea or coffee, at the moment, thank you." Tom McCardle looked out of the window to where the sun was, but could see no sign of it because of the low blanket of cloud. "It's nearly noon, by the look of it, so I can open up the drinks cabinet. Right, gentlemen, let's start by splicing the mainbrace. What'll it be?"

Tom McCardle handed Brian Epstein a Sherry and Bob Wooler a gin and tonic, then raised his own glass. Thoroughly charmed by the warmth of the Yorkshireman's greeting, the two would-be promoters raised their drinks, in silent toast, and settled back in their chairs.

"I know it's normal to keep the drinks till afterwards, like, but if you can't ring in the changes, now and then, what good is life?"

Ring in the changes? Perfect timing. Brian Epstein immediately launched into his plan to bring the world's biggest recording stars to 'the Tower'. On top of which, he added, as the

manager of The Beatles, he could guarantee the group would always appear as second on the bill. He made a particular point of
stressing the importance of Friday nights to the overall success
of the plan and finished his pitch by saying that he confidently
expected attendance would always be somewhere up around the
four thousand mark.

He was delighted to see McCardle's huge smile at mention of
The Beatles, but was confused there was no response at all at his
mention of Jerry Lee Lewis. So he smiled and slowly repeated
the legendary rock 'n' roll singer's name. Quickly adding that
he'd already spoken with Jerry Lee Lewis's representatives and
had successfully negotiated for Liverpool to be added to the
American singer's tour of England. All of which meant that the
star was now a guaranteed headliner for 'the Tower'. When he
still didn't get any response, he rolled out his next big gun. The
star he'd already lined up to follow Jerry Lee Lewis was the
young American singing sensation, hot from the charts, Bruce
Channel. Bob Wooler jumped in then and began to expound on
the importance and significance of Jerry Lee Lewis.

"Oh don't mind me, Mr Wooler," snorted Tom McCardle.
"I've got a bloody tin ear when it comes to all this 'go man, go'
stuff the youngsters go crazy over. Joe Loss and his Orchestra is
more my line. Excepting, of course, them Beatles, of yours, Mr
Epstein. Lovely bunch of lads, they are, always packing the place
out. Anyroad, that's why The Tower Company always leaves
that side of the business to you promoters. My job was to get the
place rented out. Make sure everything was always in order. The
bars all fully stocked, the toilets always clean, and not too much
blood or damage afterwards. And I were bloody good at it, too,
even, if I say so myself."

Bob Wooler butted in, again. "I'm sorry, Mr McCardle, did
you say, it *was* your job? Does that mean it's *not* your job, any
longer?"

"Aye, that's right. I'm giving up 'the Tower' and going off to
start me own club in Temple Street, in the city. There's a bloody
fortune to be made. I thought you knew, like, and were just
coming over to give me some helpful advice, seeing as how it's
more your stamping ground over there."

Brian Epstein and Bob Wooler slowly shook their heads.

"But as to your big idea of bringing in some really big names to 'the Tower', I like it, I do." Tom McCardle wrinkled his brow. "Though, you say it very definitely has to be on Friday nights?"

Brian Epstein and Bob Wooler slowly nodded their heads.

"Well, look, it's no longer up to me, like. You'll have to ask the new manager, yourselves. The company just appointed him and he starts next week. He'll be here in a minute. I told him, like, as you'd both be coming over, and he said he wouldn't miss it for the world."

"Oh, yes?" said Brian Epstein, throwing a quick glance at Bob Wooler. "And just who might that be, may I ask?"

That was the exact moment Tom McCardle's secretary, Thelma Pickles, knocked and stuck her head round the door. "Mr Leach is here, Mr McCardle. Shall I show him right in?"

HARRY LIGHTFOOT looked up from his latest copy of *Amateur Photographer* at the sound of the doorbell. He wasn't expecting any visitors. He looked around. The place was tidy. But when wasn't it? He went to the front door, hoping it wasn't one of them blessed young Americans come to save his soul again.

"Hello, Mr Makin, sir, a bit of a surprise. Do come in."

"Just passing, Harry, thought I'd pop in and see how you're doing."

"Very decent of you," he said, knowing full well Rex Makin would've had to go a very long way out of his way to end up standing on his doorstep. "Cup of tea? I'll put the kettle on. Go on through."

Rex Makin went through into the living room, put down his briefcase, a small carrier bag, and looked around. It was his first ever visit to Harry Lightfoot's house and, just as he'd imagined, everything was ship-shape and Bristol fashion. There was a big radiogram, bookcases full of books, magazines, and long-playing records. Several of the shelves devoted to sports trophies, with everything neatly arranged and polished to a shine. What really caught his eye, were the framed black and white photographs all around the walls.

All of them pictures of Liverpool—the river, the docks, Overhead Railway, people in the street, kids playing, and lines of teenagers queuing up for something—and all of them very good.

"It's that Cavern place, down Mathew Street," said Harry Lightfoot, carrying in a tea tray. "I had to have some excuse, me being outside as often as I was. Nice bunch of kids, in the main."

"You did all of these, did you?" Rex Makin turned to him, as he put down the tray. "I've seen some of your handiwork before, Harry, but these are very impressive."

He smiled, pleased. "Just whatever catches my eye, Mr Makin."

"I see you've had a couple of postcards from Hamburg."

He nodded. "Yeah, and a few letters, too. Quite touched, I was, that he bothered, like." He poured the tea. "He's a good lad, though, is young Spike. His last one said the group he was in has already gone and broken up...all of them going their separate ways, apparently."

"That's life, though, Harry, isn't it?" said Rex Makin, nodding. "And, yes, he's a good kid. I only hope he finds whatever it is he's searching for. He telephoned me from Hamburg, a little while ago, about an odd incident involving Brian Epstein. Young Spike was very worried the blackmailer might be up to his old tricks again. I told him, of course, that was highly unlikely."

Harry Lightfoot nodded and touched the scar on his cheek. "So, to what do I owe the pleasure, Mr Makin?"

Rex Makin opened his briefcase and handed him an envelope. Inside, on a single sheet of expensive headed notepaper, was a hand-written note.

Dear, Mr Lightfoot,

I've been informed that you recently rendered me, and my family, a great service. I'm so very sorry to hear that subsequently you might also have suffered some misfortune because of same. Am very pleased, however, to hear that you are now making a speedy recovery. Please accept my most heartfelt thanks.

Yours sincerely, 'Queenie' Epstein. (Mrs H. Epstein)

Rex Makin handed him a second envelope with the words 'Lloyds Bank' printed on the top left-hand corner. He opened it. Inside, was a single deposit slip made out to his personal bank account. He looked at the number printed neatly in the space at the bottom. "Really?"

Rex Makin nodded. "She's very grateful, Harry. As am I." He reached down for the little brown paper carrier bag at his feet and gave it to him. "Just a little something to be going on with."

There were two bottles of something, carefully wrapped in brown paper. One of them a bottle of 12-year old Glen Grant, single malt—his favourite tipple. "Heath covered mountains of Scotia, here I come," he said quietly. He wiped his nose with this handkerchief. "Thank you Mr Makin, sir, that's very decent of you. Now, if you'll join me in a wee dram, I think we can skip the rest of the tea."

He produced two cut-glass tumblers from out of the kitchen.

"*L'chayim*," he said, raising his glass.

"*L'chayim*." Rex Makin paused. "I did hear Joker's been pushing his weight around a good deal, recently. But, I suppose, with so many clubs and the such like popping up, everywhere, everyone's chasing after the same money."

"Yes," he said, nodding. "I did hear word a tussle had broken out in the city. And not just the usual fights between the black *shebeens*. The Chinese probably want to take over more of the gambling. I heard a good few of the drinking clubs have also got their eye on all the money being taken in by the dancehalls and music clubs. As for our Joker, all I can say is the bigger they are, the harder they bloody fall."

Rex Makin looked up, sharply. "You're not thinking of doing anything rash or foolish, are you, Harry?"

He swirled the Glen Grant around in his tumbler; the light caught in the facets of the glass, throwing a golden spider-web up across his face and pullover. "You know me, Mr, Makin, sir."

Rex Makin nodded. "I do, Harry. That's what concerns me."

SID COLEMAN said, "Good-bye," and put down the phone. It was the fourth time in as many weeks he'd heard from Brian Epstein, not counting the man's most recent unscheduled visit. He shook his head, picked up the phone, and called a number from memory.

He waited a few moments for the call to go through. "Hello, Judy. It's Sid Coleman. Is George in? And, if so, has he got a moment, by any chance?" He heard a click and waited while Judy Lockhart-Smith conferred with her boss. "Just one moment, Mr Coleman. He'll be with you, shortly." He thanked her and absent-mindedly began humming and tapping his fingers up and down on his desk. Then a voice in his ear said, "Hello, Sid, that sounds as if it's in three-four time. Something new, you're publishing, I should know about?" Sid Coleman laughed. "Hello, George, thanks for taking the call, I know how busy you are. And, no, that was supposed to be the old Gershwin tune 'Nice Work If You Can Get It' and yes, if I published it, you could have it."

George Martin chuckled. "I'm after something a little more in line with the current hit parade, Sid. It's unlikely either of us will stumble across the likes of another George and Ira Gershwin in our lifetimes."

"That's for certain. Anyway, George, I was wondering if I might ask you about that young Mr Epstein I sent over to see you. The one with the group from Liverpool who call themselves, The Beatles."

"Brian Epstein? Oh, yes. A very pleasant, if persistent, sort of chap. He's been telephoning here, daily, for weeks, apparently, and getting a bit bothersome with it, too, to tell the truth. Trouble is, he doesn't seem to have any idea about just how very busy one gets in this business. As it is, I've been working round the clock for months, up at Abbey Road. I'm sure I'll get round to giving him a call, sometime. As for that group of his, Sid, well I'm still thinking about whether I should even test them or not. There were one or two things I liked, but not much else that'd set them apart."

"Well, I rather liked a couple of the songs they wrote themselves, George, and I'd like Ardmore and Beechwood to publish them. I don't think I'd have any difficulty placing the songs. So, I was thinking. If you're going to do something, then all well and good, but if not, I'd try getting these Beatles in, over at Philips Records."

Sid Coleman paused and wondered whether he'd used the right bait or not. "Please, don't get me wrong, George. Back in February, I thought you were the best man for this Epstein to see. I still do. Only, I don't know, but I've got a funny feeling those Beatles of his have really got something. It'd be a real pity to let it all go to waste."

"Yes, yes, Sid," said George Martin, chuckling. "I hear you loud and clear. Can I jump on your hook, now?"

"You're a prince, George," laughed, Sid Coleman. "A proper angel in disguise."

"I happen to play the oboe, Sid, not the harp, but don't you worry, I'll ask Judy to give Mr Epstein a call. Then we'll set up an appointment to see these Beatles, you seem so very enamoured with, I promise."

CHAPTER TWENTY-SEVEN

Abbey Road

He'd never felt so nervous. Not in the Army when he'd been arrested for impersonating an officer. A gross misunderstanding. Not the time he'd stood in the dock in a London court accused of 'persistently importuning'. Ditto. Not even when, as 'Mr 'X', he'd been savagely cross-examined in front of a courtroom packed to the rafters with the most ghastly people one could ever imagine. All of those had been events, torments, and trials he'd had to endure. This was different. This was a test he'd set himself, to see if he really could succeed on his own terms.

He paid the taxi-driver and stood for a moment just staring at the drab two-storey, white-painted, Georgian building. It more resembled the offices of a group of solicitors or a dental practice than a major recording studio. He felt oddly deflated. He'd imagined something far more imposing. Yet it really was No.3 Abbey Road. His appointment with George Martin—he consulted his watch—was scheduled to start in less than five minutes. He crossed the forecourt and climbed the stone steps to the front door. The uniformed Commissionaire had him sign the visitors' book and then directed him to George Martin's office where, gratifyingly, he was immediately ushered inside. The hands on the wall clock, he noticed, pointing to eleven-thirty exactly.

"Brian, how nice to see you." George Martin came round from behind his file-laden desk and shook his hand. "Sorry to make you trek all the way out to St. John's Wood, but I'm right in the middle of a pile of recording projects. Please take a seat. Do excuse all the mess."

The warmth of George Martin's greeting surprised him and his spirits lifted. But when he saw the producer glance up at the wall clock for the second time, in less than a minute, his spirits promptly fell. It felt like he was being toyed with, again, and everything inside him wanted to scream in protest. Then he thought back to all the times he'd literally cried, head-in-hands, at George Martin's repeated unavailability, and he put on brave smile and got ready to hear the worst.

"Brian, I'd like to offer The Beatles a recording contract."

He froze. Afraid he'd only imagined the words. He blinked. Saw that the Head of Artists and Repertoire of EMI's Parlophone label really was nodding and smiling. His heart began beating again. "But you haven't even met The Beatles, yet, Mr Martin," he exclaimed. Then he all but bit his tongue off.

"Oh, don't worry, Brian. I'm sure we'll all get on like a house on fire. And from now on, please just call me, George."

He laughed out loud. This was he'd waited to hear. All he'd ever dreamed of for months. "That's, er…wonderful, George."

"I do hope so," said George Martin, going back behind his desk to consult his diary. "Let's say, Wednesday, 6th of June, at around seven in the evening, shall we?" The A&R man paused. "Do understand, Brian, I'm not guaranteeing them anything. I'm simply offering to test them for a recording contract. So, if you're agreeable, I'll go ahead and process all the relevant internal paperwork and have my secretary, Judy, send it to you for your lawyers to look at." George Martin glanced up at the wall clock, again. "Oh, just one other thing, Brian." The room stilled—the only sound the ticking of the wall clock. "I'd say, your Beatles have a very good friend in Sid Coleman. He'd still like to publish one or two of their original songs and I think it might not be a bad idea if you let him do it. He's a good man."

He began to breathe again. "Yes, thank you, Mr Martin, I mean, George. I'll do that. Thank you. The Beatles are in Hamburg, at present, so I'll send them a telegram, immediately. Tell them the good news. They'll be thrilled, absolutely thrilled. As am I. Thank-you."

"Jolly good. Bye-bye, then, Brian. And do please excuse me, if I now disappear. I have a session to finish with Matt Monro."

He felt like he was walking on air and he all but skipped across the courtyard to the street. And when he turned round for one last look at No.3 Abbey Road, it neither looked too small, nor too shabby, but just right. Feeling more elated than he

could ever remember being, he went in search of a Post Office
and found one in nearby Wellington Street. He telephoned his
parents to give them the good news and then sent a telegram to
The Beatles, care of the Star-Club:

CONGRATULATIONS BOYS EMI REQUEST RECORDING SESSION
PLEASE REHEARSE NEW MATERIAL = BRIAN +

After which he composed a second telegram that he sent to
Bill Harry, care of *Mersey Beat*, in Liverpool:

HAVE SECURED CONTRACT FOR BEATLES TO RECORD
FOR EMI ON PARLAPHONE LABEL 1ST RECORDING
DATE SET FOR JUNE 6TH = BRIAN EPSTEIN +

Still in a dream, he took himself off to lunch at a restaurant in
nearby Swiss Cottage. Almost too excited to eat, he ordered
smoked salmon and a glass of champagne. "To my darling boys,
The Beatles," he whispered, trying not to cry with happiness.
"With love, from me, to you." He stared out of the restaurant
window. It was far too overcast and gloomy, for May, but for
once he knew the sun would most definitely shine tomorrow.

SAM LEACH shook his head. Bob Wooler and Brian Epstein together as promoters in crime, what a shock that was. He glanced
over at the door and imagined himself walking in to his new office again. It was a sight he'd remember until the day he died.
The real bugger of it all now, though, was he had to be doubly,
doubly careful. Wooler would smile to your face and then once
your back was turned, he'd turn into your most bitter enemy.
Only now it seemed Brian Epstein was a two-faced git, as well.
Funny, how like always seems to attract like. Even so, he was
oddly disappointed in Epstein.

When Terry McCann had told him Brian Epstein had offered
him a job, and a good one at that, he hadn't wanted to believe it.
Then Terry had shown him the hundred quid he'd been given
and he knew it was true. What in hell had he ever done but offer
to help and then stand aside as the record-store owner had made
his play. And now here was The Beatles' new manager trying to
pull the small, but very effective Leach Organisation to pieces.
And the bloody funny thing was—he actually felt hurt about it
all. Not that he'd told anyone, not even Tel, otherwise people

would really think he'd gone soft in the head.

Even when Terry had sworn blind he'd never work for Brian Epstein in a month of Sundays and had taken he and Joan out for a slap-up meal, it'd done nothing to rid the bad taste in his mouth. The real kicker was, that even after all their machinations, Messrs Epstein and Wooler were still stuck with Thursday nights. He felt no little pride The Tower Company had backed him to the hilt on that decision. At least they knew the real value of The Leach Organisation and didn't want that particular boat rocked, certainly not on the inflated promises of a couple of would-be promoters. Then, again, Liverpool's 'dastardly duo' was bringing Jerry Lee Lewis to town. And a dedicated rock 'n' roller could forgive almost anything for anyone doing that. And, as manager of 'the Tower', it was also very much in his interests to see the show did well. Great balls of fire! He'd have done it, anyway, if only for the sake of meeting the 'Killer' himself— Jerry Lee Lewis.

So he'd distributed letters, handbills and posters for the special show. Gone out of his way to help in any and every way he could. Always mindful, he had his own show to promote at 'the Tower', the following night. So he didn't give all his tricks away. Such a pity, then, that the first Brian Epstein-backed 'Bob Wooler Show' had been such a huge financial flop, barely attracting two thousand punters.

When he'd bumped into Rita Shaw, from NEMS, having a drink in the Grapes, the following Saturday, she'd told him Mr Brian had been hopping mad about it ever since. "Serves him, bloody well right," he'd muttered into his glass. He'd tried to stop the would-be promoters from cutting too many corners, but his advice had fallen on deaf ears. And whatever delight he might once have taken from Brian Epstein's financial discomfort, he knew he had to find some way to work with the man, even if only for the sake of booking The Beatles on Friday nights. He knew, all too well, they were still the biggest draw on Merseyside and the true lifeblood of The Leach Organisation.

On top of all that, he had his wedding to Joan to plan and pay for. So he took a sip of cold tea and started scribbling another letter for Thelma Pickles to type up. Then he stopped and shook his head. Just think. He was 'Manager of the New Brighton Tower Ballroom'. He could hardly believe it himself, sometimes.

HARRY LIGHTFOOT drove into the city-centre and parked as near as he could to Blackler's. It wasn't the department store he wanted, but a camera shop, opposite. He still limped and didn't want to have to walk too far, but like rugby players, everywhere, he'd long learned to lock physical pain away in the back of his mind and just get on with it.

He'd known immediately what to do with the extra money he'd got from 'Queenie' Epstein—buy a new camera. He decided to stick with his old twin-lens Rolleiflex and not invest in a new 'Rollei'. Set his sights instead on one of the new Japanese 35mm SLR cameras. He'd balked at the cost of a Nikon, as much as he'd have liked one, and chose a single-lens-reflex Canon 7 as the ideal compromise, as it came with a standard 50mm lens and a built-in exposure meter. He also purchased a 35mm wide-angle lens, a 135mm telephoto lens, and had the shop 'express order' a 500mm F8 telephoto lens of the sort he'd seen newspaper photographers use at Liverpool's Anfield football stadium and Aintree racecourse. He also bought a small, lightweight tripod, an extra-long shutter-release cable, and ordered and paid for a fresh batch of three-dozen rolls of 35mm, black and white, 400 ASA Kodak Tri-X film, and asked that it be 'rush ordered' direct from Kodak's London-based distributor. *Amateur Photographer* had featured the film in several articles and photo spreads and he'd been impressed with the results people had achieved, even when pushing the film two or three stops to 800 and 1600 ASA.

As soon as the film arrived from London, he'd shot-off several test-rolls, all night studies of city streets and buildings, and once he was satisfied with the quality of the results, he adjusted his sleeping habits and got ready to work for several weeks on the night shift.

"WHERE'S THIS GEORGE MARTIN then? Hiding, is he?"

"He'll be along when he can." The Abbey Road recording engineer saw no reason to tell the musician with the funny haircut that his boss, the head of Parlophone, was in the staff canteen taking a well-earned break after yet another long and gruelling day trying to make yet another comedy record sound funny enough for repeated listening. "Let's get you all set up, first, shall we? Then I'll have someone go tell him you're here."

"Yes, let's," said John Lennon, not letting down his guard for a moment. "That's where you sit, is it? Up there, with the rest of the gods?" He pointed up to the glass-fronted control room.

The young engineer smiled and nodded, and decided to humour the young musician. After all, it was only natural he'd be feeling a mite nervous. "Up there, in the control room, with the producers? Yes."

"You don't look much like a god. What do people call you, then?"

"Er, Norman, Norman Smith. What do they call you?"

"Winston Churchill, but you can call me, John Lennon."

The engineer laughed, unused to such banter from someone about to undertake EMI's all-important 'artist's test'. Most people were too nervous to even speak. "Let's just have a quick look at your amplifiers, shall we? I need to get the balance of your instruments right."

One of the other young musicians with a funny-looking haircut, pulled the rubber covers from off the amplifiers with a flourish and stood, presenting them, as if he were a magician's assistant. "Ta-Da!"

"Blimey," exclaimed, Norman Smith. "They've seen better days."

"Haven't we all, love," said the one, called John, which set the rest of his band-mates off, laughing and giggling.

Norman Smith, however, thought they were laughing at him. So, as the drummer set up his drums and the rest of the group began tuning their guitars, he quietly got about his business— thinking that perhaps silence was the wisest course with these four young lads from Liverpool. And without another word, he carefully positioned a microphone a couple of inches in front of each of the group's amplifiers and then beckoned for Brian Epstein to join him up in the control room.

"Snotty git," muttered George.

The young engineer opened the sound faders on the mixing desk with one hand, pressed the talkback microphone with the other. "If you'll just play something, please, anything at all, we'll test for level."

The Beatles, prepared for just such a request, ripped straight into their favourite opening number, 'Some Other Guy', but the noise that erupted from out of the speakers in the control room was unspeakable.

"Hang on, hang on, hang on," shouted, Norman Smith. Then he remembered to press the talkback microphone. "Hang on, hang on. Stop it. Stop it. Stop. That sounded dreadful. Awful. Terrible."

Brian Epstein jumped up and started pacing the control room. It was bad enough Mr George-high-and-mighty-Martin hadn't deemed it an important enough occasion to attend the recording session himself. This wasn't at all how he imagined things would be going.

Down in Studio Two, The Beatles, shocked into silence by the outburst from the control room, were just as perplexed. What in hell was wrong with that? Thousands of fans in Liverpool and Hamburg had thrilled to those opening chords. Did people in London have tin ears?

Norman Smith ran down the back stairs, along the corridor, and burst into the studio. The Beatles all stared at him, warily.

"No, it's not you lot. It's your ruddy amplifiers. They're duff."

"I'll duff you, in a minute," muttered George.

The young engineer looked at his watch, bit his lip. "Look, hang on, it's late, but I'll see if our technical engineer can round up some speakers from another studio. So, just hang on, okay?"

"I would, like, if there was any rope," sighed Paul.

"I'll just hang myself and be done with it," sniffed George. "This is an awful start to things, this. Worse than bloody Decca."

"Get me some bloody rope," snapped John. "And I'll go and strangle the bugger, myself, and put him out of all our miseries."

But 'Normal' Smith, as John had already christened him, earned himself a reprieve when he another bloke produced a big Tannoy speaker as if from out of nowhere. "This is Ken Townsend. And if anyone can fix things for us, he can. What do you think, Ken?"

The young technical engineer nodded. "If I can solder a jack-socket onto the Tannoy speaker and connect it directly to your bass amplifier...as big a one as ever I've seen...homemade is it? I should be able to bypass the speaker inside that's causing all the trouble. Your amps might be okay for a dance hall, but they're no good for recording." He looked round at the other two un-happy looking guitarists. "Hang on, I'll go see if I can borrow another speaker, then I'll try and get you two set up, as well."

Impressed that people at Abbey Road were actually willing to get their hands dirty to help them succeed, The Beatles began to relax a little and to cut 'Normal' and 'Our Ken' a little more rope. So when the two engineers returned to the control room and asked them to run through some tunes again, they favoured them with an original composition, 'Love Me Do'.

Norman Smith tapped his foot and his fingers in time with the beat. Yes, the balance wasn't too bad. The drum was a bit soft, but the bass guitar sounded much better—the awful buzz-ing, crackling sounds had all but disappeared. He turned and nodded his thanks to Ken Townsend. The music didn't sound too bad, now, either. Now that he could actually hear it, he quite liked what he was hearing. In fact, he liked it a lot. It was bit raw, but it was good. So he pressed the talkback button again. "That sounded a lot better. Great stuff, really good. I'll have someone go get Mr Martin, now. I think it's time he heard you lot in living colour. Hang on."

"I'll hang on his every word, if he keeps on saying nice things like that, about us," said, George, sounding very relieved.

"It's hardly likely to be the norm, though, is it?" said, John, taking a slow steady look around the studio. "So we better be on our guard. It'd be too much to hope we'd find more nice people working in this place. After all, we are down in London."

GEORGE MARTIN looked down on the four young men from Liverpool. He had to admit, their haircuts were rather shocking, but his job wasn't to worry about their appearance. His first task was to find out which one of them was the singer; the Cliff Richard or Tommy Steele of the group; the one you stuck up front. He turned to Brian Epstein and pointed to the one pulling funny faces and generally being the centre of attention. "Which one is that, Brian?"

"That's, that's John. John Lennon, the rhythm guitarist. He's got a great voice," Brian Epstein said, sounding as nervous as a mother hen.

"Well, we'll soon find out about that. Who's the one next to him?"

"That's Paul. Paul McCartney. He plays bass and he sings, too. Paul's got a really beautiful voice."

"Okay, thank you, Brian. Let's start with him then, shall we?"

"Hello, down there in the studio. My name is George Martin and I'll be conducting this evening's test. I'll be asking each one of you to play or sing something, so we can adjust the levels a little more. Get as clean a sound balance as we can. Then, when I'm satisfied, we'll run through some of your numbers. I hope that's clear? Paul? Yes, you. We'll start with you."

The Beatles looked up at the control room to see a man even older than Brian and who more resembled a schoolteacher from some posh private school, than someone who could ever get with rock 'n' roll.

"Oh, sod," mumbled Paul. "Just take a look at him, will yer."

"God, he looks like a right toffee," said George, quietly.

"Like he's got his finger stuck-up his arse," growled John.

"Excuse me, did you say anything in there?" George Martin's voice echoed around the studio.

"Er, no, thank you, sir," said Paul. "We were just clearing our throats, like. Thank you. Shall I begin, then, Mr Martin, sir?"

"Please, if you would."

For the next hour or so the producer put each of The Beatles through an exhaustive test. He said little or nothing after each performance, just left them to stand and await his next utterance. He had them run through their repertoire of songs, all but stifling a yawn when they played old chestnuts like 'Red Sails In The Sunset' and Fats Waller's 'Your Feet's Too Big'. "Nothing frightfully original, there," he said to himself. "Not even the songs they'd written themselves." However, he recorded their original songs 'PS I Love You', 'Love Me Do', and 'Ask Me Why', as well as their version of 'Besame Mucho'. Their sound was quite interesting, in an offbeat sort of way. It was a bit raw. But might just be different enough to catch the ear. The one important question remained, though, who was the lead singer? The one called John? Or the one called Paul? George Harrison's voice wasn't bad, but it obviously wasn't strong enough to be lead. Then it struck him. Why not just let them all sing together? They harmonised well enough. That'd be a novelty in itself, a real group. He pressed the talkback button. "All right, gentlemen, thank you. That'll be all for now. I think it's time you all came up into the control room so we can have a little chat."

PAUL McCARTNEY didn't miss a thing. He took in the gold watch, the gold cuff links, the clean shirt and striped-tie, beamed his most winning smile, and proffered the tall, well-groomed man his hand. "Paul McCartney," he said in a bright, clear voice. George was a little more wary. George Martin still sounded like a right toffee, but then so did Brian. So he'd give the man the benefit of the doubt, for now. He grinned a toothy grin and stuck out his hand. "My name's George, too. George Harrison." Pete just nodded and shuffled his feet. "Er, Pete, Pete Best." But John, head back, stood stock still, and stared. It seemed he'd spent most all his life searching for someone who could say 'yes' to his dreams and just maybe this was one such a man. "George Martin, I presume. It's nice, to finally meet the man that's been making me sing and jump through hoops for the better part of an hour." He grinned. "All I can say is, I hope we passed the audition."

"We'll see," said the producer. "John Lennon, isn't it?"

John nodded, but George Martin refused to be drawn any further and John retreated behind a barely concealed frown. None of which went unnoticed by the other Beatles and, after a quick exchange of glances, they busied themselves finding something to sit on or lean against as George Martin crossed his arms and began to lecture them on the many intricacies of the recording process. The Beatles, in turn, stared back and did their level best to look attentive.

George Martin didn't talk down to them or patronise them and, pleasingly, he appeared to have the all too rare knack of making things easy to understand. What finally won them over was that the producer also treated them, if not quite as equals, then as professional musicians and they liked George Martin all the more for it. Not that the blank looks on their faces revealed any of this to him at the time.

"What you need to grasp from the very beginning is that every aspect of the recording process is replete with its own special set of problems. So, I think it might be a good idea if I run through all the different recording procedures, step-by-step, so you can get a better appreciation of it all. Okay?"

The Beatles nodded. And then all eyes glued on the record producer, they listened attentively as he explained and demonstrated what each of the switches, dials, and faders on the recording console allowed him to do with the sounds that came in from the studio. Every now and then, he turned to Norman Smith, or his assistant-producer Ron Richards, for clarification on how they'd achieve a balance between voices and instruments. Or to explain how different types of microphone produced different sounding results.

"The sound you make when you play in a dance hall or club is one thing and there's nothing at all wrong with it. Brian tells me you really work up a storm. But the sound that needs to be produced for recording purposes is another thing entirely and your equipment simply isn't capable of giving us the sound quality we need. So once we've finished, here, I can advise you on what to do about it all, if you like." He paused—looked at each Beatle, in turn. "Look, I've been going on at you all for almost an hour. So, if there's anything you don't like about me or what I've just said, now would be good a time to speak up."

The Beatles looked at one another, then back at George Martin. George Harrison nodded, slowly, as if he'd given the question considerable thought. "Well, for a start, I don't like your tie."

There was a long moment of silence. Then George Martin grinned. He couldn't help it. "Well, that's certainly one-way to break the ice," he said to himself. Then he chuckled and laughed. Then laughed some more. And once it was clear the Head of Parlophone wasn't going to throw them all out on their ears, John and Paul made great play of hitting George for being so damn cheeky. Something, Brian Epstein admitted, afterwards, he would also dearly loved to have done.

John Lennon stepped forward, grinning, and offered his hand. "You know much about rock 'n' roll, do you, Mr Martin, sir?"

George Martin grinned back. "A bit, Mr Lennon. I've record-ed a few pop hits in my time, but anything mad or unusual is definitely up my street. It looks like you and Mr Harrison, here, are the comedians of the group, so I'll just have to book the two of you for the next Goons record I do. If Peter and Spike ever decide to let me do another one, that is."

"You don't mean you know the Goons?" John Lennon asked, eyes wide. "Not Peter Sellers and Spike Milligan?"

"I do. And Harry Secombe and Michael Bentine, too."

"You recorded them all? Really? Honest?" This was beyond wonderful. It was utterly amazing. To meet someone that not only knew the Goons, but who'd actually worked with them in the flesh. It was worth coming down from Liverpool, just for this. "Oh, go on, you're joking," said John, pulling a face.

"No, I'm serious. I really did," replied George Martin, smiling.

"Go on, you didn't. Go on," quipped John, a Goon to the very life.

"No, I did, really...oh, yes, I see. Pure Sellers."

"And you really know Peter Sellers," said John, in wonder-ment. "He's one of my absolute heroes."

"Well, if it's 'The Goon Show', you want." Paul burst into strange sounding song. 'Oooh...Ying-tong. Ying-tong. Ying-tong...' John and George joined in. Suddenly, it was as if the gates of a lunatic asylum had been left open as the characters of Eccles, Neddy Seagoon, Major Bloodnok, Moriarty, and Bluebottle were all conjured up, as if out of thin air, by the three Beatles.

"Oh, you have deaded me again."

"He's fallen in the water."

"Moriarty, where are you?"

"You just can't get the wood, you know."

George Martin was taken aback, at first, by the sudden out-break of Beatles madness, but he was pleased his association with the Goons was very much appreciated. It wasn't lost on him that it'd won him some sort of instant credibility in the their eyes. "You know," he said to himself, "it might be fun working with this charming bunch of lunatics." After all, he had to find someone that could make him laugh, now that Peter Sellers had gone off to do bigger and better things.

BRIAN EPSTEIN was a little bewildered by the rapport that'd sprung up as if from out of nowhere between The Beatles and George Martin. He hadn't been able to read the producer at all during the test session and although he was genuinely pleased by the turn of events, he felt oddly jealous. Anyone who made any sort of connection with 'his boys' that he couldn't under-stand or control made him feel nervous—even now, at such a pivotal moment. The painful truth was he never ever wanted 'his boys' to feel that he didn't understand them or, worse, that he was in any way superfluous. And so, as The Beatles spent the rest of the evening telling jokes and charming everyone, he smiled, chuckled, and tried to look as if he was enjoying himself. In the end, he did finally relax. It was only then he noticed that Pete Best, probably feeling a little outshone by the other Beatles, remained quiet and reserved, almost morose, throughout the en-tire evening.

Afterwards, as The Beatles were busy packing up their equipment and preparing for the journey home, George Martin asked him if he could spare a moment up in the control room. He followed, fully believing that George Martin was going to confirm the boys' contract, but as he closed the door and sat down, the look on the record producer's face suggested some-thing else entirely.

"Brian, I know this might cause you a bit of a problem, but I'm going to have to get another drummer for the actual recording session. You can do what you like with Pete Best, on stage. In many ways, he's the best-looking one of the bunch, but he doesn't play drums very well and he can't keep in time, either. Which will mean, I'm afraid, that I'll have to bring in another drummer to play on the tracks."

He looked at George Martin and nodded, but said nothing. He was desperately trying to take it all in. He quite liked Pete and thought him rather sweet, but here was the Head of Parlophone telling him he didn't want Pete Best to play on any of The Beatles' records. Goodness gracious, what would the others say? And right then and there he decided not to tell anyone anything and not to even think about it himself until he and the group were all back in Liverpool. It felt like he'd just been handed a ticking time bomb. God only knew what would happen when it went off.

BRIAN EPSTEIN tapped his fingers up and down on the leather-edged desk blotter. There were precious few places where he had time and space to think nowadays. Driving alone in his car. At his desk, with all calls put on hold, or as now at the end of the week, after everyone had gone home and him alone with his desk diary, his personal diary, and a notepad—his islands of sanity. Making lists of tasks yet to do, underlining items that required especial attention, crossing things out when completed, gave him, however fleeting, some sense of control. He consulted that week's itemised list. First item. 'Abbey Road'. The Beatles were set to do a follow-up session with George Martin at EMI's Abbey Wood Studios. He double-checked the date. Tuesday 4th September. Made a note to book the hotel and finalise the travel arrangements. They'd all fly down together this time. Tick.

Next item. 'Hessy's Music Store'. He'd personally paid off the group's outstanding hire-purchase debts. So he ticked the item. Done. It still left the question of new amplifiers. But rather than buy them outright he wanted to look into the possibility of a manufacturer having their equipment associated with The Beatles. He'd seen such advertisements in the trade papers. And if The Shadows had Vox amplifiers then 'the boys' should, too. He made a note to explore the idea further on his next trip to London and wrote, 'New Amplifiers, Jennings Music Shop, Charing Cross Road', into his diary.

Next item. 'The Cavern Club'. He drew a circle. 'The Beatles Welcome Home' twelve-day, exclusive engagement at the club was unprecedented. Not surprisingly, Ray McFall and Bob Wooler had been more than taken with the idea. He wrote 'Cav' in the space allotted for the twelve days in both diaries.

Which brought him to 'The Tower'. He underlined the name of the venue several times. Thanks to Sam Leach, he was still stuck with Thursday nights, which of course being a work-night meant much smaller audiences. Yet even after the disastrously small turnout for Jerry Lee Lewis, he had little choice but to keep putting on shows. More important than ever now The Beatles had signed with Parlophone. That wonderful news needed to be trumpeted from the very highest tower. But, damn and blast Sam Leach, only on Thursdays!

He had the American singer Bruce Channel lined up for later in the month, with The Beatles second on the bill. That alone should ensure a high turnout, even for a Thursday. Even so, he made a note to ask Bob Wooler to get as many other top groups as possible to fill out the bill. Gerry and The Pacemakers. The Big Three. 'Kingsize' Taylor. Rory Storm and The Hurricanes. Anyone and anything that'd help bring the punters in.

Yet, even with all that, he knew how very important Sam Leach's Friday-night shows were to the continued local success and celebrity of The Beatles. There was no question but he had to keep the pot boiling until 'the boys' achieved national success. After which he could do as he pleased. So, if only for the short term, he had to call a truce, of sorts, with Sam Leach. It'd irk him. It'd be insufferably annoying. But he would do it. In time, though, there'd be any number of ways to skin that particular cat. Patience was all.

He sighed and turned to the next item on his list. 'BBC Manchester. *Teenagers' Turn*'. To ensure The Beatles' second appearance on the radio show would prove an even greater success than their first—window dressing and stage management being but two sides of the same coin—he'd called upon the newly formed Beatles Fan Club and had arranged for a special coach to take 'the boys' and their most ardent fans to Manchester. If his own experiences were anything to go by, the Liverpool fans in the studio audience would erupt into screams of delight every time it was The Beatles' turn to sing. To weigh events even more heavily in the group's favour he'd given the Fan Club's secretary explicit instructions that tickets—sold exclusively through NEMS—should only go to die-hard Cavern Club Members. And the fans had, of course, all screamed as if on cue. None of which had gone unnoticed by the BBC producers.

He sighed again and put down his fountain pen. The only real trouble had occurred after the show, when, in all the pulling, pushing, shoving and screaming, as The Beatles and their fans tried to get back onto the motor coach to go home, Pete Best had somehow got left behind. It absolutely beggared belief, but it was true. Pete had been left standing on the pavement and had had to make his own way home to Liverpool by train.

The very next morning, the three other Beatles had asked for an urgent meeting with him at NEMS. When they'd all voiced their concerns about Pete Best and his drumming. And had then told him, rather bluntly, that it was now his job to manage the problem and that he should get it resolved—and quick.

He got up from his desk, went over to the window and looked out, but it wasn't Whitechapel he saw, it was the meeting he'd had with the now very concerned John, Paul, and George.

Unusually, the situation being somewhat confrontational, it was Paul who'd spoken first. "It's dead weird, Brian. Something like that happening, so soon, after George Martin's comments about Pete's drumming, not being up to snuff. It's a sign, like."

"Almost like a sign from the Gods, Brian," George added, quietly.

"It's another bloody sign Pete's not with it," snapped John. "Thing is, 'Eppy', we just can't take the chance of us losing this bloody contract with Parlophone. Because, as we all well know, there's no one else out there will have us."

He'd started to protest. To reassure them their future success was more assured than ever, now, but John had interrupted him.

"Look, Brian, I know it's not a nice thing to do to Pete, but it's the right and *only* thing to do for The Beatles."

George had spoken up then and, even more unusually, he'd done so at some length. "What you need to understand, Brian, is I've been dead unhappy with Pete's drumming for a long time, now. He's a nice enough lad. And we've all always got on with him as best as we can, like. And it's true...he can really thump the drums. But I want something more than just 'thump-thump-thump-thump' all the time. I want us to be able to progress, musically. And while I spend all my time trying to find different ways of playing things...and Paul does, too...and John and Paul are always writing songs, like...Pete never does anything but the bare basics. And that's a real drag when the rest of us are always doing our level best to make The Beatles...the best rock 'n' roll group, not just in Liverpool, but in all of Great Britain."

How on earth could he argue with that? But feeling more than a little overwhelmed, by it all, he'd asked if he could have some time to think, as any change in the line-up would have far-reaching consequences. He'd assured them he understood their concerns about Pete and the very first thing he'd do would be to map-out some sort of timetable for the transition. And much to his surprise they'd all agreed and had continued on with the group's scheduled dates, playing on stage with Pete Best as if nothing out of the ordinary had occurred.

He smoothed his hair into place, adjusted the knot of his tie, and drew circles round and around Pete Best's name. The whole wretched affair called for some very careful handling and deep down he knew he should seek legal advice on how best to dismiss the now 'undesirable member' from the group. His mind wandering, he caught himself doodling uncontrollably and quickly lifted the nib of his pen from the notepad. He blinked. And saw that he'd drawn circle after circle after circle—some spiralling ever inwards, others growing an added dimension that turned the circles into so many sets of drums.

His telephone rang, broke his train of thought. He stared at it, oddly disinclined to answer, and he then picked it up. "Brian Epstein," he said into the mouthpiece. "Joe? Quelle surprise. No, no, just finishing up, a few things, before I go home. You what?"

He listened, his face clouding with every passing second.

"She's what? Pregnant? What? Pete's mother...Mona Best? And the father's who? Heaven forefend! You can't be serious? Neil Aspinall? Pete Best's, best friend? That's truly unbelievable. No, no, no, I won't tell 'the boys'. Thank you, Joe. I'd hate to have heard about it from anyone else but you. You're a good friend for calling me. Thank you. Yes. Yes. Goodbye."

He put the phone down and just sat and stared out of the window until everything faded into darkness. Mona Best was pregnant and not by her husband—even though they were separated, apparently. Even so, that alone could kill any chance 'the boys' might have of really hitting the big time. What a scandal the Sunday papers would make of it—the mother of The Beatles' drummer made pregnant by The Beatles' very own road manager. The backlash would be unbelievable. There was no question now—Pete Best definitely had to go.

CHAPTER TWENTY-EIGHT

The Road That Stretches Out Ahead

"Spike!" Sandra ran down the platform smiling and waving and laughing and crying. Her fella was home. The one she loved. The one she'd missed so much and dreamed about every night. The one she knew she was going to marry one day.

Spike dropped his suitcase, put down his guitar case—plastered all over with Star-Club stickers—and stood and grinned and opened his arms just as Sandra jumped into them. She hugged him and kissed him and squealed with delight and said his name over and over again and all he could do was hold on and repeat her name slowly into her hair.

They stood, hugging and kissing, on the Lime Street Station platform, for a thousand and one nights, oblivious to the bemused or scandalised stares of the crowds of people milling around them.

"Oh, I missed you. Missed you. I know you had to stay longer, but I missed you so much. I read all your letters a thousand times. 'PS, I love you', they always said. Tell me, tell me you still mean it."

"Yeah, 'course I do, my lovely, silly, adorable Sandra. It's so great to see you; so good to be back. Here, let's have a proper look at you." He released his arms and she stepped back, still holding on to his hand, almost afraid to let go. "Turn round." She let go of his hand and twirled around on the platform. He just stared at her and fell in love with her all over again. She was fabulous. And she looked at him with such delight, it intoxicated him and all he wanted to do was to make love to her right then and there. He wanted to touch her all over and have her touch him and he wanted her so badly, it hurt. He felt himself grow hard and was glad the suede coat he'd bought in Hamburg was long enough to hide the bulge in his tight black jeans. He swallowed and sighed and looked at her again and was caught by the way her hair swung and swayed, but always seemed to return to frame her face, beautifully. It made her look older, somehow, and dead sexy. "Your hair's different. It's not, all stiff, like. It looks terrific, like something from a magazine. Your new clothes are gear, too."

"Maureen did it. It's great, isn't it? Beehives are out now, anyway. And as for little me...it's how all the girls in London dress now...like little French girls...real '*modernistas*'. See? Flat shoes and a dead straight skirt." She pirouetted. "But look at you...all in black and a new suede-coat...every inch the modern musician. Only, you're so dead thin. Haven't you been eating? Oh, Spike, but you're here. You're really, really here."

"How did you know it was this train I'd be on then?"

Sandra fished in the pocket of her little, boxy, black leather jacket and held up a fan of platform tickets. "I waited for all of them, dafty."

Spike looked at her in wonder, then pulled her to him and kissed her hard on the mouth and felt her melt into him with her whole body. And as she said over and over again, how much she really, really loved him, he sighed, as much with relief, as with love.

SAM LEACH bit his lip and tried to stop fiddling with the silly-looking pen set on his desk—a parting gift from Tom McCardle. How did the old saying go? "You can take a horse to water..." The meeting hadn't been going more than five minutes and he already felt like tearing his hair out. Which would be unseemly, not to say unsightly, for the new manager of the New Brighton Tower Ballroom to do in public. Needing to play for time, he pulled a crumpled handkerchief from out his pocket and blew his nose—anything to stop from saying what he really felt like saying. He cleared his throat. Smiled. "Brian, look, I know we've had our differences, in the past, but I tell you you're making a big mistake if you cut down the number of bouncers at your Bruce Channel Show. A big name like that is going bring Teddy

Boys from miles around...all of them just itching to make a big name for themselves. And that's even before you take into account it'll be the first sighting of The Beatles at 'the Tower' since their return from Hamburg. You're going to need twice the usual number of bouncers, at the very least, not cut them by half."

Brian Epstein demurred. "It's going to be hard enough to make a profit as it is, Sam. However, if in your new capacity as manager of the Tower Ballroom you were to agree to reduce the night's rental fee it'd give me the extra funds I'd need to meet your recommendations."

It was Sam's turn to demur. "You know I can't do that Brian. Franchise lease fees are set and only negotiable on a quarterly basis, on the go forward. As the lessor, any additional cloakroom or bar-staff needed to meet increased demand are our responsibility, but all other costs, including security, are met by the lessee, you know that."

The oily rag butted in then. "Far be it from me to suggest that it's slipped your limited attention span, Leach, but it's my name on the poster this time. Top left hand corner, right before the word 'Tower', where it plainly states that it is 'A Bob Wooler Show'. So let me throw in my two-pennyworth. I say you're exaggerating the risk. Indeed, there are those who say it was your own over-reactions to the problem in the first place that's caused much of the subsequent gang trouble. All of which is to say I have to agree with Brian, here, a nominal security presence should prove more than sufficient. Especially as Bruce Channel by the very nature of his music is likely to draw the sort of crowd that more than knows how to behave itself."

"Sounds all very impressive, Bob, but it's falling on deaf ears. And as this is business not pleasure, I'll choose to ignore your acid comment about the cause of past gang troubles. The final decision is yours. It's your money, I'm just trying to warn you not to cut the wrong corners...is all."

"Thank you, Sam. Duly noted."

He nodded. What else could he do? "So be it, Brian, but I'd advise you to keep your fingers very firmly crossed on the night of the show." It worried him, though, Bob Wooler knew better, but the bloody man obviously didn't want to be seen to be disagreeing with his new business partner. Not publicly, anyway. But it wasn't Wooler or Epstein, was it, who'd be left to pick up all the pieces if everything went to hell in a handcart? He bit down on his tongue all the harder. He couldn't wait for his visitors to leave his office. He needed a drink.

The world had turned—the days come and gone—the dates duly torn from the desk calendar. If he'd had the time or inclination to keep a pocket diary he'd have torn out the pages and made a bonfire with them, so as never to be reminded of the awful train of events. Every moment dreading that he and his new job would go up in a puff of smoke. So it was just as well it was his secretary, Thelma, whose job it was to keep his desk diary up to date and to point him in the right direction. He hadn't known which way to turn, most of the time, it'd been such a bloody awful week. Or, to be more precise, two bloody awful weeks—two of the worst in living memory.

And even though Messrs Epstein and Wooler were largely at fault and there was always some joy to be had at the misfortunes of another promoter, he'd felt nothing but gut-wrenching horror at the size and intensity of the gang fight that broke out at the Bruce Channel Show. It was as ugly and dirty and vicious as anyone could ever remember. As it'd spread, inside and outside, most all the food and drink vendors in the car park had hurriedly pulled down their shutters, started up their motors, and headed for the hills. In the end everyone lost money on the show. The property damage was huge. But it was the number of people who ended up in hospital that earned the real black mark from the local constabulary. The tap dancing he'd had to do to sort it all out would've done Fred Astaire and Gene Kelly proud. He'd not only had to use all his wit and charm to placate his new bosses, he'd had to call in every favour he could to stop the local magistrate from rescinding The New Brighton Tower Company's licence to operate. It was a real close call for all concerned. Only then it'd gone from bad to worse.

At first, he'd thought nice Mr Brian Epstein had turned over a new leaf. To show his appreciation and help compensate in some small way for all the trouble that'd occurred, The Beatles' manager had agreed to a let him book 'the boys' at 'the Tower' for six Friday nights in a row. Most importantly, allowing them to perform, the following Friday, at 'Operation Big Beat III. A Cavalcade of Rock 'n' Twist'. The fly in that particular ointment being nice Mr Epstein's last minute stipulation that The Beatles be given their very own dressing room—or they wouldn't play. On the face of it an innocent enough request, but it'd all but started another bloody riot when the other groups found out about it. He'd had to promise everything but his first-born to get it sorted—even then it'd been another real close call.

The one bright spot had been his wedding, on the Saturday, when the ever-lovely Miss Joan McEvoy had made an honest man of him at Knotty Ash church. By his own admission, his finest booking to date. Anyone who was anyone on the local beat scene had been there, save for those off playing in Hamburg. Gerry Marsden, Rory Storm, and Johnny Guitar were there, as was Terry McCann, and Bill Harry and his girlfriend, Virginia. Young Spike Jones was there, with his girlfriend, along with Jimmy Molloy and Thelma Pickles—Spike having to leave early, as he was standing in for the Zodiac's bass player, at Holyoake Hall, in Penny Lane. The Beatles came to the wedding, but couldn't make the reception, either, as that night they were playing 'across the water' in Heswell, on the Wirral. Brian Epstein had politely declined the invitation to the Catholic church-service, but did attend the reception at the Crown, in Lime Street, afterwards. Bob Wooler also made a brief appearance for appearances sake.

And all to the good, but appearances can be so deceiving can't they? What is it they say in the wedding vows—for better or for worse? Well, it applied to life as well as marriage. As, out of the blue, the very next week the suddenly not-so-nice Brian bloody Epstein had telephoned him at work and, after offering only the flimsiest of excuses, had cancelled three of the remaining bookings he had with The Beatles. The bloody man called again, the next day, and asked for more money for those bookings still in the diary. Twisting the knife in, it was called. As he'd said to his lovely new wife, Joan, that very morning, as he'd set out for another hard day's night at 'the Tower', it was a very shitty way to do business, especially as it was all centred around The Beatles—real good guys, every single one of them.

HARRY LIGHTFOOT had long learned that some nights called for two Thermos flasks of coffee to get you through until morning. This night, perhaps the longest of the many he'd spent on watch over the past month, he'd been close to needing a third. But all his patience had been rewarded. All it'd taken was a helpful push and he'd at last got what he'd been hoping for all along; the sort of stuff that'd blacken a few eyes as well as nicely blacken a few reputations. He shook his head. The hours some people kept in this town, you'd have thought it was Las Vegas. He chuckled to himself. When this was all over, he might well reward himself with a trip to America. He'd never been, but he was sure he and his camera would have an interesting time over there. It'd cost a few bob, but if you looked at it as being no more than the price of a few holidays at Butlin's, it almost seemed reasonable. Anyway, if what he had planned came to pass, then a long holiday might be good for his health. Out of sight, out of mind, as they say.

He sat in his car, rewound the film, eased the roll from out the back of the camera and placed the tiny canister in the black-silk film bag with all the others. He removed the telephoto lens from the camera body, slid it into its protective case, and reattached the standard 55mm lens. With everything back in its proper place, he switched on the wiper-blades for a moment, to remove the heavy dew that'd settled on the car windscreen, and drove home through the almost deserted streets of Liverpool. It was time to catch up on his sleep.

THE GRAPES public house on Mathew Street was full to bursting. Off in the far corner, Bob Wooler was talking to three of The Beatles.

"So, my rhythmic revolutionaries, fear not, the next 'Bob Wooler Show' at 'the Tower' will be run on exemplary lines. Fisticuffs of any sort will be severely and summarily dealt with on the proverbial spot."

"So, does that mean you're going to have loads more bouncers turn up next time?" enquired George Harrison.

"Whole platoons, George...veritable companies. Nay, whole regiments of them," Bob Wooler replied, with a flourish of the hand.

"Yeah, that's what I thought you said. Only, I wanted to make sure, like. As I really dig Joe Brown and I'd hate to see anyone taking liberties with him or his Bruvvers during or after the show."

"Right," said John Lennon, impatiently. "Now, you've got that sorted out, can we get back to what we were talking about, please?"

"Yeah," piped in, Paul McCartney. "You see, Bob, everyone we've spoken to has said the same thing...Ringo's a much better drummer...one of the very best in all of Liverpool."

George nodded. "It's true, Bob. Even this fella, Roy Young, in Hamburg...who's played with everyone and was on *Oh, Boy* and *Drumbeat*, on the telly, with Tony Sheridan...when we asked him, like, he said the exact same thing...Ringo's a much better drummer."

"So, what do you think then, Bob?" said John, quietly.

"Well, I suppose, I did once call Pete 'mean, moody, and magnificent' and, of course, I meant every word of it. And, it's true, there are many of the female persuasion that, do indeed, find him attractive, in the Jeff Chandler sense, some even to the point of goggle-eyed adoration."

"Yeah...and?" said John, trying to keep his patience.

"But as to his drumming." Bob Wooler cocked his head.

"That's what we're on about, Bob, his drumming. Not his looks," sniffed George.

"Yeah, just stick to his drumming, please, Bob," said Paul.

"Well...it's good," said Bob Wooler, nodding, slowly. "It's forceful, it's pounding, it's atomic."

"Yeah...and?" said John, dangerously.

"At its best, it's as good as Ringo's." Bob Wooler turned to each of them—testing the wind, judging the mood. "That is to say, dear boys, it's *almost* as good as Ringo's, but perhaps not *quite* as inventive."

John leaned back. "You're not just saying that, because you think I'll thump you, if you get it wrong, are you, Bob?"

"My dear boy, the thought never crossed my mind." Bob Wooler said, smoothly. He gave a startled look and went up on tiptoe to peer over George's shoulder. "Oh, crimmany and cripes, I must be going."

"Why," asked Paul, "It's not your round yet, is it?"

"No, it's my nemesis."

"I never knew you had a missus, Bob," quipped, George. "I didn't even think you were married."

"No, it's my curse, my infliction, my tormentor...the thrice dreaded Sam Leach." Bob Wooler turned and reached for his coat and scarf.

"Wotcher, lads. Hello, Bob, I do hope you're leaving on my account."

"Oh, is that you, Leach?" Bob Wooler turned, feigning surprise. "I wondered why the place was clearing out so rapidly." He nodded towards The Beatles. "Goodbye, lads. Thanks for the drink. I trust my opinion was, as usual, of inestimable value." With the very slightest flick of his eyes in Sam Leach's direction, he added, as if in afterthought, "Leach." He pushed his way through the crowd, to the door.

"Pompous little git," sneered Sam Leach.

"Will you two ever kiss and makeup?" asked Paul.

"I'd rather kiss a dog's arse. Hating me, is what keeps that bugger alive," he laughed. "Anyroad, lads, I have a favour to ask."

"Concerns money, does it, young Sam?" said John, sounding like a stern Lancashire mill-owner.

"No. It's about, Brian," said Sam Leach, flatly.

"What's 'Eppy' gone and done, now?" said John, suddenly serious.

Sam Leach shook his head. "He's cancelling bookings I've got with you, right, left and bloody centre, and on the thinnest of excuses, too. I don't understand it. It's almost as if he's trying to squeeze me out. Take this month, he's only let you play for me at 'the Tower' the once and even that's because I gave way and let him put the Joe Brown show on this Friday. So, I need to ask if you'll all put in a good word for me. Otherwise, fellas, I'm well and truly buggered."

"Sure, Sam," said Paul. "We'll put in a good word. I'm sure it's only Brian trying to fit things in. We've been working our brains out, since Hamburg. He's trying to set up gigs all over the country, now."

"Yeah, Sam," said George. "Even I don't have any idea where we'll be playing next. It could be Timbuktu or Calcutta or Wales. You just never know with our Brian, these days."

"Yeah, as if I needed telling." Sam Leach pulled another face. "But I think I've come up with an idea that even your Brian's got to love."

"And what's that, Sam?"

"I want to put on 'A Festival of Beatles'. Six dates, spread over two weeks...and I want to call it, 'A Cavalcade of Beatles Magic'."

"I like it, Sam," said Paul, smiling. "It's a very catchy title."

"I've never been in a cavalcade before," said George.

"Don't you worry, Sam," said John, patting Sam on the shoulder. "We'll have a word with 'Eppy' for you. Two, if need be."

"Thanks, lads. I always know I can count on you. Oh, and thanks for the toaster, by the way. It's improved my cooking, ten-fold."

"Sam," said George, "Can I ask you something?"

"Yeah, anything for you lot, what?"

"How do you rate Ringo Starr, as a drummer?"

"BLOODY HELL, BRIAN, you should go in for boxing promotions. You'd get a much better behaved crowd. Not like this bloody rabble. They're bloody animals they are...the lot of them...un-fookin-controllable."

The vicious gang fight that'd erupted in the car park, spilled over into the entrance foyer, then surged up the main staircase, threatening to engulf the long bar and ballroom, had only been supressed by the regiments of bouncers moments before. That the intensity of the fighting had shocked the unshockable Allan Williams only added to the surreal nature of the situation.

Brian Epstein leaned back against the bar. He'd felt as afraid as ever he'd done in his entire life, but was damned if he'd let it show. After that dreadful night in Hamburg there was little now that could frighten him to death, as it were. Once you'd managed to live through the very worst of times, you tended to see life rather differently. He was oddly pleased to see the glass of rum and coke in his hand wasn't shaking even the tiniest little bit. Oddly intrigued, too, that throughout it all he'd been more afraid of what another serious disturbance could do to hurt the name of The Beatles, rather than for his own safety.

It wasn't at all what he'd had planned for 'The Joe Brown Show' at 'the Tower'. But he was learning from his mistakes and had taken no chances this time. 'Hope for the best, but plan for the worst', was his new mantra. So he'd not only rethought Sam Leach's advice on the matter, he'd also hired Allan Williams to help organise the event and assist Bob Wooler where necessary. Yet even after having more than doubled the security personnel, it still hadn't deterred the gangs of Teddy Boys from waging war. It'd been just enough, though, to stop them from entirely ruining the show and for that he was truly grateful.

"I heard from one of them bouncers, Brian, it was even worse than the gang fight you had at the Bruce Channel show. That one quickly went down in local legend, apparently, and all the Teds that missed it were hell bent on reliving it...the stupid fookers. Some of the gangs came from as far away as Stockport, Bolton, and Manchester...on motorbikes, by car, even by bloody train. All of the dozy sods determined to make trouble. Un-fookin-believable, it is."

"That's why I'm so very glad I had your expertise in security matters to call upon Allan. Thank you. Another drink for you?"

As he'd heard his father say whenever he'd needed to call in outside help. 'No need to hire a dog, then bark yourself'.

REX MAKIN was genuinely pleased to see how much more self-assured young Raymond Jones seemed. If nothing else, the lad's experiences in Hamburg had not only knocked a chip or two from off his shoulder, they'd helped cool off his anger at the world, as well. He steepled his fingers and listened intently, as young Spike—as he still insisted on being called—recounted the strange and altogether disturbing events at the Star-Club.

"Truth is, Uncle Rex, I don't know who the man in black was or even who he was aiming at. I was just stood next to him. And so when he raised his pistol and called out, I just lunged at his arm, without thinking, like. Then all hell broke loose." Rex Makin nodded, but said nothing. "Anyroad, I got smashed in the back of the head for my troubles, by one of the bouncers, probably. Got pushed to the floor and kicked a good bit, too. Then Horst Fascher appeared out of nowhere, picked me up, and pulled me out of it. He's a right scary sod, but he's got a soft spot for all rock 'n' roll musicians and The Beatles, in particular. Afterwards, he gave me this little gold Star-Club pin to wear in my lapel, for my protection. Worked like a charm, too, because I never had any more trouble in Hamburg, after that."

Rex Makin nodded again. "In your opinion, Raymond, was the man in black aiming for Brian Epstein? Or was it the Beatle, John Lennon, who you mentioned in your phone call?"

"The man shouted something I didn't catch, which may have been Mr Epstein's name, I don't know. But I definitely heard him call out, 'Is your name John Lennon?' So with John being the leader of The Beatles, it was probably some gangster trying to nobble the club's top attraction. It goes on a lot in Hamburg, apparently. Luckily, though, Horst knocked the gun out of the bloke's hand with a spring-loaded cosh before he could fire it at anyone. So, if anyone saved John Lennon's life...or Mr Epstein's life, come to that...it was Horst. Because a shot was very definitely fired and at that close range it could've killed either one of them stone dead. Horst told me later the bullet ricocheted off the floor and hit a sailor in the foot. Poor sod was so drunk, he didn't even know what'd happened, until someone noticed him leaving a trail of blood wherever he walked."

Rex Makin came round from behind his desk. "I think that about wraps it up. Thanks for coming in, Raymond...I mean, Spike...but from what you tell me, it's highly unlikely the shooting had anything to do with the case that Harry Lightfoot, you, and I were working on here, in Liverpool. Or, for that matter, was anything at all to do Mr Epstein, directly."

Spike nodded. "How is Mr Lightfoot, Uncle Rex? Is he any better?"

"Yes, he is. Still walks with a bit of a limp, but he's done remarkably well, considering. He's doing the odd bit of work for me, too. Took great delight in the letters you wrote to him from Hamburg. He's taken quite a shine to you, Spike. Thinks that deep down you're a very good sort, which let me tell you is high praise, indeed, coming from him."

His secretary buzzed though on the intercom to announce the arrival of the next appointment and he smiled and held out his hand. "Thanks, young Spike. Give my regards to your mother." He walked Spike to the door and out into the reception area—where Brian Epstein was waiting.

BRIAN EPSTEIN looked from Rex Makin to the young man. Then Rex Makin smiled and began to usher him into his office. "Brian, right on time, as usual. Good to see you. Do come in."

He turned and stared after the longhaired young man disappearing down into the stairwell that led out onto the street. "You know, Rex, I'm sure I've seen that young man, before. Funny thing, though, I can't for the life of me think where."

Rex Makin smiled. "He's sort of an ex-client of mine, Brian. I acted for his mother, some time ago, when his father was knocked down and killed. Afterwards, Mrs Makin and me took a bit of shine to the lad. Tried to help him through it all. A grand little kid, he was, so very talented. He still calls me Uncle Rex...and we decided it was perhaps best to just let that be."

"How very good and kind of you both. I'm glad to say my problem isn't a matter of life and death, even though it does involve pulling the rug out from under someone. As I mentioned, in my call, I'd very much like your advice on any legal issues that could arise from it."

The solicitor closed his office door, waved to a chair, and sat down at his desk. "I appreciate you asking my advice again, Brian. Only, I thought that perhaps after our last meeting you..."

"My mother happened to mention you'd done some especial

service for her, Rex, and for me, also. Being her usual enigmatic self she wouldn't say anything more on the matter, but she seemed so very appreciative, I felt I could no less."

The solicitor nodded and smiled at him agreeably. And the balance between them re-established, he began to outline the sequence of events that had led to the three founding Beatles' newfound dissatisfaction with their existing drummer, Pete Best. And what 'the boys' now wanted him to do about it. He paced the room as he spoke, in a vague effort to help alleviate his distress, but chose not to mention what he'd heard about Mo Best. Some things were best left unsaid—even to your solicitor.

"So what do you think, Rex? I want to do what 'the boys' want. And I'll do all I can for Pete Best, afterwards, of course." Almost absent-mindedly, he added, "Who did you say that young man was, just now? Because I think I remember where it was I saw him. It was at the opening night of the Star-Club, in Hamburg. That...that night...when...when..."

"Brian, are you all right?" Rex Makin got up from behind his desk. "Let me get you a glass of water. You look as if you've just seen a ghost."

He took a sip of water. Took a moment to regain his composure. Then he told Rex Makin all he'd witnessed 'that night' in the Star-Club, in St. Pauli. "So you see, Rex, I'm certain that young man saved John Lennon's life. And in all probability, mine, too. All I know is, since then, I've been galvanised into action by the very thought of what could've happened that night."

Rex Makin shook his head, smiled. "You know, Brian, I don't know whether you believe in coincidences or not, but young Mr Jones was telling me the exact same story, just before you arrived. And what a story it is, too. All I can say is I'm just very glad nothing untoward happened to you, or to Spike, or to this John Lennon person. That would've been truly awful for everyone." The solicitor cleared his throat, picked up a file from his desk. "But to the matter at hand. I've given considerable thought as to how you should dismiss Mr Peter Best...'the undesirable member'...from the group, given that The Beatles are now, to all intents and purposes, a legal partnership."

PAUL McCARTNEY pressed his foot down hard on the accelerator and, wheels spinning, tyres screeching, his 'new' Goodward-green Ford Consul Classic shot forward from the traffic lights. There wasn't a minute to lose. He and John had left Liverpool at the crack of dawn to make the 160-mile journey, across country, to the seaside resort of Skegness. Only this was no pleasure trip, but a rescue mission. To rescue themselves, their group, and the recording contract that was almost certainly now within their grasp. The sole reason they were speeding to the Butlin's Holiday Camp, located on the east coast of England, to pick up Ringo Starr. And once they'd got both him and his drums packed safely inside the car and the trunk, they'd turn right round again and make the long journey back home.

Paul had decided not to go via Manchester and Sheffield, but opted instead for the more southerly route through Warrington, Stockport, and Chesterfield, before finally making for Lincoln and Skegness. "It'll be much faster that way. Less traffic."

"The speed you drive, Paul, I'm surprised we're not already meeting ourselves coming back. Just get us there in one piece, will yer?" John yawned and poured himself another cup of coffee from the Thermos flask Paul's dad had given them. "Incidentally, your dad could've put some bloody milk in here," sniffed John. "It's just like that Nazi crap we drank in Hamburg."

"Well if you'd just like to step outside the car and get yourself some, John, I'll be back this way in about five or six hours."

"Ha, bloody, ha, but no complaints, it'll do till we get there. Anyroad, I'm just really glad Ringo said, yes, to our 'Eppy'."

"Me, too, as it's clear Pete can't help get us where we're going to." Paul glanced over at his friend. "So, you're okay with it, now, John?"

"What? The coffee?"

"No, dafty, what we're doing now...dumping Pete for Ringo."

"Yeah, I am." John nodded. "But only because of the group, Pauly, nowt else. You've always got to think of the group, first. That's what I did when I first met you. You could play better than me, so I didn't hesitate, the group was that much stronger with you in it."

Paul nodded and smiled. "I'm glad you did, Mr Lennon. Only, that's what our George has been on about, all this time, isn't it?"

"Yeah, it is. I thought he was a right drag, going on and on about it, at first, but after both Decca and EMI, well, I changed my mind."

"Funny, our George, then George Martin coming to the same conclusion...both pushing for a change so the group could sound better."

"But that's it, Pauly, us being better as a group. We've always got do that, you and me, or what's the bloody point? Just playing the same old things, the same old way, would get us nowhere. It'd kill me, for sure. Kill us, too. And that's not what it means to be a Beatle."

"It's like when we write our songs...always trying to make them better than the last one...then trying to make them better each time we play them. Like that harmonica piece you worked out on, 'Love Me Do'. It made the song sound so, so much better...real bluesy, like."

"That was from me listening to that Delbert Clinton play harmonica for Bruce Channel. What a terrific bloke he was. He showed me some real nice licks on the harp. That's what I mean, you see, it's always searching for what'll make what's good sound that much better."

Paul ripped right into 'Searchin'—the root of anything and everything good yet to come.

John started in on 'One After 909'—one of the first songs he'd ever written that he thought was any good.

Paul joined in—right on track—harmonising—seamlessly.

Paul laughed. "Right, then, you bugger, now one of mine." And then he lit straight into 'I Saw Her Standing There'.

John nodded, imagined, reached for new and different notes, and harmonised in fourths, as Paul sang in fifths. It sounded great. They both nodded, then. Yeah, that's a real keeper.

And that's how they went on for miles and miles. The two of them singing and laughing and joking and thinking and smoking and chatting—in between challenging each other with their favourite songs. Some of which they'd written together.

On the outskirts of Chesterfield, Paul looked over at John. "So that's really it, then? Bye, bye Pete Best."

"Look," said John, reaching for the dashboard cigarette lighter. "Pete was good enough for what we needed when we needed it, but it's different now. And if Pete's not good enough for us to make records, then he's not good enough to be a Beatle." He took a drag of his cigarette. "Truth is, I suppose, he never really fit in. So the writing was always on the bloody wall, even before all this latest nonsense."

"Yeah," said Paul, running a hand back through his hair. "What do you think Mo's going to say when she hears he's been thrown out of the group?" He threw a glance at John.

John opened the window a little, so the cloud of cigarette smoke got sucked out. Wound it up again. "Not that that's the only thing she's got to worry about at the moment, but she's going to shit a brick. She'll go bloody spare. But that's the ever-lovely Mo for you. If she'd only shurrup for a mo' and let Pete get a word in edgewise, he might not have ended up being so bloody shy and reserved, all the time."

Paul rolled his eyes. "Don't you mean 'mean and moody'?"

John stubbed out his cigarette. "It's his drumming I'm on about, not his bloody looks, despite what Bob Wooler and Bill Harry think."

"Yeah, it's a bit rich, isn't it? Bill always saying in *Mersey Beat* about us being Pete's group?" Paul bit his lip and shook his head.

"He's worse than Mo, sometimes, he is. It's not Pete's bloody group. It's not even my group...it's all of us. You, George, me, and whoever the hell the drummer is...that's The Beatles."

"It's always 'Congratulations, Pete and the boys', lately, though, isn't it?"

John turned, exasperated. "Bill's bloody had his knickers in a twist ever since this last Hamburg trip. Probably thinks I don't appreciate him, as I didn't send him over any of me poems and postcards and all the rest of the crap I normally send when we're away. But I couldn't, I just couldn't. Just thinking of Bill and Stu and me, altogether, drinking ourselves silly, down Ye Cracke, or the three of us just messing about in the college canteen. It brought it all back and I just had to lock it all away. So a few times since we've been home, when I've seen Bill, in the Grapes, I've had to leave. He probably thinks that I just cut him dead or me head's got too big." He sighed. "I suppose I should sit down and explain how I feel or give him something for his bloody paper, but it's still all too close. Stu's death left a hole the size of Lancashire, inside me. Bloody hell, Pauly, I never thought anyone dying would hit me so bad, ever again, but it did."

"Yeah, it's a real drag," said Paul, softly. And for a time they drove on in complete silence, but as they turned off the A57, at Lincoln, and made for the A158 and the last leg of their journey to Skegness, the talk turned back to Ringo Starr. "What do you think our Rory's gonna say when he finds out we've come to Butlin's and swiped Ringo away from under his nose? And before The Hurricanes have finished their season, too."

"He'll g-g-go-go bloody spare he w-w-will, b-b-but he'll get over it, as soon as he gets himself and The Hurricanes another drummer. He's known Ringo has had itchy feet for months. Ringo even told 'Eppy', when he called him on Tuesday, that 'Kingsize' Taylor had just offered him twenty-quid a week to become one of The Dominoes."

"What did Brian say to that?"

"He offered Ringo twenty-five quid a week to become a Beatle. Told him we also had a recording contract all lined up. So Ringo said he always liked us and was dead flattened and didn't need any time to think. Asked 'Eppy' when did he want him to start being a Beatle."

"He's a lad, isn't he?"

"He will be, once he gets rid of his beard, his sidies, and gets his hair cut like the rest of us." John sniggered. "I'll tell him he can keep his bloody rings. It wouldn't be Ringo, without them."

"He's a funny looking bugger, though, isn't he? What with that big hooter of his," said Paul, laughing, as he banged out a drummer's tattoo on the motorcar's horn.

"Yeah, but one look at him and we'll always know we're not geniuses...we're just Beatles. Anyroad, I think he's got a lucky face."

"He better have. Anyway, we'll drop him and his drums back at his house, tell him to rest up, then we can practice together Saturday afternoon, before we go over to Port Sunlight, for Saturday night's gig. Then our Ringo will be a fully qualified Beatle."

"Where are we going to fellas?" John shouted.

"There's only the two of us in the car, John," retorted Paul.

"Well, bloody improvise, then, you Scouse bastard," John said laughing. "But just you keep your bloody eyes on the road, as you do." He rolled down the car window and let the rush of fresh air hit him full in the face. Then stuck his head out and shouted, gleefully, into the wind. "I said…where we going toooo fellaaas?"

"To Skegness, Johnno," Paul shouted at the top of his lungs.

"And which Skegness is that, Pauly?" yelled, John—the wind ripping at his words and scattering them out into the passing countryside.

"The one down by the seaside, where our Ringo is, John."

"And which Ringo is that, Pauly?" shouted John, right into Paul's ear, almost causing his now closest friend to jump right out of the driving seat.

"The Ringo Starr that's going to take us where we're going to, if you don't make me drive off the bloody road, you daft sod."

"He must be a real bloody star already, then, mustn't he?"

"The topper-most-drummin-most star there is, Johnno."

And they both yelled and banged their hands up and down on the dashboard and the steering wheel like a pair of madcap drummers.

"All the same, McCartney," said John, laughing; gasping for breath; "Your dad could've still put some bloody milk in this coffee."

"Hang on then, farmer Lennon," laughed Paul. "I'll stop at the next cow we come to and you can get out and milk the bugger, yourself."

CHAPTER TWENTY-NINE

Drumbeats, Rolls, And Fills

Pete Best peered at his watch and wished the hands would stop. Brian Epstein was always such a bloody stickler for punctuality—even if only for another informal meeting to discuss future Beatles' business.

He looked at Neil Aspinall driving like a madman through the early morning streets of Liverpool. Beatles' roadie, best mate, lodger, Mo's what—boyfriend? What to call him now? He couldn't call him 'step-dad'. That'd be plain daft. Truth was, even he couldn't believe what'd happened—a brand new little baby brother, Roag, right out of the blue. But what did any of it matter, just so long as Mo was happy. Especially after dad had upped and left her the year before. Somehow though she'd kept cheerful, kept them all laughing, kept the family going. Kept the Casbah and Casbah Promotions going, too. Even as young as he was, he knew that in tough times you took your comfort wherever you could find it. She was a bloody wonder, was Mo. It was funny, though, the way the world turned, sometimes.

"I'll have you there in considerably less than two ticks."

"Thanks, there, Nell, but let's all get there in one piece. There's a lot riding on both of us, these days. Wonder what our Brian wants to talk about. He didn't say much last night, at the Cav."

"I don't have a clue, Pete. So, look, I'll just drop you, go park, then come back and have a quick shuffty at all the latest jazz records, downstairs. Here we are. See you later, alligator."

He exited the van and glanced up at the sign on the front of the building: N.E.M.S. What was it that Bob Wooler called Brian these days? 'Nemperor!' Well, thumbs up, to that. Humming to himself, he pushed open the big plate glass door and ascended the stairs to the offices on the first floor.

" 'Lo, Beryl. Mr Epstein asked me to come see him."

"Er, yes, he's expecting you, Pete. A moment." Beryl Adams pressed the intercom button. "It's Pete Best for you, Mr Brian."

He heard the familiar voice. "Thank you, Beryl, send him in."

Beryl Adams smiled, got up from behind her desk, opened the door to her boss's office and there stood Brian, an odd look on his face.

"Hello, Brian, you wanted to see me?"

"Yes, er…good morning, Pete. Thank you for coming. A drink?"

"No, thank you, Brian. A bit too early."

"How are you this morning, Pete? Okay, are you?"

He nodded—couldn't think of what else to say.

"Funny weather we're having, doesn't seem to know whether it wants to rain or shine."

"Er, yes. What's up Brian, something bothering you? Another promoter not wanting to pay the increased fees you're asking for us? Is that it? Mo was only saying this morning, about how she'd heard a few of them grumbling about it, but she thought it'd soon blow…"

"No, er, not that. How is your dear mother by the way?"

"She's well, thank you, Brian. Still The Beatles' number one fan."

"That's good, that's good. Just as long as she's well."

Now he was puzzled. Brian Epstein always came straight to the point. For no reason at all, he glanced over at the clock.

"Pete, I have some bad news for you. The boys want you out. And they want Ringo in. They don't think you're a good enough drummer." There was a long pause—four bars, at least. "George Martin didn't think you were a good enough drummer, either."

There was a sound like a rim-shot somewhere inside his head and he heard himself saying, "Does Ringo know about this, yet?"

A distant voice said, "He's joining the boys, this Saturday." But all he could hear were drumbeats and cymbal crashes. Then, somewhere, over on the far side of the world, there was the sound of bells ringing and he saw Brian Epstein pick up the telephone. He glanced over at the clock again, but the hands were motionless, as if time had suddenly run out of reasons to tick on into the future.

Brian Epstein's mouth opened and closed. Opened and closed. "Sorry about this." But the words meant nothing now. "Beryl, I expressly said, no calls. Oh...yes...put him through." Sound of fingers tapping—on the desktop. "No. I'm with him, at the moment." Strange words. Even-stranger silences. "Yes, just now. No, I don't know yet. Yes, later. Yes. Goodbye."

But no more words for him, now, only words for someone else.

It felt like he'd been punched in the stomach. He could hear his heart thumping in his chest, the rush of blood beating in his ears, but it was no rhythm he recognised. He was hit by a sudden thought that sent him reeling again. Was this Brian taking revenge? He tried to swallow, but couldn't. He forced himself to think. Why risk breaking up the group? Was it because he'd once turned down Brian's amorous advances?

He hadn't told, anyone. It was just the one time, in Brian's car, one night, after they'd had dinner together. Brian had told him how much he admired him and asked whether he'd like to spend the night in a hotel, somewhere. He'd just stared straight ahead, his hands on the dashboard, said he'd had a terrific night, but he'd better get on home. Thanks for asking, like. It wasn't until later he'd even allowed himself to think of what Brian had really been asking. He'd blushed, felt a bit queasy, but the next day Brian had just smiled, as if nothing had happened. Since when he'd thought the whole thing had simply been put to bed, so to speak. But now what was he to think? He swallowed. Felt sick. He knew full well Brian wouldn't break up the group without the explicit agreement of the other three Beatles.

He thought of John and Paul and George. He'd been through thick and thin with them for two, long, hard-slog years. On their very first visit to Hamburg, he and Paul had even been thrown into a St. Pauli prison cell, together, after they'd been accused of having started a fire at the Bambi Kino. And John? What about all the things he'd got up to in Hamburg with John that'd never bear repeating? So what'd he done wrong? What the fook had he done wrong?

He looked at Brian's mouth opening and closing on the far side of the desk—a million miles away. He glanced at the clock again. The hands still hadn't moved. He was still lost in time.

"So you see, Pete, there are a couple of venues left before Ringo joins and I was hoping you'd still play. It'd be such an enormous help if you would. Then, next week we can get together over lunch and discuss your situation, see if we can set you up in another group. I happen to know The Merseybeats are looking for a first class drummer and I thought you might perhaps consider joining..."

He heard himself shouting. "I'll play your bloody dates, for you, Brian, but I'm bloody shattered the lads didn't have the guts to tell me themselves. It's not right. I deserve better. It's trial, without jury. Think how you'd feel, Brian. Just think how you'd bloody well feel, being on trial for who and what you are and not even being given the chance to defend yourself."

Brian Epstein simply nodded, his face full of sympathy. "Next week, Pete, we'll talk again, I promise."

BRIAN EPSTEIN waited for Pete Best to depart, scanned the items on his notepad, reached for his pen and drew a line through Pete's name. The telephone call had come from Paul McCartney, in a phone box, in Skegness. To tell him Ringo Starr had definitely joined the group, they'd shaken hands on it, had sorted things out with Rory Storm, and were on their way back to Liverpool. Ringo would follow on, later, and be back in Liverpool, by Saturday. Good. No last minute problems there. He put a tick next to Ringo Starr's name.

Next question. Would Pete play the next two engagements? Pete had said he would. So that item got a tick, as well. Tomorrow he'd send over an official NEMS press release to Bill Harry for inclusion in next week's *Mersey Beat*. The boys would practice on Saturday afternoon. Ringo would officially start with the group on Saturday night. Good. Now he had to attend to a really ticklish problem. He tapped his fingers on his notepad, swallowed, straightened the knot of his tie, and had Beryl Adams put in a call to the local Town Hall.

SAM LEACH scratched his chin. The Beatles had been as good as their word. He'd managed to get six dates out of Brian Epstein, as well as a promise that none of them would be cancelled, this time. So, The Beatles would be playing—well, three of them would, with a sit-in drummer—and Sam Leach and 'the Tower' were both still standing. Only trouble now was Liverpool's bloody jungle drums. Word must've already got round that something was up, because ticket sales were way down. There'd been no official announcement, as yet, so most fans wouldn't have heard about the sacking of Pete Best. If he knew, though, it stood to reason others did. He could imagine the whispers, drifting like a thick fog all across Merseyside. It meant he wouldn't see anything like the profits he'd been counting on, which added the threat of imminent penury to personal injury.

Christ, but dealing with Brian Epstein was bloody torture. In return for 'his boys' performing, soddin' 'Eppy' had extracted one Friday night a month from him for so-called 'special' events. It was the thin end of the bloody wedge, of course, but he had no choice. Not if he wanted to fill the Tower's coffers, as well as his own pockets. At least he still had the upper hand at 'the Tower'. He'd also cornered the Majestic Ballroom and the Rialto. So his 'Beatles Festival' was as good as all lined up, which was ace. It still didn't rid him of the very itchy feeling between his shoulder blades. He sniffed the damp night air—time for a drink—a real bloody stiff one.

HARRY LIGHTFOOT gave himself the whole weekend to develop and print his rolls of film. No need to rush. Not now he had the cat in the bag, so to speak. He'd 'pushed' the film and now had to overdevelop it, so as to compensate. He consulted his test-film notes and set the clock. A few twists and turns of the developing tank, followed by the stop bath and the fixer, a wash and a rinse, then the film could be hung up to dry. Afterwards, he cut each roll of developed film into strips and printed off a contact sheet to see what he'd captured.

He peered through a loupe, marked a dozen or so pictures with a china pencil, and made a set of full-size prints. He'd sacrificed some detail, but the contrast was there, and he concentrated on making the faces in the photographs clear and distinct. He looked at the set of prints in the red light of the darkroom, nodded, and then pinned them all up to dry. Later, he spread the prints out on the kitchen table and examined them again. He discarded two of the pictures, then returned to the darkroom and made six copies of each of the others.

He poured himself a glass of Glen Grant, got his notebook, a biro and a notepad, and sat down to look at the rows of prints again. He took a sip of single malt. Nodded. Yes. A story there even a blind man could follow. It'd taken a couple of small 'Molotov cocktails' as the real clinchers, but needs must when the devil drives. He'd used beer bottles of the sort The Joker's Club always had stacked up, outside, in wooden crates. Filled them both with petrol. Stuffed petrol-soaked rags down inside. Set one alight. Hurled it. Then hot-footed it—hot-limped more like it—around to the back of the building, set the other bottle alight, and hurled that. Then he'd disappeared back into the shadows and got himself nicely positioned and all ready to shoot.

He'd practised on old doors out at an abandoned factory site, up the estuary, to gauge the right amount of petrol. Not enough to do any real damage, just enough to bring certain people out of the club and the City Fire Brigade to the scene. The arrival time of the fire engines a sure way to get the illicit goings-on at the club on official record. The fact the flames had given him a good light to shoot by was an added bonus. His only worry had been that someone in the Liverpool City police force might question the exact order of events. Knowing them, though, he doubted anyone would suspect that the anonymous caller who'd dialled 9-9-9 to report the fire, from a phone box on Edge Lane, was the self-same person that only a few minutes later had thrown petrol bombs at the club's front door, as well as its secret exit door at the rear.

He took another sip of Glen Grant, rolled it slowly around his tongue, licked his finger, leafed through his notebook, and began copying out times, dates, places, names and, whenever necessary, rank and serial number. He painstakingly typed everything onto 3 x 5 file cards, then stapled each card to the back of its corresponding photograph. When he'd finished, he dou-ble-checked all six sets, then placed a full set of photos inside six large buff-coloured envelopes. He closed and sealed them, poured himself another whisky, consulted his notebook again and addressed each envelope in turn. Just how damaging it'd all prove to be was now in the laps of the Gods or, rather, the six Fleet Street editors who'd soon be the lucky recipients of all his—of necessity, very anonymous—hard night's work.

RINGO STARR couldn't believe it. Here he was, Sunday night at the Cavern. It might just as well have been *Sunday Night at the London Palladium* given the number of times he and The Hurri-canes had played there, which was hardly ever. This was Remo Four, Bluegenes, Gerry and The Pacemakers territory—Red Riv-er Jazzmen, Yorkshire Jazz Band country. No wonder Rory hated the place, there was hardly enough room to swing a cat, let alone a microphone stand. The fans here made the holiday-makers at Butlin's seem like candidates for an old people's home. They were raving mad. Hopping mad, too, about Pete Best being gone. Well bugger the whole lot of them. Elsie Stark-ey's little boy, Ritchie, has got a bloody job to do.

I'm up here, if they all but bloody knew it, drumming like mad, bashing on me bloody skins, as if me bloody life depended on it. Which it does, of course, and likely always will. Other than that, just like everyone else, he'd always been waiting for some-thing to happen. Something worth getting up in the morning for—something that'd make life worth living—anything, but life in some bloody factory or engineering works. Spend his life as an apprentice joiner? No bloody thanks. That's why he'd been drumming for five years, non-bloody stop. Same old clubs, same old faces and places. He was right bloody browned off with it. Not the drumming. That's what he did best. No, it was the walls he didn't like. All the bloody walls that'd hemmed him in since he was a nipper: bedroom walls, hospital walls, school walls. That's why he spent so much time bashing against doors to be let out. That's why, once upon a time, he'd written off to Texas, to the Houston Chamber of Commerce, with big dreams of cowboy country with big open spaces.

He just wanted to get out, get away. Even bloody emigrate, for good, if he had to. That's why he'd left The Hurricanes and gone back out to Hamburg to play with Tony Sheridan. Hoping for a wind of change. Not wanting to be a Hurricane anymore or play another bloody season at Billy bloody Butlin's bloody Holiday Camps. Hell—he really would go mad if he had to do that, year in, year out. In the end, he'd re-joined The Hurricanes for just one more holiday season. Then 'Kingsize' Taylor had wanted him to join The Dominoes. Then The Beatles and Brian Epstein had come a-knocking with an extra five-pound a week, which was certainly nothing to sneeze at.

America was still the big dream. That's where it'd all started. Country. Western. Rock 'n' Roll. Rhythm-and-Blues. That's where it all happened—cowboys, big cars, and big, big, beautiful women. That's where he'd go one day. Yesireee! That's where the future lay. He only hoped there was enough room for him. "Pete Best Forever! Ringo Never!" All the girls, down in front, had shouted at him—some of the boys, too—all of them shoving, pushing, yelling. "Down with Ringo!" "Down with Ringo!" Well, not if little Ritchie Starkey has anything to do with it. Just you wait and see. "Give it a bash," George Harrison had said just before some bugger in the crowd had bashed the poor lad in the eye. Give it a bash? There was nothing on God's green that was going to stop him from bashing up a bloody storm.

John had his back to him, so he looked at George, even as he tried to hear Paul's bass. Catching their nods and winks and foot-stomps that told him when to change beat. But he'd already changed a whole lot, as it was. He'd already cut off his sideburns, combed his hair forward—all in an effort to look like a Beatle. He'd known the moment he'd joined the group, the three of them had been together for years, like a gang, and he was the new boy and always would be—never any changing that. And there it was. Dead funny. He was an apprentice joiner, after all. But it was the right drum-stool to be sitting on, no doubt about that. The Beatles were going places. And now he was going with them, too. So he'd smile and nod and shake his head in time and see just how far it took him.

He looked over at George Harrison, again, winking and blinking his bruised blackened eye at him. Nodding in time, chin going up and down, pointing to the next change in tempo. Breaking into a lop-sided toothy grin to signal the drum break. Time for another Ringo roll, another Ringo fill, time for his drumbeats and backbeats to earn Elsie Starkey's little boy his ticket to ride.

BRIAN EPSTEIN smiled at the young bouncer, named Mal, and stared at the proffered stick of Wrigley's gum. He nodded, took the foil and paper-wrapped packet delicately between his thumb and forefinger and began to unwrap it. "Thank you," he said. "Perfect timing. That's exactly what I need." Chewing gum wasn't at all his usual habit, but then what was happening wasn't at all usual. So he rather self-consciously popped the gum into his mouth and began to chew. And was soon chewing, repeatedly and relentlessly—in the manner of a true American manager—to help stop his nerves from becoming overstretched.

"Don't you mind them rowdies, Mr Epstein, I'll bear-hug them off the floor and have them up the stairs...all sprawled out on Mathew Street if they make too much noise."

"Er...thank you...Mal...is it? I'd be forever grateful."

Granada Television had come all the way from Manchester to film The Beatles playing a Wednesday lunchtime session at the Cavern. All down to members of The Beatles Fan Club writing to the North's independent television station to ask them to put their favourite group on 'the telly'. Increasingly on the look out for things that'd appeal to the region's teenagers, Granada's producers had sent people to see The Beatles perform—twice. And duly impressed, they'd dispatched a TV crew to film 'the North's Top Group'—his touch that—in performance for future transmission in the news program *Know The North*.

The Cavern was packed, of course, with most of the fans on their best behaviour. Most still seemed unaware Pete Best had been dismissed from the band and replaced by Ringo Starr. There were a good few who did, however, and he'd been booed to his face a number of times. One or two fans had even tried to punch him. He'd simply ignored it all, but had the burly, young bouncer, Mal Evans, standing close by, just in case. As long as 'his boys' remained unharmed he was fine. And he did all he could to look cool and composed—just like managers were always supposed to look. After one particularly noisy outburst, he'd even calmly turned to the Granada TV producer and told him that any booing he might hear was simply the sort of friendly rivalry that erupted, occasionally, between fans of different local groups—just teenagers letting off steam. And, again, the right word at the right time appeared to have worked wonders.

Then with a quick nod from the cameraman and the sound engineer—and one from him—The Beatles lit into a medley of Little Richard songs. George and John's flourish of opening guitar chords, he noted, sounding particularly bright and brilliant on their new Vox AC-30 amplifiers. Paul immediately capturing the Cavern crowd with his very first scream of..."Kansas City." Effortlessly hitting high notes, growling with passion, forever building excitement. "Yeah, yeah." Howling into George's solo. Pleading. Calling. "Hey-hey-hey." John and George singing "Bye-bye" and "So long" over and over until the Cavern was one, head-nodding, foot-tapping mass. On and on until a roll and a snap and a thunderous double clap of Ringo's bass drum brought everyone back home.

It had all sounded very good to his ears. Ringo had fit in very well. And he looked over at the director, who looked over at the cameraman, who gave a quick nod. "Good." The director turned to the sound engineer, who adjusted his headphones and waggled his hand, as if to say 'maybe'. "Not good." He chewed on and on—his eyes not missing a thing.

Then after another minute or so of talking amongst themselves, but not long enough for the crowd to get too restless, the director twirled a finger and nodded to his crew, then back at him. Still chewing gum like there was no tomorrow, he nodded curtly to John and Paul and George. Paul turned to Ringo—nodded. Ringo counted the group in on his sticks. "One-two-three-four." And, as one, George, John, and Paul hit into 'Some Other Guy' and sang and played the sure-fire crowd-pleaser through to its end—a reprise of the intro kicked to a finish by

Ringo's bass drum. Everything then neatly wrapped up by George's very special 'Gretty' chord. He smiled. "Very good. Very good, indeed." But in that split-second—before the Cavern crowd yelled and screamed their appreciation—a lone voice yelled out: "We want Pete!"

BRIAN EPSTEIN adjusted the white carnation on the lapel of his dark blue pinstriped suit so that it lay 'just right'. Appearance was everything. Especially when you were the 'best man' on your way in a chauffer-driven car to pick up the bride-to-be and take her on to the register office.

He'd known something was up the moment John Lennon had called and asked for a 'private word'. He'd first thought it might be John having second thoughts about the sacking of Pete Best, but it'd turned out to be an altogether different magnitude of problem. John's girlfriend, Cynthia, was pregnant and John had decided to do the decent thing and marry her. All very laudable, but so inconvenient, as it didn't do for any rising young pop star to have a steady girlfriend, let alone for them to be married. As for fathering children, that was anathema, it sent completely the wrong message. A pop star had to be openly available to all the hopes and dreams of his legions of adoring female fans.

Of course, he'd told John not to worry, offered his congratulations, and had then immediately taken charge. He'd chosen the registry office, pulled every string possible to get the special marriage licence, in time. He'd even decided to let John and Cynthia have the use of the fully-furnished flat he kept in Faulkner Street, as a wedding present. He'd miss the convenience of having his little private 'bolthole', but again there were appearances to keep up. It was no hardship at all, really, not if it helped John in his predicament and helped keep the world at bay. Even so, it peeved him that the shoes that seemed to be forever dropping from on high were baby shoes. First, there'd been Mo Best, Pete's mum, with a child born out of wedlock, fathered by none other than Neil Aspinall, the boys' road manager of all people. And now this: another unplanned-for pregnancy.

Where on earth, he wondered, was it all going to end?

SPIKE JONES raised his beer glass, in celebration. "Congratulations, Jimmy. And the very best of British luck to you both."

"Yeah, should be good. She's a good girl, is Thelma. Well, I mean, I got right browned off having to do me courting in the backseats at the cinema or the backseat of me car. The sofa in the living room at home was no bleedin' better, neither, as I could never get me mum and dad or any of me bleedin' brothers out of the house for long enough. So, God's honest, that's why me and Thelma got engaged, no other reason."

Spike looked over the edge of his glass. "She's not...you know?"

"No, Thelma's not bleedin' well pregnant. You're as bad as my little brother, you are, Spikey. He asked the same soddin' question. Only, when I told him 'No, that's not the reason we're getting married,' the little sod put on a Welsh accent and ran round the house yelling, 'There's posh, then, isn't it?'"

"What's so posh, then?"

It was Thelma and Sandra, hair newly titivated, lipstick freshly applied, returned from a visit to the Ladies.

"Er...that engagement ring Jimmy bought you, Thelma," Spike said, quickly. "There's no posher jewellers in all Liverpool, than Messrs Boodle and Dunthorne. Everyone knows that."

"Only the very best for our Thelma," Jimmy said, nodding thanks for Spike's quick thinking. "Start as you mean to go on, I always say."

"And very nice, too," sighed Sandra, taking hold of Spike's hand.

Spike raised his glass again. "Sounds like real love, if you ask me. So, 'cheers', you two, from the two of us."

He meant it, too, oddly glad his friends hadn't been shotgunned into marriage—a real passion killer if ever there was one. He squeezed Sandra's hand. Their day would come.

CHAPTER THIRTY

Tutti-Frutti

Sam Leach put his head in his hands and groaned. "That's all I need, a couple of dead Beatles on me hands."

Word on the street was that a gang of Toxteth Teddy Boys was going attack The Beatles when they played the Rialto, because of what they'd done to Pete Best. And they didn't ever fookin' mess around in Toxteth. They were all as hard as six-inch fookin' nails.

The Beatles had heard the rumours. And Brian Epstein had telephoned to say that if 'his boys' were in any sort of danger they wouldn't appear. "As I'm sure you of all people appreciate, Sam, there's been far too much violence at recent concerts. And if The Beatles were shown to have been the direct cause of yet another serious disturbance, the damage to their reputation could be crippling, especially if it made the newspapers."

The plain truth was, he'd be crippled, too, if The Beatles failed to show. Attendance at the first four 'Beatle Festival' shows had been way down because of the fall-out over Pete Best. And if his final two shows at the Toxteth Rialto and 'the Tower' weren't both sell-out successes, he'd have a twenty-four-carat-gold-plated bloody disaster on his hands. He wracked his brains. Nothing. Then it hit him. Of course! Allan-bloody-Tanner—'The Black Bomber'—the pride of Toxteth. He put an immediate call in to the ex-boxer who he'd first met working as a bouncer at the Iron Door Club. "Allan, me old mate, got a big favour to ask." He quickly explained the situation. "So will you have a word with the locals for me? See what the score is?"

He put down the phone, stared into space, and began to chew his nails down to the nub. And when Allan Tanner at last called back, he listened so hard his ears rang, then let out a huge sigh of relief. The rumours were false. A number of local hard cases had even promised that for the good name of the area, they'd ensure nothing bad happened. And if anyone did start trouble, they'd be very quickly dragged to another part of the city and severely dealt with.

He put down the telephone, rubbed his head vigorously with his fingers, slapped himself in the face to get the blood circulating again, and put in a call to NEMS. "Er, is that Beryl? Sam Leach, here. I need to see Mr Epstein as soon as possible. Yes, it's dead important." The line clicked. He waited. "Yes. Yes, okay, I can come right over."

He dashed down the stairs, jumped into his new second-hand motorcar—his new driving license burning a hole in his pocket—and sped like a madman through the Mersey Tunnel. Everything was on the line and he prayed his news would be enough to swing it his way. Just in case, though, he'd add another Sam Leach touch and arrange for each Beatle—and Brian Epstein, too—to be accompanied at all times by two handpicked bouncers. He parked, hurriedly, and dashed into NEMS.

"So you see, Brian, the rumours are completely false. There's nothing for anyone to be worried about. Not a thing."

Brian Epstein steepled his fingers and shook his head. "No. Sam. Thank you for trying, but I daren't take the risk. The safety of The Beatles is paramount. I simply can't allow them to perform." He glanced over at John and Paul standing by the window. "I'm sure you understand," he added.

John shuffled his feet, looked down at his shoes. "Sam's word has always been good enough for us, 'Eppy'," he said, quietly. "If Sam says it's safe...it'll be safe. So we'll just go ahead and play, if that's okay with you?"

Paul scratched his chin with his forefinger, nodded. "Yeah. We can't not play, Brian, especially, as we're top of the bill."

Even from where he was standing, Sam could see Brian Epstein's neck begin to colour. He waited for the bomb to go off.

"Very well, as you both wish," 'Eppy' said, very calmly.

SAM LEACH pressed the stub of pencil to his tongue and re-did his sums. 'The Beatles Show' at the Rialto had gone off without a hitch. The Beatles—with none other than Ringo Starr on drums—had been given a tremendous reception, with no hint of trouble from the fans. The turnout, though, had been bloody awful and no matter how he added it all up, there was no way he could cover his costs. He'd already paid the three supporting-groups and told them to get off home. All he had to do now was square things away with the lads—*pro-tem*.

He heard the wave of cheering, shouting, and applause get louder and louder. Then The Beatles crashed through the door and into the dressing room. He turned to face them. "Welcome back, lads. Good news, another toppermost performance. Bad news, I'm short and can only pay you half of the agreed £40 fee, tonight. I'll make up the rest tomorrow night, at 'the Tower', I promise. Scout's honour."

John, Paul, and George looked at him, laughed, and nodded. This wasn't the first time, nor would it be the last. Ringo said nothing, just smiled. Brian Epstein, however, was livid. "No. No. No. This sort of behaviour is unacceptable. It's far more than you taking The Beatles for granted, again, Mr Leach. It's abuse, verging on the criminal."

He felt the colour drain from his face and couldn't speak a word. So he turned to each Beatle in a desperate silent plea.

John rolled his eyes, shook his head. "Sam's okay, 'Eppy', really he is, even if his hair always looks untidy. He'll pay us tomorrow night." He pulled a funny face, waved a fist. "Won't you, Leachy?"

Everyone laughed, even Ringo, but Brian Epstein just glared. "I think I really need to talk to you, Mr Leach," he said, his voice clipped and cold. "Please come to my office, first thing, in the morning." Then, without another word, he turned on his heel and left the dressing room. The Beatles all looked at one another and shook their heads and, in complete silence, followed their manager out the door. Paul McCartney held back a moment, turned to him, and put a hand on his shoulder. "Hey, don't you worry, none, Sam. We'll sort things out with Brian on the way home, we will. Promise. Scout's honour."

SAM LEACH knew something was up. The pained look on Rita Shaw's face said it all. He'd had a funny feeling he should pay a

quick visit to the NEMS ticket agency counter at the Whitechapel store, prior to going up to the office. Fighting back tears
of embarrassment, her voice quivering, she told him that Mr
Brian had demanded the withdrawal of all tickets for any and all
'Sam Leach Promotions' and that the staff were to inform customers who wanted tickets, that The Beatles would no longer be
appearing for The Leach Organisation at 'the Tower' or anywhere else.

He climbed the stairs to Brian Epstein's office in a complete
daze and stood there, like a lemon, while Beryl Adams introduced him over the intercom, then ushered him into her boss's
inner sanctum.

Brian Epstein barely even bothered to look up from his desk.
"Either you pay me nineteen pounds, immediately, Mr Leach, or
The Beatles won't be appearing for you this evening. Nor will
they appear in any future shows with which you are concerned."

Sam couldn't believe his ears. It made no sense. It certainly
made no business sense. He wiped a hand across his face—tried
to stop shaking. "But...but Brian, as it does every Friday, the
NEMS ticket agency will sell tickets well in excess of the money
owed. You could take that as payment."

This time the bloody man didn't even bother to glance up at
him. "No, no, no, Mr Leach, I'm afraid that won't be possible."

He realised then it wasn't about the money. It'd never been
about the money. It was all about Brian Epstein asserting his authority—to show who was really in charge. He'd caused The
Beatles to question and overturn one of Brian Epstein's deci-
sions and now Mrs Leach's naughty little boy had been served
notice. It was never going to be allowed to happen again.

He staggered back down Mathew Street, visibly shaking, and
sought refuge in the Grapes. He ordered a whisky. Downed it in
a single gulp. Ordered another. What the hell was he going to do
now? He'd have to pay out hundreds of pounds in refunds for
that night's show and be stuck with masses of other debts, none
of which he'd be able to pay. It'd bankrupt him. Finish him in
the business. If not for good, then at least as far into the future
as his addled brain could imagine. Brian Epstein had won the

war and he'd done it by simply taking The Beatles away from him. The only thing he'd ever truly lost any sleep over.

All he could think of now was just how fast he could drink himself into complete and blessed oblivion. Then from over the rim of his whisky glass—of all the people, in all the gin-joints in all the world—he saw Paul McCartney come into the Grapes. He nodded, tried to put on a brave face, keep a stiff upper lip, but was pouring out his tale of woe before he even knew it. After all he had nothing else left to lose, certainly not his pride.

The usually unshakable Paul, shocked and saddened by what he heard, shook his head, stuck his hand in his pocket and bought him another whisky—and a double one, at that. The sort of thing you did prior to a funeral. "You hang on here, a bit, Sam," Paul said, softly. "I'll go have a word with Brian. This is getting too silly for words."

He watched the big-brown-eyed Beatle go and wondered whether he'd see him or John or George—or even Ringo—ever again. "A life without Beatles. What a fookin' horrible thought." He stared into his drink. What was it they said? 'One was never enough, three was one too many'. He reached for the whisky intent on sinking a whole damn bloody bottle, if need be. And then a shadow loomed over him.

"Okay, Sam. We play."

He looked up, but all he could see was a slim dark shape against a greater darkness. He blinked. "Who? What? What's that you say?"

"Tonight, Sam. We'll play. The Beatles will play 'the Tower'."

He tried to get to his feet, but couldn't. Nothing worked. Nothing. He couldn't even manage a teensy-weensy tiny smile of gratitude. All he could feel were the salt tears running down his cheeks.

SAM LEACH rubbed his head. How did the bloody song go? Smile when your bloody heart is breaking? All the rest of that long hard day he'd tried his best to put on a happy face. Hoping against hope that grey skies were going to bloody cheer up. Only they never ever did. It was as if everything he did or touched was stuck under a dark thunderous cloud.

Once again, rumours The Beatles wouldn't be playing—rumours he was sure originated not a million miles away
from Bob Wooler's turntable—had had the desired effect.
Throw in the continuing unrest over the sacking of Pete Best
and attendance at 'the Tower' that Friday night was a total loss.
Nevertheless, he approached Brian Epstein just before The Beatles were due to go on and offered him the nineteen pounds still
due from the previous evening's show at the Rialto.

But the bloody man just refused to take the money.

"I want payment in full, Mr Leach, for last night, as well as
tonight. No instalments, no bit-by-bit, but the full fee due The
Beatles...all fifty-nine pounds of it. And I'll take it, now, if you
please."

Sam just stared at him. No group was ever paid before they
went on stage. Promoters weren't that daft. Brian Epstein knew
full well The Leach Organisation wouldn't have anywhere near
that amount of ready cash on hand. It'd be there, by the end of
the night, from additional ticket sales, but not at that moment.

"Oh, come on 'Eppy', be bloody reasonable," John muttered.

"Yeah, 'Eppy', Sam'll pay us, in full, later, he will," said
George.

"No, that's out of the question now. I want fifty-nine pounds,
in cash, now, Mr Leach, or The Beatles will not appear tonight."

"Brian, it'll be alright. Sam gave his word," said Paul. "And,
look, if it'll make any difference, like, I'll give up my share of tonight's fee. Sam and 'the Tower' have been very good to us."

"No. That's very generous of you, Paul, but it misses the
point."

And that was it—a stand off, a stalemate, and The Beatles due
on stage any minute. Sam had to do something or he'd feint
clean away. "Er, look, lads, give me five minutes. I'll go check
the box-office."

"Yeah, okay, Sam. You go do that," said John, quietly.

Sam all but ran to the box-office. Looked at the meagre takings and knew he was dead in the water. He turned and saw
Ringo Starr walking up and down the corridor with a scribbled
placard that read '*No Pay! No Play!*' and his heart all but sank and

drowned. And in the space of a couple of heartbeats, the tide of bad news reached the furthest corners of the Tower Ballroom. "The Beatles weren't going to appear!" And, suddenly, waves of people converged on the box-office to demand their money back.

Hearing all the commotion, John and Paul dashed out into the corridor, waving their arms and shouting, "Hey-hey-hey. We're going to play. Don't take your money back or Sam won't have enough to pay us."

That's when Brian Epstein played his trump card. He called John, Paul and George back into the dressing room—waved Ringo away. Sam followed them in and quietly closed the door behind him. This time, The Beatles' manager ignored him totally and turned instead to face 'his boys'.

"You defied my wishes, last night, at the Rialto. And if you do so again, tonight, then it's all over between us." The look on his face said he meant every word. And that was it. The line had finally been drawn. It was no longer a nasty little spat between Messrs Epstein and Leach. The whole future of The Beatles was on the line, now, as well.

No one moved. No one said anything. It was as if time itself had suddenly stopped. Sam felt his legs start to give way. It felt as if the whole bloody Tower had toppled down on top of him. He tried to breathe, tried to speak, but nothing happened. Finally, he managed to draw in a lungful of air. He coughed, tried to clear his throat, but when he spoke his voice was thick with emotion. "John, Paul, George, hold on a mo." Slowly, he turned to face Brian Epstein. "As for you, you just fook off out of it...out of my Tower...before I do something to you I might live to regret."

The bloody man just looked at him—cool, calm, and very collected—and walked to the door. "As you wish," he said. Then Epstein stopped and turned to face the three Beatles. "The decision is now yours, gentlemen," he said, and then was gone from out the room.

Sam peered at John, Paul, and George through watery eyes and bit down hard on his lower lip. "Whatever else I might think of him, lads, that lousy bugger's obviously the one that's going to get you to where you're going to. I wish I could, but I can't. Not in this lifetime, anyway. Nor can anyone else around Merseyside, for that matter." He swallowed hard, shook his head, tried to sniff up whatever was blocking his nose. "What I want to say is, thanks-a-million, fellas. Thanks for always trying to help. You've all been great, you really have. You gave us all a shot of rhythm-and-blues none of us will ever forget and I've loved every single rockin' minute of it. You richly deserve whatever success comes your way and it will come, we all know it, we all of us feel it, but now our roads must part." He shook hands, clasping each of theirs in both of his. "Now bugger off, you magical sods, before I really make a bloody fool of myself."

All three Beatles nodded, each one of them seemingly too overcome to say anything more. And with heads down, they quietly filed out into the corridor and, in less time than it takes for a heart to beat, were gone from 'the Tower'.

GEORGE MARTIN was taking no chances. In many ways he'd already gone way out on a limb for The Beatles. People had laughed when he'd told them the name of his latest signing. "Beetles? Another one of your *Goon Show* larks, is it, George?" "Spike Milligan in disguise?" He'd just shrugged it all off. There was just something about The Beatles—something special. They had that indefinable something called 'star quality'. All it needed was a 'hit' single and the rest of Britain would know it, too. That's why he was taking no chances when it came to The Beatles' first record.

The session, the week before, had been a mite disappointing. The Beatles hadn't been at their best, not by a long chalk. And having listened repeatedly to their attempts at Mitch Murray's sure-fire hit 'How Do You Do It?' it was all too painfully clear he'd never get anything more out of John Lennon and the boys than a very bad Buddy Holly impersonation. He didn't want to risk killing the magic, quite yet. So he was going to let The Beatles record two songs they'd written themselves. The new drummer, Ringo Starr—a name that'd caused almost as much derision along the corridors of EMI as 'Beatles'—was another matter, entirely. Starr had sounded no better than Pete Best. So he'd called in a session drummer who could keep perfect time and who would draw and bind the three Beatle guitarists together and give them a rock solid base to work from. The Beatles weren't ready to be given their heads, quite yet. Not unless he wanted upper management to hand him his own head on a plate. Life was much too short, as it was.

RINGO STARR was hopping mad and it was all he could do not to go thump Mr George high-and-bloody-mighty Martin on the bloody nose. It'd been like an ambush out of a cowboy movie. The session drummer, Andy White, had been laying in wait inside Abbey Road Studio Two, already sat in the saddle of his pearly white drum set. So what else could he think, but that the bastards were doing a Pete Best on him? And that hurt. A lot. Little Ritchie Starkey might well be a left-handed drummer who played a right-handed kit, but no one had ever complained about his drumming before. No one.

What made it worse, the three other Beatles hadn't even been able to look him in the face since the session started. And the more he was asked to just hit a tambourine—"twice on every third beat, if you please"—or shake his maracas on the backbeat, while nice polite Mr White politely played the bloody drums, the more he was convinced he was about to get pushed out of the group before he'd even had a proper chance to prove himself. He was that mad, if the tambourine wasn't the only one he owned, he'd have punched his fist right through the bloody thing.

"Ringo?" George Martin's marbles-in-the-mouth voice echoed down from the control room.

"Er, yes, Mr Martin, sir?"

"We're going to try to record two versions of each song; the first version with Andy White and the second version with you. Okay?"

"Er, yes, Mr Martin, sir."

"So take over now on 'Love Me Do'. Then Andy will try 'PS I Love You'. Then we'll switch to you, again. And then if we have time, we'll do the same with 'Please Please Me'. Okay?"

"Er, yes. Thank you, Mr Martin, sir."

"And, Ringo, please, just call me, George."

"Er, thanks, there, George," he said, but in his mind, he was yelling. "Just let me drum me stuff, you sod. I'll call you anything you bloody well like, then. Even, Sir George, if that's your bloody fancy."

LOSING THE BEATLES felt like losing both arms and both legs; money-wise, that was. It was all so very obvious now that Brian Epstein's little tricks had had but one aim, all along—to rob him of his Friday night franchise at 'the Tower'. "Well, fook you, Mr Brian bloody Epstein. Takes more than a posh bloody Yid to crush Mrs Leach's little boy." Truth was, though, he'd really have to put on his thinking cap if he was to make up for lost revenue. He had to come up with a really big idea—and no messing.

So he did what he always did when he wanted to give himself time and space to think—he pushed away all the office paperwork on his desk and had Thelma bring him a cup of tea and a plate of biscuits and he had a read of the trade papers. He reached for the *New Musical Express*, turned a page, reached for a digestive biscuit, and nearly bit through his tongue. Little Richard was coming to England!

He started to choke, his mind racing. "Remember to swallow, you stupid sod. You'd be no use, to you, Joan, or anyone else, you falling down stone dead on the carpet. But 'Good Golly, Miss Molly!' Little-bloody-Richard! They didn't come any bigger than that!" He scoured the paper for more details, then got up and walked around his desk, trying not to let his growing excitement get the better of him. "Calm down, calm down, you silly sod. No need to give yourself a heart attack."

Once he'd calmed down, sufficiently, he put on his other hat, and The Leach Organisation put in a call to the Don Arden Agency, in London. "Hello. Yes. Good morning. This is The Leach Entertainments Organisation, in Liverpool. I just saw a little piece in the *New Musical Express* and had to call you immediately. Could you confirm the report that Mr Richard Penniman, known also as 'Little Richard', is shortly coming to

England? He is? How very wonderful. Are there, perchance, any available dates where he might be booked to play at the fabulous Tower Ballroom, here in Liverpool? There are? Yes. Please hold while I check my diary."

He held the phone at arm's length, tried to catch his breath, again, and stop his heart from completely bursting out of his chest. "Yes, that date will work. May I enquire as to the required fee? Three-hundred-and-fifty pounds? Yes, yes, of course, that's all very acceptable and within budget. After all, how can one put a price on genius? Yes, I'll confirm in writing."

He gave the office telephone number should they require any further information. Said 'thank you' several times and gently replaced the phone back down in its cradle. Then he punched the air with a yell of triumph as might have awoken the dead.

His office door flew open and Thelma Pickles poked her head around. "Did you want something, Mr Leach? Only, I heard you shout."

BRIAN EPSTEIN stared at the half-page advertisement in the *Liverpool Echo* and couldn't stop blinking. "Damn the man. Would he never go away? Sam Leach had pipped him to the post, yet again, and this time, with none other than, Little Richard. Even he knew they didn't come much bigger than that. He tapped a forefinger against his chin and re-scrutinised the ad. "Attack is always the best defence," he said aloud, as he leaned forward and touched the intercom button. "Beryl, put in a call to the Don Arden Agency, in London. Tell them I need to speak to Mr Don Arden, himself. Say it's important. Then buzz me when you have him on the line."

He sat as still as cat eyeing a mouse and stared off into the distance, seeing nothing, hearing nothing, but the murmur of his secretary's voice outside his office door. He had the telephone to his ear almost before she pressed the intercom. "Yes, thank you, Beryl. Mr Arden? Good morning, my name is Brian Epstein, owner and managing director of NEMS Entertainment Enterprises. It concerns a newspaper advertisement I saw this morning to do with an artist that you represent, Little Richard, and his proposed appearance at the Tower Ballroom, here, in Liverpool. I feel it only right and proper to inform you of the true financial circumstances of Mr Sam Leach, the would-be promoter. Not to put too fine a point on it, but he has no money in the world to speak of. I had unfortunate dealings only very recently with the said Mr Leach regarding lack of full payment of fees due. Yes, most regrettable. I simply thought you should know. Yes, you're welcome, goodbye." He put down the phone, shot his cuffs, straightened his tie, and waited for the wheels of commerce to turn.

He didn't have to wait long. Only the call, this time, was from Don Arden's secretary who informed him that her boss had spoken personally to Mr Sam Leach at the offices of The Tower Company and that the matter had been agreeably resolved. Mr Leach had given every assurance the agreed-to fee of £350 could and would be paid. He muttered some inanity about how very glad he was to hear that the issue had been satisfactorily dealt with. Thanked her for calling back. Then he leaned forward in his chair and started tapping his fingers, furiously, up and down on his desktop.

A quarter of an hour later, he buzzed through to Beryl Adams. "Beryl put in another call to the Don Arden Agency for me, will you, please. Tell them I'd like to speak to Don Arden, again. Thank you." He was busy making minute adjustments to the things on his desk, when the call came through.

"Thank you for taking the call Mr Arden. Look, I don't want to be a bother, but I've been thinking. As Little Richard's appearance will be such a signal event for Liverpool, I'd really hate for anything untoward to occur at the last moment. What would you say to NEMS Enterprises offering you a fee of £500 to book Little Richard?" There was a protracted silence at the end of the phone. "Mr Arden?" He listened to what the London agent had to say for a full minute or so. "Yes, I appreciate your position. No contract has been signed yet. And, yes, it's only right that you must offer Mr Leach the first right of refusal. Yes, of course, I'll await the outcome. Thank you for even considering my offer. Goodbye."

He got up from his desk, went over to the window, and looked out across the grim, grey Liverpool skyline. For a moment, there appeared the very faintest gleam of September sunshine. He shot his cuffs, touched his tie, and patted an errant lock of hair into place. "That's you damned and done-for, Sam Leach. Now just you try and eel your way out of that."

SAM LEACH felt confused, disappointed, and very angry. Don Arden, himself, had called The Tower Company to enquire whether The Leach Organisation would be prepared to match NEMS Enterprises' offer. And, of course, he was in no position to, especially as the fee also had to be paid in advance and in full. Within minutes of him putting the phone down, one of Don Arden's secretaries had called back to confirm that the contract to present Little Richard at 'the Tower' had passed directly to NEMS Enterprises. And as much as he hated to admit it, there was bugger all he could do about it. Brian Epstein had beaten him, yet again. He blinked and blinked again. Or had he?

He marched down the corridor to tell Bill Roberts, The Tower Company's chairman all about "that bastard Epstein" stealing away Little Richard from under his very nose. But the bloody man just shook his head and shrugged. Said there was really nothing he could do about it, as it was company policy never to get involved in contractual disputes between artists or promoters. He heard the words and knew what was really being said. The Tower Company could refuse any booking they damn well pleased. But everyone there knew The Leach Organisation had lost The Beatles and would no longer be able to fill 'the Tower' on the all-important Friday nights. So it was very much in their interests, to stay out of any dispute between him and Brian Epstein.

It was all simply business, of course, nothing personal.

"Nothing personal, my arse," Sam muttered as he walked back to his office. He knew, then and there, what he had to do—must do—but he wanted to go home and talk to Joan about it first. After all, wasn't that what it said in the marriage lines—'for better or for worse'.

The very next day, he handed in his notice as manager of 'the Tower' and officially gave up his option on the Friday night franchise. Then he put in calls to thank all the groups that'd ever played for him at the venue. Even releasing one group from a long-term contract they'd only just signed with him and the Tower Company, so as to free them up to play elsewhere.

The following week, he cleaned out his desk, left the building for the last time and, much to his surprise, was met by a line of stallholders who worked 'the Tower' car park. The owner of the hot dog stand, immaculate in smart suit and trademark bowler hat, was stood on an upturned beer crate. The little man waved for silence and raised his hat. "Thank you, folks. Hush now. We all know why we're here. It's to say a real big thank you to Mr Sam Leach for all the custom he's brought each and every one of us, over the past year. We've none of us, ever seen anything like it, God's honest. And we know there've been ups and downs, and such, but it's never ever been his fault. He's always been there for all of us. And so, Mr Leach, we all of us just want to wish you all the very best of luck with whatever comes next."

Sam nodded and smiled at the crowd, not quite sure what else to do. Then the midget gave another little wave of his hand, the line parted, and one of the better-looking women stallholders came forward and presented him with a wooden box containing three bottles of champagne—and not cheap stuff, either. Then everyone who was there clapped and the little man stood on tiptoe and—waving his hat—led all the stallholders in a round of cheers. "Three big cheers for Mr Leach! Hip-hip...hooray! Hip-hip...hooray! Hip-hip...hooray!"

Sam nodded, touched beyond measure, and bit down hard on his lip. "Thanks, Titch," he said, quietly.

The midget looked up at him. "We all mean it, Mr Leach." He adjusted his hat, held out a tiny hand. "Here, give us a hand down off this thing, will you?" The little man walked along beside him—serious, now. "You know, me and a lot of the other stallholders are thinking of packing this patch in. 'The Tower' won't be the same with you gone. You made money for all of us, you did. Never seen such crowds. And God bless you for it. But it'll all go down hill, now that you're leaving, you just watch."

Sam bit down hard again. "Good knowing you, too, Titch. Your burgers and hotdogs were top-rated by all the groups. You go safe, now, and be sure to watch out for those bloody Teds."

"Ta, Mr Leach. Please give my regards to Mrs Leach." The midget touched a finger to the brim of his hat. "And do remember there's always a hot dog or hamburger waiting for you at my stall, wherever I set up around the 'Pool. All the toppings you ever want, too. As much as you like, as often as you like."

Sam nodded his 'thanks', too overcome to say anything more, and walked away, his thoughts trying to get into step with his now uncertain future. There had to be bigger, more important things in life than the New Brighton bloody Tower. Had to be.

He thought of Joan, at home, happy and very pregnant, and he smiled. Said aloud: "That's what's most important...your wife...your family. Nothing else even comes close."

He stopped and turned for one last look. Funny. 'The Tower' already seemed a lot smaller than he remembered it being. He sniffed again, wiped his nose on the back of his hand, brushed a thumb under both eyes, turned his back on 'the Tower' and slowly made his way home.

CHAPTER THIRTY-ONE

The Girl Can't Help It

Spike stepped forward, threw out his left arm, thrust his right arm skywards, and stood as if gazing out on some far distant horizon; the very image of the statue towering over the entrance to Lewis's department store.

"You big dafty," said Sandra, pulling on his sleeve.

"Just call me 'Nobby Lewis'," Spike said, laughing. He peered up at the statue. How in hell he'd once had the nerve to climb from out a nearby window, just to stick one of Sam Leach's 'Operation Big Beat' posters on the bloody thing, he'd never know. He shook his head. "Good old Sam. Where would we all be without him? He's far more worthy of the name 'Liverpool Resurgent' than Jacob Epstein's naff bloody statue."

"What was that Spike?"

"Oh, just me thinking about Sam Leach. Hoping everything goes well for him, now he's left 'the Tower'. Fancy a quick coffee at the Kardomah, San? Or shall we just go straight to NEMS?"

"Let's just go get 'Love Me Do' and catch a bus to your mam's...have tea there." She looked up at him, with a coy, mischievous smile. He kissed her gently on the lips. Then the two of them walked hand-in-hand down Ranelagh Street and headed for Whitechapel. Totally lost in each other, they arrived home, in Huyton, with The Beatles' new record in a NEMS paper-bag, without being at all conscious of how it or they'd got there.

Sandra made tea. Spike switched on the radiogram in the living room, so the big tube amplifier inside had time to warm up. He held The Beatles' first real record with reverence "Well done, lads," he whispered as he gazed at the bright red Parlophone label. On the record sleeve it said: THIS RECORD MUST BE PLAYED AT 45 R.P.M. He shook his head. They must think we're bloody daft. What else do they think we're going to do with it? Eat our bloody beans-on-toast off of it?

He turned the disc over. 'P.S. I Love You'. Saw that John and Paul had composed both sides. He pulled the shiny black disc from its paper sleeve, put it on the record player's centre spindle and gentled it down onto the turntable. Leaving the balance arm up and to one side, he pushed the switch to automatic, watched as the tone arm rose and moved across to the edge of the disc. He waited until he heard the crack and hiss of the stylus as it kissed the plastic and was drawn into the groove. Then he looked back at Sandra and smiled.

John Lennon's harmonica wailed out of the radiogram's speaker like a clarion call to another world. Then John and Paul were singing in sweet harmony. The eternal plea: "Love me do." The eternal reason: "I love you." The eternal promise: "I'll always be true." They listened to the song over and over and over again, then turned the disc over and played the 'B' side. Dancing ever more closely, round and around, in front of the electric fire. Transported with delight. The Beatles—their very own Beatles—had made a record. And it was totally fab.

Sandra half-sang half-whispered: "Love, love me...I love, love you...I do, I do, I do." And as the song ended she pressed her head into Spike's shoulder and said, very softly, "Please, please, love me do, Spike. You know I love you and I'll always be true, don't you?" She looked up into Spike's face. The gaunt look he'd had when he'd come back from Hamburg was gone. It was her Spike—her Raymond—just as he'd been the very first time she'd ever set eyes on him, the moment she'd fallen in love with him. "Please, please, tell me you love me in the same way you always told me in your letters."

"What? 'P.S. I Love You'?" Spike said, his voice a whisper. "You know P.S. stands for 'Pretty Sandra', don't you?" She shook her head; thrilled at the secret code now revealed. "P.S. My pretty little Sandra...my little taste of honey...I...love...you."

They kissed, their lips locked together, as they oh so slowly descended onto the sofa. They pushed their bodies into each other and with each thrust kissed harder and longer. Spike moved a hand up towards Sandra's left breast and gently caressed it, the palm of his hand moving round and round in a never-ending circle. Then he slid his hand to her other breast.

He swallowed hard. Sandra began to move under him. She whispered, "Oh, Raymond." He swallowed again. "San," he croaked. His hand moving oh so slowly down the length of her body and along her thighs until it touched the hem of her skirt. He moved his weight, pressing, pushing with his knee, and Sandra, moving beneath him, opened her legs. Then slowly, so very slowly, his hand began to move up, beneath her skirt, sliding over her stockings, stroking and caressing between her legs, in ever-decreasing circles, until his fingertips came to the end of her stocking tops and to the soft secret flesh of her inner thighs.

Sandra moved, slowly, her breathing deep and fast, and she pushed against his hand as his fingers ran along the ruched elastic of her knickers. A finger slid slowly underneath the edge. Touched. Moved the tiny curls of pubic hair. Spike swallowed hard. Sandra's breath caught in her throat.

He caressed, rubbed, probed, and then slowly slid a finger inside her. Sandra moaned and said his name. He slid a second finger inside her and tried to imagine and understand what it was he was feeling. Very gently, he withdrew his hand and slid it, fingers sticky wet, across the soft swell of her belly. Then slowly, very slowly, he began to pull her knickers down. Sandra jerked—went suddenly rigid. "No, don't. No. Stop! No! Raymond. No!" She twisted away, almost violently. "Oh, Spike, no. Stop! Please."

"What? What?" Spike's voice was thick with emotion, his erection a constant, throbbing ache. "What? What?" He rolled off the sofa and over onto the floor. He leaned back on his knees, looked at Sandra, slowly ran a hand back across his face and then through his hair.

Sandra stared at him, a look of utter desperation on her face.

"Spike, I can't. I want to, but I can't. Not now. Not yet. It's...it's...I'm sorry...sorry." Tears began to trickle down her cheeks.

"What's up, San? What?"

"It's...it's just that I've...I've been afraid...for so very long."

"What? What do you mean afraid? Afraid of me?"

"No, no, no...not you, Spike, not you. It's...it's...it's..." Sandra buried her face in her hands and began to sob, uncontrollably.

Spike just stared at her. He felt deflated, irritable, puzzled. Then he simply felt confused and oddly concerned and not a little ashamed. He pushed himself upright, crouched down beside her, and gently stroked her arms, her shoulders. And then he gently pulled her to him. "There. There." And with her head nestled on his chest, he stroked her hair. "There, there, San. Whatever it is, it'll be okay. It will. It will."

She shook her head. "No, no it won't. Not ever. It's...it's me dad."

Spike froze. "Your dad? What do you mean?"

Her voice sounded small and weak, like a tiny kitten mewing. "He tried to...has...you know...tried to fiddle...with me." She began to sob—softly—gasping for air in short breaths. "He's...he's done it for years. Saying it was because he loved me. That I was his favourite li...lit...little girl." She sat, lost in time, tears and mascara running down her cheeks.

Spike couldn't breathe. He was shocked beyond belief. His head was spinning. He was spinning. "Bloody hell, San. I'm...I'm so sorry. I had no..."

"It's...it's why my sister, Maureen, left home. It's why I...I..."

"Does your mam, know any of this?"

"Yeah...no. I don't know. I think she must...only she...she..."

"I'll fookin' kill him." Spike's voice was thick with anger. "I'll murder the bastard." He suddenly thought of his own father. He'd never once felt afraid. Even when he'd been dead naughty and his dad had shouted at him—he'd always known he was loved. Even when his dad had taught him to box or they'd played soccer—he'd always felt safe. Now his dad was gone forever and he felt like crying, too. Only, Sandra was already doing enough crying for both of them. He gently stroked her hair. "There, there, San. It'll be all right. Honest. I'm here now, don't you worry. No one's going to harm you...ever again."

Sandra nodded, took a deep, deep breath, and reached for her purse. As she turned, to dab away her tears, Spike was suddenly aware of The Beatles still singing 'Love Me Do' on the radiogram and the tea gone stone cold in the cups. "I'll...er...I'll get us some more tea."

He needed some time to think and he knew Sandra did, too.

Sandra gave him a tiny smile and disappeared up into the bathroom. And by the time Spike came into the living room with some freshly brewed tea, she was sitting, just staring at the electric fire. He handed her a hot cup of tea. She nodded without even looking at him "I told me dad I'd kill him if he ever tried to touch me again. I'd stick a knitting needle in his ear when he was asleep and kill him dead." She sipped her tea. "I told him I'd run and tell all the neighbours and all his friends down the docks what he'd done. Shame him to the world. He's left me alone ever since."

Spike just stared at her. Still stunned. Still unable to believe what he'd heard. "I'm so sorry, San. Really I am. I understand now, I do. But you're safe now...safe...I promise."

He saw her that first night at 'the Tower'. Fearless. Facing down the gang of Teds who'd attacked the midget all by herself. Bloody hell, what a living hell she'd had to put up with, at home, yet she'd never once talked about it. Never once let on. No wonder she was always dreaming about escaping off to London or travelling on a train to some far away place.

"I'll try, next time, I will." She looked at him, her eyes red-rimmed from crying. "I want to. I want to make love to you. I really do."

Spike shook his head. "It's not important, San. You are."

"It is though, Spike. It's because I love you, that I want to."

He was silent for a good minute or two. "I was going to tell you, mum's going to be away in Llandudno, next weekend, on some training course for the Royal Liver Company. You could stay the night."

She blinked, bit her lip, and nodded. "I'll just have to tell me mum I'm staying with Thelma for the weekend, then, won't I?"

SPIKE was in heaven. Or as close to it as he was ever likely to get, given where he stood in the pecking order of Liverpool's ever-growing hosts of beat musicians.

Out on stage was a lone black grand piano. Lined up behind it was Sounds Incorporated: two sax players, a guitarist, a bass player, drummer, and keyboard player with a Vox Continental electronic organ. All the musicians white guys, yet they looked so damn cool, so hip, in shiny Italian suits and real American 'shades'. Their bodies, heads, hands, feet in ever-fluid locomotion, readying the audience for what was to come. Pumping out a single, pulsing, bass-heavy chord, over and over again, that made everything electric.

The atmosphere fully charged, crackled for release.

Bob Wooler's voice purred into the microphone. His dulcet tones like shiny-black fur on a cat. A sudden wave of clapping and cheering, all but eclipsed his words: "Ladies and Gentlemen, NEMS Enterprises presents 'A Bob Wooler Production'." A roar erupted, enough to blow the roof off. "It's the King of Rock 'n' Roll! It's...Little Richard...at the Tower!"

Then there he was. Little Richard.

Twisting. Twirling. Leaping. Strutting. Careening from one side of the stage to the other. And not one word yet, sung or screamed. There was only him—Little Richard. Black. Beautiful. Hair 'conked', moustache pencil-thin, smile utterly radiant; a rocking body not of this world; a whirling mass of energy— whooping, wheeling, waving, and bouncing nonstop. His shark-skin suit, shiny, sharp, attracting all eyes, both male and female.

And just when it seemed that nothing could cut through the riot and pandemonium in the auditorium, Richard skidded to a stop, twirled, and screamed: "Do you wanna hear it?"

The drummer cracked the snare. Richard screamed: "Yeah!" Everyone in the place screamed: "Yeah!"

Richard twirled, dived; screamed again: "Do you gotta hear it?" Screamed again: "Yeah?" Everyone screamed back: "Yeah!"

Richard shouted: "Do I gotta give it to you?" The crowd shouted: "Yeeeah!"

Then Richard let lose with a scream to end all screams—a long, drawn-out sound that slid up the scale, higher and higher and higher, until it broke into: "Lordy, Lord-dee, Lord-deee, Lord-deeee...*Yeeeeaaaah!*"

Before the sound had time to echo off the walls, Little Richard ran full-pelt across the stage—sliding, sliding, sliding—until, magically, he came to a stop right beside the grand piano.

He spun around, hit every note on the keyboard with a thundering hand and just stopped dead, a lone finger sounding, ringing out the lowest bass note. Then he threw back his glistening head and gave forth with a wild fevered cry that hit you like a drumstick in the eye. *"Aaaah-wop...bop-aah-wop!"*

Saxes, guitars, electronic organ, and drums slammed down the first beat of the bar. A wall of rocking, rolling, pulsating sound crashed over him like a tidal wave heralding the end of the old world and the coming of the new.

"Aaaah...Tutti-Frutti..." The magical incantation repeated over and over and over again until the last incandescent full-throated call for everyone to rock 'n' roll.

"Aaaah-wop...bop-aah-wop...bop-aah...Whoooooo!"

Little Richard stood at the keyboard his hands pounding up and down like pneumatic drills. Tireless. Relentless. Unstoppable. Hammering on and on and on. Smashing the piano keys with fists, elbows, his backside and his feet. Screaming, calling, whooping, squealing, singing songs Spike had only ever heard coming out of jukeboxes and record players. Singing with such force, such passion, such belief, it turned rock 'n' roll into a living breathing entity you'd willingly give your life to for as long as you lived.

Richard sang all his hits. He rocked it up. He ripped it up. He shook it up. He balled it up. He sang so long and so loud it made Spike's ears ring and his head spin. And the only prayer Spike could pray was: "Dear God, please never ever let Little Richard finish. And if I gotta die, take me right now, right out of this towering cradle of rock."

Boom-boom-boom-boom...Aaaah-lop-bam-boom!"

PAUL McCARTNEY was in seventh heaven because, after Elvis, Little Richard was his 'number one man' and he the 'number one fan' and every time Richard squealed, whooped or screamed, he did, too. And for one magical moment, he was free to be a rocking schoolboy, again, his heart filled to bursting with happiness and joy. Unable to contain himself, wanting to share the moment, he glanced over at John, a huge grin on his face.

JOHN LENNON stood, arms crossed, eyes narrowed, a huge grin on his face, too, oblivious to all but Little Richard. Nodding in time to the beat. Not missing a thing. Marvelling at the black singer's effortless display of command. Full of admiration at how Richard could hold the entire audience with a look, a nod, a grin, or a sneer. Then get everyone going again with a single shake of his head or a simple falsetto 'Whooooooo!'

BRIAN EPSTEIN nodded his head, almost in time with the beat. He couldn't help but smile and feel more than a little pleased with himself. His 'boys' were playing the same stage as the great Little Richard and had more than held their own. It was nothing less than the passing of the torch, from one legend to the next, just as he'd always envisioned. Smiling, he turned, and stopped short, and stood staring at a good-looking young man in an ill-fitting stage suit. It was the same boy he'd seen coming out of Rex Makin's office; the one he'd seen that night, in Hamburg; the one he'd been meaning to call. "Excuse me, but I think we've met somewhere, before, haven't we?"

The young man spun round, still laughing at having just discovered he and the bass player for The Dakotas had the same name. "Er, yeah, hello. It's Mr Epstein, isn't it? Fab show. He's just fantastic, isn't he?"

He smiled and leaned forward so as to be heard. "Yes, he's quite the showman. Only I've been meaning to call you ever since I saw you at Rex Makin's office. I didn't realise you played in a group? Er, Mr...who...?"

"Er, Spike Jones, Mr Epstein. And, no, I don't play in a group full-time. I'm just standing in for The Coasters' bass player, as he's out sick, tonight, with bronchitis."

"So you're backing Billy Kramer, tonight? I see." He liked the look of young Billy Kramer, but he hadn't been too impressed with The Coasters, which would partly explain why he hadn't also noticed the young man before. He took out slim, leather card-case and handed the young man one of his business cards. "Do please give me a call."

The young man took the card and nodded, but before he could say anything, Bob Wooler appeared as if from out of nowhere. "Excuse me, Brian. Have you got a moment?"

"Certainly, Bob." He turned back to the boy; touched his arm. "Must dash, but do call me."

JOHN LENNON raised his glass in acknowledgement and pitched his voice so it could be heard above the noise of the after-hours drinking crowd at the Blue Angel.

" 'Eppy'...that was truly epic. There's nothing little, at all, about Little Richard, there were moments I thought he'd bring the whole bloody Tower crashing down around our ears."

Paul piped in then. "Yeah, Brian, that was great...a dream come true. We all of us were like kids, seeing Richard, on stage. Really couldn't believe it, like, even while it was happening."

George mashed the remains of his cigarette into an already full ashtray. "Everyone was scrambling to have a photo taken with him afterwards...me, included...and he doesn't even play the guitar."

"Having Little Richard play 'the Tower' was a brilliant idea of yours, 'Eppy'. That's what I call some real bloody managing. Us being headliners on the same bill as him is really starting to get us up there...to the toppermost of the poppermost."

Brian Epstein looked at John from over the rim of his gin and tonic and smiled enigmatically. He put his drink down on the table. "You'll be pleased to hear, then, John, that Little Richard was so thrilled by his tumultuous welcome from the Liverpool fans, he immediately agreed to return for a second engagement. And if I can manage it, next time, somewhere in the city centre. Hopefully, at the Empire."

"You're not serious? He's coming back? For a second time?"

"Yes, Paul, I am. And he is. And, with luck, in a couple of weeks."

"That's the cherry on top of the cake, that is, Brian."

He nodded his head, reached for his glass. "Two cherries on the cake, don't you mean, Paul?"

"Blimey, 'Eppy', a double slice of Little Richard. That's really having your cake and eating it, too."

"You should always try for two bites of the cherry, if you

can, John. You can never have too much of a good thing, you know."

John Lennon all but snorted up his rum and coke trying to think up a suitable retort to that.

BRIAN EPSTEIN dropped John Lennon back at the flat on Faulkner Street and drove away feeling rather pleased with the way things had gone. Most pleasing of all, 'the boys' had applauded him on how well he was managing things. It was true, he was doing rather well, but it was all very nice they'd acknowledged it. In turn, he was extremely proud of them. The audience's ear-splitting response to 'Love Me Do' had rivalled that for any of Little Richard's songs, even 'Tutti-Frutti'. There'd also been warm applause for Ringo Starr. Which hopefully meant the whole Pete Best affair could finally be put to rest. He'd been pulling strings like mad all week to have Pete join Lee Curtis and The All-Stars, get them on the bill and on the road to success. Aided and abetted, yet again, by his good and dear friend, Joe Flannery.

He drove back into the city centre with every intention of going on to Feather's Club, but as he continued along Mount Pleasant, up towards Lime Street, he decided that perhaps he'd already had quite enough excitement for one night. His celebratory drink at the Blue Angel, with The Beatles after the show, had been a perfect ending to an altogether perfect day. Why chance meeting someone at Feather's who—intentionally or not—might just go and spoil it all? He took the turn up towards Edge Lane and began the long, fast sweep round to Queens Drive, and home.

He began to hum 'Baby Face'. Odd, but there was a time, the only thing he would've deigned to hum would've been some favourite light classical piece. He smiled. There'd been so many changes since he'd first met The Beatles. He realised just how much comfort he took in the new contract he and the boys had signed only ten days earlier, when they'd all instantly agreed to him raising his commission to twenty-five per cent. Their trust in him had done wonders for his confidence.

"Just you keep doing, what you're doing, 'Eppy', and we'll all be bloody rich," John had said, as the three other Beatles scrawled their signatures over the sixpenny-postage stamps of the Queen. This time he'd made sure to sign the contract himself. They were all bound together for the next five years, at least. And forever afterwards, too, if all that he had planned for them came into being.

He truly felt like a man of destiny. The Beatles were going to be bigger than Little Richard—bigger even than Elvis Presley. That was why he now had to be so much more discreet about everything. Why he always made a point to have a 'girlfriend' or even his secretary accompany him to Beatles' dates—all to give the right impression. It was why he'd given up his flat to John and Cynthia. And if ever he needed something or someone special, then he'd just have to look further afield. Go to Spain again or to London, Paris, Amsterdam, even Hamburg. Yes, Hamburg. He'd go out to Hamburg with 'the boys' when they fulfilled their next booking there. There were always so many delicious ways to enjoy oneself in St. Pauli.

He tapped his fingers up and down on the steering wheel. Narrowed his eyes. He'd never allow anyone to take advantage of The Beatles, not ever. They were too big an act to be paid off in bags of small coins, as some petty promoters had tried to do. There'd be no short-changing 'his boys', either. No more Sam Leach. He shook his head. To think, he'd once offered Leach a third ownership of NEMS and the stupid, stupid man had turned him down flat. He'd been angry about it at the time, but was only too thankful now for the way it'd turned out. Even so, it'd been a genuine offer on his part, one made in good faith, but there was just no helping some people, sometimes.

He held his hands lightly on the steering wheel, peered out into the night not seeing houses or streets only the bright future ahead. A fast-approaching distant light caught his eye and he pressed his foot down hard on the accelerator and rushed to meet it, delighting in the smooth power of the motorcar's engine. The point of light up ahead was like a bright star in the darkness, a promise of things yet to come, and it grew and grew and grew until it split into two and became a furniture removals van. His shiny Zephyr and the shadowy pantechnicon passed, uneventfully, like two ships in the night. He laughed. Flashed the car's main beams in sheer devilment. Stars, ever-twinkling points of light, were made to hold back the dark. And wasn't that the very thing he was doing now, giving birth to stars?

He laughed again and thought of Billy Kramer, a nice looking boy with an interesting voice and bags of sex appeal. Yes, very definite possibilities there. Less so, Kramer's backing group, The Coasters. The Dakotas were a much more impressive group, even if their singer, Peter something or other, was rather weak. With a little rearranging, here and there, he might just have another star in the making. He was already talking with Gerry Marsden, but it wouldn't hurt to have another star waiting in the wings. After which, there was that other young man, from Hamburg, the one he owed so much to. How very nice that he'd suddenly appeared out of the blue—and a musician, no less. Yes, it was all starting to come together nicely. He began humming again—Mozart's 'A Little Night Music' this time—and he turned right onto Queens Drive and was soon safely home.

SPIKE had been given two tickets for the eight o'clock show as a surprise birthday gift, and he and Sandra were stunned to find they were sitting in the best seats in the orchestra stalls. "That Mr Epstein really came up trumps. He must really like you a lot," said Sandra. "Yeah," said Spike. "He reckons I did someone some good when I was out in Hamburg, but I told him he was mistaken. Fab seats though, aren't they?" Sandra nodded and turned round to see if she could see Jimmy and Thelma seated way up in the balcony. Their friends had queued in line and paid for their tickets and she felt strangely odd at not being up there with them. Then she just felt glad they were all there, anyway. The NEMS big-name 'Pop Package Show' was a complete sell out. And given who was on the bill, the only thing that really mattered was that you were there at all.

It'd been a little over two weeks since Little Richard's knockout show at 'the Tower' and now here he was, back in Liverpool, topping the bill at the Empire Theatre. Sandra looked through the program, knowing full well Spike already knew it by heart. She glanced at him and the look on his face said it all. It didn't matter that he wasn't filling-in for any of the bass players in the groups. This time round he was going to get to see Little Richard, front and centre. And nothing could be better than that, unless, of course, it was also seeing The Beatles play at one of the city's most prestigious venues.

Sandra slipped her arm through Spike's and cuddled up. She'd never felt so happy. She sighed and as if in response the houselights dimmed and a slow, pulsing, bass-heavy chord began to sound, over and over again. The audience set up such a roar that the very tumult alone seemed to cause the heavy red velvet and gold-tasselled curtain to ascend to the heavens. And, soon, like everyone else in the house, Sandra was on her feet screaming and shouting with joy. Her happiness, beyond measure. And she was lost and found and born again in the music and before she knew it, another once-in-a-Merseyside lifetime, never-to-be-missed event had come to an end, seemingly, before it'd ever even begun.

The crowd of deliriously happy punters spilled out of the Empire Theatre, into the Liverpool night. Sandra held onto Spike very tightly so as not to get separated and arm-in-arm they walked down Lime Street in the direction of the railway station. "That was totally fab," sighed Sandra. "One of the best shows...ever. Our very own Beatles on the same stage as Little Richard. And some of those other acts weren't too bad, neither."

Spike ran his hand through his hair. "That Jet Harris used to be The Shadows' bass player, San, but he sounded more like a second-rate Duane Eddy to my ears. Didn't reckon him half as much as I thought I would. Our Paul can play rings around him."

She looked up at her Spike, suddenly feeling fiercely proud of him. "You could play rings around him, if you wanted to."

Spike grinned at Sandra's obvious bit of flattery, but he loved her for saying it, because it was true, his musicianship had improved in leaps and bounds. He couldn't imagine playing anything but the bass now and was having the time of his life filling in for different Merseyside groups and being widely re-

garded as the 'one' to call if you were stuck for a bass player. A
number of beat-groups had even asked him to join them full-
time, but he'd turned them down. He'd had enough of being
stuck in a band, at least for the time being. He'd experienced
first hand the sort of animosities and rivalries that could spring
up from out of nowhere. On the very brink of success, Fras,
Cliff, and Dave had fallen out with Roy Young, then with one
another, and then with him. Maybe one day he'd pick up again
with his old band-mates, but for now he was still learning. Stealing ideas like mad from every bass player he came across. He
hoped one day he'd be able to play as good as Johnny Gustafson
of The Big Three, but there was only ever one 'number one man'
in his eyes. The one who'd first inspired him, the man who really knew how to make the bass sing and in a whole new different
way. If he dreamed of Sandra every single night, then every single day he daydreamed of playing bass guitar like Paul
McCartney.

THE TWO LOVEBIRDS pulled their collars up against the wind
and made their way down Renshaw Street, all the time hoping
for a bus, even if only to save them a few minutes walking, but
they'd passed the Adelphi Hotel and Lewis's before one appeared. Spike shook his head. There was never a bloody bus
when you needed one. He glanced over at the offices of *Mersey
Beat* across the street and wondered if the photo of him—with
all the other musicians gathered around Little Richard, everyone
grinning like mad—was ready to be picked up. Then Sandra gave
his arm a short sharp tug. There were seven or eight of them.
Teds. Spread across the pavement some thirty yards ahead.

The Odd Spot club, on Bold Street, was the nearest refuge,
but as the gang was standing on the corner of Slater Street,
blocking the way, that was out. Best bet was to cross the street
and continue on down towards Berry Street and make for the
Blue Angel, on Seel Street.

"Just keep your head down, San. Don't look them in the face,
no matter what they say." They crossed over and Spike moved
so as to position himself between Sandra and the gang of Teds.

"Er, got a light, there, la'? Or a burn, maybe?"

Spike and Sandra kept on walking—picked up their pace.

"Hey, I'm talking to you. Are you hard of hearing or something? Or is that long fookin' hair of yours making you deaf?"

They pushed on. Every sound magnified, ears on full alert, Spike heard the scrape and squeak of boots and shoes and the swelling tide of jeering that told him the gang were following and closing in fast.

"Hey, you. Are you a fookin' fella or what? Or are you two a pair of fookin' judies?"

A brick thudded to the pavement close to Sandra's feet, as the shouts behind them got louder and even more raucous.

"Hey, are you two a couple o'fookin' Lime Street brasses? 'Cos if you are, like, we really fancy the small one."

"Seel Street's not far, San, let's run for it. Ready? Go."

They set off, like hares, not even daring to look back. Then Spike started laughing. Adrenaline coursing through him, like fire. "I'm dead glad you're wearing them flat shoes of yours, San. We'd have been right buggered if you'd had your high heels on."

Sandra started giggling, then. "Don't Spike, don't. I...I can hardly run, as it is. But...but you could always beat them off with...with that new guitar strap I got you for your birthday."

They made the corner of Seel Street and dashed across the road to the safety of the Blue Angel. Spike pushed Sandra inside and turned to see the Teds all milling around the lamppost on the corner, angrily shaking their fists and gesticulating wildly with wave after wave of obscene V-signs.

"I'm fookin' gonna have you, pal," one of the Teds shouted as another brick crashed to the ground near Spike's feet.

"Fook off, you pathetic buggers," Spike yelled. "Just fook off."

"You okay, young Spike? Only you're lowering the tone of the place, something awful." It was John Lennon, standing behind him, in the club's doorway, glass in one hand, cigarette in the other. "Leave 'em be, you daft sod. That little gold Star-Club pin doesn't work in Liddypool. None of them stupid gits speak bloody German anyway. Zo, kommen zie, inside, mein Herr, und get ein stiff drink down your neck und quick."

CHAPTER THIRTY-TWO

Chains Of Love

John Lennon eyed his fellow Beatles. "I'm bloody knackered with all this bloody travelling. But 'Eppy' says we need to be out on the road, pushing the disc up the charts, winning over new fans. Gig-by-gig. Club-by-club. Ballroom-by-bloody-ballroom. Here, there, and everywhere. All of which means we've got to keep on bloody doing it, be it Manchester, London, or bloody Bristol. We've got to get as much exposure on the radio and the telly as is inhumanly possible. But I'd go on *Coronation Street* or *Gardener's Question Time*, I would, if it helped get our record heard by more bloody people."

Paul nodded. "It's pretty amazing, our 'Eppy' buying up thousands of copies of 'Love Me Do' to make sure it got into the record charts."

"That's what you call bloody managing, Pauly, and why ever not? It's how them Tin Pan Alley bastards do things in London."

George lit another cigarette. "The drag is, despite our record being 'number one' on *Mersey Beat*'s Top Twenty pop charts since the day of its release, it's still struggling to get into the Top Forty everywhere else. And now Hamburg's looming again."

"Aye, two weeks in horrible Hamburg and all the '*Mach shau! Mach*-bloody-*shau!*' we can bloody stomach. Makes me bloody wonder if we'll ever get free of the bloody place."

"We did give our bloody word, though, didn't we?" offered Paul.

"And 'Eppy's got us more money this time, too. Six hundred Deutsche Marks, per Beatle, per week. So we have to go play."

"Yeah. You're right, George. In for a pfennig, in for six hundred soddin' Deutsche Marks! *Sieg Heil! Sieg Heil! Mach Schau!*"

Ringo Starr chimed in. "There is a bright side, fellas. Being in Hamburg will give me time to get your lengthy repertoire under me skins. I've always done 'Matchbox', like, but as you want me to do 'Boys' and all them other songs, I'll have time to learn all the new words. On top of which, I did hear Little Richard's heading the bill, this time, too, so we'll be able to watch him till the cows come home, we will."

"Yeah, there is that. Yeah, good one, Ring."

"Yeah, rip up 'The Ring Cycle' and tell Miss Molly the news."

JOHN LENNON had the wit to smile as he said it, but he knew he was skating on thin ice. "But as we keep on telling you, George, we don't want to do it. We don't like it. It isn't us."

George Martin lowered his chin, raised an eyebrow, and stared at the stubborn Beatle. "When you boys can give me a song as well written as this one by Mitch Murray, then we'll record it. Otherwise, 'How Do You Do It?' is going to be your next record." He folded his arms. "Look, I know we couldn't agree on you doing it, before, but with 'Love Me Do' still struggling to make the Top Thirty, let alone the Top Ten, I'm looking for something that'll really break through next time."

"We hear you, George, honest we do," said Paul McCartney, silkily. "But if you'd let us, like, we'd like to try a number you said wasn't good enough last time." Paul looked across at John. "But, er, what we've done, while we were away in Hamburg, like, is speed it up just a tiny bit."

George Martin narrowed his eyes. "What? 'Please Please Me'?"

"Yeah, George," said George Harrison, grinning a toothy grin. "We'd like to please you. If you're open to being pleased that is."

John jumped in to the fray. "I've added a harmonica part I think works quite nicely. I think you'll quite like it, too, George."

George Martin looked at The Beatles as he would a pack of cocker spaniels. He shook his head; tried to keep a straight face. "Okay, gentlemen, we'll try a run through, but it better be good."

"It'll be better than good, it'll be great, George," offered George Harrison. "It'd have to be, with you producing it."

"I think that's enough flattery for one day, Mr Harrison. May I suggest you pick up your guitar and convince me that way?"

George Martin perched himself on a high stool, every inch

the music teacher waiting to be impressed. John and George picked up their Gibson acoustic guitars. All three Beatles gathered round. George and John played the opening notes and chords. Then John and Paul lit straight into the first verse. John singing melody; Paul harmonising on a repeated note, high above it. The two of them sounding like the Everly Brothers, only much more raw and urgent. On into the bridge, an ardent call to 'come on' from John, swiftly echoed by Paul and George, their twin harmonising gritty and powerful. Through to the chorus when all three Beatles exploded into a three-part harmony. A heartfelt plea to 'please, please me'. And as he heard their combined voices break into a repeated cry of 'Woaaah...Yeah' the hairs stood up on the back of his neck. There it was—the hook, fully barbed and rounded and ready to stick in the mind.

George Martin liked what he heard. He liked it a lot. The song *was* much stronger. It had great pace, nice guitar lines. His only complaint, at just over a minute in length, it was far too short. He asked George to play the song again and for John to show where he'd add the harmonica part. He listened to it and liked it even more. "You know, it's a vast improvement over what you played me before. I think if we double John's harmonica with George's intro, which we can do as an overdub afterwards. Repeat the first chorus at the end. Have Ringo really drive it along. I think we may have something." He nodded, smiled, got off his stool and went back up into the control room. He pressed the talkback button. "Let's practice it once or twice, get the levels right. Then we can try lay one down. Okay?"

He stared down at The Beatles, as they readied themselves to play for him again. He turned to Ron Richards, his assistant producer. "They're a bloody extraordinary bunch. I gave them a problem and they went away and fixed it and came back with something a hundred times better. I don't know where they're going to end up, but it's going to be fascinating being along for the ride." He pressed the talkback button again. "Okay. Thank you. Let's try 'Please Please Me'. When you're ready. Take One."

He listened to The Beatles come together in the studio. It was almost eerie the way they suddenly became more than the sum of the parts they each played.

He studied Ringo Starr. Head rocking from side to side, a big grin lighting up his face, completely at one with the group. He listened intently to the drum pattern and nodded, satisfied. There was something very interesting happening there, almost as if Ringo had a perfect feel for the right drum sound for the song. Perhaps that was it, a drummer who was there to serve the song, rather than simply show off his skills. Very much like the role George Harrison seemed to play in the group, always searching for just the right little touches to lift a song.

George Martin smiled. Wasn't that exactly the role he'd chosen for himself at Abbey Road? To help all the stars he came into contact with interpret a song or piece of music—or comedy sketch for that matter—in the best way possible. All the while keeping himself very firmly in the background, so that the stars could shine all the brighter. That was when Ron Richards unwittingly broke into his train of thought to ask whether he was satisfied with 'Take One'.

"Yes, yes, thank you. It was very good," he said, almost absent-mindedly. Then he thought. "No, it wasn't just good...it was wonderful...super...really, really great." The first take of 'Please Please Me' had been astoundingly bright, joyful...brilliantly alive. He pressed the talkback microphone button, paused to catch his breath. "Gentlemen," he said, "I think you've just made your first 'number one' hit."

HARRY LIGHTFOOT stared at the brightly coloured posters in the travel agent's window. The people in them looked like they'd never done a decent day's work in their lives. But nice work, if you could get it, like. He had to admit he did fancy the idea of a bit of blue sky and a bit of sun, now that Liverpool and the rest of Britain were readying for another awful winter. It was already blowing that cold, it was even-money there'd be snow soon and lots of it. That alone made it an opportune time to take the little holiday he had planned. But it was more the premonition he had about things becoming excessively hot for a lot of people in the city, that gave the very idea of an extended Christmas and New Year holiday abroad its increasing appeal.

He glanced at the Butlin's holiday camp poster that always seemed to be the same one, year after year—happy couples and families in bathing suits, not a goose-pimple in sight. '*Whatever the weather, it's fine at Butlin's*'. "Yes," he thought, "and just you read between those lines. Stuck inside for two solid weeks, drinking yourself witless with people you couldn't stand, while every single day it pissed down with rain outside."

No, he wouldn't be going back there again.

He looked at the Sky Tours posters for the new all-in package holidays to Spain, Italy, and Greece. And at the picture-posters of all the destinations British European Airways flew to in Europe, all of them telling you to come fly with wonderful BEA. There were some lovely pictures and very nice photography, but his heart and camera were already set on America. The picture he had in mind was Frank Sinatra on the cover of an LP he had at home. A brilliant blue sky, a waiting aircraft, and '*Come fly with me*' all the way to New York, Florida, and Miami. Funny, the power a good picture had in a newspaper or magazine, on a record cover, or on a poster on a wall. If it was right, it tickled the imagination something wonderful and you filled in all the rest of the story yourself. His eyes lit on a poster for Pan American World Airways and he pushed open the glass door of the travel agency and, whistling tunelessly to himself, went inside.

PAUL McCARTNEY pulled the microphone closer. "And now here's the B-side of our very first record on the Parlophone label, a song we wrote ourselves, called 'P.S. I Love You'. Especially for them two lovebirds over there, Spike and Sandra."

He sang engagingly about writing a special love letter to the one you loved and nodded to acknowledge the happy young couple waving madly back at him. He'd always dreamt of having a song of his and John's in the Hit Parade. The only trouble now was their record hadn't made it into the Top Twenty, even though they'd been working nonstop to help push it up the charts. It was all so never ending. They'd just played the Cavern. Zipped round the corner and up Church Street for an engagement at the '527 Club'. It wasn't really a proper club, though; it was the restaurant on the top floor of Lewis's department store pressed into service by the young members of staff for their 'Young Idea Dance'. But then as John had said to Brian, "We'll play bloody anywhere if it helps gets us top of the Hit Parade."

'Eppy' had them working day and night now. Not only lunchtimes, but twice, even three times in an evening. He knew the week's typewritten list of engagements almost as well as he knew the night's set list: Tomorrow night, Birkenhead; Friday lunchtime, the Cavern, again; Friday evening, the 'Big Beat Show' in Newton-le-Willows. Saturday night, over to North-wich, in Cheshire, then straight back up to Liverpool to play a late show at 'the Tower'. Come Sunday morning, yet another long, dreary drive across country. Peterborough, this time, to play two 'package shows' that evening with the Australian pop star, Frank Ifield. Not exactly his cup of tea, but Brian was all for it as the gig could open up a whole new booking circuit. So be it. Sing on McDuff.

"Thank you, much. We're glad you enjoyed our song. So now, to finish, we're going to do another original song...the one on the A-side of our record...called 'Love Me Do'. And this time it's for each and every one of you '527 Club' lovebirds out there, tonight. And if you haven't done it already, like, why not pop along to NEMS and buy yourself a copy so you'll always remem-ber this very special evening."

NEIL ASPINALL glanced over at his brand new part-time assis-tant. "You're not at the Cavern now, you know, Mal. There's no just standing around looking tough...you've got to work for a liv-ing...even when you're sitting on your arse in this old bone-heap. And you can unwrap that bloody stick of Wrigley's, for me, for starters. I daren't take my bloody eyes of the road when I'm following Paul and 'Eppy' in their flash motorcars. They both of them drive like bloody maniacs and I can hardly keep up with them in this old Commer van, as it is." His eyes not leaving the A41 trunk road, for an instant, he bit into the gum and began to chew. "Okay. Ta. So, look, you best get a sense of what you've signed up for. Take a shufti at what's in that envelope on the dashboard...the one with my name typed on it. 'Eppy's latest memo of who and what...when and where...and be a good lad, Mal, read it out loud for us."

Mal Evans wiped his sweaty palms on his trousers, reached for the envelope and opened it. He unfolded the sheet of paper, stared at it for an age, then cleared his throat and began to read. "Bristol, first. For *Discs A Gogo* at the Television Centre. Then across to Wembley Studios, London, for another TV show. Back up to Liverpool for lunchtime and evening gigs at the Cav. On, up to Southport, the following day, for a gig that evening. Back down to Liverpool for another Cav lunchtime session. Same evening they top the bill at 'the Tower' at Bob Wooler's 'Big-Beat Spectacular'. Next night, they're off to Manchester, to the Oasis Club. Sunday night. They're at the Cav again. Bloody hell, Neil, don't they ever rest?"

"Not for now, they don't. Not if 'Eppy' has his way. There are another eight or nine gigs...here, there, everywhere...before they fly off to Hamburg, again. And the very last thing the lads need to worry about is 'the what' and 'the where' and 'the how' of their guitars, amps, and drums. That's all down to you and me, now. Making sure everything's all right on the night, so to speak. So are you still all right with all this, are you, Mal, being an assistant road manager? Bet nobody told you there'd be days, like these?"

JOHN LENNON yawned long and hard and wiped the sleep from his eyes with the back of his hand. "Not the bloody A580 trunk road again? Manchester, here we go round the bloody mulberry bush until 'a-tishoo, a-tishoo', we all bloody fall down dead. Hell...the rate we're going we haven't even got time to go down with the bloody flu, as is happening in the rest of the country, the bloody germs can't keep up with us. Not sure I bloody can, either."

"Still a damn sight better than driving a fork-lift at Garston Bottle Works, John," offered George, helpfully, from the back seat. He yawned. "Anyroad, I reckon it's Ringo's loud and incessant drumming that's keeping all the flu germs away. Too noisy for them to be able to exist, like."

Paul, eyes firmly fixed on the road ahead, chuckled. "It's a good thing we've got the little lad along with us, then, isn't it?"

John swallowed down the remains of another throat lozenge, belched, and banged his chest. "I wish he'd stuck his bloody drum sticks right up the noses of them po-faced gits, back in Peterborough. God, it still gets me. That was the worst bloody audience we've ever played to. The stuck-up gits just sat there in stony silence. We might as well not have been there. The whole lot of them should be shipped off to Australia, along with Frank Ifield and his bloody yodelling."

"Yeah," sniffed George. "The reporter from the local rag said we failed to excite. That we were barely tolerable. And castigated Ringo for making far too much noise and thinking it was his job to lead the group."

"It's that reporter that needs castigating...the stupid git knows fook-all about our kind of music." John looked back over his shoulder. "How is our intrepid new leader, by the way?" But Ringo didn't say anything. He was dead to the world—head resting on a rolled-up overcoat, nose pressed hard up against the car window.

BRIAN EPSTEIN bid 'adieu' with a wave of his hand to George Martin and his secretary standing on the steps of the Adelphi Hotel. Then he accelerated away into the night, up Brownlow Hill, towards Edge Road, all set for another fast drive home. Then he remembered himself, eased his foot off the accelerator and reduced his speed to something like the posted limit. His love of fast cars was well known amongst his close circle of friends, but ever since he'd signed his latest management contract with the newly revamped Beatles, he was taking care not to drive too fast, even if he was driving himself all the harder.

Truth was he'd never felt so driven. With the prospect of success now so very close, all it needed was one last concerted push to go from nothing to something very real—from ignominious failure to celebrated success. And now with definite talk of 'the boys' recording an LP as well as a second single as a follow up to 'Love Me Do', there was nothing for it but to push all the harder, push himself all the more and if need be push 'the boys' to their very limits. Time and tide wait for no man. He was sure they'd thank him for it in the end. And the only sure way for The Beatles to break through was for them to be so good they couldn't be ignored—by anyone, anywhere. And the key to future success was maximum exposure. That's why there could be no void. No vacuum. No empty spaces. Their diary had to be kept full for weeks and months ahead.

That's why 'the boys' not only had to look smart; they had to be seen to be true show-business professionals. They had to turn up on time and start and finish on time. They could no longer eat or drink or lark about on stage. Nor could they shout and swear and joke with the audience. Professionalism was everything, as had been proven that very evening. George Martin had travelled up to Liverpool specifically to see whether it was possible to record a live album at the Cavern and The Beatles had all but blown the whitewash off the ceiling. They'd been absolutely brilliant. Yet, as genuinely impressed as he'd been—especially the wild response of the fans—George Martin had decided the Cavern was a 'no go'. The club's three interconnected brick arches made it an acoustic nightmare, totally unfit for recording purposes. The record producer had promised, however, that when he came to record The Beatles' first LP he'd do his utmost to capture the raw excitement of their live act.

And all to good, but all of it still way in the future. The 'boys' had lots of engagements to fulfil before their next recording session. Every single booking, an important step towards them becoming more widely known. He didn't know many of the venues he'd booked the group into. He'd never had occasion to visit any of the places before, but he knew the roads you had to travel to get there. And he saw them in his mind's eye—each one overlaying the next—one long and winding road, disappearing off into the distance, extending far into the future.

New bookings across the river in Runcorn and Birkenhead, down in Shrewsbury, then as far south as Bedford. Back up to Liverpool for the first ever *Mersey Beat* Poll Awards Show, on the Saturday night, and then another gig at the Cavern on the Sunday evening. Over to Manchester, again, early the next day, for a third appearance on Granada Television's *People and Places*. Then back to Liverpool to pack their suitcases as they were due to fly out to Hamburg, the next day. He'd booked them to play the Star-Club for the two weeks over the Christmas and New Year holidays—at a substantially increased fee—and, yes, under the circumstances, perhaps a little difficult for John to be away from home. But they daren't let up now for anything. Not when everything seemed to be gathering speed. He had to keep driving forward. Keep the momentum going.

JOHN LENNON glanced at the sign to the airport, wound down the car window, and threw his chewing gum out onto the road. "Speke bloody Airport here we come again," he groaned, winding the window back up, his breath steaming in the cold air. "What 'Eppy' doesn't bloody seem to appreciate is that it's not just about us making bloody money, any which way we can, any more, it more about us getting our record heard and more of our records bought. 'Love Me Do' barely made it into the *Melody Maker*'s Top Twenty and is already sliding back down the charts. So, now, again, thanks to our clever dick of a manager's bloody mismanaging we're going to be away in bloody Hamburg the very moment we should be here, at home, playing more dates, doing more radio, more television. Doing any soddin' thing we can to keep the momentum going."

"We're already doing all we bloody can, John. We've all been knackering ourselves silly to try keep everything going."

"I know, Pauly, only now we'll be bloody knackering ourselves for four bloody hours, night after bloody night, for thirteen bloody nights, straight, and for what? And the real bastard is we'll all be away from home over Christmas and New Year and my Cyn will be home, all alone, in Faulkner Street...and with her expecting, too."

"It's a real drag you being away from Cynthia, for Christmas, John. But we can't break the contract even though we might want to. So let's all just try and make the best of it, okay? As George said, it's much better than us having to work in some factory or office somewhere."

"No one's ever going to see me punching a bloody time clock in some factory or office. Not in this life, anyway. Still and all, at times like these, I could give 'Eppy' a right royal thumping."

"The money's still dead important, John. We all of us need to make as much of it as we can. As we all of us know this isn't going last forever. So we've got to make hay when the going's good, even if it is in Hamburg. And let's not forget our 'Eppy' managed to get us 750 DM a week, each, this time, from Herr Manfred Weissleder. That's nothing to sneeze at."

"Of course the money's bloody important George, I'm not daft. It's just me pushing back on things. Trying to stay bloody sane. I mean, I put up with Brian's bloody typewritten lists, the Little Lord Fauntleroy suits, us bowing at the waist at the end of every song or set, and all the bloody rest of it. The do bloody this, the do bloody that, the go bloody here, the go bloody there. Don't bloody swear, John. Don't bloody fart out of tune, John. And now with us going back to Hamburg, again, it feels like we're just going backwards. So all I'm saying is that this definitely has to be the last bloody time we play the bloody Star-Club, in bloody Hamburg. Or I really will go bloody spare. Is that clear enough now? We've got London to conquer, yet. The bloody Germans couldn't ever do it, but The Beatles bloody will. Only this time, it'll be a lot less *Sieg Heil! Sieg Heil!* and a lot more *'Please, Please Me!'*"

SPIKE stared up at the sign through tired red-rimmed eyes, eyes that felt full of grit. 'WILLKOMMEN NACH HAMBURG'. It didn't seem so strange this time, but it still felt odd. In Liverpool, one minute, the next walking out of the Hamburg-Hauptbahnhof, looking for a taxi, which given all the slush and snow on the ground looked a very tall order indeed. He stood in the taxi line, pulled his coat collar up around his ears, and gazed enviously at the black leather peaked caps a lot of Hamburgers were now wearing to keep their heads warm.

He was there to fill-in for The Undertakers' bass player who'd slipped on the ice in the street and broken his wrist. All of which, had led to a crack-of-dawn telephone call promising him the earth if only he'd come out to Hamburg on the next train. He'd said 'Yes' even before thinking about it. Told his mother he was going—as ever, to stony silence—packed a suitcase, taken a taxi to Lime Street, left everything in the left-luggage office, then dashed round to Lewis's to break the news to Sandra. Who'd been none too pleased. In fact, she'd been good and mad. It meant he'd be away for Christmas and New Year and they'd already planned on going down to London to stay with her sister, Maureen, for the holidays. So he'd done what he always did to make Sandra laugh, he struck the pose of 'Liverpool Resurgent', a pained look of remorse on his face. Then he'd almost gone and blown it by singing a few bars of 'Chains', a song he'd been learning. And she'd narrowed her eyes and told him in no uncertain terms she didn't need any bloody chains to lock him to her side.

He'd been really contrite. "It's just me, Sandra, your brown-eyed stupid man. Sorry, love. I just didn't think." She'd tried to look stern. "If I didn't love you so much, Spike Jones, I'd just tell you to hit the road and don't come back. Only, you better do or I'll hit you with the heel of my stiletto shoe." So he'd pulled a face, tried to look suitably terrified, then he'd laughed and pulled her to him, hugged her tight.

Sandra's boss, a nice woman he'd sat next to at the 'Young Idea Dance', let Sandra take an early lunch-break so she could see him off. And as they'd walked up towards Lime Street Station, oblivious to the bitter cold wind, he'd told her he loved her, that she was the only one, and that when he got back from Germany, they'd go down to London, together, for a short break. Even talk about moving there for good.

Then there they were, again, in the railway station, amidst all the noise and bustle. They found themselves by the instant-photo booth and without a word being said, they were suddenly sitting on the bench inside, the curtains drawn, kissing like there was no tomorrow. Then Sandra pulled away and said she should brush her hair and as she'd done so, he'd run a quick hand through his. He produced a two-bob piece from his jacket pocket, waited for her to nod she was ready, then leaned forward and pushed the coin into the slot. Then he turned round, pulled her to him again and kissed her, passionately. Their lips locked together. A brilliant white light flashed four times. A single kiss captured in four different photographs. She'd called his name. He'd whispered hers. And with no more words said, they both knew they were going to be together forevermore.

There was a sudden urgent knocking on the outside of the photo-booth and the privacy curtains rippled on both sides. A trembling, high-pitch, treble voice said, "Er, excuse me, mister, miss, but are you twos finished in there, like? Only I want to have some pictures taken of me, me brother, and me dad, before he goes away, like." Another little voice piped in then. "Yes, and his train's going in five minutes, so can you hurry please?"

They'd groaned and laughed. He'd called out, "Yes, we're finished." Then he'd turned to Sandra, kissed her hard on the lips, and said, "No, we've only just begun." Then they'd pulled back the curtains, either side, exited the booth, and stood and waited the three long minutes for the instant-picture strip to develop. Then there it was—the kiss—the two of them, their lips locked together, a moment captured forever. Sandra held it up, reverently. "I'll paint a picture of that for you, one day, San," he whispered, his lips brushing her hair, "just like the first time." Then Sandra very carefully folded the photo-strip in half and gently tore it in two. She handed him the first two photos of 'the kiss' and kept the other two for herself. Then she looked up at him and said, oh so very softly, tears in her eyes, "From now on, that's the only way you'll ever be parted from me, Spike Jones."

JOHN LENNON adjusted the toilet seat around neck, the symbolism beyond blatant now. It was going to be another crap night. He didn't give a stuff what others might think. He'd outgrown the place. Had his fill. And just like in *Alice Through The Looking Glass* he could all but feel his head and feet bursting through the roof and doors of the Star-Club. Acting the Goon on stage. Standing in his underwear on the Reeperbahn, a Tyrolean hat on his head, a small pig on a lead, whatever the hell it was, it was all just grist for the bloody misery mill. Anyroad, it was soon going be all over and done with. They were off home tomorrow. Thank God, Martin, and Luther.

He growled into the microphone. "That was 'Roll Over Bee-thoven'. Chuck Richard's famous light opera about German berry-pickers, sung as ever by my friend George H. Goering, here. This next number is a cha-cha-cha dedicated to that great tenor saxophone player, Adolf-big-lips-Hitler...'There Was Peace, Till There Was You'."

'Eppy' had gone back to Liverpool, just before Christmas, looking very pleased with himself, even if a bit shagged out. And for one last time, The Beatles were off the leash and free from the chains no one else could see. For starters, they'd been eating and drinking on stage, telling jokes, talking amongst themselves, and generally behaving like the leather-clad rock 'n' roll louts they really were. And with it being New Year's Eve, you could even belch into the microphone, just as long as you raised your glass of beer and smiled and yelled, "Cheers, you Nazi-fookers!"

They'd even called their friends to join them up on stage, one of Brian Epstein's biggest taboos. They'd had 'Kingsize' Taylor, minus his Dominoes; Adrian Barber, ex-lead guitarist of The Big Three, now the Star-Club's stage manager; both of them jacked into the club's cream-coloured Fender amplifiers, trading guitar licks with George Harrison, showing everyone how it should be done. Roy Young had thumped the grand piano and done his Lit-tle Richard. Tony Sheridan had wiggled his hips and done Jerry Lee Elvis. A great looking bit of stuff, Carol Elvin—who sang with Roy's Star-Combo and who everyone wanted to shag like mad—shimmied and shook until they had to beg her to get off as she was driving people crazy with deeply lustful thoughts. Jackie Lomax, got up and sang, his wrist still in a cast. Then that young fella, Spike, the one standing in for Jackie, had gone head to head with Paul, the two of them hammering away like mad on 'I Saw Her Standing There'. Then Bugs Pemberton of The Domi-noes and Brian Redman of The Undertakers had both set up stools next to Ringo and they'd all battered and bashed their drum skins until it seemed the skyscrapers painted on the stage backdrop would peel off and collapse into rubble.

"This one's 'Little Queenie' by Chuck Berrystein, a born Scouser who's got bent legs, wavy hair, and likes yobbos."

As for, himself—John Lennon of Liddypool—he was both ringmaster and stationmaster—the heavy-lidded eyes at the centre of the storm. And what fookin' fun it was. What fookin' larks! So fookin' what they were trying to record it all on some fookin' Telefunken tape recorder. No one would ever want to hear it. It was total crap.

"This next one's by John Winston Lennon. That great, Russian revolutionary who got full marks for missing the last train from Lime Street. It's time to rock the 'One After 909'."

The number 'nine' figured hugely in is life—always had, always would—therefore why not sing about it? So he did. And when he'd come to the end of the line, he grabbed the microphone again.

"Und zo meine Damen und Herren before you all start marching round and murdering 'Auld Lang Syne'...this next song is for all you crips who walk with a limp. And if you haven't got a limp you soon will have if you don't clap for this song by Gene Vincent, because it's going to be sung for you now by the Star-Club's very own rock 'n' roller in chief...the man who can really belt out the hits. It's the one...the only...Herr!...Horst!...Fascher!"

Horst ran out onto the stage to cheers, whistles, and thunderous applause, waved his arms over his head like a champion boxer and grabbed the microphone. He gave a curt nod, swivelled his hips, and shot out an arm, finger pointed straight at Ringo. Ringo kicked out the beat. "Well...Be-bop-a-lula..." Then there was no doubt about it. Horst Fascher was finally up there, where he always dreamed he'd be—in rock 'n' roll heaven—singing and playing amongst the stars.

"Be-bop-en-Hamburg...dem Himmel sei Dank!"

"SANDRA! Happy New Year, love...hope it's a good one...lots and lots of love, to you, from the both of us. Cheers."

Maureen raised her glass of Babycham, held her innermost feelings in check, and squeezed her husband's hand so tightly it almost made him wince.

"Happy New Year, Morr. Happy New Year, Jack. Cheers to you both." Sandra held up her glass, swallowed hard, and tried to hold back her tears. "Thank you, you two lovely people, for letting me come stay for Christmas in your beautiful London home. I hope it turns out to be a Happy New Year for us all."

"You deserve it to be, Sandra, love." Maureen turned and smiled at her husband, "Will you give us a minute, Jack?"

Jack nodded. "Sure, I'll go put the kettle on, make us all a cuppa." He left the living room and closed the door behind him.

"Look, Sandra, love, me and Jack have been talking. We haven't got a lot, what with moving into the house and everything, but if you need the money it's there and whether you decide to have the baby or put it up for adoption we'll do everything we can to help. And if you do decide to have an abortion and you haven't got too long to make up your mind, then I know someone at work that knows of a private clinic in Harley Street that deals with that sort of thing. You've got to decide what you want to do."

Sandra sat stunned, speechless, what an awful predicament she was in. Far worse than the bitter Christmas weather, had been the bitter realisation that the sickness she'd suffered almost every morning since she'd arrived at her sister's house was an early sign she was pregnant. It was Maureen who'd first noticed and commented upon it and they'd taken the calendar down off the kitchen wall and worked out the dates with pencil and paper. After which, Maureen had taken Sandra round to see a doctor who'd confirmed that Sandra was indeed expecting. But beyond listing her options and giving them both a strict talking to, he'd offered little or no real help.

"It's my fault," said Maureen. "I shouldn't have encouraged you."

"Don't be daft," said Sandra. "It's nobody's fault, but mine."

Even so, her sister and brother in-law's generous offer of support was totally unexpected and she felt not a little humbled and ashamed at having put such a burden upon them. It'd all been so very lovely, though, that weekend with Spike. Just the two of them, alone in his mother's house, just the two of them, together, like a real married couple, able to enjoy their very own Friday night, Saturday night, and Sunday morning. And Morr had been right, it had felt a little odd at first, but then, just as she'd said, it felt really, really wonderful, and they'd made love six or seven times. And, well, it was just that her handbag had always seemed to be somewhere else in the house or, simply, that she hadn't ever wanted it to stop.

"When does your Spike get back from Hamburg?"

"Not till the end of the first or second week in January."

"You better stay here until then. We'll call Lewis's, say you've got very bad bronchitis, the doctor says you mustn't travel and you're staying here until you're better. Or you can just send in your notice by letter, but either way when you do go home you and Raymond have got to make up your minds, pretty damn quick."

"Yes, I know, but I must talk to Spike, first, Morr. Thank you for everything, big sister. I don't know where I'd be without you, I don't."

Maureen sighed. "Well, who knows, San? You might not have gone and got yourself pregnant if I'd just minded me own bloody business."

"But you've always helped me get through things, Morr, always shown me the way, and what to do, ever since I was little."

"That's what I mean, love. I can't bloody help it. I've always got to try and help, because you're my lovely little daft duck of a sister."

The two sisters held on to one another and cried in the New Year.

CHAPTER THIRTY-THREE

Thank Your Lucky Stars

Brian Epstein arrived at Dick James's office a good forty minutes before his eleven o'clock meeting. He was seething. The first music publisher he'd had an appointment with hadn't even bothered to come in. And when the receptionist had had the temerity to suggest that he might like to play his demo disc for the office boy, he'd stormed out.

He wouldn't allow The Beatles' next single 'Please Please Me' to be taken lightly by anyone. He'd been very disappointed by Ardmore & Beechwood's feeble efforts with 'Love Me Do' and was looking for a more committed music publisher. He'd thought of offering the music publishing rights to Hill & Range, the American company that represented the Elvis Presley song catalogue, but George Martin had advised against it, suggesting he look for a company that was hungry, not so well established, and a little closer to home. "Find someone that'll work really hard for you, Brian. I'll give you some names. You can even try my old friend, Dick James. He's the one that offered us Mitch Murray's 'How Do You Do It?' On that side of the business, there's no one I'd trust more."

Dick James was also feeling more than a mite disappointed that morning. He hadn't long left a big music-publishing house to start his own company and he was finding it very tough going. So when George Martin had called to tell him that even though The Beatles had recorded 'How Do You Do It?' the group didn't like the end product and that Parlophone had decided not to release it, it wasn't at all what he needed to hear. Like everyone else, he very badly needed a hit.

Having an A-side in the Hit Parade is what brought in the money, and he'd staked his reputation on 'How Do You Do It?' being a sure-fire hit. Now, George Martin had set up a meeting for him with The Beatles' manager, so that he could listen to the 'acetate' of a song the group had composed themselves. Artistes writing their own tunes? It didn't bode at all well. That was the job for a professional Tin Pan Alley songwriter. His receptionist knocked on his door and said his eleven o'clock appointment had arrived early and asked whether he was available. He nodded, dropped the paperclip he'd been toying with into a box in his drawer, stood up, and got ready to smile. The things one did for colleagues in the business.

"Mr Epstein? Please, come in. What can I do for you, sir?"

After a few minutes of exchanging pleasantries, most of them about George Martin, Brian Epstein handed him the demo disc and sat back, nervously, on the edge of his chair. He held the acetate by the edges, like a true professional, and carefully placed it onto the tiny Dansette record player he kept in his office. Then he turned the switch to automatic play, stepped back, crossed his arms, and waited.

It was just as well he'd remained standing, for after a single hearing of 'Please Please Me', he felt like jumping for joy.

"What do you think?" asked Brian Epstein, his voice strained.

He could hardly contain himself. "I think it's a 'number one' record, if ever I heard one, Mr Epstein." He paused, shook his head. "And I'll tell you straight, I think it's even better than 'How Do You Do It?' Much better. Fresh. Raw. Amazing."

Brian Epstein beamed with pleasure. "Yes, the two Beatles who wrote it, John Lennon and Paul McCartney, are very, very talented."

"Well, if you'd consider letting me publish 'Please Please Me' for you, Mr Epstein, I'd work on it personally and do everything I possibly could to promote it into the Hit Parade. I would. I promise."

Brian Epstein narrowed his eyes. "That's exactly what Ardmore and Beechwood said they'd do with the last record, but I have to say, I'm extremely unhappy about how little they accomplished in the end."

Dick James was undeterred. "Well, look, let me phone a friend of mine, right here and now, and see what we can do." He picked up the phone and dialled a number from memory. Brian Epstein looked at him; knowing full well that he'd done exactly the same sort of thing to impress people in his own business dealings. He sat back and waited.

"Philip Jones, please." He looked up, nodded, smiled. "Hello Phil. It's Dick. Got a minute? I've got something rather special here, from a fabulous new pop group, and I know you're going to thank me when you hear it." He carried the telephone over to the record player, held up the receiver to the speaker and played 'Please Please Me' at full volume. "Well, what do you think? It's coming out week Friday, on the eleventh." He listened for a few moments. "Didn't I tell you? It's 'number one' hit material. By a new group called The Beatles. Yeah, catchy song and a catchy name that'll stick in people's minds. Yeah. Yeah. You're right. You're right. So then you'll book them on the show, two weeks, this Saturday? And record the show up in Birmingham, Sunday week, on the thirteenth? Okay. Great. Terrific. Thanks, Phil. Did I say you're a prince? Yeah. Yeah. Yeah. Bye."

Dick James put down the phone and looked over at Brian Epstein, who now seemed more dazed than bemused. "That," he said, "was Phil Jones, the producer of a very important pop music show called *Thank Your Lucky Stars* that gets broadcast nationally over the entire independent television network on Saturday evenings. Once you get your artistes on the show, you're pretty much assured of a hit record the following week. All the teenagers tune into it. It's all the rage."

Brian Epstein knew all about *Thank Your Lucky Stars*. At this stage of the game, a spot on the show was more than he could ever have hoped for. It would give The Beatles national exposure. It certainly wasn't the sort of opportunity you got handed to you on a plate every day. "That was most impressive, Mr James. *Thank Your Lucky Stars*. I'm sure 'the boys' will be very impressed and very pleased. I know, I am."

"Do I take it, then, Mr Epstein, that I can publish your song?"

SAM LEACH lit a ten-shilling cigar and puffed on it proudly. The New Year had been just thirty-three minutes old when his wife Joan gave birth to a little girl, Debbie. "Joan's finest performance and my best ever production," Sam said, gazing up at the stars in the night sky. "Better than The Beatles at their absolute best. Thank you, God."

Come the cold light of morning, however, he knew he had to redouble his efforts at finding work. He still had a mountain of debts to clear from his many ventures and was determined to pay them off, in full. So he'd taken a job as a cost clerk at the huge Automatic Telephone factory on Edge Lane and put in as much overtime as he could. Seeing how tight things were for the young couple, Joan's mother had invited them to move in with her. So that's what they'd done.

Nevertheless, to keep some vestige of the flame alive he continued to devour *Mersey Beat* and the *New Musical Express*. And when it was announced The Beatles were to play their first Liverpool engagement in nearly a month, he bought tickets the day they went on sale. On the night of the show, he stood in line with all the rest of the punters, outside the Grafton Rooms, on the West Derby Road. One of the evening's highlights, The Beatles singing their soon-to-be-released, new song, 'Please, Please Me'. It stunned the crowd, it was that good, and a lot of people couldn't believe the boys had written it themselves. "Absolutely bloody amazing! A 'number one' record, if ever I heard one," he said to anyone who could hear him amidst all the cheering and clapping and whistling.

It was Ringo Starr who spotted him in the crowd as The Beatles came off stage at the end of their set and made their way to the dressing room protected by a wall of bouncers. None of whom Sam knew. "Hey 'oop, Sam. What you doing there?" Ringo called out. And before he'd even had time to reply, the Beatle had thrust a drumstick into his hand and said to the nearest bouncer, "Hey, he's one of our roadies, he is. Be so kind as to let the gentleman through."

And, suddenly, there he was, back again inside The Beatles' inner sanctum. The boys were absolutely delighted to hear the news about the birth of his daughter, but were equally dismayed to hear he was stuck in some stuffy office as a bloody cost clerk.

George Harrison shook his head. "It's not you, Sam."

Paul McCartney felt the same. "No, it's not for you, Sam."

It was John Lennon who seemed most annoyed and quick as a flash he turned and levelled a finger at him. "Bloody hell, Sam. I've never known you to quit on anything. Not once. So just you get your arse back in the business, before it's too bloody late."

"It's not as easy as you might think, John," he shot back.

"Don't bloody give me that," snapped, John. "Just go bloody do it, Sam. Go promote something, even if it's only at Knotty Ash Hall."

"Yeah, you're right," he said, smiling. "When I do get back on my feet, like, I hope you fellas won't be too big to play for me?"

John pulled a face. "Look, that's between you and 'Eppy'. We all of us, always liked playing for you, Sam, you know that."

Something in him bubbled back up to the surface. "Yeah. I suppose that means now you lot have had a song of yours in the Hit Parade, you'll be wanting something ridiculous, like fifty-quid a night?"

George laughed. "Brian charges fifty quid for people to just watch us blow our bloody noses, now."

That was when Brian Epstein walked into the dressing room.

The bloody man completely ignored him. Just told The Beatles it was time to go. Not wanting to cause any more embarrassment, he quickly shook hands with John, Paul, George, and Ringo. "Thanks for the boost, fellas. I promise, I'll be back up there in business again, within the week, see if I'm not." He gave them one last smile.

The very next day he went in search of a new venue. It would've been more fun if Terry McCann was around, but he couldn't blame his old mate for having gone back to London. "It's just no fun, anymore, Sam," Tel had said. "It's getting far too cut throat, what with you losing 'the Tower' and all. Everyone seems to be doing the dirty on everyone else these days. So I'm off back to me own turf. Go do a bit of minding, down in the Smoke, but I'll be in touch, for sure."

Those had been good days with Tel, the best. Maybe things could be like that again one day. Then right out of the blue— almost as if it'd been pre-ordained—after a long, frustrating, unsuccessful day of enquiries, he was told that Mo Best had given up her option on Friday nights at Knotty Ash Hall. It was a great hall, popular with all the groups, and Mo had built up a strong local following for the place. It was certainly not the sort of opportunity you got handed to you on a plate every day. And as luck would have it, too, the bloke responsible for the hall was on the premises. So he quickly came to an agreement to take over the Friday-night franchise. Shook hands on the deal.

He immediately called 'Kingsize' Taylor, told him he'd got Friday nights at Knotty Ash. Asked when he was next free. "Friday," came the reply. "What? This next Friday, Ted?" "Yeah, this Friday, Sam. How many bloody Fridays are there in a week?"

So then he called Rory Storm and got the exact same answer.

Un-bloody-believable! He punched the air. Kissed the sky. He was back in business and with two of Merseyside's top rockin' bands! "Good Golly, Miss Molly! But God's in his heaven and life's suddenly very, very good."

BRIAN EPSTEIN turned to 'his boys'. "I'm so very, very proud of you. I've been pushing you relentlessly and your response has been nothing less than stellar. Only now I believe all of your hard work is about to start paying off. This appearance on *Thank Your Lucky Stars* is of tremendous importance. I know it may not seem like it on such a bleak Sunday afternoon, in a cold TV studio, on the outskirts of Birmingham, with you about to mime to your record in front of a small studio audience, but just remember it is your very first nationally networked television broadcast. The very first opportunity for the whole country to see The Beatles and hear 'Please Please Me'. So just be yourselves and perform and play with the same feeling, the same joy, you had that very first time I saw you at the Cavern."

He paused. Looked at each one of them in turn.

"The TV camera is the eye of the world and you're now at the very eye of the coming storm of beat music. And so when the show they're taping this afternoon is transmitted next Saturday night, just before six o'clock," he paused to consult his typed-copy of the coming week's agenda, "when you'll be preparing to play the Town Hall Ballroom, in Pauls Moss,

Dodington, in Shropshire." He smiled as John and George gave out with loud groans. "I promise you, it will be the real start of everything you've ever dreamed of." He held up a paper cup in salute. "And even though there's only tap water for me to toast your future success with, and not champagne, it in no way reduces the significance of today's occasion, for this, now, is the turning point."

The Beatles looked at him, smiled, and shuffled their feet.

So, this was it then, it was happening, at last. No wonder they were all feeling so bloody nervous—far worse than anything they'd felt before.

'Eppy' looked at them, smartly dressed in velvet-collared suits and black ties, 'Beatle' haircuts, and Cuban-heeled boots, and he knew enough about the theatre to realise that for a few moments, at least, he needed to take their minds off their coming performance. "Have you boys given any thought to the future and what it might bring? Because you're about to open up 'Pandora's Box', you know, you really are."

George rubbed his chin and grinned his toothy grin. "Well, Brian, I don't know about any Pandora, but if as you say now's the real beginning, then I only hope we can start making some real money. I know we're good. And if we ever got to be a big as Cliff Richard and The Shadows, that'd be really great. But I reckon if you can manage it so we can tour and make records for three or four more years, that'd be great, too. Then I'd be able to buy myself a few nice guitars and a new car, and a bus for me dad and a new house for me mam. After that, Brian, I don't really know. Just make us enough money so we don't have to worry about our families. I'd be a very happy man, then."

Brian smiled and looked at Ringo. And Ringo pointed one of his drumsticks at himself, as if to say: Who me? Then he laughed and tilted his head to one side. "I know I'm still the new boy," he grinned at the others, "but I'd rather be in this group, eight days a week, than be in any other group or band anywhere else in the whole wide world."

"Good one, Ring," chuckled, Paul. "We're all very glad you've joined the group."

Ringo scratched his head. "But, er, as to the future, like? Well, a string of hairdressers, maybe, seeing as how I know someone in that line of business. Not the old-fashioned type of place, mind, more one of them modern ones that does men's hair as well as ladies." He shook his head so his haircut swung out like a curtain, waited for it to resume its shape again. "See, it's the coming thing. Before long everyone will want a 'Beatle' haircut like mine." Then he grinned again and laughed. "Failing that, of course, there's always America."

"Just remember to turn left at Greenland," said Paul.

"What about you, Paul?" said Brian, softly.

"Me? Well, Brian, I think the same as George. It can't last forever, maybe three or four years if we're dead lucky. But I'll go on writing songs with John whatever happens. I love doing that. Then who knows, maybe even do a musical or something. That'd be good. Anything, really, just as long as I can keep on performing and playing and writing music."

John Lennon snorted. "Yeah, I can just see the two of us walking down Tin Pan Alley with all the other boring old farts." Paul looked at him sharply. "No, don't worry, Pauly, it's only me being me. We'll run rings round the bloody lot of them and dance all the way to the bank, too. We'll rake the bloody money in. We'll all be millionaires."

"You will you know, you all will." Brian said, looking at each one of The Beatles in turn. "I believe there's absolutely nothing can stop you, now. You can be as big as you want, for as long as you want. Be bigger than anyone has ever dreamed of being."

"Right," said George, "I think I better go and have a quick pee. What with all this water I've been drinking, I wouldn't want it to look as if I've been caught short when I go out there, start tapping my feet."

"Er, good idea, la'. Always go where nature calls," said Ringo.

"It's the natural thing to do," said Paul, "Lead on MacDuff!"

George, Ringo, and Paul pulled agonised faces, filed out of the dressing room, and went in search of the toilets. John wrinkled his nose, turned, and peered at Brian. "What did you mean, 'Eppy', when you said, 'You can be as big as you want for as long as you want'? Don't you think we'd all want it to go on forever?"

"The lightning is about to come out of the bottle, John. The Beatles are about to electrify the world. And you're the only ones now that can ever stop it. Or ever break it apart. No one else can, not even me."

"So you're saying we're all stuck with one another, 'Eppy'?"

"That's it, exactly, John. Somehow, Ringo was the perfect finishing touch. It's odd, but something extraordinary happens now when you all start playing together. It's as if you're complete, somehow. You don't look as if you need anyone or anything and, what's more, it looks as if you don't give a damn about what anyone might think or say about it all. And that's what makes you all so very attractive to everyone. The only thing the rest of us can do now is stand back and watch and listen, in awe."

"Bloody hell, 'Eppy', I thought we were just a band that wanted to get big enough to get out of Liverpool and go top the pops in London. It's funny, though, what you're saying. George says it feels odd, sometimes, when we start to play, it's like we're all one person."

"The four of you are simply perfect together, John. You're the whole thing. Complete. In the way you look and the way you sound."

"I've always thought of The Beatles as being a bit like a gang and that no one of us is The Beatles, we all are. To me, it's the group as a whole that's important, as none of us can do it on our own. Not me, not Paul, not George, not Ringo. And you're right, it does seem as if we've been looking for the perfect drummer from the very beginning. So, yeah, 'Eppy', The Beatles is all four of us, and always will be. All for one, and all that stuff."

"George is right, John, you do all come together like one person." He paused. "George is…is unquestionably the soul of the group. Paul is the heart…its warm, welcoming, ever-beating heart. Ringo…Ringo is the body, its flesh and blood, its bones and its sinews. And you, John, you're its mind…bright and piercing and perceptive…and you always will be. And if ever one of you stops…or leaves…or breaks away…there'll be no more Beatles and the whole magical thing will fall apart and the whole world will be the poorer for it."

"Blimey, 'Eppy', I think I need go take a pee, now, as well. Otherwise I'm not sure which will burst first, me bladder or me bloody head. I'll be back in a minute. Then I think I need to ask everyone, just one more time, where we're all going to."

"I'll pour us all some more water, so we can all toast to the future, together. But from now on, I promise, it'll only be the very best champagne, all the way."

"It better be, 'Eppy', it better be, for all our bloody sakes."

Brian Epstein sat alone, but he no longer felt alone. He was as close as anyone could ever be to The Beatles without actually being a Beatle. And there was nowhere else he'd rather be. Or anyone else he'd rather be with. 'The boys' completed him, too. They made him feel whole. With The Beatles, the missing part— deep, deep, deep down inside him—was at last fully fulfilled.

He closed his eyes and was enveloped by darkness. But it brought no fear to him now. For in that darkness shone John, Paul, George, and Ringo—ever-brighter pinpoints of light that pushed back any and all thoughts of interminable blackness and the innumerable horrors hidden therein. As long as he focussed purely on 'his boys' he could avoid the dread dark void beyond—the emptiness—the nothingness—that for so long had been the herald of so many dreadful nightmares. He was free now to create even more stars to shine alongside The Beatles and, safe among them, no dark shape could ever come to haunt or threaten to destroy him ever again. He had so much now to be thankful for. A galaxy of twinkling stars that all promised the sun would shine tomorrow and forever afterwards.

SANDRA AND MAUREEN sat in front of the telly watching the commercials. It would be a while yet before Jack came home. He was out with his mates. No doubt, in some pub, somewhere, having gone to watch his local team Chelsea playing against Arsenal, at Highbury. And 'Murray-mints may be the too-good to hurry mints', but the TV adverts couldn't end fast enough as far as Sandra was concerned. So when the multi-pointed star whirled and spun on the screen to announce the start of the next programme, she was so focussed she'd almost forgotten the heavy weight she carried inside her. She glanced at the clock.

Five minutes to six. She looked back at the screen and there it was, *Thank Your Lucky Stars*. She knew Spike would be watching, too. She imagined him sitting in front of the telly, in the living room of his mother's house, just as she'd so often done herself. Where they'd kissed and cuddled and where she wished with all her heart she was now.

She tried not to be so impatient, but all the other singers on the show looked and sounded so old-fashioned, they were a total drag. When would The Beatles be on? She wanted the whole world to see 'the boys' from Liverpool. It was as if she was pregnant with the secret of them, too.

SPIKE felt suddenly electrified. Chair pulled up in front of the TV, he'd sat through as much of the show as he could and in the end turned the sound off. The acts had been so lame. Then, without warning or fanfare, Brian Matthews, the compère, was introducing The Beatles and he lunged forward, turned up the sound, and just stared at the screen. The Beatles looked so damn good in black and white—it was almost as if they'd been made for television. They sang 'Please Please Me' and the music he thought he knew so well hit him full blast. It sounded so raw, so tough, in comparison with everything that'd gone before, that it was almost like he was hearing the group again for the very first time. He could tell they were miming, though, their guitars weren't even plugged into their amplifiers, but they did it so well, with such charm, such finesse, it didn't matter. They looked like real professionals—like proper *bona fide* stars.

And as The Beatles sang the song's final refrain, he found himself moving closer and closer to the TV screen. He wanted to touch the four figures he knew so well, touch them for luck, touch them for love, for he knew that somewhere, down in London, Sandra was doing the same. "So I can feel close to you," Sandra had said. And as The Beatles bowed in unison at the end of their song and the studio audience whistled and clapped and cheered he said softly, "I love you Sandra. So, so very, very much." His whispered words drowned out by all the girls on the television screen screaming for more Beatles.

SPIKE telephoned Sandra very early the next morning.

"Weren't they fab, Spike? Oh, our Paul looked really lovely."

"Yeah, they looked great, didn't they? John, Paul, George and...and Ringo. He looked like he really belonged in the group, didn't he? As if he'd been drumming with them forever."

"And I love their new record, 'Please Please Me'. I haven't heard them even sing it before. It must be dead new."

"Yeah. It was released a week last Friday and after last night I bet it won't be long before it makes 'number one'. I've got a copy of it here, now. The other side's called, 'Ask Me Why'. And don't ask me why, but I think you and me will be playing it over and over again, every single day and night, next week. We'll wear it right into the rubber mat of the turntable."

"How did it go last night? Where did you play?"

"The gig? Yeah, it went great. Played Aintree Institute for The Strangers. I wish you'd been there, San. I can't wait to see you."

Sandra's heart fluttered and ached. "Oh, I've missed you, too, Spike, so much. It's been such a long time. I've still got your Christmas present for you, you know. I'm bringing it with me. Do you want to know what it is?"

"No, surprise me. I like your little surprises." The line went dead for a moment, as if someone had put a hand over the receiver. "San? Are you still there? I thought the connection had broken. Everything all right with your sister? Yes? Good. What I started saying was, talking of surprises, Jimmy rang to tell me he and Thelma have set the date for them to get married. It's the anniversary of the day we all met, that first time, at 'the Tower'."

Sandra's heart beat faster and though she was thrilled for her best friend, a pang of jealousy pierced her heart. She'd dreamed of marrying Spike since that very first night. Her Spike—her Raymond—was the one person who would make her life complete. She swallowed. "Yeah, Thelma rang and told us. It's dead great, isn't it? They want to take us for a meal to celebrate and go see *Lawrence of Arabia* afterwards. I'm so happy for Thelma, but mostly I'm so very happy I'm coming back home today. It's been such a long time. I love you. And I can't wait to see you."

REX MAKIN put down the *Sunday Telegraph* and reached for the *News of the World*. His wife, Rachel, had long given up trying to get him to stop reading at the Sunday breakfast table, but the practice had become a weekly ritual—both sacred and profane. As he'd explained to her on numerous occasions, as a solicitor, it was a professional necessity for him to keep up with all many scandalous and scurrilous goings on in the world-at-large.

That particular day his interest had been drawn to a front-page news item detailing reports that, following recent exposures in a number of national newspapers, the preliminary inquiry into accusations of police bribery and corruption in Liverpool had now given rise to a full-scale citywide investigation. It added that, pending further inquiries, a number of senior Liverpool police officers had already been suspended and that a number of establishments had been raided and officially closed, including several reputed brothels and unlicensed gambling clubs. Most notorious of which, was after-hours drinking club run by an un-named local black businessman who—it was inferred—had close links with both the police and the criminal underworld. The Head of Lancashire Constabulary was quoted as saying that more heads would definitely be rolling.

Rex Makin put his cup to his lips, only to find the tea had gone stone cold. Still deep in thought, he put his teacup down and reached for the marmalade and another slice of toast. He chuckled as he picked up his butter knife. As for real-life bloody drama, this was even better than watching *Z-Cars* on the telly. He pulled a face—something between vengeance served and unconfined glee—and thanked his lucky stars he'd never given cause for Harry Lightfoot to come looking for him, with malice aforethought.

"Another cup tea, darling?" his wife asked, sweetly.

Hello, Goodbye

Sandra heard Spike's voice and pushed a shilling into the slot. "Hello Raymond? Spike? Hello. Yes, it's me. I'm at Euston Station, waiting for me train. Dialled you myself from one of them new direct-dial phone boxes, didn't I? Yes, clever little me. Oh, I miss you so much. I'm so glad I caught you. There might be a delay. Yes, dead cruel, but it won't be long, now, my love, until I get home to you. And I've got so much to tell you. I do. I do. Oh, you must come down and visit London...it's dead fab, it is. Oh, wait a minute. I think they're saying something about my train over the loudspeaker. Hold on."

She pushed open the kiosk door a little, listened hard, and heard the announcement was for a different train. Then she caught the sound of 'pips' coming from the telephone handset signalling time was running out and that she should insert more coins. She screeched. "Oh, please, no. Hold on!"

Frantically, she pushed a six-penny piece into the slot, and then another. "Hello? Hello? Oh, good, Spike, you're still there." She wanted to tell him right then and there that she was pregnant, but she caught herself just in time. She and Maureen had agreed it was something best said, face-to-face. Then suddenly she was saying it, blurting it out, in a torrent of excitement and dread and hope. "Raymond. Raymond, I'm pregnant." But the long piercing shriek of a guard's whistle and the crackly sound of another train departure announcement over the Tannoy system, drowned out all her words.

She heard Spike shouting that he'd missed what she'd said and could she repeat it. And she said, simply, "Raymond Jones, I love you. I love you. I love you. Hang on a mo, that sounds like my train they're talking about." She listened. "Yes it is. So it must mean it's leaving on time. Great. Can't wait to see you at Lime Street. I love you. I love you. Bye-ee."

She turned and it was only then she caught the end of the station announcer's message.

"*...due to work on the line at Edge Hill, in Liverpool, the Liverpool train, standing at Platform Seven, will now not be going into Lime Street Station, but will arrive, instead, at Liverpool Central Station. We apologise for any...*"

She gripped the receiver even tighter, in some vague hope it might hold the connection. "Oh, no, no, no, no. Raymond! Spike! Spike!" she shouted. "It's been changed. I'll be coming in to Central now." But the line was dead. Frantically, she pushed another coin into the slot and redialled the number for Spike's home, but all she heard was the dreadful dispiriting high-pitched noise that told her the number was now engaged and the line unobtainable.

SPIKE put down the phone. He'd thought it might be Sandra calling back again, for some reason, but the telephone hadn't stopped ringing since her last call. There'd been umpteen calls for his mother, a wrong number, a neighbour calling to ask whether he'd seen her missing cat, someone calling to confirm a gig on the Tuesday night. The last call was someone who said their bass player had just called in sick and could he step in that night, at the Cavern. He'd said, no, he was sorry he was already booked. They'd asked, who with, and he'd said the name of the first group that came into his mind and they'd said he should drop them because they were such a crap group. And he'd said, no, he couldn't because he'd given his word, and they'd said, sod off then, and they probably wouldn't be calling him ever again. And he'd thought, well sod you and all, but he wasn't going to miss meeting Sandra for anything. He'd not seen her for nearly six weeks, as it was, and he was just dying to see her.

He went back to his room and a copy of *Mersey Beat* he'd carried all the way to Hamburg and back, caught his eye. It was still folded over to the editorial: THE RAT RACE. As usual, Bill Harry had hit the nail smack on the head. It'd certainly firmed-up his own views and thoughts about the future. Liverpool had changed—and not for the better. The 'Rocking City' wasn't rocking anymore. The good old days had got old very quickly. He snatched up the paper and scanned the article again: *Acid tongues prevail…murmurs of discontent, whispered rumours, and sarcastic comments…all motivated by petty jealousies…all polluting the atmosphere…all the having a laugh and drinking together, or giving each other a helping hand have all gone…now if one group suffers misfortune of any kind other groups are glad.*

People had talked about nothing else back in Hamburg. The consensus being that it was The Beatles and their success that'd caused the rot. They'd got a record in the Hit Parade. They were getting more and more work outside Liverpool. They'd been to London. They'd been on the radio, as well as the telly. Now, word was, Brian Epstein had signed Gerry Marsden and that he and The Pacemakers were going to make a record down in London, too. The cry was all but universal, 'Why them, why not us?' People had even complained that *Mersey Beat* should be renamed *Mersey Beatle,* because Bill Harry spent so much time writing about the group.

Spike shook his head. What the fookin' hell did people expect? The Beatles *were* the best and not just in Liverpool. Whatever '*it*' was—they had '*it*' in spades. Even though he'd got to know them a little bit, and had played on stage with them at the Star-Club, he couldn't put his finger on what '*it*' was exactly. He just knew that whenever they played it stirred something in him, something joyful. It made him want to be a better bass-player. Made him believe that anything was possible. Beyond that, it was best to enjoy it, like they always did. That's why he was content moving from one group to another; playing a night here, a night there; being on the outside of all the squabbles and bickering; being free of it all, always above the fray.

Even when Roy Young had asked him to stay on in Hamburg, as part of Star-Combo, and both Adrian Barber and Tony Sheridan had urged him to say, 'yes', he'd turned them down flat. Great blokes and musicians as they undoubtedly were—and as much as he'd grown to love Hamburg—he knew if he stayed, he'd never leave. In the end, all the drink, all the Prellies, all the St. Pauli girls—all the goings on—behind the stage, in some bunk, or in some girl's crumpled bed—all the throwing up and the falling down drunk—didn't make for a full life. All he knew was that he wanted more out of life. The fact he didn't have an inkling, yet, what that 'more' was, didn't matter a jot. All that mattered was that he kept on going, kept on trying to be better at whatever he did. And for now that meant him playing the bass guitar every day and him getting better at it every day.

Roy Young had all but said the same. As disappointed as he'd been by Spike's decision not to join Star-Combo, the bandleader had encouraged him to keep on with it all. Had told him about session musicians who got work at recording studios. Told him, that if he was really serious about playing the bass, he should go to London and get as much experience under his guitar strap as he could—maybe even learn to sight-read music. After which, he should just try to pick up any and all work he could; learn to play anything, for anybody, anywhere, anytime. He'd even mentioned that he'd heard Spike's old friends, Fras and Dave, were in London, playing the clubs, and that Cliff had got married and left the business altogether.

So, yeah, London was calling. Funny that. Maybe it'd always been on the cards, what with San always wanting to go there and now him wanting to go there, too. So what was to stop them? He looked at the clock. Bugger. He might just be able to get a local train into town. Failing that, it would have to be a taxi from Huyton station. That's if he could even bloody well get one in all the soddin' rain.

SPIKE sat back in the seat, tried to catch his breath, and stared out the taxi window at a dark rain-swept Liverpool. Places and local landmarks he'd known all his life passing before his eyes like fleeting shadows, every single one of them freighted with some family memory or other. His mam and dad—school-friends—him on his bicycle or with a sketchpad—bus-rides—long walks home in the wee hours, more often than not carrying an increasingly heavy guitar case—and even with all that—the only thing he could think about—could focus on—was Sandra.

He knew how much she loved him and that every little thing she did, she did for him. People had told him he was lucky guy, a hundred times over. Jimmy Molloy mostly—he never ever let telling him about it. And it was true. He was an incredibly lucky guy. It struck him, then, that when he was with her, walking beside her or simply having a cup of tea, she filled up the awful emptiness he'd carried deep down inside since his dad had died. Sandra made him complete, somehow, and he suddenly realised with a startling clarity that with her by his side he could achieve absolutely anything he set his heart and mind on. The one thing in his life he was completely sure of now, was that he would love her forever and their love would never die.

Lime Street Station loomed out of the darkness. The taxi screeched to a stop and he hurriedly paid his fare and jumped out. A big sign proclaimed: 'Sunday Rail and Bus Service'. An oxymoron if ever there was one. Something was always being cancelled or worked on every day of the bloody week. Thank Christ for taxis, as expensive as they were. So which platform was it? Left? Platforms 1-to-6? Right? Platforms 7-8-9? Bugger! He dashed over to the lines of notice boards displaying all the different train timetables and searched frantically for one headed: 'To And From London'. He found it, ran a shaky finger down the incredibly small lines of type, but found it impossible to see straight. Starting to panic, he remembered the big main concourse notice board. Oh, hell. Sandra's London train wasn't even listed on it. He looked round for a special notice board, somewhere, anywhere, but saw nothing. He stared at his watch. It was already nine o'clock! Oh, bloody hell. He looked up, saw a station porter and ran up to him. "The London train, which platform, please, mister?"

"What the next one? Well, there's the mail train that goes...let me see, now...in about an hour and a bit."

"No...the one...the one due in from Euston, about now."

"Nay, lad, you've got the wrong location. That one's going into Central Station that one is. It's not coming in here. There should be a sign up, somewhere. Where is it now? Only it seems they're behind schedule with all this new-fangled electrification business. Why? Are you meeting someone?" Spike nodded, trying not to look too impatient, just praying the silly old sod would just bloody well hurry up. The man scratched his chin.

"Well, now look here. Knowing as how they usually work it at the main signal box, at Edge Hill Junction, just to be on the safe-side, like, they'll make it wait a bit. So the Euston train will probably be delayed and will have to wait on the line. Let me see, now." The rail-man took a silver fob watch from his vest pocket, consulted it, looked up at the station clock, and nodded. "Yes, I reckon as they'll have to wait for the 9:09 local to clear. So that means they'll be on the one coming in after that, the one after 9:09, which should get them into Central...oh, gone quarter past...say around nine-twenty. Have you got that?"

But Spike was already sprinting back towards the entrance. "Thanks, mister," he yelled over his shoulder.

SANDRA sighed a weary sigh. The train had been stopped for almost twenty minutes. It seemed so cruel to be caught in limbo between here and there, so near, yet still so far away from home. She was impatient to arrive, desperate to arrive, desper-ate to see her lovely Raymond again, but she was also dreading it and was frightened of what might happen now after six long and lonely weeks apart. Six weeks that'd changed her life forever.

She tried to calm her fluttering heart and still her restless mind. Throughout the entire journey all she'd heard, over and over again, in her head, as the train wheels had clattered over and over the tracks, was '*Will he stand by me, stand by me, stand by me? Or will he leave me forever and go?*' '*Will he stand by me, stand by me, stand by me? Or will he leave me forever and go?*' She dabbed at a lone tear with a mascara-stained hanky and remem-bered the first time they'd kissed and that last, long, lovely kiss at Lime Street Station. She sighed a gentle sigh that for a mo-ment left her breathless and stilled the ache in her heart. Strengthened, she reached inside her purse and pulled out the little red leatherette photo-wallet and opened it and stared at the photos again. The first kiss and the last kiss—nothing in the world could ever change that. She put her hand flat on her belly and tried to picture the baby growing inside her, the little life that would be the living image of her and her darling Spike, her beloved Raymond Jones. "Oh, Raymond, what are we going to do?" she whispered. She turned and looked out of the window, at the world seemingly stopped forever in its tracks. The raindrops glistening on the glass mirroring the tears trickling down her cheeks. Lost in thought, lost in time, oblivious to all of the other passengers in the carriage.

SPIKE stopped dead at the sight of the Teds.

"Hey, you. Yeah. You. Don't like your hair. It's dead poncey, like a fookin' tart's. Don't yer agree, like, it looks like a fookin' tart's?"

There were four of them. He stared at their faces, at the dirty red bandana tied around the neck of the tallest of them, knew he'd met them all before and enough times for it to seem like a recurring nightmare.

There was a flicker of recognition in the gang leader's eyes and then a grin slowly spread across his pimply pockmarked face. "Oooh! You! Oh, this is too bloody good to be true, this is. I've waited forever to do you over, I have. Hey, fellas, it's that long-haired fooker that was always giving us so much fookin' bother at 'the Tower'."

"Oh, yeah, him, yeah!" The other Teds all chorused, shaking their shoulders and seemingly shivering with glee. They howled and whooped with anticipation of what was about go to down. This was going to feel so good—so bloody fookin' good—it almost hurt.

Spike glanced left—right—quickly realised he was trapped. On one side he was hemmed in by the line of notice boards displaying train timetables, on the other by a line of trolleys and carts piled high with mailbags awaiting the night train to London. The line of carts much too long to run around; the mailbags piled too high to scramble over. They'd have grabbed his legs and pulled him back down long before he'd managed to get a foot over the toppermost one.

He took a quick look behind. Fook it. Blocked by the soddin' instant photo-booth, of all things. The curtains were closed, too, with a couple inside, blocking the way. He could still try and push through to the other side. Otherwise, he was well and truly and totally buggered.

The Teds knew it, too. And they leered at him, confident they had him trapped and that this was going to be easy meat.

Spot lit by the overhead neon lights, all four Teddy Boys stepped forward in a line. Stepping in time, like a would-be beat group strutting a going-nowhere Shadows-walk at some crappy village dancehall. This time though they didn't all step back, in unison, but continued moving forward. Then they all shook their hands as if about to click their fingers in time to the beat. Only these clicks were spring-loaded. He blinked. Saw four slim fingers of steel all pointed directly at him—the long thin evil blades sharp and cold in the yellow light of Lime Street Station.

As he turned to run he counted them off...

"One. Two. Three. FOUR!"

And in the brilliant white flashes of light that followed—
all he could see was Sandra's face that first time at 'the Tower' on that magical Liverpool night he saw her standing there, when she was just seventeen.

Raymond Jones

"What's more, Raymond, you saved John Lennon's life. And because you did, one day, the whole world is going to remember and revere the name of Raymond Jones."

He paused, took a sip of water, smiled his infectious smile; his slightly crooked front teeth making him appear impossibly boyish.

"As I said, Raymond, I want to do something for you...help you, in some way. You seem to know all about the music: the groups, the clubs. So I'm sure we can find some way for you to come and work for me at NEMS Enterprises. I know that, as we get bigger, I'm going to need to call on people I can trust. I have a good sense of people: a good sense of you. And, as you play the bass guitar, I could even build a group around you, if you so desired." He saw the incredulous look on Raymond Jones's face. He smiled. "Just think about it, that's all. I don't want to rush you. I simply want you to know I'll never ever forget what you did."

"But as I keep telling you, Mr Epstein, I didn't..."

"Let me stop you for a moment. I assure you, I will neither be overruled, nor dissuaded in this matter. So please, Raymond, just humour me in this, if you would. And always remember you can always call on me. Is that clear?"

"Yes, yes it is. Okay, then. Thank you, Mr Epstein."

"Now tell me something. When is your birthday, exactly?"

"Er, 28th of October...the day of the Little Richard concert."

"You like Little Richard, don't you?"

"Yes. He's really great."

He nodded in agreement and held up a hand. "Excuse me, a moment." He reached forward and pressed the intercom.

"Beryl. Please call down to the ticket office and get two, twelve-and-sixpenny tickets for the Little Richard Show, at the Empire. The very best orchestra seats available for the eight o'clock show. Then bring them right up, please. Thank you."

He looked at his wristwatch, then the clock on his desk, and wrote something in his notebook. "October 28th...at three o'clock, exactly. Excellent."

"I can't think why anyone would ever need to remember that date and time, Mr Epstein."

"One day, you will, Raymond. And so will the rest of the world."

On 11 May 1963 The Beatles' debut LP *Please, Please Me* topped the British album charts and stayed there for thirty weeks. On Saturday, 3 August 1963, The Beatles made their 292nd and last appearance at the Cavern Club.

On Sunday, 13 October 1963, The Beatles appeared on *Sunday Night at the London Palladium*, an enormously popular television variety show broadcast live, nationally, each week, from the famous West End theatre. More than 13 million viewers watched the show. The next day, most all of the London-based national newspaper reported on the riotous scenes of hordes of screaming fans greeting The Beatles' arrival at the theatre. One of the newspapers dubbed it '*Beatlemania*'.

Two weeks later, on Monday, 4 November 1963, The Beatles appeared at the annual *Royal Command Performance,* at the Prince of Wales Theatre, in London. This was the occasion of John Lennon's famous remark: "For our last number I'd like to ask your help. Would the people in the cheaper seats clap your hands and the rest of you, if you'll just rattle your jewellery." After the show was broadcast to the nation the following Sunday evening, '*Beatlemania*' engulfed all of Great Britain.

Three months later, on Sunday, 9 February 1964, The Beatles appeared on *The Ed Sullivan Show*, an enormously popular television variety show broadcast live to a nation-wide audience, each week, from New York City. The event set a new world record for the largest-ever TV audience. Over 73 million people all across America watched the show. Smashing to pieces the previously held record, the television debut of Elvis Presley on *The Ed Sullivan Show*. And the rest, as they say, is...history.

AUTHOR'S ACKNOWLEDGEMENTS

The One After 9:09, although a work of fiction, would have been impossible to write, but for the extraordinary wealth of memoirs, chronicles, and original research concerning The Beatles and their times published over the last fifty years. A number of books proved absolutely essential and need to be singled out for special acknowledgement. My debt of gratitude to all of the many individuals concerned is total.

Bill Harry. *Mersey Beat* on the early Liverpool days, still a work of wonder. His encyclopaedic works on The Beatles—beyond scholarly.

Astrid Kirchherr and Jürgen Vollmer. Their photographs of The Beatles' Hamburg days are a continuing joy—incomparable.

Mark Lewisohn. An astonishing body of work. From *The Beatles Live!* through to *The Beatles Recording Sessions* and *The Complete Beatles Chronicle*—to the first of his three-volume *magnum opus*: *The Beatles: All These Years: Tune In*. Definitive, indispensable—always a complete joy.

Ian MacDonald. *Revolution In The Head: The Beatles Records and the Sixties*. A masterpiece—*sans pareil*.

Michael Braun. *"Love Me Do!" The Beatles' Progress*. There's no better fly-on-the-wall account of the band's early days.

Philip Norman. *Shout* and *John Lennon*. First and last words.

Jonathan Gould. *Can't Buy Me Love*. Essential reading. Hugely insightful views into The Beatles' music, as well as a very nuanced appreciation of the group's extraordinary influence and affect on post-war society in both the UK and US.

Hunter Davies. *The Beatles*. The first and best 'inside story'.

Bob Spitz. *The Beatles: A Biography*. A treasure trove.

Andy Babiuk. *Beatle Gear*. A true revelation—and such fun.

Peter Frame. *The Beatles and Some Other Guys*. Frame's 'Rock Family Trees' are a never-ending magical mystery tour.

Spencer Leigh. *The Beatles in Liverpool* and *The Beatles in Hamburg*—although both late to the party—were most welcome guests. A real 'Fab' time. And by a real Liverpudlian, to Bootle.

Martin Lewis moved mountains to get Brian Epstein's auto-biography *A Cellarful of Noise* (1964) republished in 1998. His introductory essay '*With A Little Help From Their Friend...*' is simply terrific. Lewis was a tireless advocate for Brian Epstein to receive greater recognition. It's largely due to his efforts that The Beatles' late manager was finally inducted into the Rock 'n' Roll Hall of Fame in 2014. Knockout work.

Ray Coleman. Of the many chroniclers of The Beatles, I developed a special affection for Coleman's work, especially in regard to his twin-biographies on John Lennon and his biography on Brian Epstein. The latter book, particularly, because it was what first keyed me in to 'the Sam Leach Affair'.

Sam Leach. Originally, *The One After 9:09* concerned the intertwined stories of The Beatles, Brian Epstein, and the 'mythical' Raymond Jones. Sam Leach was but a minor figure, at best. However, on reading his book, *The Birth of The Beatles* (Published in the UK as *The Rocking City*.) Sam walked into the story, glass of whisky and cigarette in hand, with tickets to the New Brighton Tower in his pockets, and demanded that it be re-written to include him. His book is a marvellous record of the times: warm, generous, untidy, and very, very funny—much as, I suspect, is Sam Leach himself. He comes across as being utterly irrepressible—some would say an incorrigible dreamer—but what towering dreams. I hope I've managed to capture the unique magic of the man, whom I believe to have played—along with such Liverpool luminaries as Bill Harry and Bob Wooler—a hugely significant role in the early life of The Beatles and a signal part in the rise of the whole Mersey beat scene. He deserves to be lauded for that. Most of the incidents involving Sam Leach in *The One After 9:09* are based upon events recounted by him in his autobiography. I urge you to read it. It merits a much wider audience and an honoured place on every 'Beatles bookshelf'.

One minor point: Sam Leach's memory of The Beatles singing 'Twist and Shout' at the first all-nighter at the Iron Door on Saturday 11 March, 1961 is a little flawed; The Isley Brothers' record wasn't released until the following year, when Mark Lewisohn lists it as being included in The Beatles' 'Live' repertoire.

However, in *The One After 9:09* I chose to stay with Sam's sometimes-imperfect memory, as opposed to Mark Lewisohn's always-immaculate research.

The 'fab' photographs at Sam Leach's 'Battle of The Bands' in Aldershot, 9 December, 1961, were actually taken by his friend, Liverpool photographer Dick Matthews, not Raymond Jones.

Rex Makin—still a highly regarded and much-respected figure in Liverpool civic and legal circles—certainly never knew Raymond Jones or Harry Lightfoot. It's highly likely, though, that having been for all his professional life the champion of the underdog, he met or had dealings with their counterparts.

George Harrison, Brian Epstein, and George Martin all remarked on the phenomenon of The Beatles resembling a 'single entity' or 'complete person' when they performed together. However, in all my Beatle-ing, the idea was never better articulated than in a scene in Richard Marquand's 'fab' film *Birth of The Beatles* (1981). Since the film was first screened on British television I've often quoted the observation attributed to Brian Epstein and I drew upon the spirit of it for my novel. Especial thanks then to screenwriters John Kurland and Jacob Eskendar for their inspiration.

A special salute to *A Hard Day's Night*—a uniquely 'fab' experience. Thanks to director, Dick Lester; screenwriter, the late Alun Owen; producer, the late Walter Shenson; and actor, and very much a personal favourite, the late Victor Spinetti.

Particular thanks to 'Auntie Beeb'. The BBC's documentary departments are without peer. Even so, the BBC TV *Arena* programme '*The Brian Epstein Story*'—produced by the late Debbie Geller and directed by Anthony Wall—and on which Geller's excellent book of the same title was also based—is truly exceptional. Also of special note—the BBC Radio documentaries: *Merseybeat, All Night Long, The Inner Light (of George Harrison.)*

A special tip of the hat to UK music magazines: *Mojo, Uncut,* and '*Q*' for their many excellent articles and special editions about The Beatles and their times. Ditto *Rolling Stone* in the US. Many thanks, too, to the dedicated fanzines: *Daytrippin'* and *Beatlefan*. Thanks a bunch, there, fellas. Love yer work.

The birth of The Beatles began with a sequence of '*lighting bolts from the Gods*' that defies all probability. | John meets Paul | Paul leads to George | George leads to Ringo | The Beatles lead to Brian Epstein | Brian Epstein leads to George Martin | Five signal events, without the occurrence of any one of which, The Beatles, as we knew and loved them, would never have existed.

Thanks to George Martin—*the fifth 'bolt' if not the fifth Beatle.* Unique, in terms of both the times and place, he had the smarts, the skills, and 'the ears' to help produce, as well as introduce The Beatles and their music to the world. His book, *All You Need Is Ears*, warm, witty, wonderful. *Produced by George Martin: 50 Years In Recording* (6 CDs) a revelation. Rock on, George.

Thanks to the late Brian Epstein, who by all the evidence was a man of great charm and style and singular vision—as well as of extraordinary perseverance and dedication—and about whom Paul McCartney said, not quite twenty years ago today: "*If anyone was the fifth Beatle, it was Brian.*" 'Nuff said.

Thanks to George Harrison. What a lovely man he was. His musicianship, song writing, driest-of-dry wit, and 'unique soul' are forever inspiring. '*Namaste...George*'.

Thanks to the one and only Ringo Starr for not only being uniquely and irrepressibly 'Ringo', but also for always being—and providing—the full fulfilment of the missing part. Thanks a million, Ritchie. Keep on bashing those skins.

And lastly: Thanks to John Lennon and Paul McCartney for their sublime body of work. If John's song 'One After 909' was the genesis of the book—then Paul's 'I Saw Her Standing There' was what gave it its tone and form. My heartfelt thanks to both men: to the memory of the one taken from us all, all too soon; and to the other musical genius who—to everyone's delight—is still rockin' as hard as ever he did; twin legends in their own time—in my life—and for evermore.

Tony Broadbent | January 2015

Especial thanks to those 'Beatle buddies' who helped keep me going on the long and winding road to *The One After 9:09*— Andrew Tonkin, Barry Tomalin, John Morrell, John Lawton, Kirk Russell, Adrian Muller, Dave Quayle, Fras Britton, and—as ever—my brother, Seth.

"Viel dank" to Nicky and Bettina Zurek—for their memories and 'vernacular' of Hamburg.

Thanks to everyone I ever played in a band with, some of who have already left the building—notably demon drummer Cliff Pocock, who I hitchhiked to Hamburg with when we were both sixteen. It's so inspiring to know that many of the lads are still performing—in pubs, clubs, village halls, and music festivals—the songs that so moved and inspired us all those many years ago.

I'd like to believe there really was a 'Raymond Jones' and that he did venture into NEMS and set the whole magical mystery into motion. And so myth or no: "Thanks, Ray, whoever you are...or were."

Never-ending thanks to my wife, Christine, for understanding that The Beatles 'really had a hold on me' and meant so much more to me—and to the youth of post-war Sixties Britain—than might initially have been conveyed to American ears by their magical music alone.

And, lastly, a thank you to my mum and dad who bought me my first electric guitar and amplifier, and The Beatles' first LP, and who, most importantly, 'got' The Beatles and didn't mind at all when I combed my hair down over my forehead and— London grammar schoolboy that I was—began speaking with a cod Liverpudlian accent, insisting all the while that they now call me by my first name—Paul.

Lightning Source UK Ltd.
Milton Keynes UK
UKOW02f2159120915

258489UK00002B/52/P